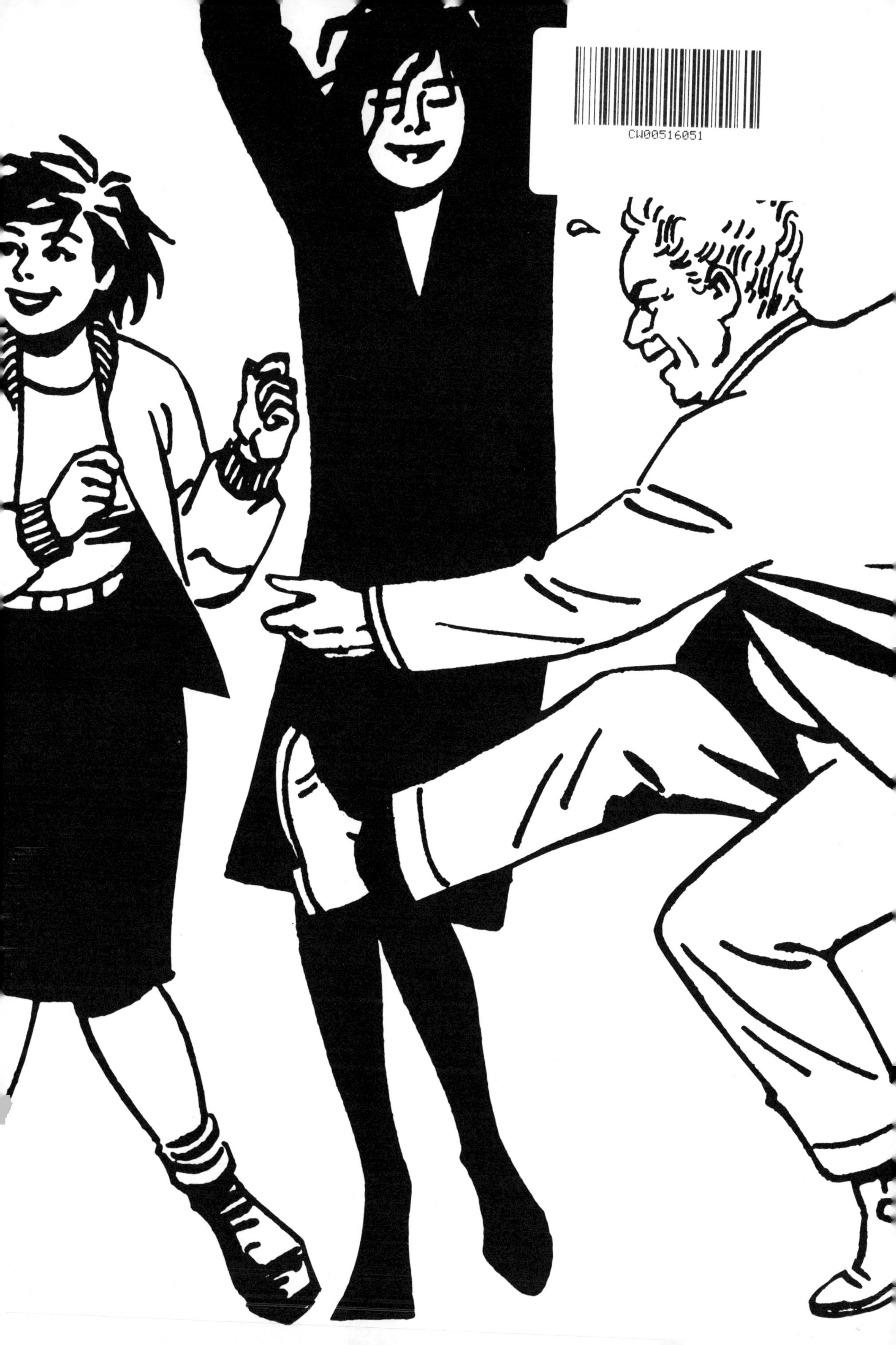

APE SEX
(LOVE AND ROCKETS VOLUME THREE)
ISBN 1 85286 171 1

Published by Titan Books Ltd
58 St Giles High St
London WC2H 8LH
First edition June 1989
10 9 8 7 6 5 4 3 2 1

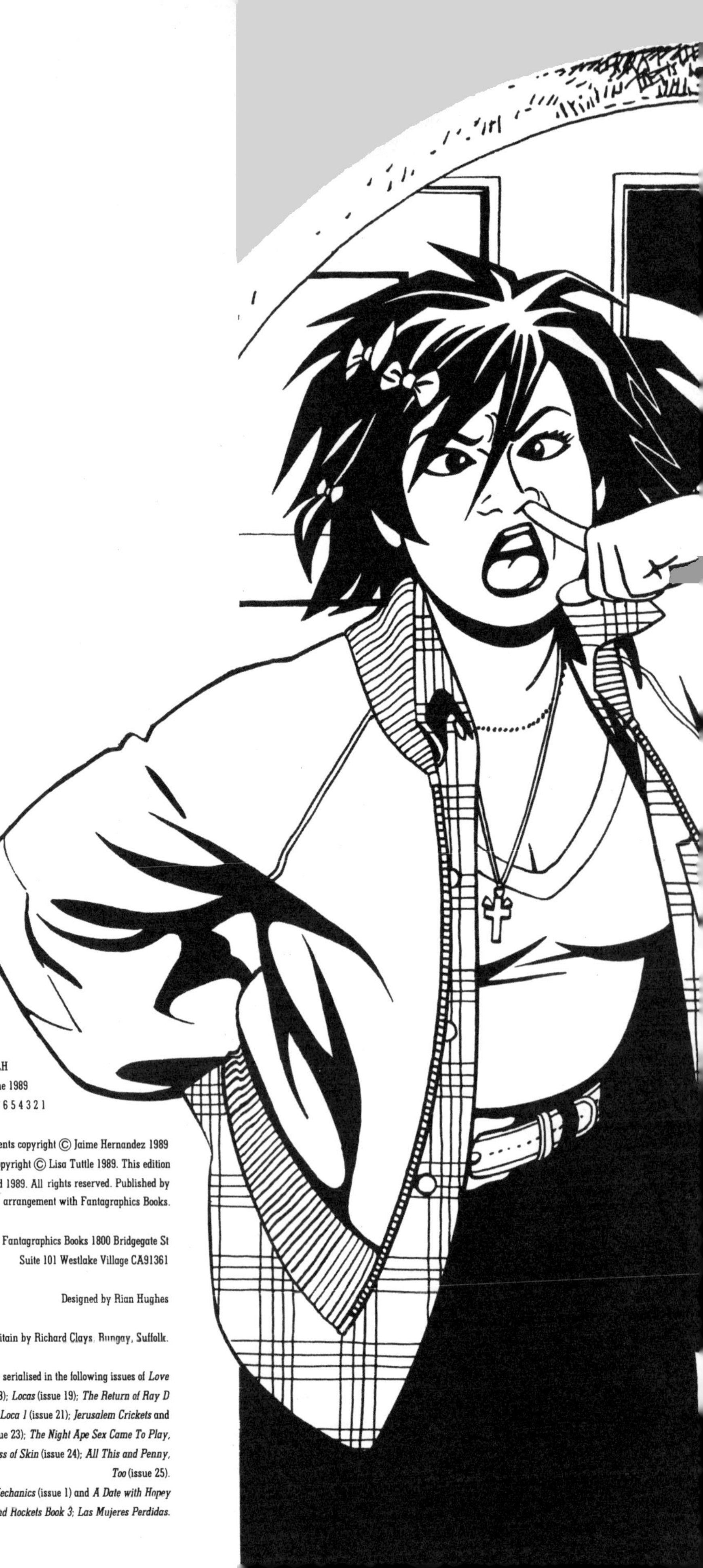

Originally published in the US by Fantagraphics Books 1800 Bridgegate St Suite 101 Westlake Village CA91361

Designed by Rian Hughes

Printed and bound in Great Britain by Richard Clays, Bungay, Suffolk.

The contents of this book were originally serialised in the following issues of *Love and Rockets: Locas 8.01-11.15* (issue 18); *Locas* (issue 19); *The Return of Ray D* (issue 20); *Jerusalem Crickets* and *Vida Loca 1* (issue 21); *Jerusalem Crickets* and *Vida Loca 2* (issue 22); *Vida Loca 3* (issue 23); *The Night Ape Sex Came To Play, Jerry Slum and the Crickettes* and *A Mess of Skin* (issue 24); *All This and Penny, Too* (issue 25).

Hey Hopey originally appeared in *Mechanics* (issue 1) and *A Date with Hopey* originally appeared in *Love and Rockets Book 3: Las Mujeres Perdidas.*

JAIME HERNANDEZ

Ape Sex

A LOVE AND ROCKETS GRAPHIC NOVEL
TITAN BOOKS

JAIME HERNANDEZ was born in Oxnard, near Hollywood, California, in 1959, one of six brothers who were all encouraged to draw by their mother, herself a fan of comic books. He went on to study classical figure drawing at Ventura College in California, and to devour popular culture such as comics, pulp science fiction movies and rock music. However, it was punk together with the publication of the American *Heavy Metal* comic magazine that really made him realise that, creatively, anything was possible. Beginning in 1980 to draw from his own life he began to create the contemporary characters which people the fantastic but solidly urban reality of his *Love and Rockets* strips. These were self-

published in a magazine of the same name also containing work by his brothers Gilbert and Mario, and a copy was sent to Gary Groth, the publisher of Fantagraphics' *The Comics Journal*. He immediately offered to publish their work regularly and, since then, *Love and Rockets* has grown in popularity on both sides of the Atlantic, being translated into four languages. With his brothers, Jaime has also drawn for the first four issues of *Mister X* (published during 1984 in Canada by Vortex Comics and collected into a single edition by Titan Books, entitled *The Return of Mister X*). This is the third *Love and Rockets* collection published by Titan; the previous two were titled simply *Love and Rockets* and *Mechanics*. He has also produced strips for *Silverheels, Vortex* and *Anything Goes*, along with poster pages for DC's *Who's Who* and pages for *The Rocketeer* graphic novel. Jaime continues to write and draw *Love and Rockets* from his home in Oxnard.

How can I explain what's so great about *Love & Rockets*? Comics fans don't need me to tell them. Comics fans, I suspect, have their own language, a shared world of reference for comparing, contrasting and describing. But I've never been a comics fan, and the fascination for superheroes remains incomprehensible to me. During the last few years, however, has come the 'graphic novel' boom, and some very talented artists and writers who are redefining the form, opening it out, moving beyond the self-referential fannish world. Jaime Hernandez, author of this volume, is one of the most interesting of these new talents.

Jaime Hernandez grew up in California, surrounded by comic books which were brought home, read and collected by his older brothers. Like them, encouraged by his mother (herself a fan of comics) and a father who painted, he began drawing as a child. Although he went on to study art at college, it was the comics he devoured as a child — *Superman, Fantastic Four, Archie, Dennis the Menace* — which have been the most obvious influence on his work.

As a child I read comics, too, as I read everything which came into my orbit, although I was probably finishing with them at about the same time young Jaime was learning to read. Superheroes disappointed me early. No matter how I tried, I couldn't identify with Supergirl or Wonder Woman. I couldn't believe in them; how could I care what happened when it was clear from the start that nothing would ever affect or change them? Love comics promised a glimpse of real life, but the world depicted in those strangely ritualistic strips was just as unreal, just as unbelievably one-dimensional as all the others.

It wasn't 'realism' I was looking for, I hasten to add. I've always had a problem with so-called realism, because it doesn't reflect what I think of as reality. Realism diminishes reality by denying the importance of imagination in our lives — the dreams, fantasies, coincidences and general weirdness which surrounds us all just as certainly as family, furniture and jobs.

So I didn't want a more 'realistic' comic, but a more truthful one. (Fact and truth, as William Faulkner said once, don't really have much to do with each other.) What I wanted, although I didn't know it, was *Love & Rockets*. Of course, even if I'd known, it wouldn't have done me any good, as it didn't then exist. So I had to wait twenty years. So, it was worth it.

Out there in California, the Hernandez brothers (Mario, Gilbert and Jaime) were doing their own thing. They created their own characters, in their own style, putting them in situations they found interesting, without considering whether these comic strips were commercial. They decided to self-publish, and in 1981 brought out a collection of their work titled *Love & Rockets*. They were hoping to find an audience, but because their work didn't fit into the drug-orientated underground comics scene, and because it didn't look like a Marvel comic, they knew they couldn't count on pleasing anyone but themselves. 'I had my little universe, but I didn't think it was going to go anywhere, so it was going to be all my own,' as Jaime Hernandez explained in a recent interview.

His universe encompasses small-town life in present-day California — an ordinary world where young people work as waitresses and play in punk rock bands, get drunk, pick fights, fall in love and hang out. And in another part of the world, the very same characters work as 'pro-solar mechanics', fixing rockets, riding hover-bikes, falling in love, picking fights, hanging out, and dealing with a few left-over dinosaurs. Undeniably an original and personal vision, but it's one which transcends the merely personal with resonances for a lot of readers. I certainly recognized it. OK, it's not *exactly* the world I live in, but it's a lot more like what I know of life than what usually passes for it on television or in comics. Jaime Hernandez created his own little universe, as plenty of people have done before, but his is the talent of the best of novelists, to make it real outside his own mind, to make you recognize it as true. What makes his characters outstanding, and what makes *Ape Sex* more like a novel of the old-fashioned, non-graphic kind, is that Maggie and Hopey and Danita and Doyle and Ray and Speedy and Esther and others are *people*. They're not just funny costumes, or pegs to hang a joke or an adventure on, they're people with their own reality, their own particular habits, relationships and pasts and futures as well as a present. In an interview, Jaime Hernandez has said that friends and real people were his inspiration, not imaginary superheroes. You can tell that Jaime Hernandez believes in these people he's drawing — he *knows* them — and his belief compels ours.

Am I making this all sound too serious for a book called *Ape Sex*? (That title has got to be a set-up: Oh, Mr. Hernandez, I just love your...ulp!) It's true, but *Love & Rockets* is also always a lot of fun, and this latest instalment is no exception. The previous volume, *Mechanics*, was concerned mostly with what Penny Century (a would-be superhero, that groovy chickadee a.k.a. Beatriz Garcia) so aptly described as 'the stuff comics are made of'. That is, chases, explosions, rescues, escapes,

love and rockets. Maggie was a mechanic, working in a dinosaur-infested swamp for that gorgeous hunk Rand Race, writing letters home about her adventures to Hopey and her other pals. The strips collected in this current volume don't have much to do with rockets, but a lot more to do with life... crazy life ('*Vida Loca*'). Maggie has come home. She's lost her comic-book job (and also her comic-book figure). She's living with her aunt (a former women's wrestling champion), and it's Hopey's turn to have adventures (of a grubbier, more realistic kind) as she goes on the road with a band.

Although he enjoys drawing dinosaurs and rocket ships — all that comic book stuff — Jaime Hernandez has said that his interest was always in his characters and their reactions to their situations. Their situations have changed not so much because he is pursuing some limited idea of 'realism' than because he found the fantasy elements got in the way of readers caring deeply about what happened to the characters. Superheroes never die... and so the trappings of the superhero comic distance the reader, who is made a voyeur instead of a participant, unshockable and essentially uninvolved. Although I'd hate to lose the rockets entirely (putting a character as contemporary, female, and richly human as Maggie into the traditional settings of pulp fiction is such a wonderful idea), I understand the author's concern, and he's obviously right. People get shot in comics all the time, and it means nothing. When it happens in *Ape Sex* it matters, and you feel hurt.

I still haven't managed to explain what makes *Love & Rockets* so great. Gilbert Hernandez (author of *Heartbreak Soup*), talking about the music that he and his brothers love, and trying to explain why, said, 'The best of rock and roll cannot be articulated. You can't say Elvis was good because of this or that. It's not going to work. You either get it or you don't. You have to hear it; *feel* it.'

And the same is true, despite all the critical theory in the world, for all popular culture, and for all art. I can't tell you why *Love & Rockets* is good — you'll have to feel it for yourself. All I can do is urge you to find out; turn the page; read on.

Lisa Tuttle
March 1989

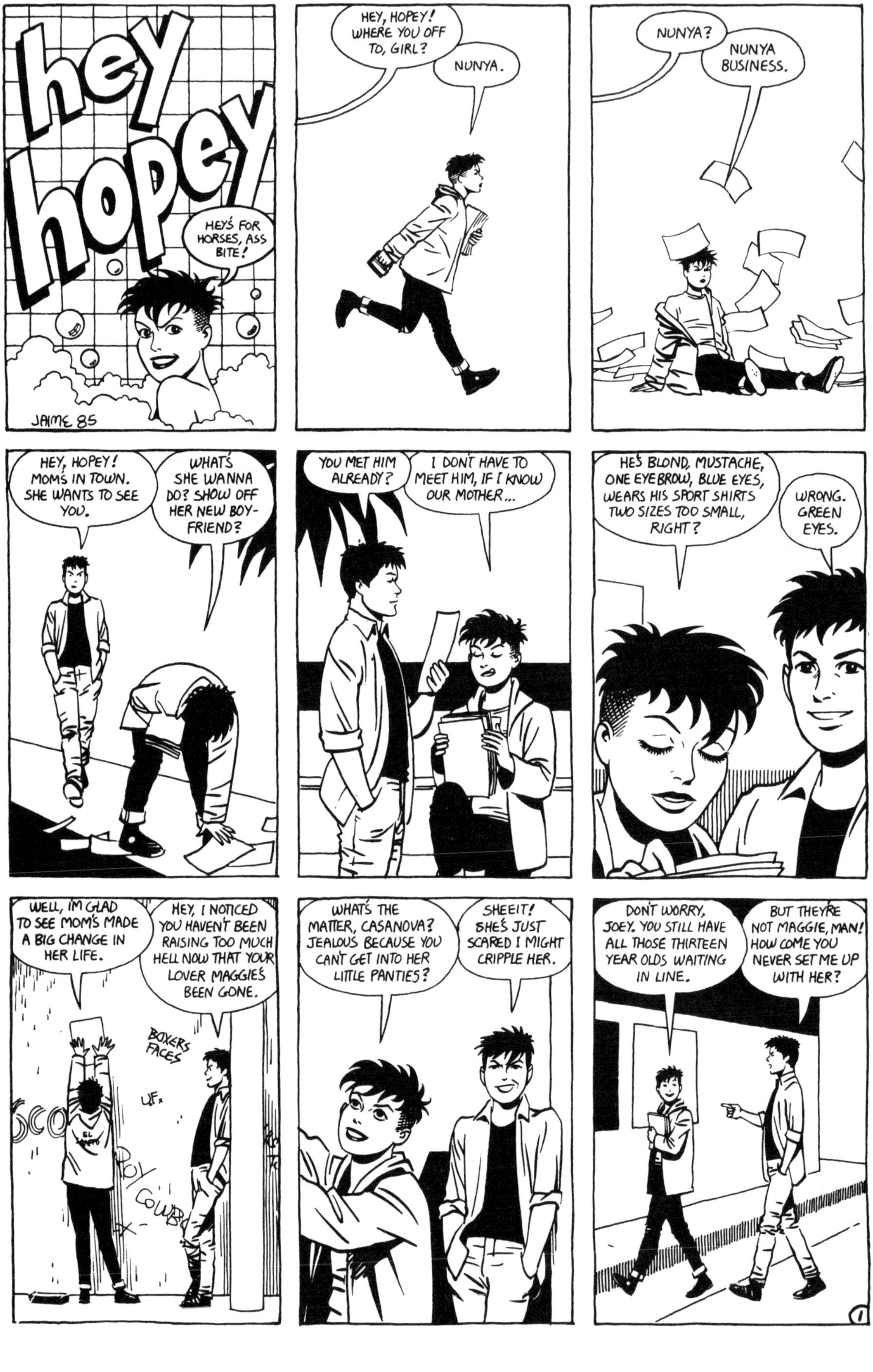
hey hopey
HEY'S FOR HORSES, ASS BITE!
JAIME 85
HEY, HOPEY! WHERE YOU OFF TO, GIRL?
NUNYA.
NUNYA?
NUNYA BUSINESS.
HEY, HOPEY! MOM'S IN TOWN. SHE WANTS TO SEE YOU.
WHAT'S SHE WANNA DO? SHOW OFF HER NEW BOY-FRIEND?
YOU MET HIM ALREADY?
I DON'T HAVE TO MEET HIM, IF I KNOW OUR MOTHER...
HE'S BLOND, MUSTACHE, ONE EYEBROW, BLUE EYES, WEARS HIS SPORT SHIRTS TWO SIZES TOO SMALL, RIGHT?
WRONG. GREEN EYES.
WELL, I'M GLAD TO SEE MOM'S MADE A BIG CHANGE IN HER LIFE.
HEY, I NOTICED YOU HAVEN'T BEEN RAISING TOO MUCH HELL NOW THAT YOUR LOVER MAGGIE'S BEEN GONE.
BOXERS FACES
WHAT'S THE MATTER, CASANOVA? JEALOUS BECAUSE YOU CAN'T GET INTO HER LITTLE PANTIES?
SHEEIT! SHE'S JUST SCARED I MIGHT CRIPPLE HER.
DON'T WORRY, JOEY. YOU STILL HAVE ALL THOSE THIRTEEN YEAR OLDS WAITING IN LINE.
BUT THEY'RE NOT MAGGIE, MAN! HOW COME YOU NEVER SET ME UP WITH HER?
1

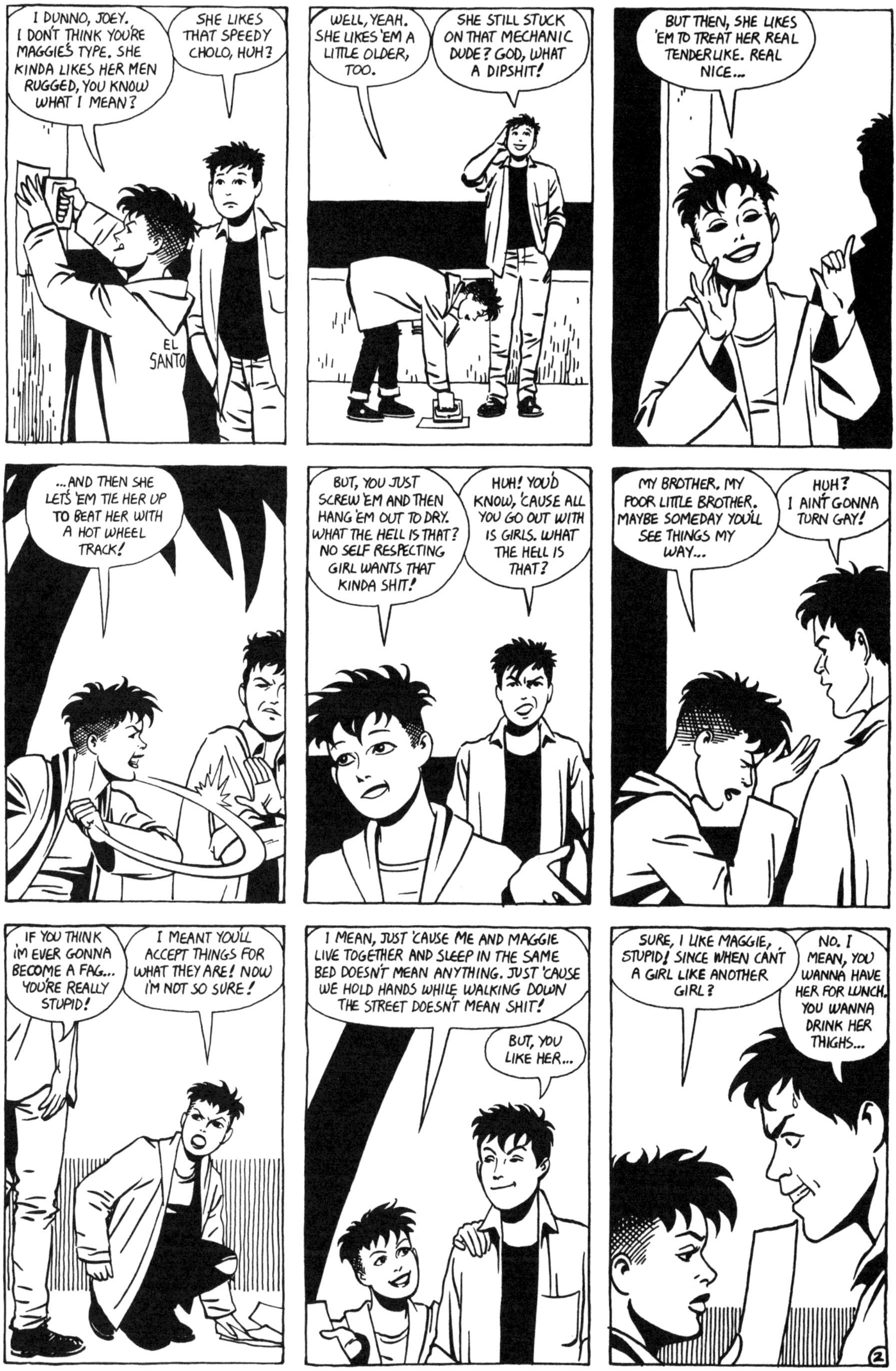
I DUNNO, JOEY. I DON'T THINK YOU'RE MAGGIE'S TYPE. SHE KINDA LIKES HER MEN RUGGED, YOU KNOW WHAT I MEAN?
SHE LIKES THAT SPEEDY CHOLO, HUH?
EL SANTO
WELL, YEAH. SHE LIKES 'EM A LITTLE OLDER, TOO.
SHE STILL STUCK ON THAT MECHANIC DUDE? GOD, WHAT A DIPSHIT!
BUT THEN, SHE LIKES 'EM TO TREAT HER REAL TENDERLIKE. REAL NICE...
...AND THEN SHE LET'S 'EM TIE HER UP TO BEAT HER WITH A HOT WHEEL TRACK!
BUT, YOU JUST SCREW 'EM AND THEN HANG 'EM OUT TO DRY. WHAT THE HELL IS THAT? NO SELF RESPECTING GIRL WANTS THAT KINDA SHIT!
HUH! YOU'D KNOW, 'CAUSE ALL YOU GO OUT WITH IS GIRLS. WHAT THE HELL IS THAT?
MY BROTHER. MY POOR LITTLE BROTHER. MAYBE SOMEDAY YOU'LL SEE THINGS MY WAY...
HUH? I AIN'T GONNA TURN GAY!
IF YOU THINK I'M EVER GONNA BECOME A FAG... YOU'RE REALLY STUPID!
I MEANT YOU'LL ACCEPT THINGS FOR WHAT THEY ARE! NOW I'M NOT SO SURE!
I MEAN, JUST 'CAUSE ME AND MAGGIE LIVE TOGETHER AND SLEEP IN THE SAME BED DOESN'T MEAN ANYTHING. JUST 'CAUSE WE HOLD HANDS WHILE WALKING DOWN THE STREET DOESN'T MEAN SHIT!
BUT, YOU LIKE HER...
SURE, I LIKE MAGGIE, STUPID! SINCE WHEN CAN'T A GIRL LIKE ANOTHER GIRL?
NO. I MEAN, YOU WANNA HAVE HER FOR LUNCH. YOU WANNA DRINK HER THIGHS...
2

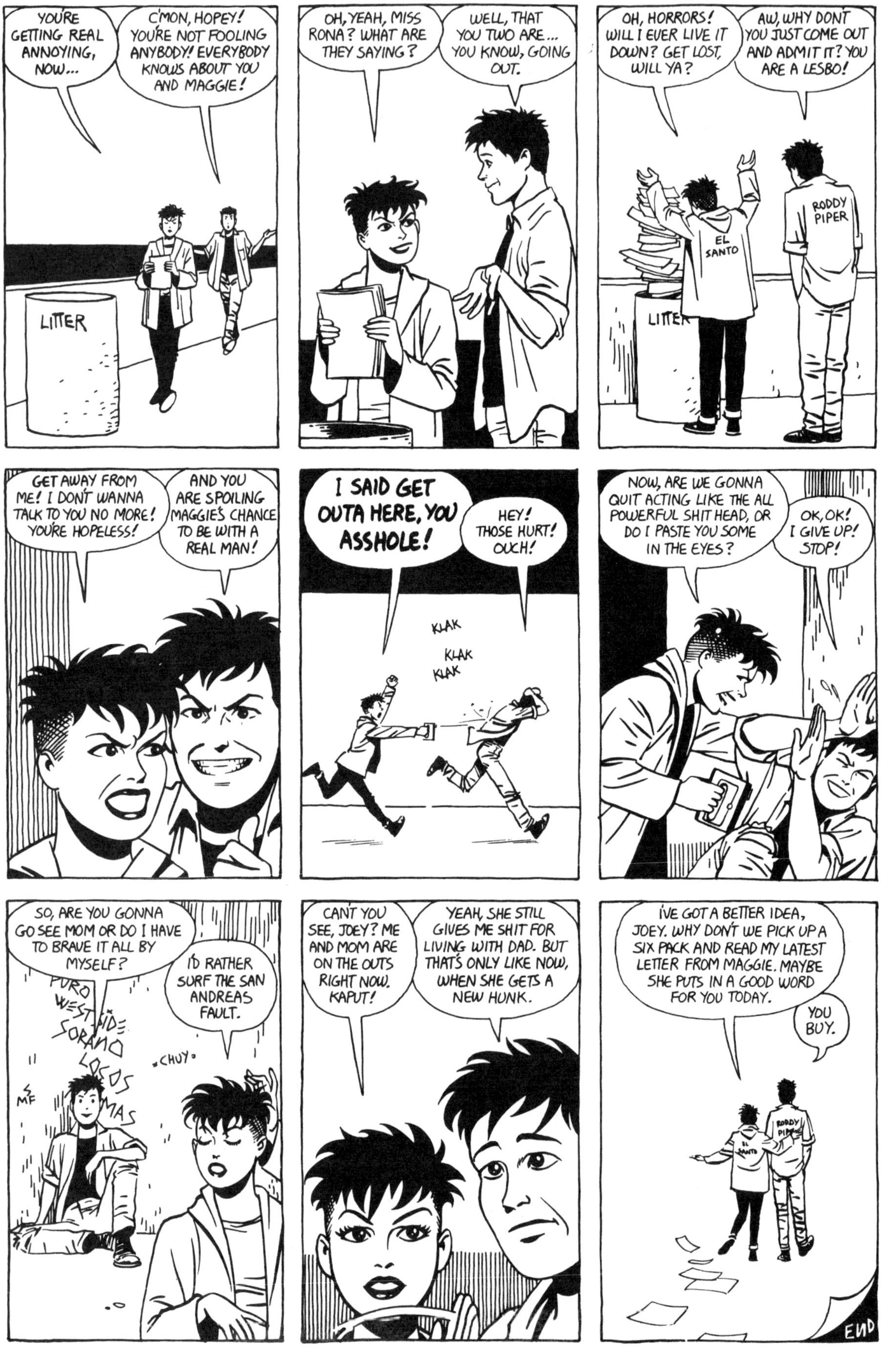
YOU'RE GETTING REAL ANNOYING, NOW...
C'MON, HOPEY! YOU'RE NOT FOOLING ANYBODY! EVERYBODY KNOWS ABOUT YOU AND MAGGIE!
LITTER
OH, YEAH, MISS RONA? WHAT ARE THEY SAYING?
WELL, THAT YOU TWO ARE... YOU KNOW, GOING OUT.
OH, HORRORS! WILL I EVER LIVE IT DOWN? GET LOST, WILL YA?
AW, WHY DONT YOU JUST COME OUT AND ADMIT IT? YOU ARE A LESBO!
EL SANTO
RODDY PIPER
LITTER
GET AWAY FROM ME! I DON'T WANNA TALK TO YOU NO MORE! YOU'RE HOPELESS!
AND YOU ARE SPOILING MAGGIE'S CHANCE TO BE WITH A REAL MAN!
I SAID GET OUTA HERE, YOU ASSHOLE!
HEY! THOSE HURT! OUCH!
KLAK
KLAK
KLAK
NOW, ARE WE GONNA QUIT ACTING LIKE THE ALL POWERFUL SHIT HEAD, OR DO I PASTE YOU SOME IN THE EYES?
OK, OK! I GIVE UP! STOP!
SO, ARE YOU GONNA GO SEE MOM OR DO I HAVE TO BRAVE IT ALL BY MYSELF?
I'D RATHER SURF THE SAN ANDREAS FAULT.
PURO WESTSIDE SORANO LOCOS
CHUY
CAN'T YOU SEE, JOEY? ME AND MOM ARE ON THE OUTS RIGHT NOW. KAPUT!
YEAH, SHE STILL GIVES ME SHIT FOR LIVING WITH DAD. BUT THAT'S ONLY LIKE NOW, WHEN SHE GETS A NEW HUNK.
I'VE GOT A BETTER IDEA, JOEY. WHY DON'T WE PICK UP A SIX PACK AND READ MY LATEST LETTER FROM MAGGIE. MAYBE SHE PUTS IN A GOOD WORD FOR YOU TODAY.
YOU BUY.
EL SANTO
RODDY PIPER
END

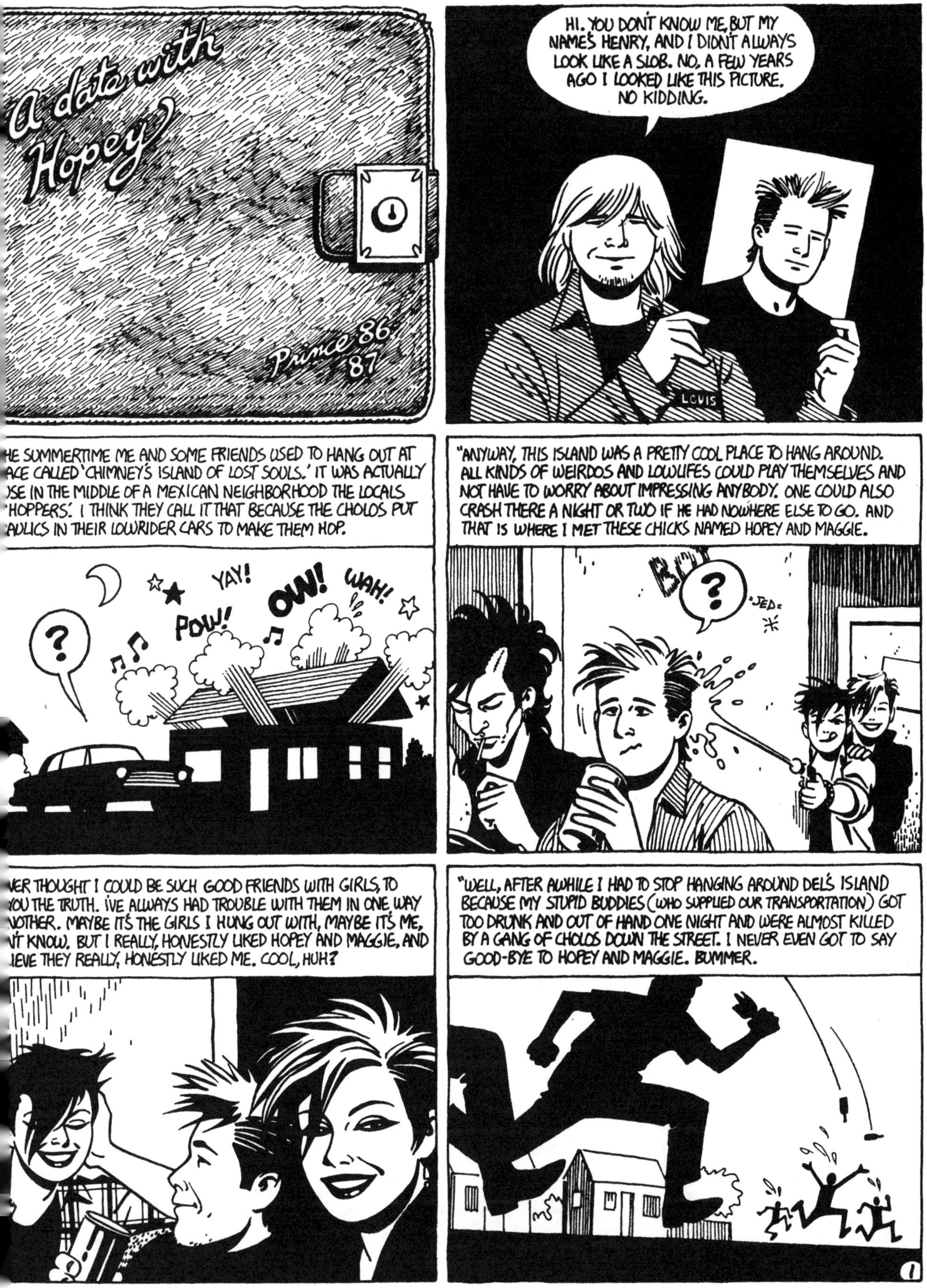
A date with Hopey
Prince 86-87
HI. YOU DON'T KNOW ME, BUT MY NAME'S HENRY, AND I DIDN'T ALWAYS LOOK LIKE A SLOB. NO, A FEW YEARS AGO I LOOKED LIKE THIS PICTURE. NO KIDDING.
LOUIS
HE SUMMERTIME ME AND SOME FRIENDS USED TO HANG OUT AT ACE CALLED 'CHIMNEY'S ISLAND OF LOST SOULS.' IT WAS ACTUALLY OSE IN THE MIDDLE OF A MEXICAN NEIGHBORHOOD THE LOCALS 'HOPPERS.' I THINK THEY CALL IT THAT BECAUSE THE CHOLOS PUT AULICS IN THEIR LOWRIDER CARS TO MAKE THEM HOP.
"ANYWAY, THIS ISLAND WAS A PRETTY COOL PLACE TO HANG AROUND. ALL KINDS OF WEIRDOS AND LOWLIFES COULD PLAY THEMSELVES AND NOT HAVE TO WORRY ABOUT IMPRESSING ANYBODY. ONE COULD ALSO CRASH THERE A NIGHT OR TWO IF HE HAD NOWHERE ELSE TO GO. AND THAT IS WHERE I MET THESE CHICKS NAMED HOPEY AND MAGGIE.
?
YAY!
POW!
OW!
WAH!
?
JED
VER THOUGHT I COULD BE SUCH GOOD FRIENDS WITH GIRLS, TO YOU THE TRUTH. I'VE ALWAYS HAD TROUBLE WITH THEM IN ONE WAY NOTHER. MAYBE IT'S THE GIRLS I HUNG OUT WITH, MAYBE IT'S ME, N'T KNOW. BUT I REALLY, HONESTLY LIKED HOPEY AND MAGGIE, AND IEVE THEY REALLY, HONESTLY LIKED ME. COOL, HUH?
"WELL, AFTER AWHILE I HAD TO STOP HANGING AROUND DEL'S ISLAND BECAUSE MY STUPID BUDDIES (WHO SUPPLIED OUR TRANSPORTATION) GOT TOO DRUNK AND OUT OF HAND ONE NIGHT AND WERE ALMOST KILLED BY A GANG OF CHOLOS DOWN THE STREET. I NEVER EVEN GOT TO SAY GOOD-BYE TO HOPEY AND MAGGIE. BUMMER.

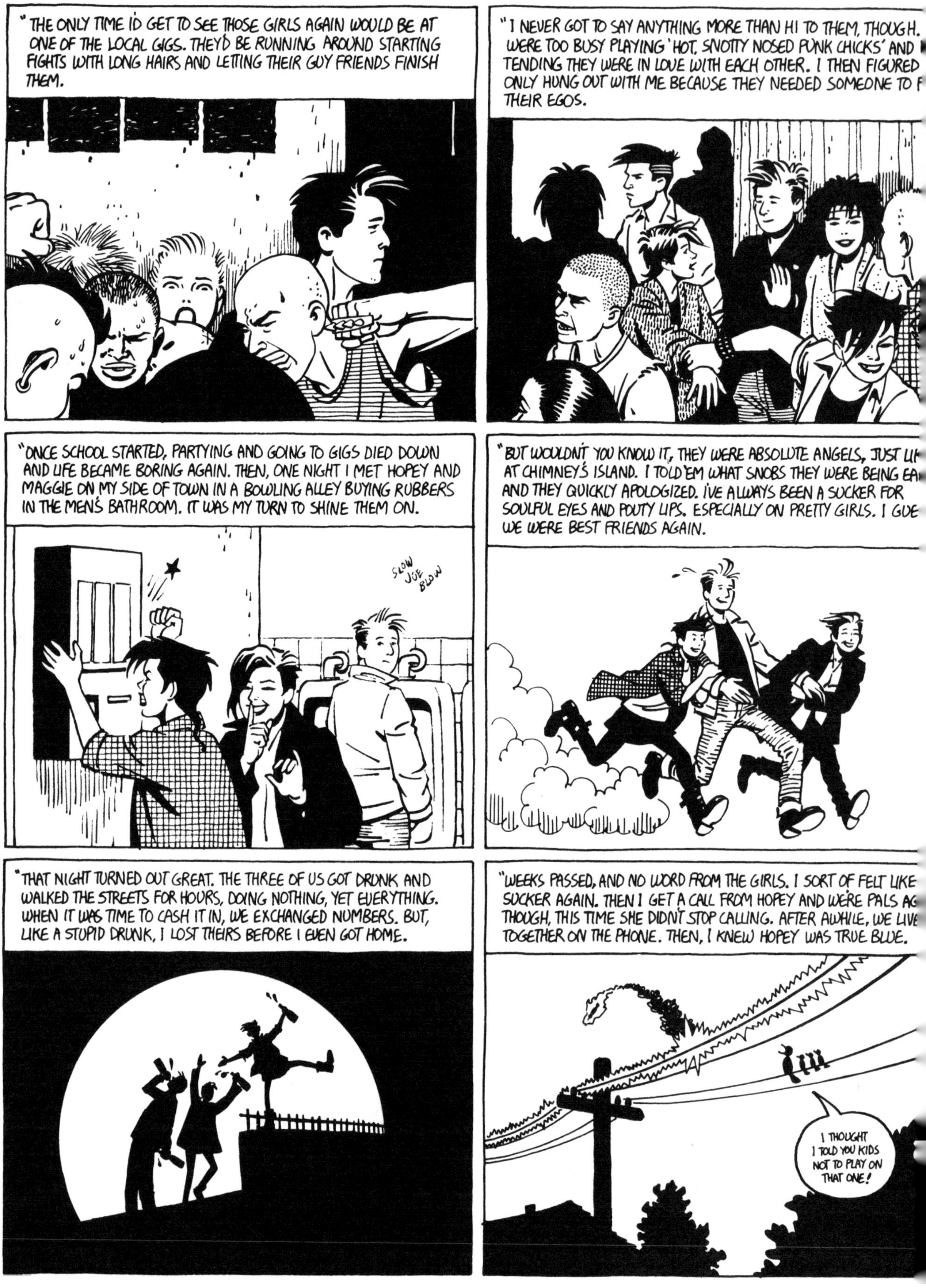
"THE ONLY TIME I'D GET TO SEE THOSE GIRLS AGAIN WOULD BE AT ONE OF THE LOCAL GIGS. THEY'D BE RUNNING AROUND STARTING FIGHTS WITH LONG HAIRS AND LETTING THEIR GUY FRIENDS FINISH THEM.
"I NEVER GOT TO SAY ANYTHING MORE THAN HI TO THEM, THOUGH. WERE TOO BUSY PLAYING 'HOT, SNOTTY NOSED PUNK CHICKS' AND TENDING THEY WERE IN LOVE WITH EACH OTHER. I THEN FIGURED ONLY HUNG OUT WITH ME BECAUSE THEY NEEDED SOMEONE TO THEIR EGOS.
"ONCE SCHOOL STARTED, PARTYING AND GOING TO GIGS DIED DOWN AND LIFE BECAME BORING AGAIN. THEN, ONE NIGHT I MET HOPEY AND MAGGIE ON MY SIDE OF TOWN IN A BOWLING ALLEY BUYING RUBBERS IN THE MEN'S BATHROOM. IT WAS MY TURN TO SHINE THEM ON.
SLOW JOE BLOW
"BUT WOULDN'T YOU KNOW IT, THEY WERE ABSOLUTE ANGELS, JUST AT CHIMNEY'S ISLAND. I TOLD 'EM WHAT SNOBS THEY WERE BEING AND THEY QUICKLY APOLOGIZED. I'VE ALWAYS BEEN A SUCKER FOR SOULFUL EYES AND POUTY LIPS. ESPECIALLY ON PRETTY GIRLS. I WE WERE BEST FRIENDS AGAIN.
"THAT NIGHT TURNED OUT GREAT. THE THREE OF US GOT DRUNK AND WALKED THE STREETS FOR HOURS, DOING NOTHING, YET EVERYTHING. WHEN IT WAS TIME TO CASH IT IN, WE EXCHANGED NUMBERS. BUT, LIKE A STUPID DRUNK, I LOST THEIRS BEFORE I EVEN GOT HOME.
"WEEKS PASSED, AND NO WORD FROM THE GIRLS. I SORT OF FELT LIKE SUCKER AGAIN. THEN I GET A CALL FROM HOPEY AND WE'RE PALS THOUGH, THIS TIME SHE DIDN'T STOP CALLING. AFTER AWHILE, WE TOGETHER ON THE PHONE. THEN, I KNEW HOPEY WAS TRUE BLUE.
I THOUGHT I TOLD YOU KIDS NOT TO PLAY ON THAT ONE!

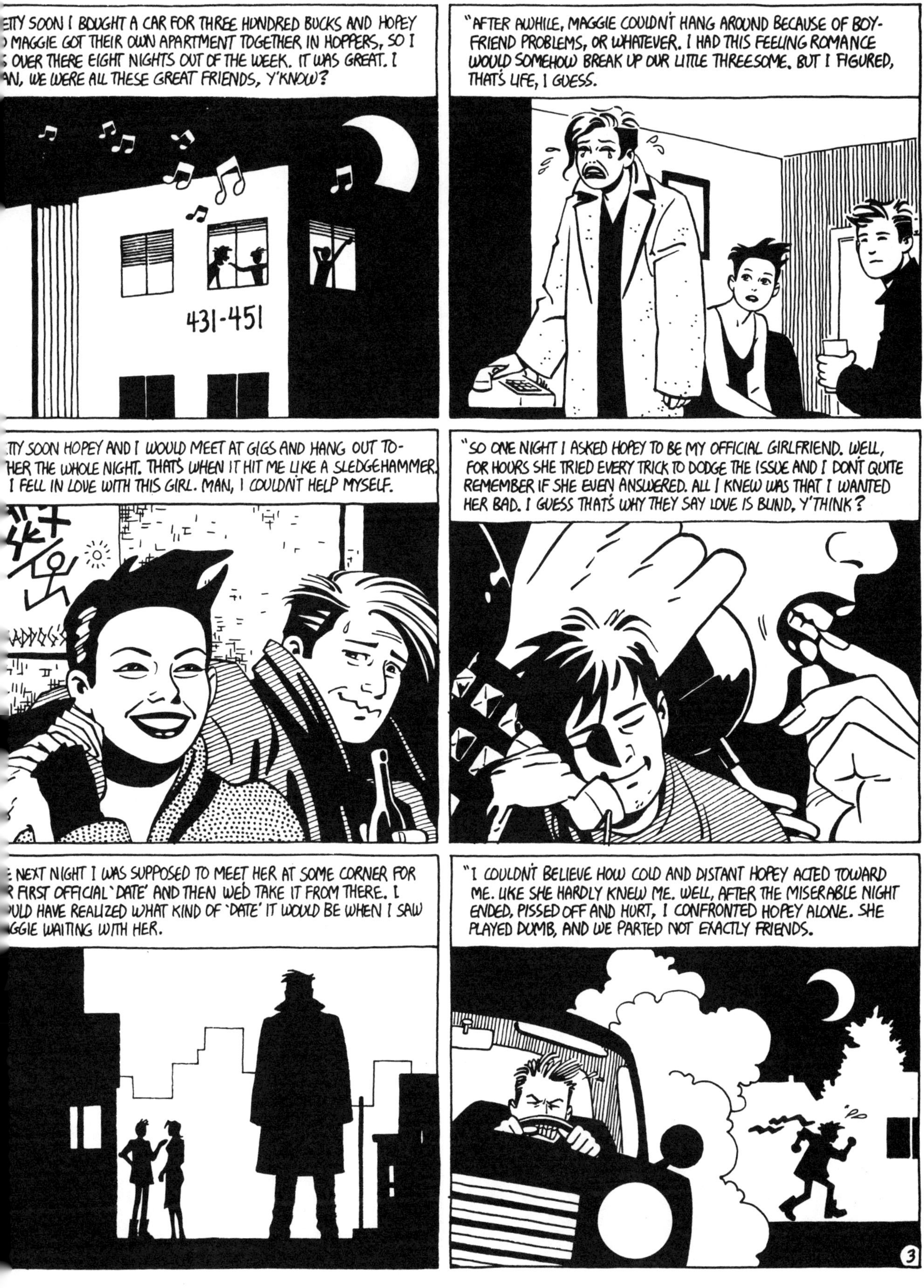
ETTY SOON I BOUGHT A CAR FOR THREE HUNDRED BUCKS AND HOPEY
MAGGIE GOT THEIR OWN APARTMENT TOGETHER IN HOPPERS, SO I
OVER THERE EIGHT NIGHTS OUT OF THE WEEK. IT WAS GREAT. I
AN, WE WERE ALL THESE GREAT FRIENDS, Y'KNOW?
431-451
"AFTER AWHILE, MAGGIE COULDN'T HANG AROUND BECAUSE OF BOY-FRIEND PROBLEMS, OR WHATEVER. I HAD THIS FEELING ROMANCE WOULD SOMEHOW BREAK UP OUR LITTLE THREESOME. BUT I FIGURED, THAT'S LIFE, I GUESS.
ETTY SOON HOPEY AND I WOULD MEET AT GIGS AND HANG OUT TO-
HER THE WHOLE NIGHT. THAT'S WHEN IT HIT ME LIKE A SLEDGEHAMMER.
I FELL IN LOVE WITH THIS GIRL. MAN, I COULDN'T HELP MYSELF.
"SO ONE NIGHT I ASKED HOPEY TO BE MY OFFICIAL GIRLFRIEND. WELL, FOR HOURS SHE TRIED EVERY TRICK TO DODGE THE ISSUE AND I DON'T QUITE REMEMBER IF SHE EVEN ANSWERED. ALL I KNEW WAS THAT I WANTED HER BAD. I GUESS THAT'S WHY THEY SAY LOVE IS BLIND, Y'THINK?
E NEXT NIGHT I WAS SUPPOSED TO MEET HER AT SOME CORNER FOR
R FIRST OFFICIAL 'DATE' AND THEN WE'D TAKE IT FROM THERE. I
OULD HAVE REALIZED WHAT KIND OF 'DATE' IT WOULD BE WHEN I SAW
GGIE WAITING WITH HER.
"I COULDN'T BELIEVE HOW COLD AND DISTANT HOPEY ACTED TOWARD ME. LIKE SHE HARDLY KNEW ME. WELL, AFTER THE MISERABLE NIGHT ENDED, PISSED OFF AND HURT, I CONFRONTED HOPEY ALONE. SHE PLAYED DUMB, AND WE PARTED NOT EXACTLY FRIENDS.

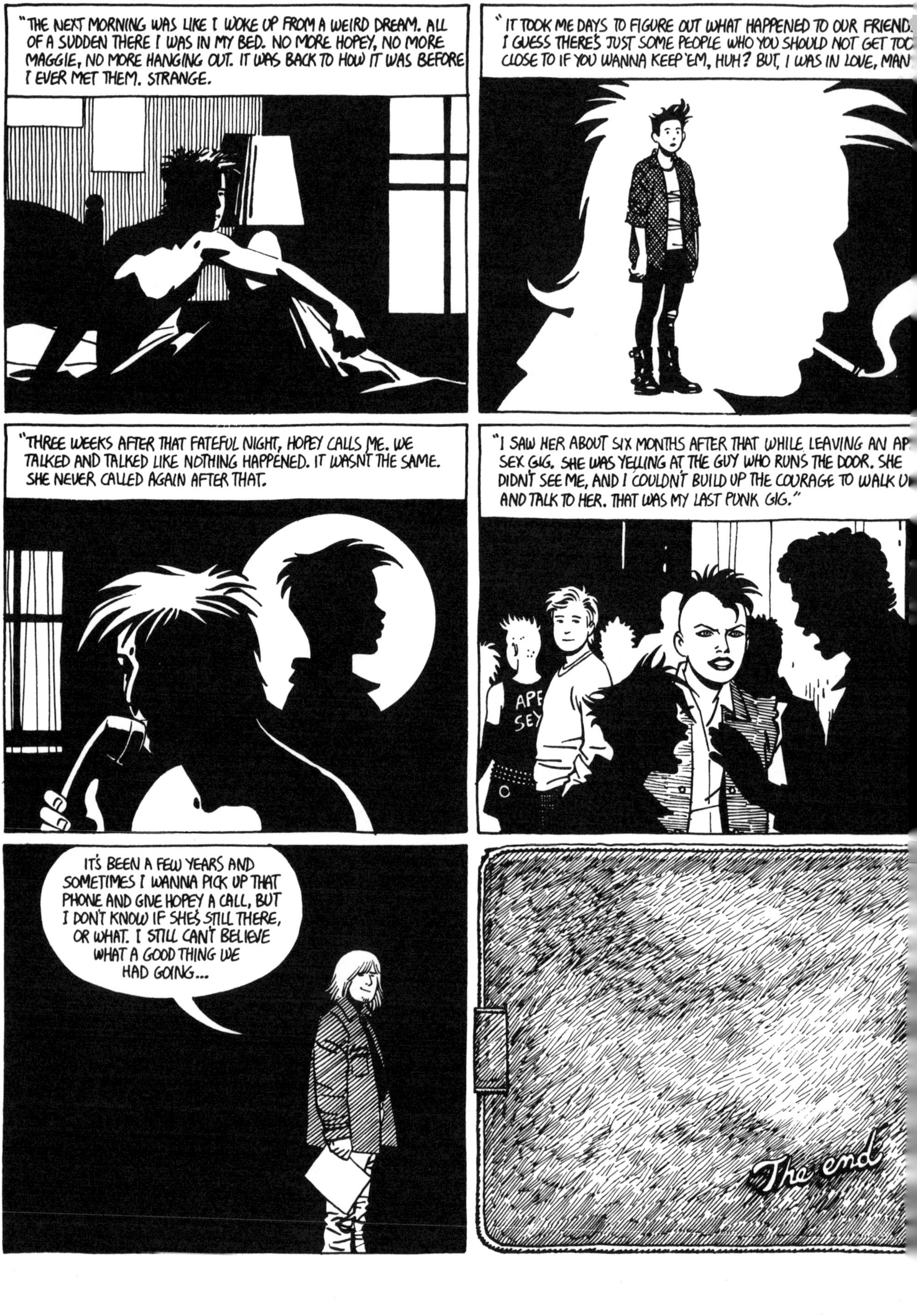
"THE NEXT MORNING WAS LIKE I WOKE UP FROM A WEIRD DREAM. ALL OF A SUDDEN THERE I WAS IN MY BED. NO MORE HOPEY, NO MORE MAGGIE, NO MORE HANGING OUT. IT WAS BACK TO HOW IT WAS BEFORE I EVER MET THEM. STRANGE.
"IT TOOK ME DAYS TO FIGURE OUT WHAT HAPPENED TO OUR FRIEND. I GUESS THERE'S JUST SOME PEOPLE WHO YOU SHOULD NOT GET TOO CLOSE TO IF YOU WANNA KEEP 'EM, HUH? BUT, I WAS IN LOVE, MAN
"THREE WEEKS AFTER THAT FATEFUL NIGHT, HOPEY CALLS ME. WE TALKED AND TALKED LIKE NOTHING HAPPENED. IT WASN'T THE SAME. SHE NEVER CALLED AGAIN AFTER THAT.
"I SAW HER ABOUT SIX MONTHS AFTER THAT WHILE LEAVING AN AP SEX GIG. SHE WAS YELLING AT THE GUY WHO RUNS THE DOOR. SHE DIDN'T SEE ME, AND I COULDN'T BUILD UP THE COURAGE TO WALK U AND TALK TO HER. THAT WAS MY LAST PUNK GIG."
APE SEX
IT'S BEEN A FEW YEARS AND SOMETIMES I WANNA PICK UP THAT PHONE AND GIVE HOPEY A CALL, BUT I DON'T KNOW IF SHE'S STILL THERE, OR WHAT. I STILL CAN'T BELIEVE WHAT A GOOD THING WE HAD GOING...
The end

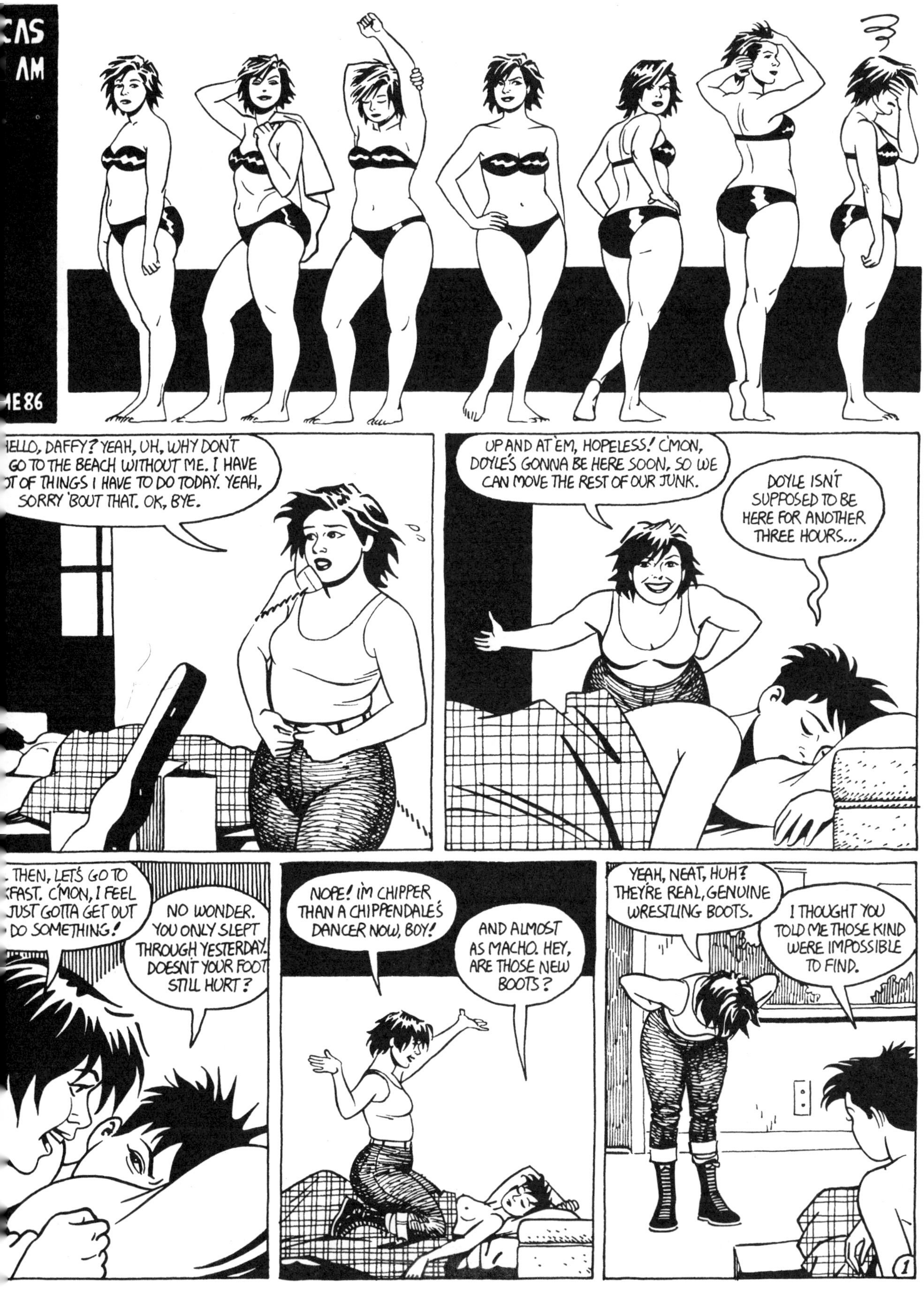

CAS
AM
ME86
HELLO, DAFFY? YEAH, UH, WHY DON'T GO TO THE BEACH WITHOUT ME. I HAVE OT OF THINGS I HAVE TO DO TODAY. YEAH, SORRY 'BOUT THAT. OK, BYE.
UP AND AT 'EM, HOPELESS! C'MON, DOYLE'S GONNA BE HERE SOON, SO WE CAN MOVE THE REST OF OUR JUNK.
DOYLE ISN'T SUPPOSED TO BE HERE FOR ANOTHER THREE HOURS...
THEN, LET'S GO TO KFAST. C'MON, I FEEL JUST GOTTA GET OUT DO SOMETHING!
NO WONDER. YOU ONLY SLEPT THROUGH YESTERDAY. DOESN'T YOUR FOOT STILL HURT?
NOPE! I'M CHIPPER THAN A CHIPPENDALE'S DANCER NOW, BOY!
AND ALMOST AS MACHO. HEY, ARE THOSE NEW BOOTS?
YEAH, NEAT, HUH? THEY'RE REAL, GENUINE WRESTLING BOOTS.
I THOUGHT YOU TOLD ME THOSE KIND WERE IMPOSSIBLE TO FIND.

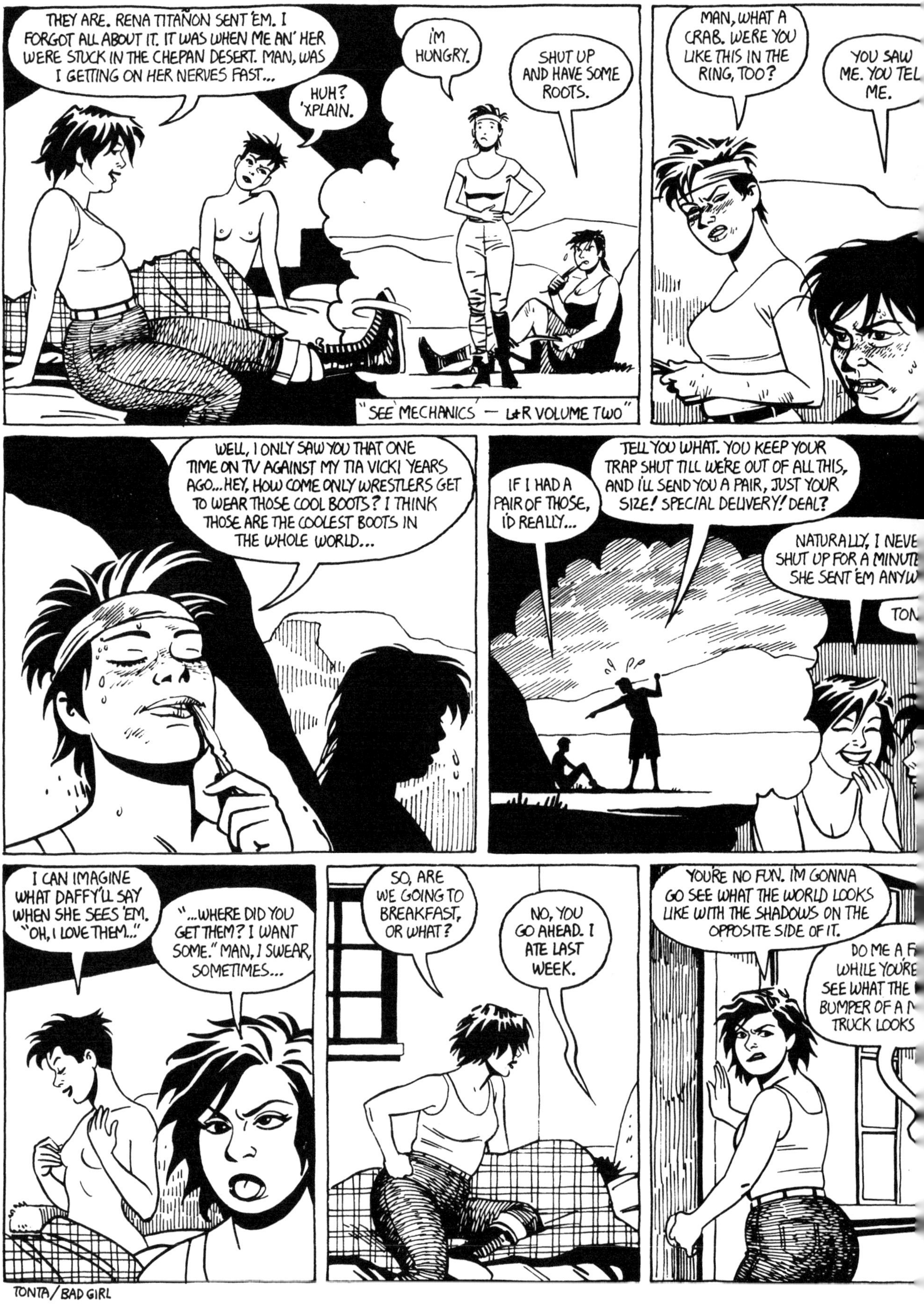
THEY ARE. RENA TITAÑON SENT 'EM. I FORGOT ALL ABOUT IT. IT WAS WHEN ME AN' HER WERE STUCK IN THE CHEPAN DESERT. MAN, WAS I GETTING ON HER NERVES FAST...
HUH? 'XPLAIN.
I'M HUNGRY.
SHUT UP AND HAVE SOME ROOTS.
"SEE 'MECHANICS' — L&R VOLUME TWO"
MAN, WHAT A CRAB. WERE YOU LIKE THIS IN THE RING, TOO?
YOU SAW ME. YOU TEL ME.
WELL, I ONLY SAW YOU THAT ONE TIME ON TV AGAINST MY TIA VICKI YEARS AGO... HEY, HOW COME ONLY WRESTLERS GET TO WEAR THOSE COOL BOOTS? I THINK THOSE ARE THE COOLEST BOOTS IN THE WHOLE WORLD...
IF I HAD A PAIR OF THOSE, I'D REALLY...
TELL YOU WHAT. YOU KEEP YOUR TRAP SHUT TILL WE'RE OUT OF ALL THIS, AND I'LL SEND YOU A PAIR, JUST YOUR SIZE! SPECIAL DELIVERY! DEAL?
NATURALLY, I NEVE SHUT UP FOR A MINUTE SHE SENT 'EM ANYW
TON
I CAN IMAGINE WHAT DAFFY'LL SAY WHEN SHE SEES 'EM. "OH, I LOVE THEM..."
"...WHERE DID YOU GET THEM? I WANT SOME." MAN, I SWEAR, SOMETIMES...
SO, ARE WE GOING TO BREAKFAST, OR WHAT?
NO, YOU GO AHEAD. I ATE LAST WEEK.
YOU'RE NO FUN. I'M GONNA GO SEE WHAT THE WORLD LOOKS LIKE WITH THE SHADOWS ON THE OPPOSITE SIDE OF IT.
DO ME A F WHILE YOU'RE SEE WHAT THE BUMPER OF A M TRUCK LOOKS

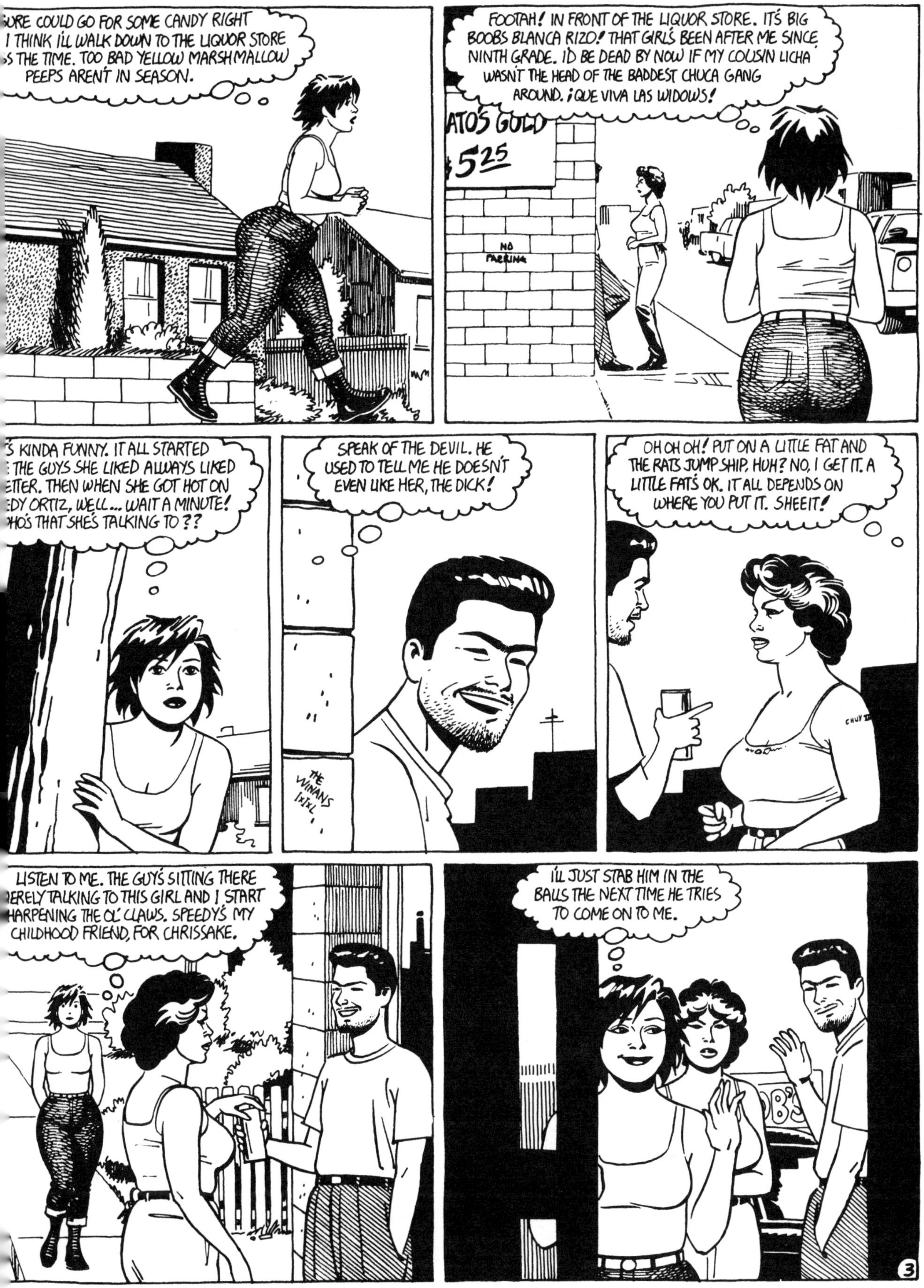

SURE COULD GO FOR SOME CANDY RIGHT
I THINK I'LL WALK DOWN TO THE LIQUOR STORE
S THE TIME. TOO BAD YELLOW MARSHMALLOW PEEPS AREN'T IN SEASON.
FOOTAH! IN FRONT OF THE LIQUOR STORE. IT'S BIG BOOBS BLANCA RIZO! THAT GIRL'S BEEN AFTER ME SINCE NINTH GRADE. I'D BE DEAD BY NOW IF MY COUSIN LICHA WASN'T THE HEAD OF THE BADDEST CHUCA GANG AROUND. ¡QUE VIVA LAS WIDOWS!
ATO'S GOLD
5 25
NO PARKING
'S KINDA FUNNY. IT ALL STARTED THE GUYS SHE LIKED ALWAYS LIKED ETTER. THEN WHEN SHE GOT HOT ON EDY ORTIZ, WELL... WAIT A MINUTE! HO'S THAT SHE'S TALKING TO??
SPEAK OF THE DEVIL. HE USED TO TELL ME HE DOESN'T EVEN LIKE HER, THE DICK!
THE WINANS
OH OH OH! PUT ON A LITTLE FAT AND THE RATS JUMP SHIP, HUH? NO, I GET IT. A LITTLE FAT'S OK. IT ALL DEPENDS ON WHERE YOU PUT IT. SHEEIT!
LISTEN TO ME. THE GUY'S SITTING THERE MERELY TALKING TO THIS GIRL AND I START SHARPENING THE OL' CLAWS. SPEEDY'S MY CHILDHOOD FRIEND, FOR CHRISSAKE.
I'LL JUST STAB HIM IN THE BALLS THE NEXT TIME HE TRIES TO COME ON TO ME.

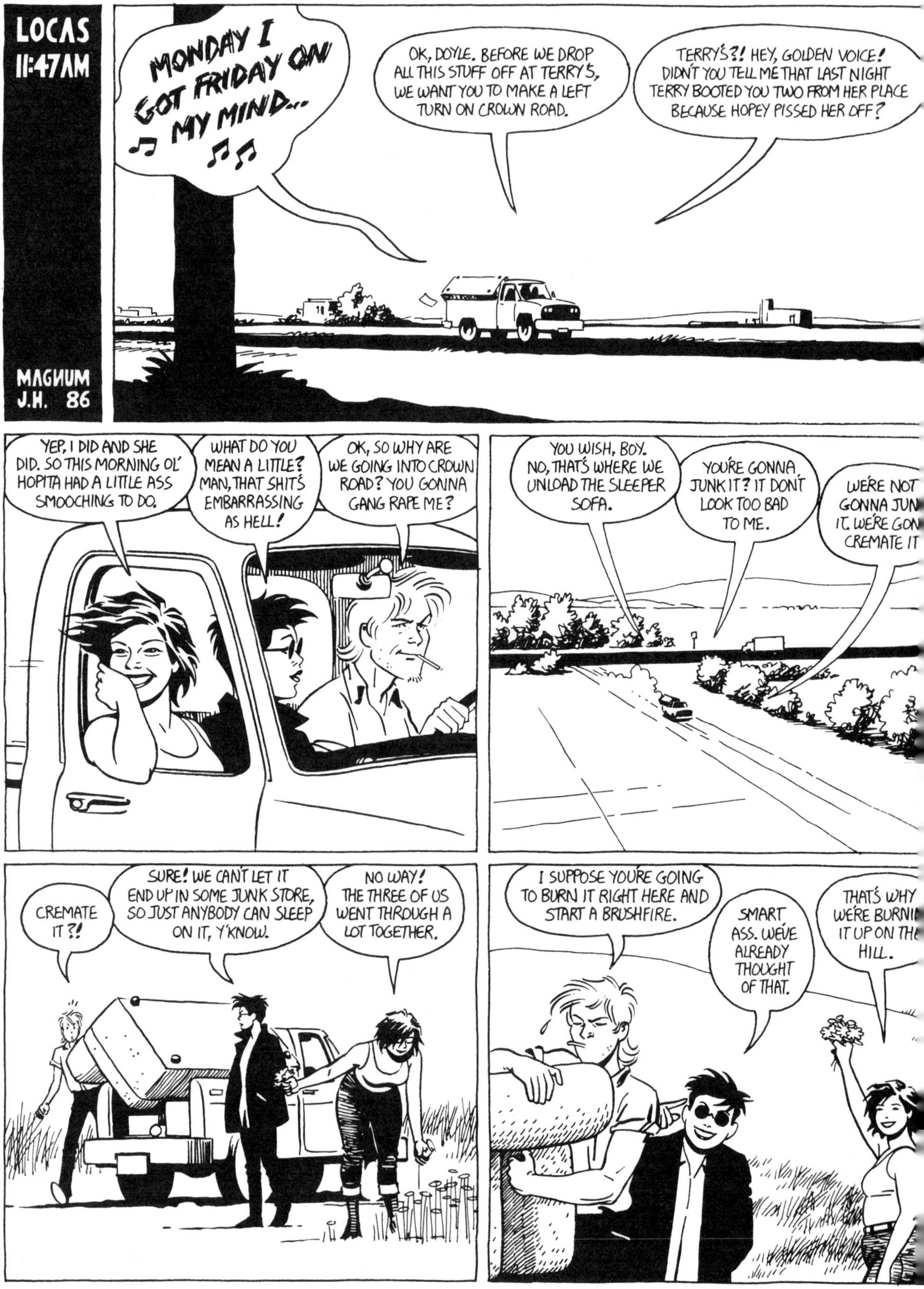
LOCAS
11:47AM
MAGNUM
J.H. 86
MONDAY I GOT FRIDAY ON MY MIND...
OK, DOYLE. BEFORE WE DROP ALL THIS STUFF OFF AT TERRY'S, WE WANT YOU TO MAKE A LEFT TURN ON CROWN ROAD.
TERRY'S?! HEY, GOLDEN VOICE! DIDN'T YOU TELL ME THAT LAST NIGHT TERRY BOOTED YOU TWO FROM HER PLACE BECAUSE HOPEY PISSED HER OFF?
YEP, I DID AND SHE DID. SO THIS MORNING OL' HOPITA HAD A LITTLE ASS SMOOCHING TO DO.
WHAT DO YOU MEAN A LITTLE? MAN, THAT SHIT'S EMBARRASSING AS HELL!
OK, SO WHY ARE WE GOING INTO CROWN ROAD? YOU GONNA GANG RAPE ME?
YOU WISH, BOY. NO, THAT'S WHERE WE UNLOAD THE SLEEPER SOFA.
YOU'RE GONNA JUNK IT? IT DON'T LOOK TOO BAD TO ME.
WE'RE NOT GONNA JUN IT. WE'RE GON CREMATE IT
CREMATE IT?!
SURE! WE CAN'T LET IT END UP IN SOME JUNK STORE, SO JUST ANYBODY CAN SLEEP ON IT, Y'KNOW.
NO WAY! THE THREE OF US WENT THROUGH A LOT TOGETHER.
I SUPPOSE YOU'RE GOING TO BURN IT RIGHT HERE AND START A BRUSHFIRE.
SMART ASS. WE'VE ALREADY THOUGHT OF THAT.
THAT'S WHY WE'RE BURNI IT UP ON TH HILL.

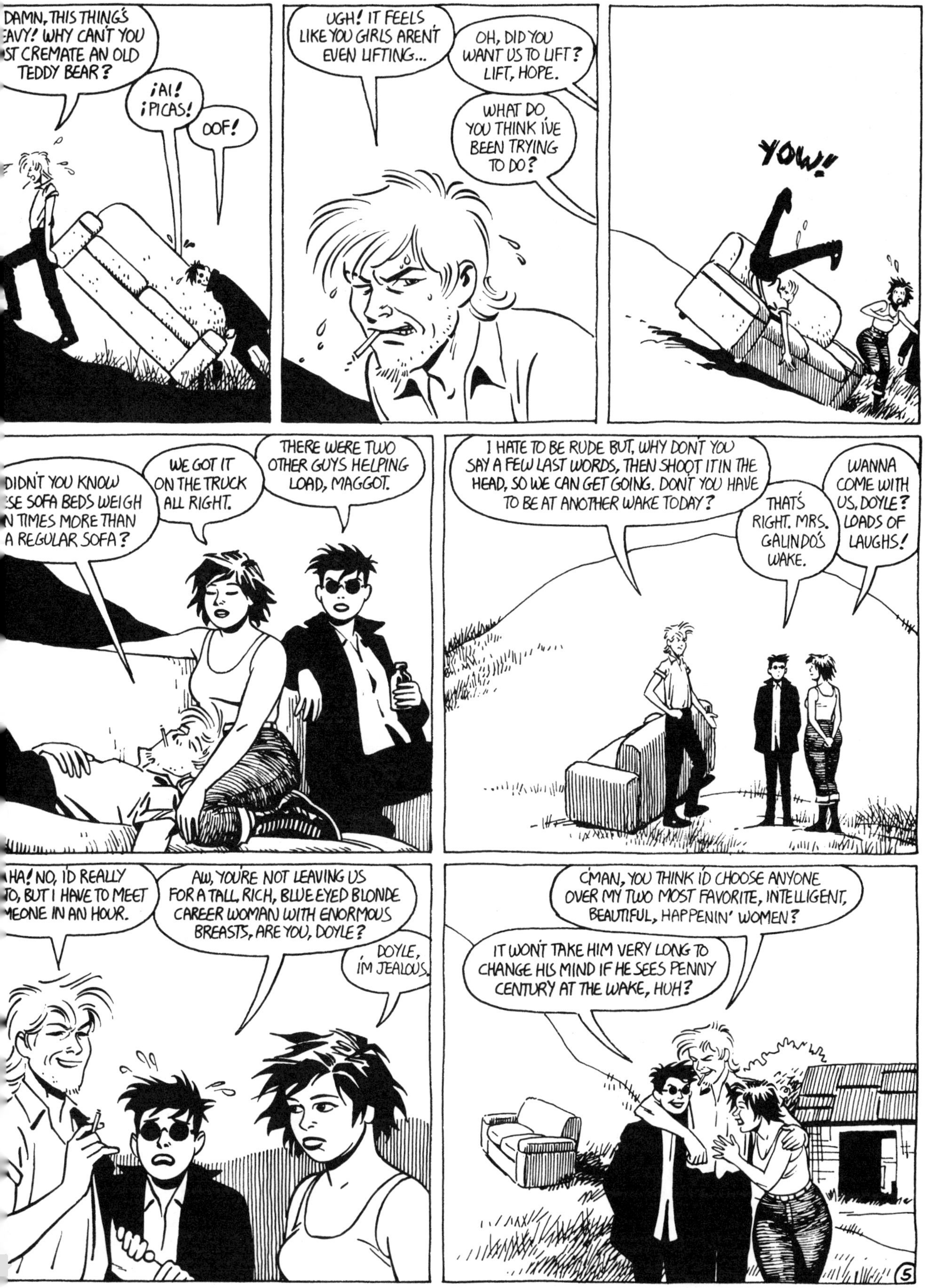
DAMN, THIS THING'S
EAVY! WHY CAN'T YOU
ST CREMATE AN OLD
TEDDY BEAR?
¡AI! ¡PICAS!
OOF!
UGH! IT FEELS LIKE YOU GIRLS AREN'T EVEN LIFTING...
OH, DID YOU WANT US TO LIFT? LIFT, HOPE.
WHAT DO YOU THINK I'VE BEEN TRYING TO DO?
YOW!
DIDN'T YOU KNOW
ESE SOFA BEDS WEIGH
N TIMES MORE THAN
A REGULAR SOFA?
WE GOT IT ON THE TRUCK ALL RIGHT.
THERE WERE TWO OTHER GUYS HELPING LOAD, MAGGOT.
I HATE TO BE RUDE BUT, WHY DON'T YOU SAY A FEW LAST WORDS, THEN SHOOT IT IN THE HEAD, SO WE CAN GET GOING. DON'T YOU HAVE TO BE AT ANOTHER WAKE TODAY?
THAT'S RIGHT. MRS. GALINDO'S WAKE.
WANNA COME WITH US, DOYLE? LOADS OF LAUGHS!
HA! NO, I'D REALLY
TO, BUT I HAVE TO MEET
MEONE IN AN HOUR.
AW, YOU'RE NOT LEAVING US FOR A TALL, RICH, BLUE EYED BLONDE CAREER WOMAN WITH ENORMOUS BREASTS, ARE YOU, DOYLE?
DOYLE, I'M JEALOUS.
C'MAN, YOU THINK I'D CHOOSE ANYONE OVER MY TWO MOST FAVORITE, INTELLIGENT, BEAUTIFUL, HAPPENIN' WOMEN?
IT WON'T TAKE HIM VERY LONG TO CHANGE HIS MIND IF HE SEES PENNY CENTURY AT THE WAKE, HUH?

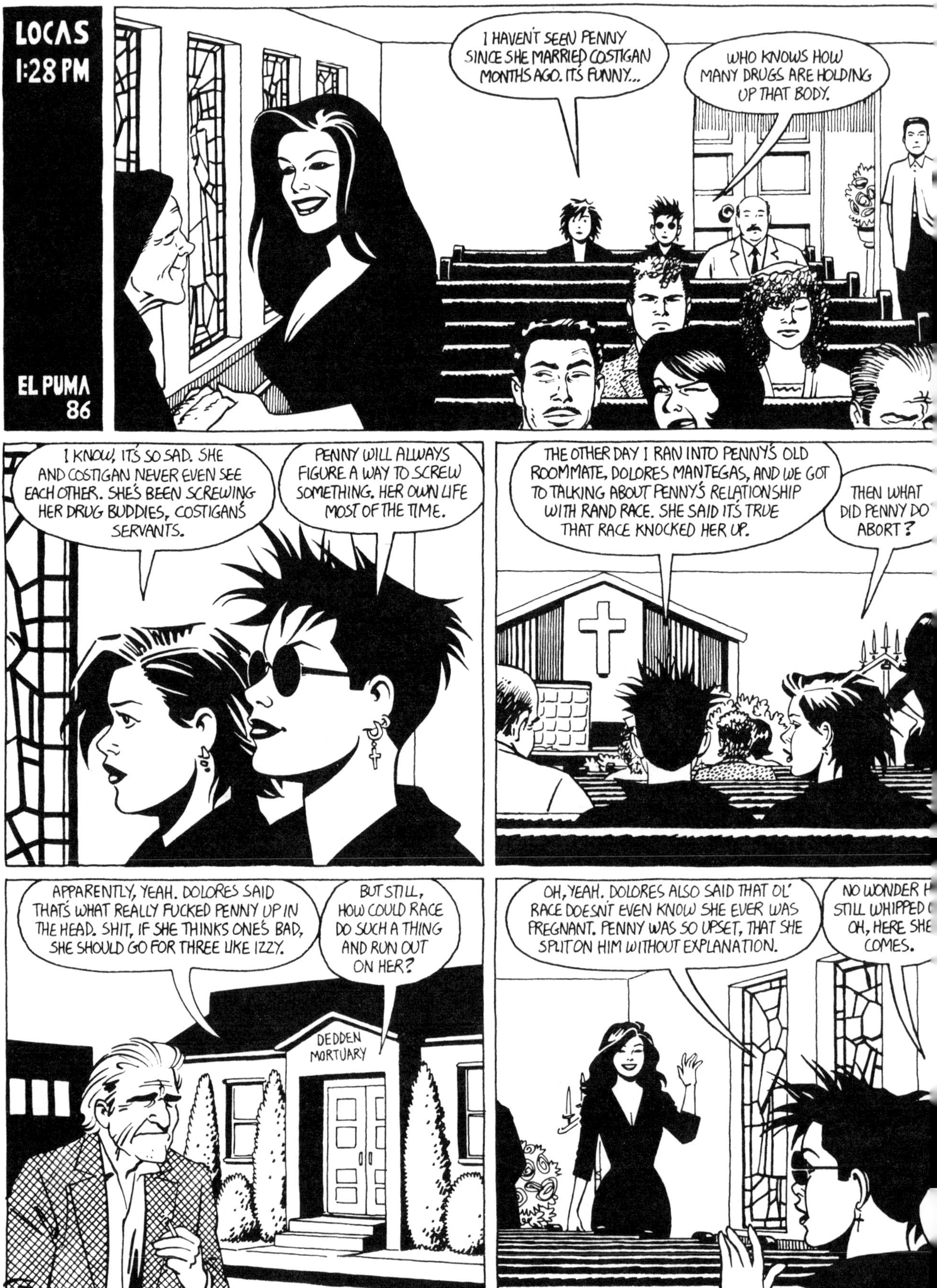
LOCAS
1:28 PM
EL PUMA
86
I HAVEN'T SEEN PENNY SINCE SHE MARRIED COSTIGAN MONTHS AGO. IT'S FUNNY...
WHO KNOWS HOW MANY DRUGS ARE HOLDING UP THAT BODY.
I KNOW, IT'S SO SAD. SHE AND COSTIGAN NEVER EVEN SEE EACH OTHER. SHE'S BEEN SCREWING HER DRUG BUDDIES, COSTIGAN'S SERVANTS.
PENNY WILL ALWAYS FIGURE A WAY TO SCREW SOMETHING. HER OWN LIFE MOST OF THE TIME.
THE OTHER DAY I RAN INTO PENNY'S OLD ROOMMATE, DOLORES MANTEGAS, AND WE GOT TO TALKING ABOUT PENNY'S RELATIONSHIP WITH RAND RACE. SHE SAID IT'S TRUE THAT RACE KNOCKED HER UP.
THEN WHAT DID PENNY DO ABORT?
APPARENTLY, YEAH. DOLORES SAID THAT'S WHAT REALLY FUCKED PENNY UP IN THE HEAD. SHIT, IF SHE THINKS ONE'S BAD, SHE SHOULD GO FOR THREE LIKE IZZY.
BUT STILL, HOW COULD RACE DO SUCH A THING AND RUN OUT ON HER?
DEDDEN MORTUARY
OH, YEAH. DOLORES ALSO SAID THAT OL' RACE DOESN'T EVEN KNOW SHE EVER WAS PREGNANT. PENNY WAS SO UPSET, THAT SHE SPLIT ON HIM WITHOUT EXPLANATION.
NO WONDER H STILL WHIPPED OH, HERE SHE COMES.

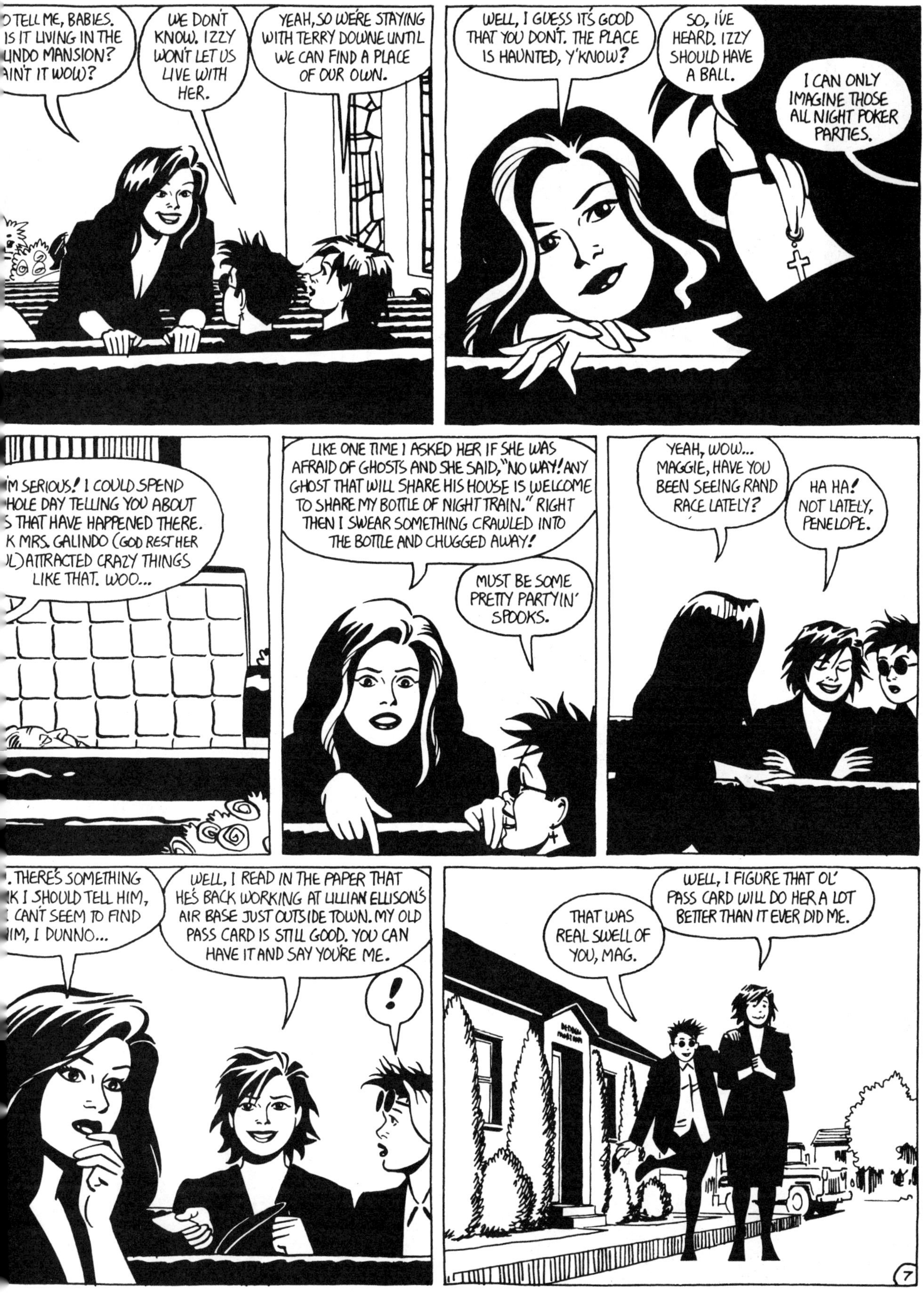
O TELL ME, BABIES. IS IT LIVING IN THE LINDO MANSION? AIN'T IT WOW?
WE DON'T KNOW. IZZY WON'T LET US LIVE WITH HER.
YEAH, SO WE'RE STAYING WITH TERRY DOWNE UNTIL WE CAN FIND A PLACE OF OUR OWN.
WELL, I GUESS IT'S GOOD THAT YOU DON'T. THE PLACE IS HAUNTED, Y'KNOW?
SO, I'VE HEARD. IZZY SHOULD HAVE A BALL.
I CAN ONLY IMAGINE THOSE ALL NIGHT POKER PARTIES.
I'M SERIOUS! I COULD SPEND HOLE DAY TELLING YOU ABOUT S THAT HAVE HAPPENED THERE. K MRS. GALINDO (GOD REST HER IL) ATTRACTED CRAZY THINGS LIKE THAT. WOO...
LIKE ONE TIME I ASKED HER IF SHE WAS AFRAID OF GHOSTS AND SHE SAID, "NO WAY! ANY GHOST THAT WILL SHARE HIS HOUSE IS WELCOME TO SHARE MY BOTTLE OF NIGHT TRAIN." RIGHT THEN I SWEAR SOMETHING CRAWLED INTO THE BOTTLE AND CHUGGED AWAY!
MUST BE SOME PRETTY PARTYIN' SPOOKS.
YEAH, WOW... MAGGIE, HAVE YOU BEEN SEEING RAND RACE LATELY?
HA HA! NOT LATELY, PENELOPE.
. THERE'S SOMETHING K I SHOULD TELL HIM, CAN'T SEEM TO FIND HIM, I DUNNO...
WELL, I READ IN THE PAPER THAT HE'S BACK WORKING AT LILLIAN ELLISON'S AIR BASE JUST OUTSIDE TOWN. MY OLD PASS CARD IS STILL GOOD. YOU CAN HAVE IT AND SAY YOU'RE ME.
!
THAT WAS REAL SWELL OF YOU, MAG.
WELL, I FIGURE THAT OL' PASS CARD WILL DO HER A LOT BETTER THAN IT EVER DID ME.

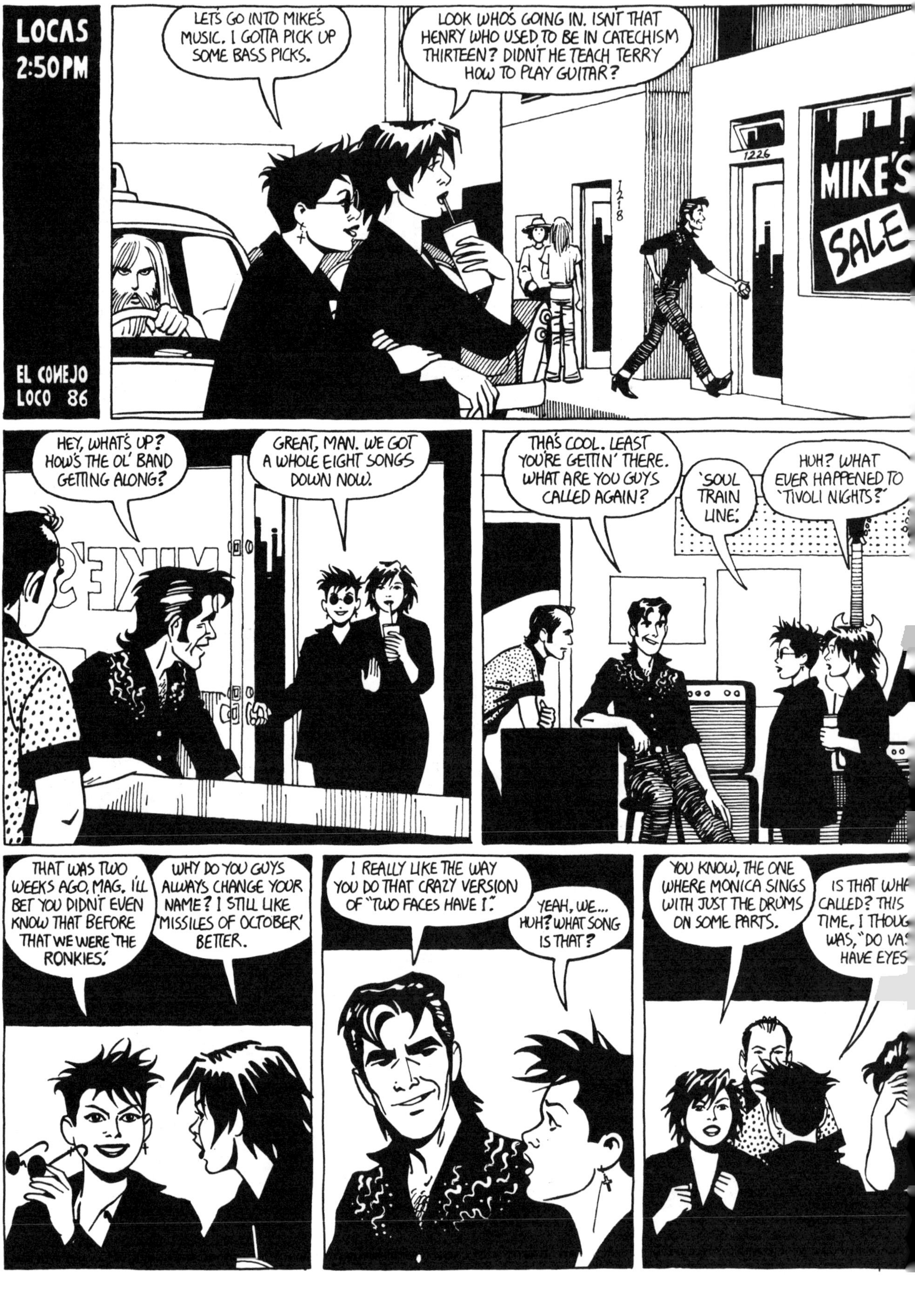
LOCAS
2:50 PM
EL CONEJO LOCO 86
LETS GO INTO MIKE'S MUSIC. I GOTTA PICK UP SOME BASS PICKS.
LOOK WHO'S GOING IN. ISN'T THAT HENRY WHO USED TO BE IN CATECHISM THIRTEEN? DIDN'T HE TEACH TERRY HOW TO PLAY GUITAR?
1218
1226
MIKE'S
SALE
HEY, WHAT'S UP? HOW'S THE OL' BAND GETTING ALONG?
GREAT, MAN. WE GOT A WHOLE EIGHT SONGS DOWN NOW.
THA'S COOL. LEAST YOU'RE GETTIN' THERE. WHAT ARE YOU GUYS CALLED AGAIN?
'SOUL TRAIN LINE.'
HUH? WHAT EVER HAPPENED TO 'TIVOLI NIGHTS?'
THAT WAS TWO WEEKS AGO, MAG. I'LL BET YOU DIDN'T EVEN KNOW THAT BEFORE THAT WE WERE 'THE RONKIES.'
WHY DO YOU GUYS ALWAYS CHANGE YOUR NAME? I STILL LIKE 'MISSILES OF OCTOBER' BETTER.
I REALLY LIKE THE WAY YOU DO THAT CRAZY VERSION OF "TWO FACES HAVE I."
YEAH, WE... HUH? WHAT SONG IS THAT?
YOU KNOW, THE ONE WHERE MONICA SINGS WITH JUST THE DRUMS ON SOME PARTS.
IS THAT WHA CALLED? THIS TIME, I THOUG WAS, "DO VAS HAVE EYES

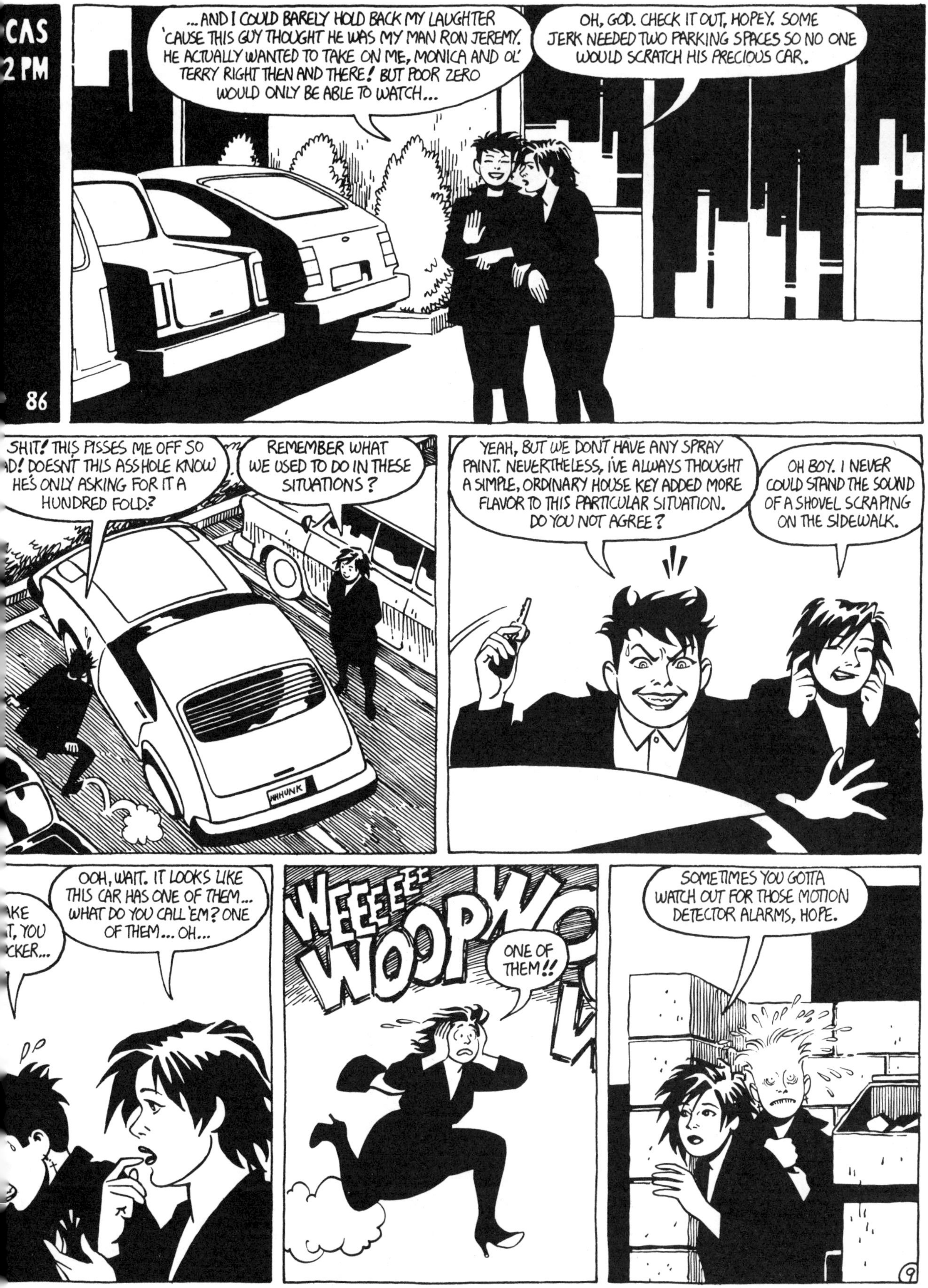
CAS
2 PM
...AND I COULD BARELY HOLD BACK MY LAUGHTER 'CAUSE THIS GUY THOUGHT HE WAS MY MAN RON JEREMY. HE ACTUALLY WANTED TO TAKE ON ME, MONICA AND OL' TERRY RIGHT THEN AND THERE! BUT POOR ZERO WOULD ONLY BE ABLE TO WATCH...
OH, GOD. CHECK IT OUT, HOPEY. SOME JERK NEEDED TWO PARKING SPACES SO NO ONE WOULD SCRATCH HIS PRECIOUS CAR.
86
SHIT! THIS PISSES ME OFF SO AD! DOESN'T THIS ASSHOLE KNOW HE'S ONLY ASKING FOR IT A HUNDRED FOLD?
REMEMBER WHAT WE USED TO DO IN THESE SITUATIONS?
HHHUNK
YEAH, BUT WE DON'T HAVE ANY SPRAY PAINT. NEVERTHELESS, I'VE ALWAYS THOUGHT A SIMPLE, ORDINARY HOUSE KEY ADDED MORE FLAVOR TO THIS PARTICULAR SITUATION. DO YOU NOT AGREE?
OH BOY. I NEVER COULD STAND THE SOUND OF A SHOVEL SCRAPING ON THE SIDEWALK.
AKE T, YOU CKER...
OOH, WAIT. IT LOOKS LIKE THIS CAR HAS ONE OF THEM... WHAT DO YOU CALL 'EM? ONE OF THEM... OH...
WEEEEE-WOOP
ONE OF THEM!!
SOMETIMES YOU GOTTA WATCH OUT FOR THOSE MOTION DETECTOR ALARMS, HOPE.
9

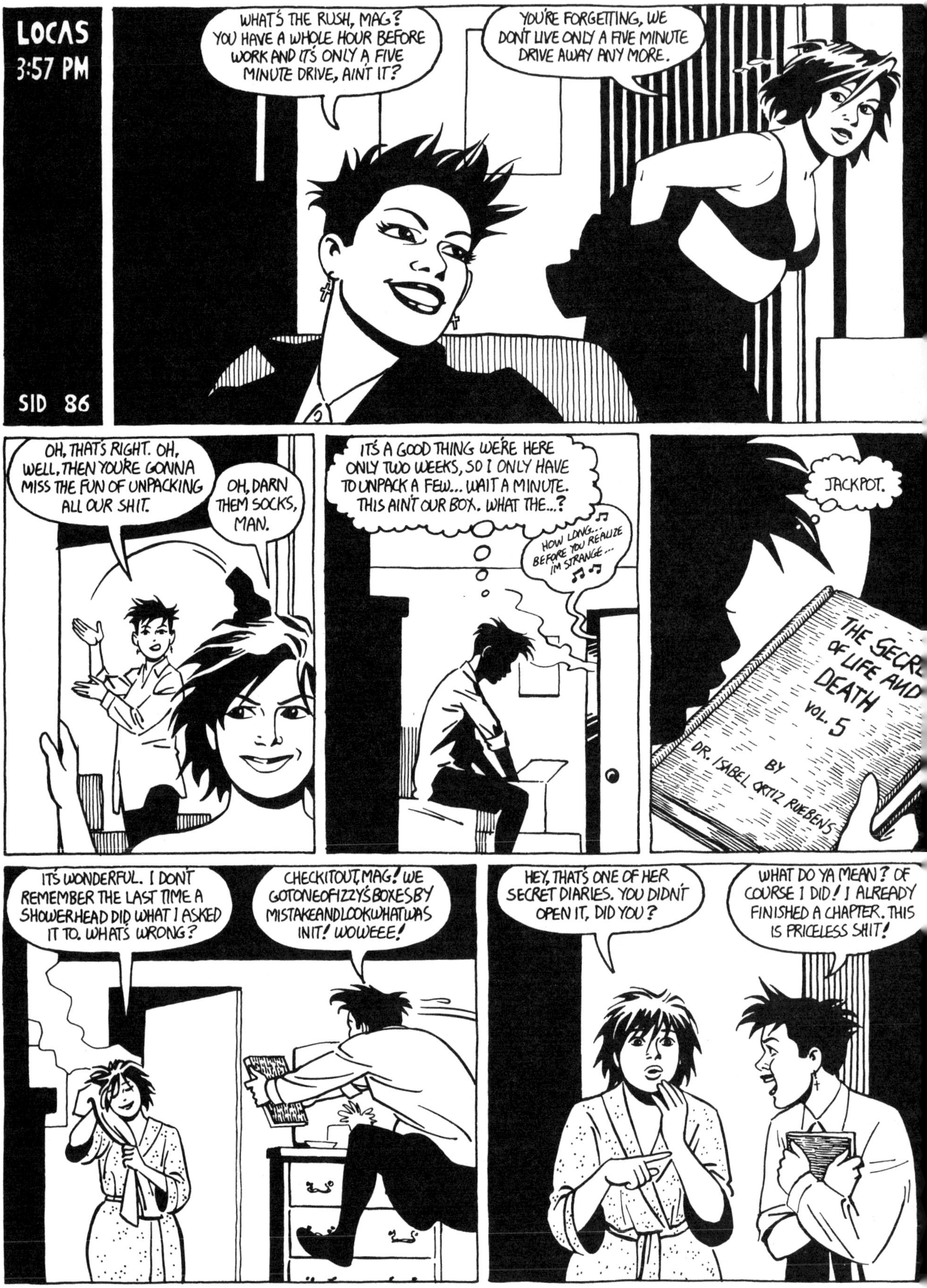
LOCAS
3:57 PM
SID 86
WHAT'S THE RUSH, MAG? YOU HAVE A WHOLE HOUR BEFORE WORK AND IT'S ONLY A FIVE MINUTE DRIVE, AIN'T IT?
YOU'RE FORGETTING, WE DON'T LIVE ONLY A FIVE MINUTE DRIVE AWAY ANY MORE.
OH, THAT'S RIGHT. OH, WELL, THEN YOU'RE GONNA MISS THE FUN OF UNPACKING ALL OUR SHIT.
OH, DARN THEM SOCKS, MAN.
IT'S A GOOD THING WE'RE HERE ONLY TWO WEEKS, SO I ONLY HAVE TO UNPACK A FEW... WAIT A MINUTE. THIS AIN'T OUR BOX. WHAT THE...?
HOW LONG... BEFORE YOU REALIZE I'M STRANGE...
JACKPOT.
THE SECR OF LIFE AND DEATH VOL. 5 BY DR. ISABEL ORTIZ RUEBENS
IT'S WONDERFUL. I DON'T REMEMBER THE LAST TIME A SHOWERHEAD DID WHAT I ASKED IT TO. WHAT'S WRONG?
CHECKITOUT, MAG! WE GOTONEOFIZZY'SBOXESBY MISTAKEANDLOOKWHATWAS INIT! WOWEEE!
HEY, THAT'S ONE OF HER SECRET DIARIES. YOU DIDN'T OPEN IT, DID YOU?
WHAT DO YA MEAN? OF COURSE I DID! I ALREADY FINISHED A CHAPTER. THIS IS PRICELESS SHIT!

HEY, WHERE YOU GOING? AREN'T YOU GONNA READ ME SOME?

I THOUGHT YOU HAD TO GO TO WORK?

AW, COME ON HOPEY! DON'T FUCK AROUND!

YOU GOTTA KISS MY BUTT FIRST.

OK OK! OUCH! HEY, WHERE'D YOU GET MUSCLES?

MAKIN' THEM FRENCH FRIES AIN'T NO SISSY SHIT, CHICK!

CHECK IT OUT. THIS VOLUME WAS WRITTEN ABOUT THE TIME ME AN' YOU FIRST STARTED HANGING AROUND. SEE, SHE WRITES ABOUT THAT TIME WE FOUND THAT BIG OL' PURSE SITTING IN THAT LADY'S BIG OL' CAR...

YOU GUYS SHOULD HAVE WAITED FOR ME TO GET HOME, THEN WE COULD HAVE HAD US A THREESOME.

HI, TERRY.

OH, MAGGIE. BEFORE I FORGET, ISABEL TOLD ME TO TELL YOU THAT YOUR AUNT VICKI WANTS TO SEE YOU AT HER HOME AS SOON AS YOU CAN.

VICKI GLORI? SHIT!

YOU'VE HAD IT NOW, MAG...

NO, THIS IS SERIOUS SHIT. IT'S REALLY CRAZY. AND SHE LOST HER WRESTLING TITLE THE OTHER DAY. WHO KNOWS WHAT KIND OF CONDITION SHE'S IN RIGHT NOW...

IT'S TRUE, Y'KNOW...

ONE TIME SHE CHASED ME AN' DEL CHIMNEY OUT OF HER HOUSE AND DOWN THE STREET WHEN MAGGIE USED TO LIVE WITH HER.

I'LL GO AND SEE HER AFTER WORK. SHOOT, MAN...

IT'S BEEN NICE KNOWING YOU, GIRLS.

REMEMBER, MAG. IF SHE TRIES ANYTHING, RAKE THE EYES.

11

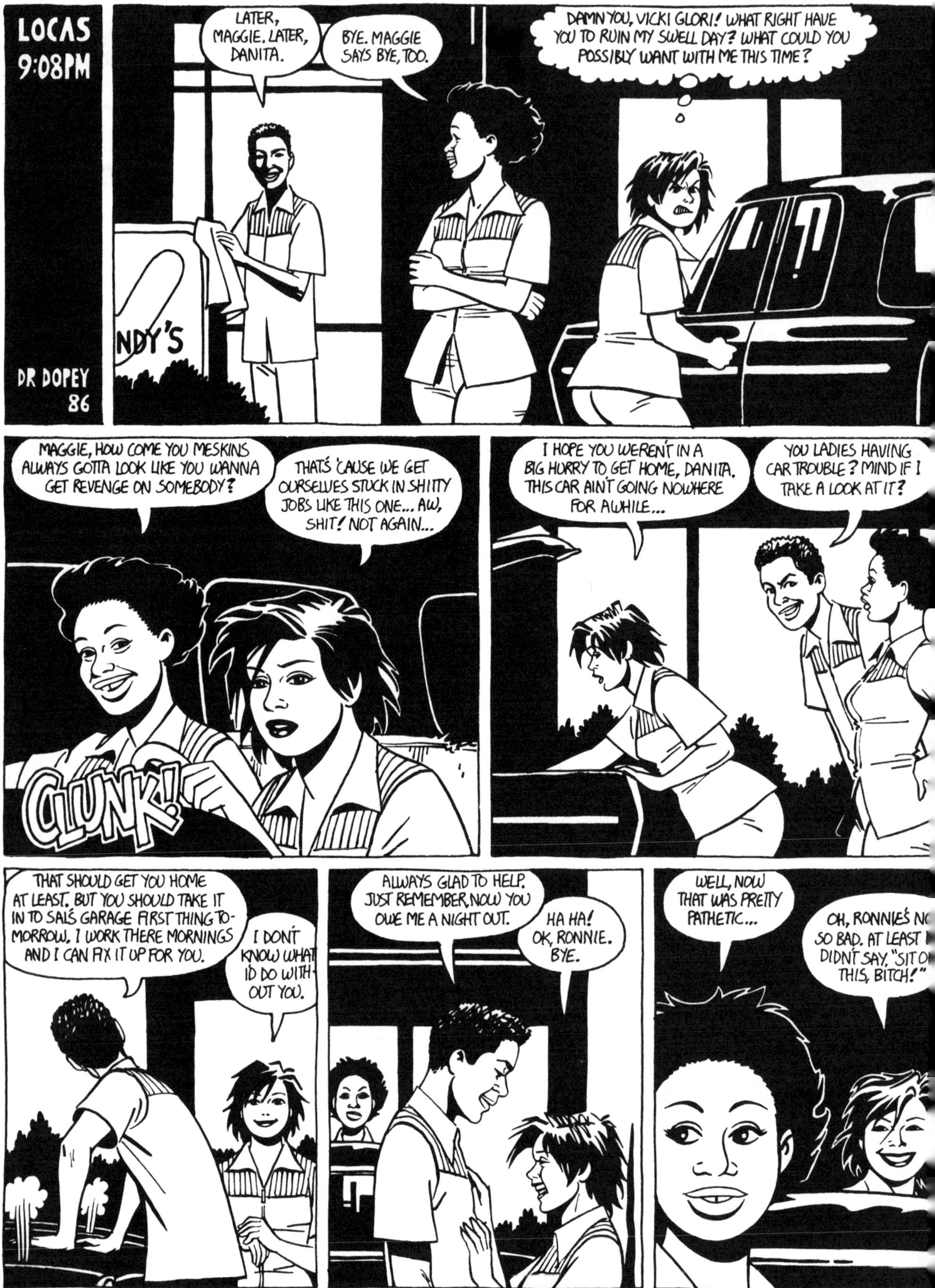
LOCAS
9:08PM
DR DOPEY
86
LATER, MAGGIE. LATER, DANITA.
BYE. MAGGIE SAYS BYE, TOO.
DAMN YOU, VICKI GLORI! WHAT RIGHT HAVE YOU TO RUIN MY SWELL DAY? WHAT COULD YOU POSSIBLY WANT WITH ME THIS TIME?
NDY'S
MAGGIE, HOW COME YOU MESKINS ALWAYS GOTTA LOOK LIKE YOU WANNA GET REVENGE ON SOMEBODY?
THAT'S 'CAUSE WE GET OURSELVES STUCK IN SHITTY JOBS LIKE THIS ONE... AW, SHIT! NOT AGAIN...
CLUNK!
I HOPE YOU WEREN'T IN A BIG HURRY TO GET HOME, DANITA. THIS CAR AIN'T GOING NOWHERE FOR AWHILE...
YOU LADIES HAVING CAR TROUBLE? MIND IF I TAKE A LOOK AT IT?
THAT SHOULD GET YOU HOME AT LEAST. BUT YOU SHOULD TAKE IT IN TO SAL'S GARAGE FIRST THING TO-MORROW. I WORK THERE MORNINGS AND I CAN FIX IT UP FOR YOU.
I DON'T KNOW WHAT I'D DO WITH-OUT YOU.
ALWAYS GLAD TO HELP. JUST REMEMBER, NOW YOU OWE ME A NIGHT OUT.
HA HA! OK, RONNIE. BYE.
WELL, NOW THAT WAS PRETTY PATHETIC...
OH, RONNIE'S NO SO BAD. AT LEAST DIDN'T SAY, "SIT O THIS, BITCH!"

MESKIN/MEXICAN

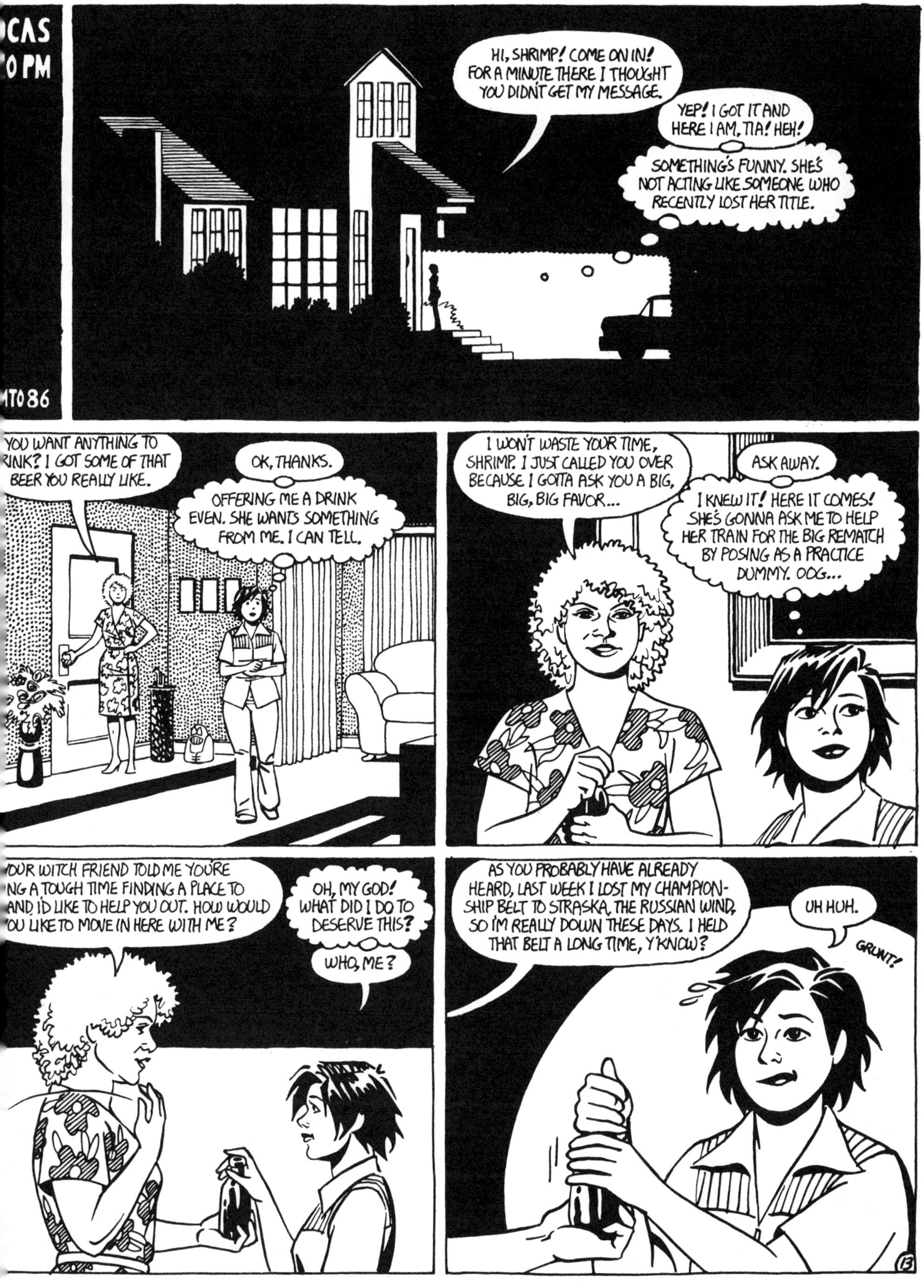
CAS
0 PM
TO 86
HI, SHRIMP! COME ON IN! FOR A MINUTE THERE I THOUGHT YOU DIDN'T GET MY MESSAGE.
YEP! I GOT IT AND HERE I AM, TIA! HEH!
SOMETHING'S FUNNY. SHE'S NOT ACTING LIKE SOMEONE WHO RECENTLY LOST HER TITLE.
YOU WANT ANYTHING TO RINK? I GOT SOME OF THAT BEER YOU REALLY LIKE.
OK, THANKS.
OFFERING ME A DRINK EVEN. SHE WANTS SOMETHING FROM ME. I CAN TELL.
I WON'T WASTE YOUR TIME, SHRIMP. I JUST CALLED YOU OVER BECAUSE I GOTTA ASK YOU A BIG, BIG, BIG FAVOR...
ASK AWAY.
I KNEW IT! HERE IT COMES! SHE'S GONNA ASK ME TO HELP HER TRAIN FOR THE BIG REMATCH BY POSING AS A PRACTICE DUMMY. OOG...
OUR WITCH FRIEND TOLD ME YOU'RE NG A TOUGH TIME FINDING A PLACE TO AND, I'D LIKE TO HELP YOU OUT. HOW WOULD OU LIKE TO MOVE IN HERE WITH ME?
OH, MY GOD! WHAT DID I DO TO DESERVE THIS?
WHO, ME?
AS YOU PROBABLY HAVE ALREADY HEARD, LAST WEEK I LOST MY CHAMPIONSHIP BELT TO STRASKA, THE RUSSIAN WIND, SO I'M REALLY DOWN THESE DAYS. I HELD THAT BELT A LONG TIME, Y'KNOW?
UH HUH.
GRUNT!

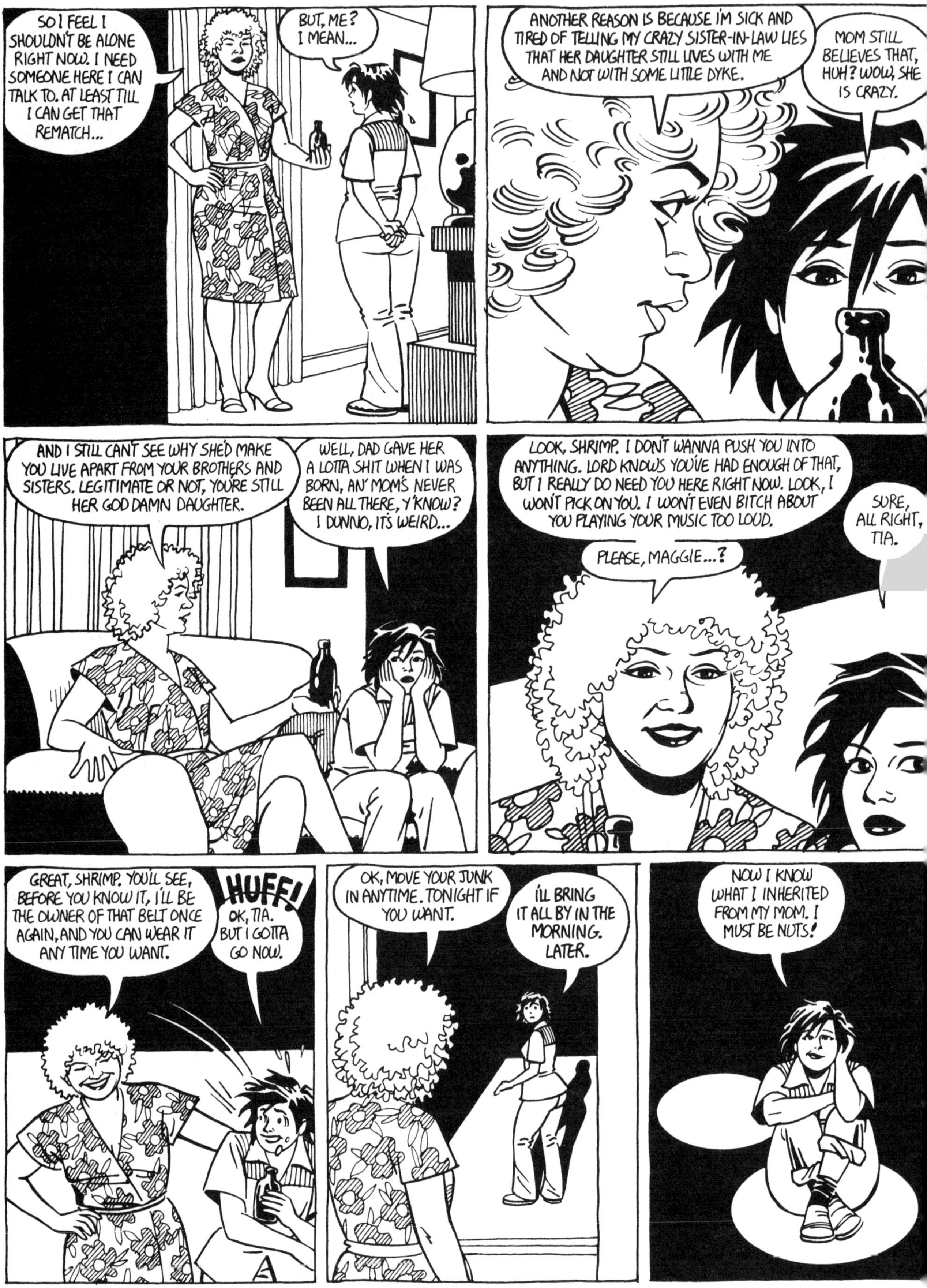
SO I FEEL I SHOULDN'T BE ALONE RIGHT NOW. I NEED SOMEONE HERE I CAN TALK TO. AT LEAST TILL I CAN GET THAT REMATCH...
BUT, ME? I MEAN...
ANOTHER REASON IS BECAUSE I'M SICK AND TIRED OF TELLING MY CRAZY SISTER-IN-LAW LIES THAT HER DAUGHTER STILL LIVES WITH ME AND NOT WITH SOME LITTLE DYKE.
MOM STILL BELIEVES THAT, HUH? WOW, SHE IS CRAZY.
AND I STILL CAN'T SEE WHY SHE'D MAKE YOU LIVE APART FROM YOUR BROTHERS AND SISTERS. LEGITIMATE OR NOT, YOU'RE STILL HER GOD DAMN DAUGHTER.
WELL, DAD GAVE HER A LOTTA SHIT WHEN I WAS BORN, AN' MOM'S NEVER BEEN ALL THERE, Y'KNOW? I DUNNO, IT'S WEIRD...
LOOK, SHRIMP. I DON'T WANNA PUSH YOU INTO ANYTHING. LORD KNOWS YOU'VE HAD ENOUGH OF THAT, BUT I REALLY DO NEED YOU HERE RIGHT NOW. LOOK, I WON'T PICK ON YOU. I WON'T EVEN BITCH ABOUT YOU PLAYING YOUR MUSIC TOO LOUD.
PLEASE, MAGGIE...?
SURE, ALL RIGHT, TIA.
GREAT, SHRIMP. YOU'LL SEE, BEFORE YOU KNOW IT, I'LL BE THE OWNER OF THAT BELT ONCE AGAIN, AND YOU CAN WEAR IT ANY TIME YOU WANT.
HUFF!
OK, TIA. BUT I GOTTA GO NOW.
OK, MOVE YOUR JUNK IN ANYTIME. TONIGHT IF YOU WANT.
I'LL BRING IT ALL BY IN THE MORNING. LATER.
NOW I KNOW WHAT I INHERITED FROM MY MOM. I MUST BE NUTS!

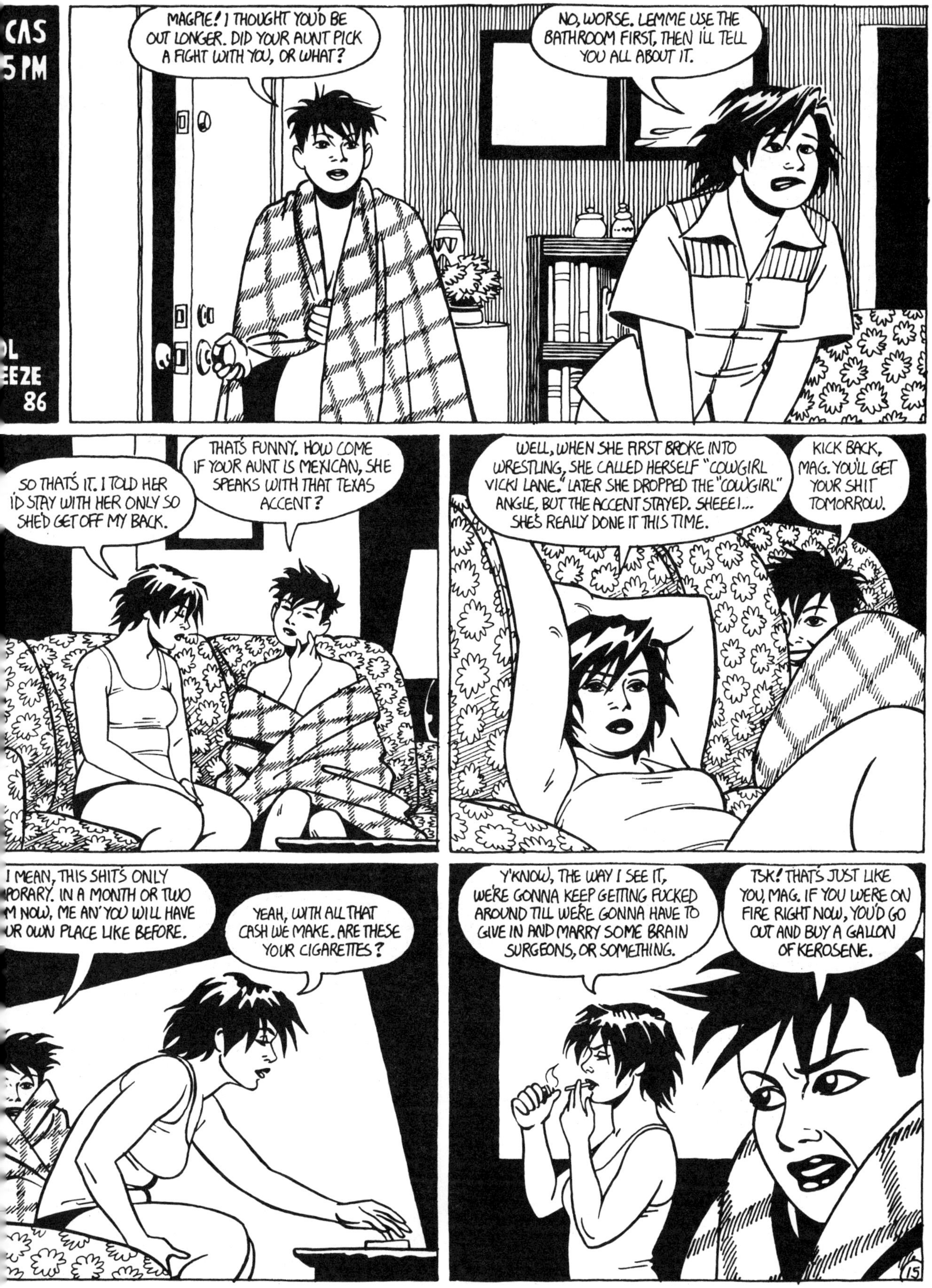
CAS
5 PM
L
EEZE
86
MAGPIE! I THOUGHT YOU'D BE OUT LONGER. DID YOUR AUNT PICK A FIGHT WITH YOU, OR WHAT?
NO, WORSE. LEMME USE THE BATHROOM FIRST, THEN I'LL TELL YOU ALL ABOUT IT.
SO THAT'S IT. I TOLD HER I'D STAY WITH HER ONLY SO SHE'D GET OFF MY BACK.
THAT'S FUNNY. HOW COME IF YOUR AUNT IS MEXICAN, SHE SPEAKS WITH THAT TEXAS ACCENT?
WELL, WHEN SHE FIRST BROKE INTO WRESTLING, SHE CALLED HERSELF "COWGIRL VICKI LANE." LATER SHE DROPPED THE "COWGIRL" ANGLE, BUT THE ACCENT STAYED. SHEEEI... SHE'S REALLY DONE IT THIS TIME.
KICK BACK, MAG. YOU'LL GET YOUR SHIT TOMORROW.
I MEAN, THIS SHIT'S ONLY
PORARY. IN A MONTH OR TWO
M NOW, ME AN' YOU WILL HAVE
UR OWN PLACE LIKE BEFORE.
YEAH, WITH ALL THAT CASH WE MAKE. ARE THESE YOUR CIGARETTES?
Y'KNOW, THE WAY I SEE IT, WE'RE GONNA KEEP GETTING FUCKED AROUND TILL WE'RE GONNA HAVE TO GIVE IN AND MARRY SOME BRAIN SURGEONS, OR SOMETHING.
TSK! THAT'S JUST LIKE YOU, MAG. IF YOU WERE ON FIRE RIGHT NOW, YOU'D GO OUT AND BUY A GALLON OF KEROSENE.
15

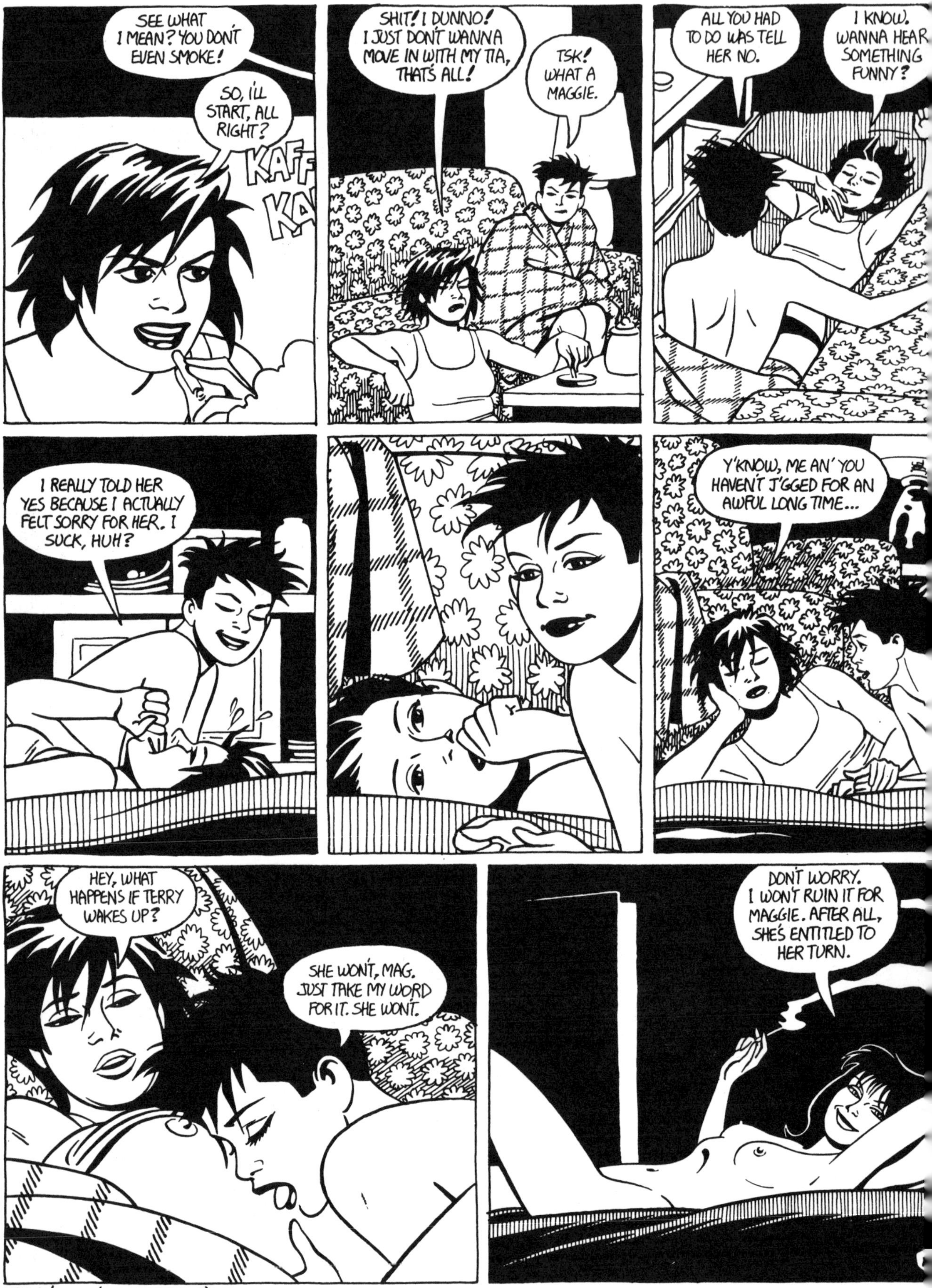

SEE WHAT I MEAN? YOU DON'T EVEN SMOKE!
SO, I'LL START, ALL RIGHT?
KAFF KA
SHIT! I DUNNO! I JUST DON'T WANNA MOVE IN WITH MY TIA, THAT'S ALL!
TSK! WHAT A MAGGIE.
ALL YOU HAD TO DO WAS TELL HER NO.
I KNOW. WANNA HEAR SOMETHING FUNNY?
I REALLY TOLD HER YES BECAUSE I ACTUALLY FELT SORRY FOR HER. I SUCK, HUH?
Y'KNOW, ME AN' YOU HAVEN'T J'GGED FOR AN AWFUL LONG TIME...
HEY, WHAT HAPPENS IF TERRY WAKES UP?
SHE WON'T, MAG. JUST TAKE MY WORD FOR IT. SHE WON'T.
DON'T WORRY. I WON'T RUIN IT FOR MAGGIE. AFTER ALL, SHE'S ENTITLED TO HER TURN.

J'GGED/JUGGED (PRONOUNCED JIGGED)

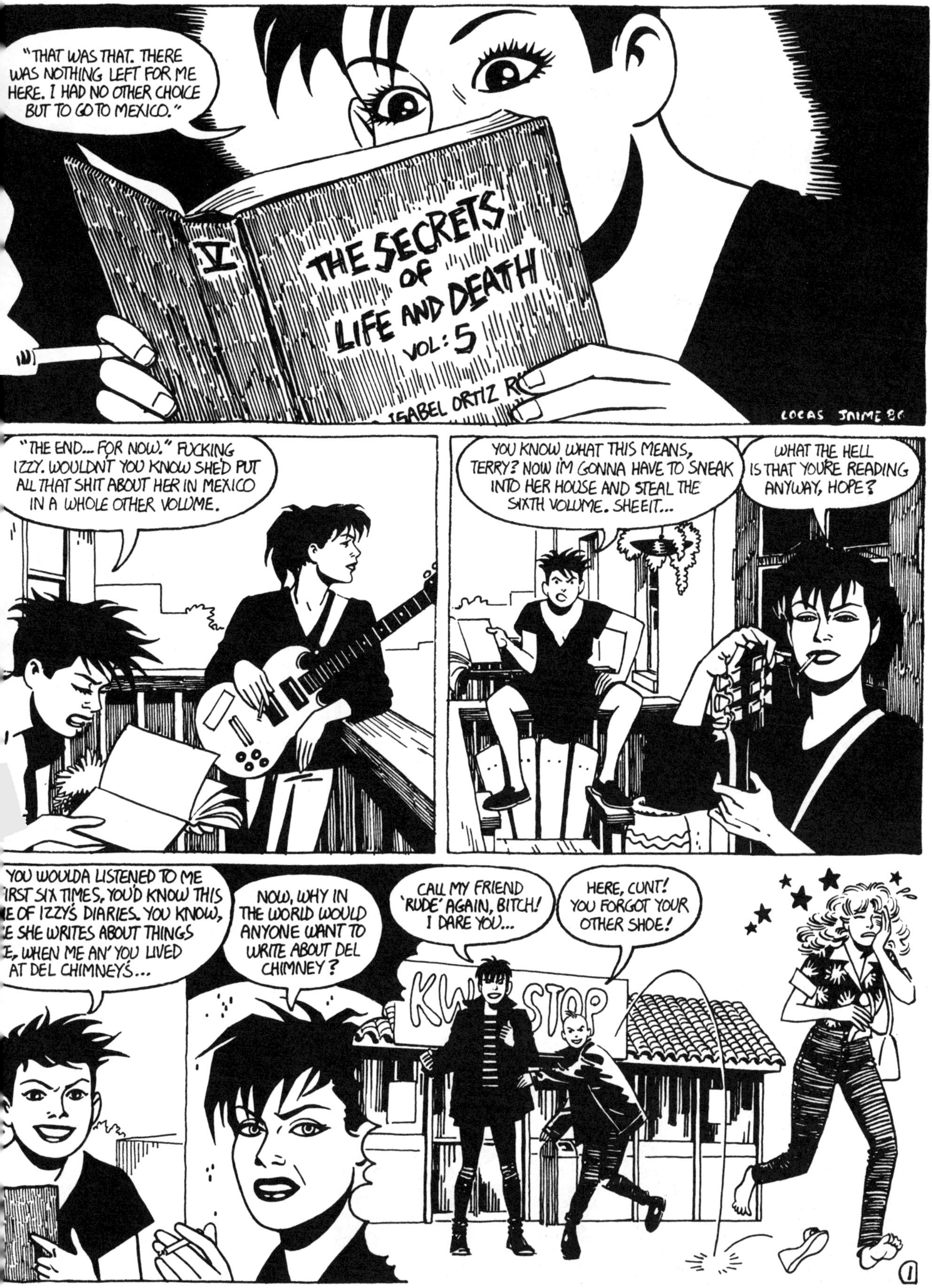
"THAT WAS THAT. THERE WAS NOTHING LEFT FOR ME HERE. I HAD NO OTHER CHOICE BUT TO GO TO MEXICO."
VI
THE SECRETS OF LIFE AND DEATH VOL: 5
ISABEL ORTIZ R
"THE END... FOR NOW." FUCKING IZZY. WOULDN'T YOU KNOW SHE'D PUT ALL THAT SHIT ABOUT HER IN MEXICO IN A WHOLE OTHER VOLUME.
YOU KNOW WHAT THIS MEANS, TERRY? NOW I'M GONNA HAVE TO SNEAK INTO HER HOUSE AND STEAL THE SIXTH VOLUME. SHEEIT...
WHAT THE HELL IS THAT YOU'RE READING ANYWAY, HOPE?
YOU WOULDA LISTENED TO ME
IRST SIX TIMES, YOU'D KNOW THIS
E OF IZZY'S DIARIES. YOU KNOW,
E SHE WRITES ABOUT THINGS
E, WHEN ME AN' YOU LIVED
AT DEL CHIMNEY'S...
NOW, WHY IN THE WORLD WOULD ANYONE WANT TO WRITE ABOUT DEL CHIMNEY?
CALL MY FRIEND 'RUDE' AGAIN, BITCH! I DARE YOU...
HERE, CUNT! YOU FORGOT YOUR OTHER SHOE!
STOP

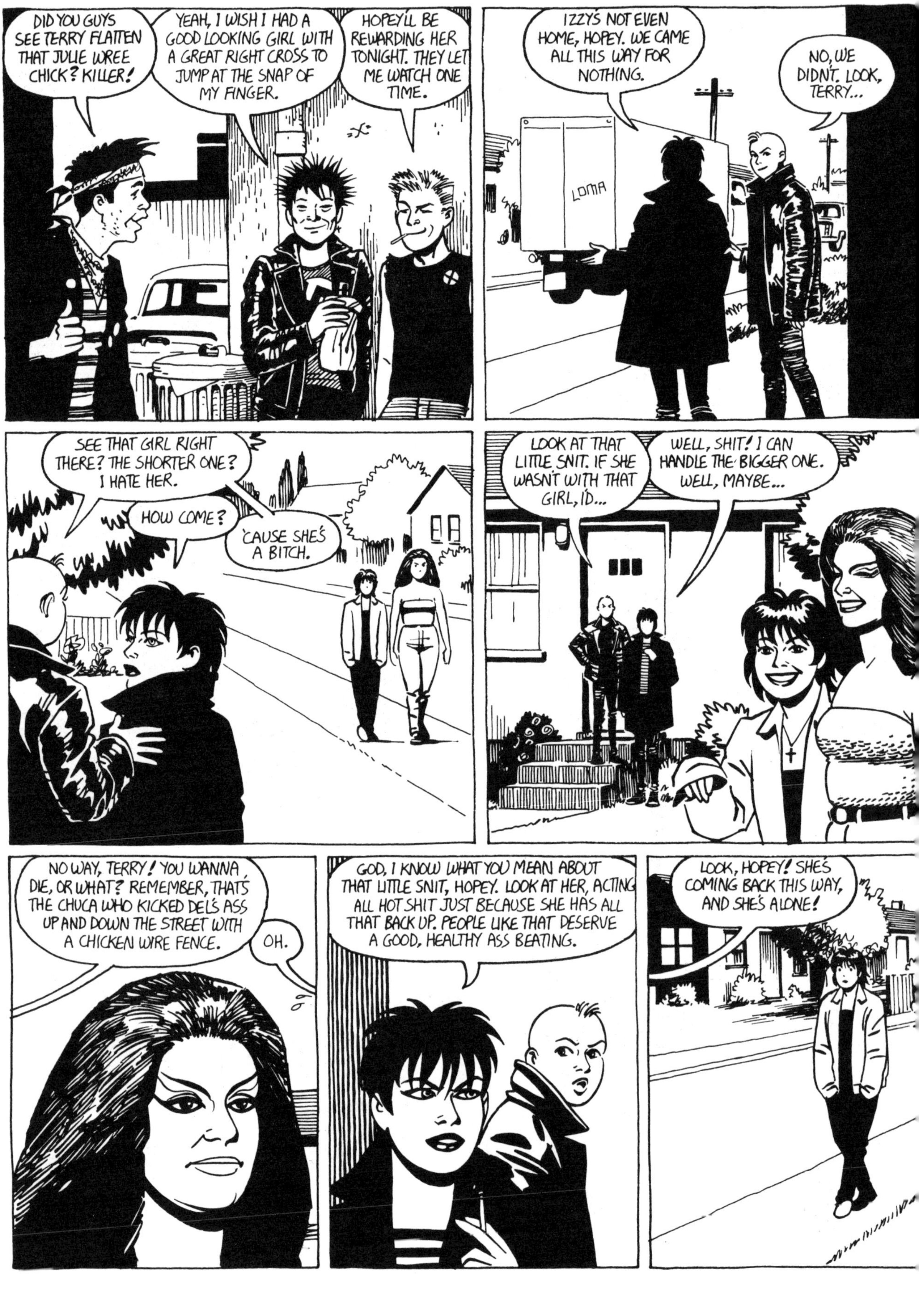
DID YOU GUYS SEE TERRY FLATTEN THAT JULIE WREE CHICK? KILLER!
YEAH, I WISH I HAD A GOOD LOOKING GIRL WITH A GREAT RIGHT CROSS TO JUMP AT THE SNAP OF MY FINGER.
HOPEY'LL BE REWARDING HER TONIGHT. THEY LET ME WATCH ONE TIME.
IZZY'S NOT EVEN HOME, HOPEY. WE CAME ALL THIS WAY FOR NOTHING.
NO, WE DIDN'T. LOOK, TERRY...
LOMA
SEE THAT GIRL RIGHT THERE? THE SHORTER ONE? I HATE HER.
HOW COME?
'CAUSE SHE'S A BITCH.
LOOK AT THAT LITTLE SNIT. IF SHE WASN'T WITH THAT GIRL, I'D...
WELL, SHIT! I CAN HANDLE THE BIGGER ONE. WELL, MAYBE...
NO WAY, TERRY! YOU WANNA DIE, OR WHAT? REMEMBER, THAT'S THE CHUCA WHO KICKED DEL'S ASS UP AND DOWN THE STREET WITH A CHICKEN WIRE FENCE.
OH.
GOD, I KNOW WHAT YOU MEAN ABOUT THAT LITTLE SNIT, HOPEY. LOOK AT HER, ACTING ALL HOT SHIT JUST BECAUSE SHE HAS ALL THAT BACK UP. PEOPLE LIKE THAT DESERVE A GOOD, HEALTHY ASS BEATING.
LOOK, HOPEY! SHE'S COMING BACK THIS WAY, AND SHE'S ALONE!

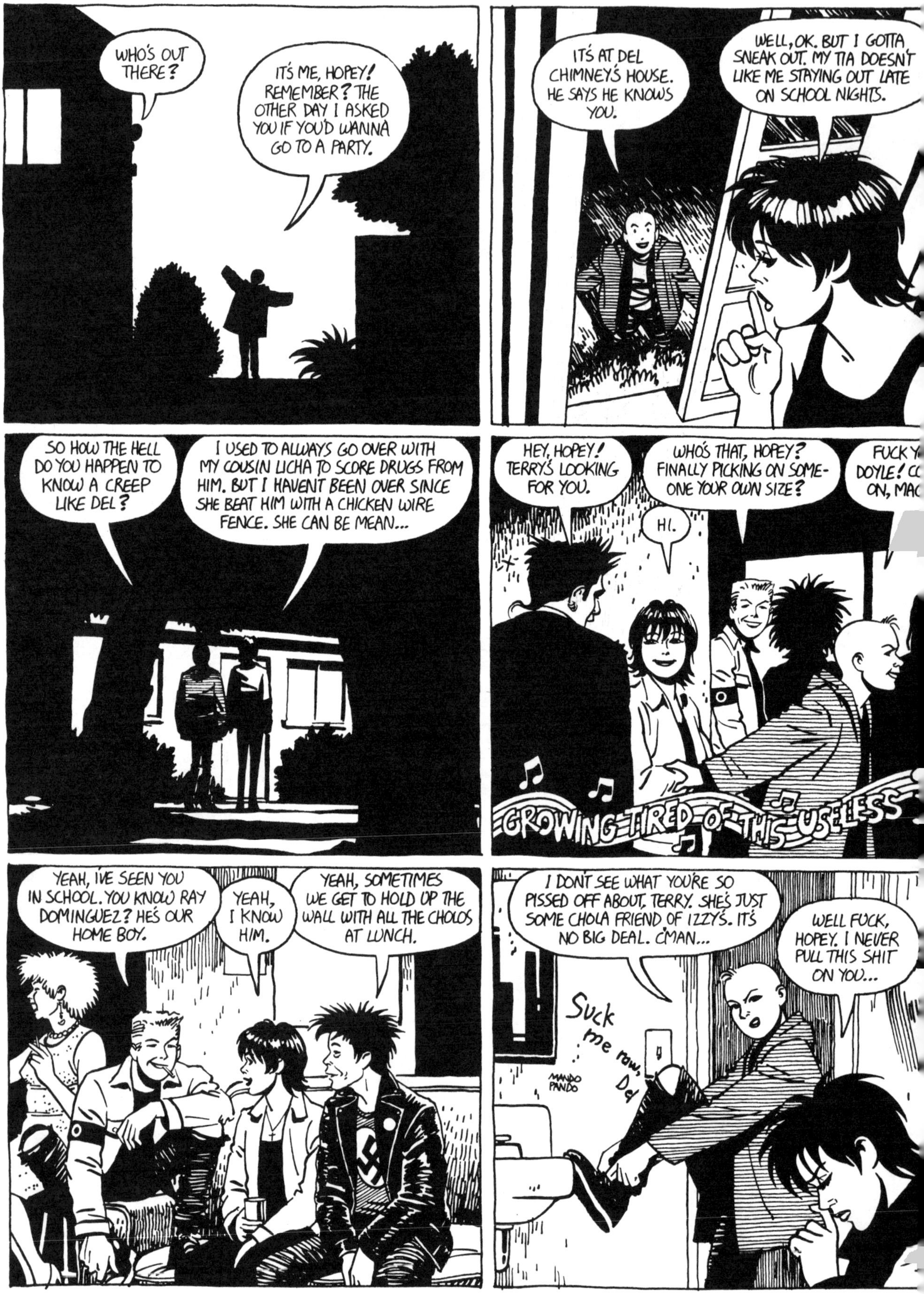
WHO'S OUT THERE?
IT'S ME, HOPEY! REMEMBER? THE OTHER DAY I ASKED YOU IF YOU'D WANNA GO TO A PARTY.
IT'S AT DEL CHIMNEY'S HOUSE. HE SAYS HE KNOWS YOU.
WELL, OK. BUT I GOTTA SNEAK OUT. MY TIA DOESN'T LIKE ME STAYING OUT LATE ON SCHOOL NIGHTS.
SO HOW THE HELL DO YOU HAPPEN TO KNOW A CREEP LIKE DEL?
I USED TO ALWAYS GO OVER WITH MY COUSIN LICHA TO SCORE DRUGS FROM HIM. BUT I HAVEN'T BEEN OVER SINCE SHE BEAT HIM WITH A CHICKEN WIRE FENCE. SHE CAN BE MEAN...
HEY, HOPEY! TERRY'S LOOKING FOR YOU.
WHO'S THAT, HOPEY? FINALLY PICKING ON SOMEONE YOUR OWN SIZE?
HI.
GROWING TIRED OF THIS USELESS
YEAH, I'VE SEEN YOU IN SCHOOL. YOU KNOW RAY DOMINGUEZ? HE'S OUR HOME BOY.
YEAH, I KNOW HIM.
YEAH, SOMETIMES WE GET TO HOLD UP THE WALL WITH ALL THE CHOLOS AT LUNCH.
I DON'T SEE WHAT YOU'RE SO PISSED OFF ABOUT, TERRY. SHE'S JUST SOME CHOLA FRIEND OF IZZY'S. IT'S NO BIG DEAL. C'MAN...
WELL FUCK, HOPEY. I NEVER PULL THIS SHIT ON YOU...
Suck me now, Del
MANDO PANDO

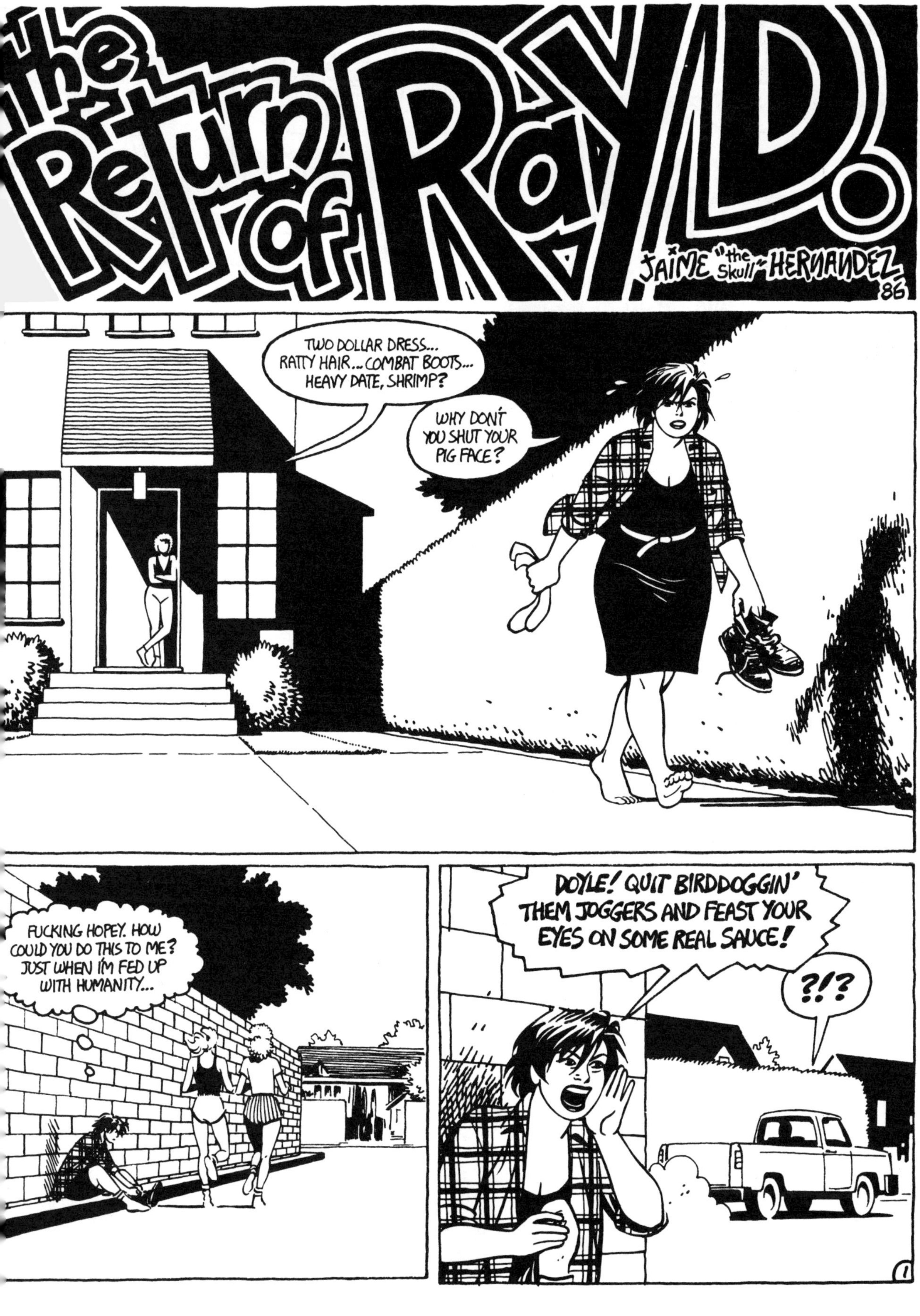
the Return of Ray D.
JAIME "the Skull" HERNANDEZ 86
TWO DOLLAR DRESS... RATTY HAIR... COMBAT BOOTS... HEAVY DATE, SHRIMP?
WHY DON'T YOU SHUT YOUR PIG FACE?
FUCKING HOPEY. HOW COULD YOU DO THIS TO ME? JUST WHEN I'M FED UP WITH HUMANITY...
DOYLE! QUIT BIRDDOGGIN' THEM JOGGERS AND FEAST YOUR EYES ON SOME REAL SAUCE!
?!?
1

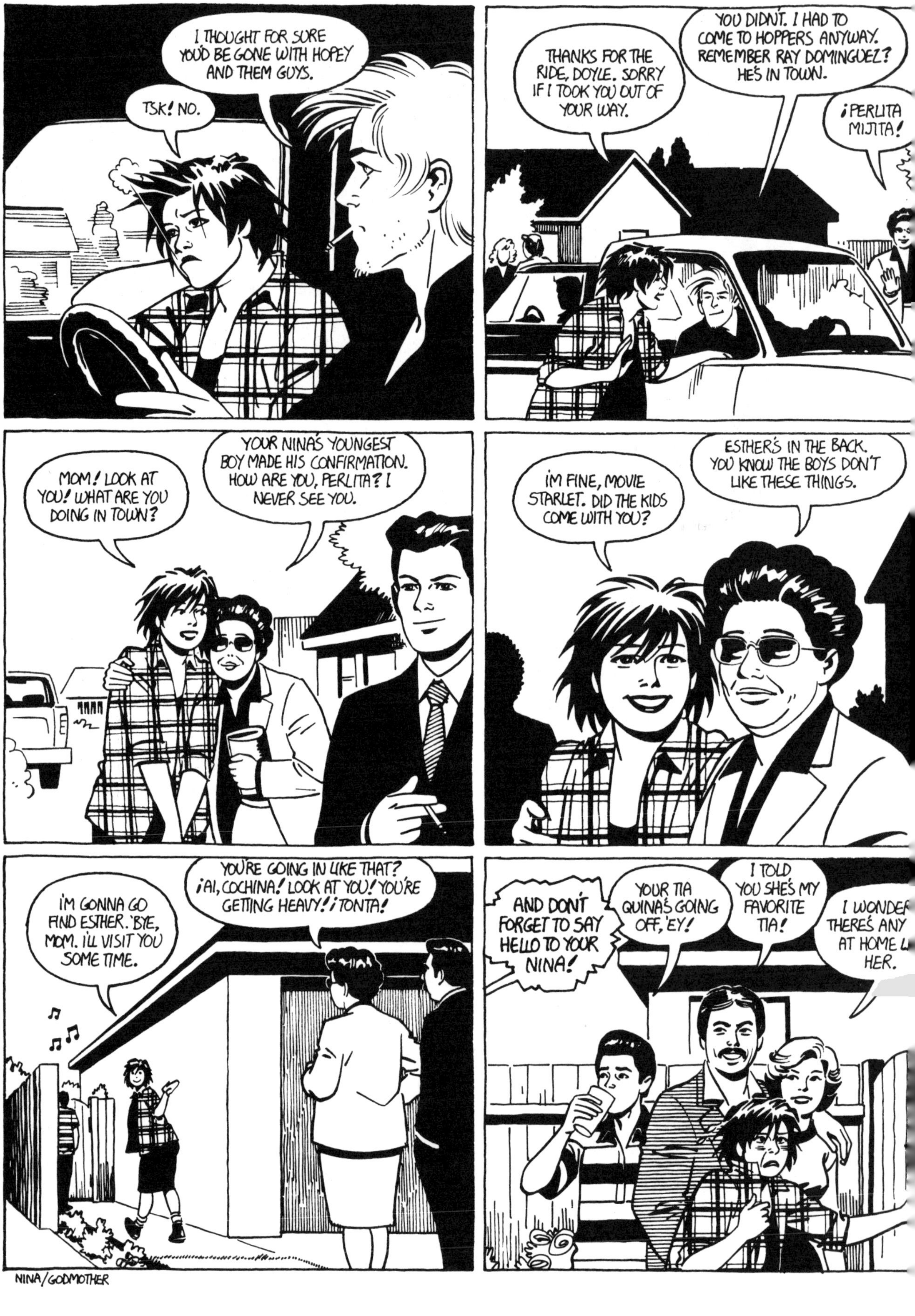
I THOUGHT FOR SURE YOU'D BE GONE WITH HOPEY AND THEM GUYS.
TSK! NO.
THANKS FOR THE RIDE, DOYLE. SORRY IF I TOOK YOU OUT OF YOUR WAY.
YOU DIDN'T. I HAD TO COME TO HOPPERS ANYWAY. REMEMBER RAY DOMINGUEZ? HE'S IN TOWN.
¡PERLITA MIJITA!
MOM! LOOK AT YOU! WHAT ARE YOU DOING IN TOWN?
YOUR NINA'S YOUNGEST BOY MADE HIS CONFIRMATION. HOW ARE YOU, PERLITA? I NEVER SEE YOU.
I'M FINE, MOVIE STARLET. DID THE KIDS COME WITH YOU?
ESTHER'S IN THE BACK. YOU KNOW THE BOYS DON'T LIKE THESE THINGS.
I'M GONNA GO FIND ESTHER. 'BYE, MOM. I'LL VISIT YOU SOME TIME.
YOU'RE GOING IN LIKE THAT? ¡AI, COCHINA! LOOK AT YOU! YOU'RE GETTING HEAVY! ¡TONTA!
AND DON'T FORGET TO SAY HELLO TO YOUR NINA!
YOUR TIA QUINA'S GOING OFF, 'EY!
I TOLD YOU SHE'S MY FAVORITE TIA!
I WONDE THERE'S ANY AT HOME HER.

NINA/GODMOTHER

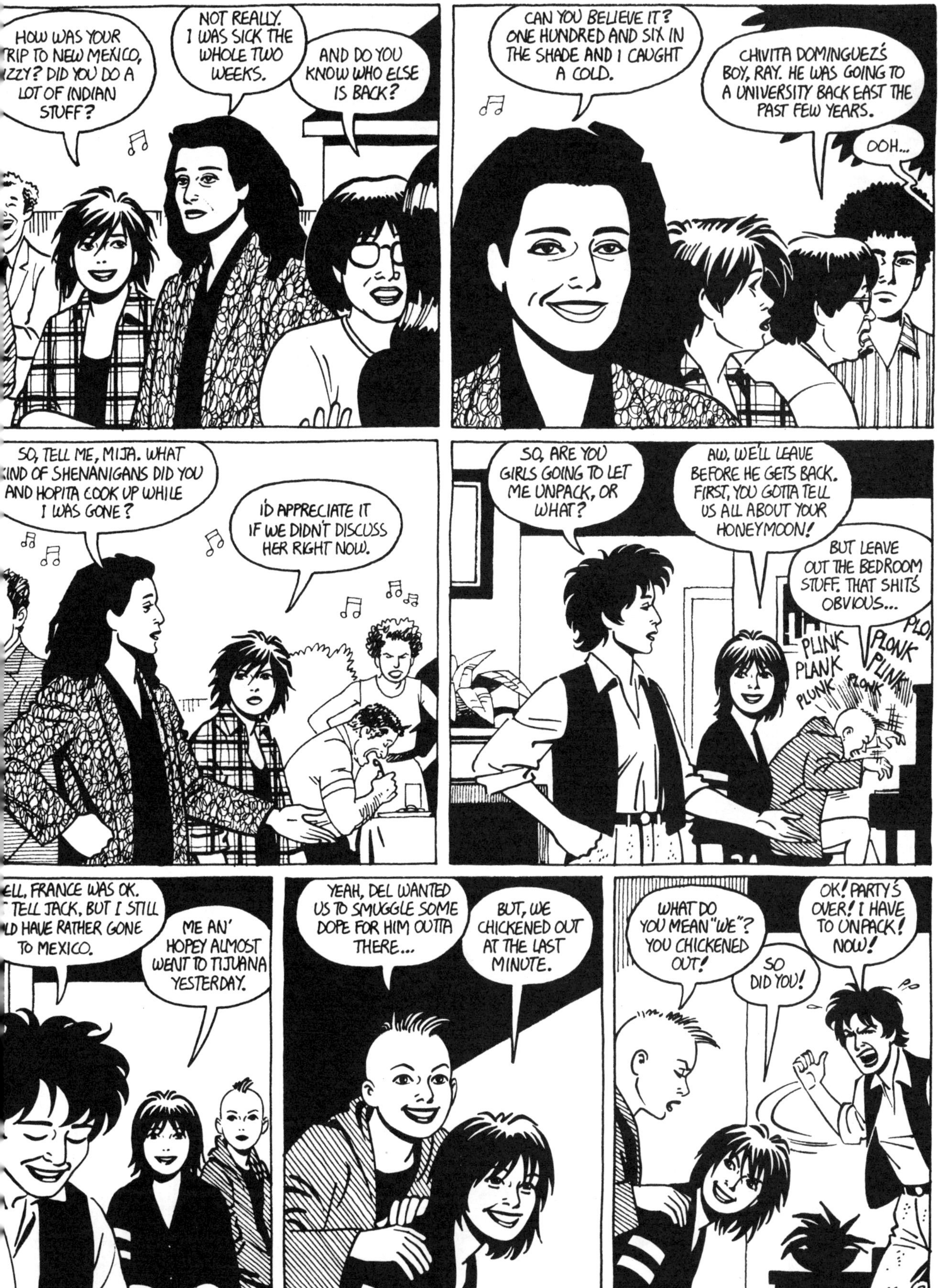
HOW WAS YOUR TRIP TO NEW MEXICO, IZZY? DID YOU DO A LOT OF INDIAN STUFF?
NOT REALLY. I WAS SICK THE WHOLE TWO WEEKS.
AND DO YOU KNOW WHO ELSE IS BACK?
CAN YOU BELIEVE IT? ONE HUNDRED AND SIX IN THE SHADE AND I CAUGHT A COLD.
CHIVITA DOMINGUEZ'S BOY, RAY. HE WAS GOING TO A UNIVERSITY BACK EAST THE PAST FEW YEARS.
OOH...
SO, TELL ME, MIJA. WHAT KIND OF SHENANIGANS DID YOU AND HOPITA COOK UP WHILE I WAS GONE?
I'D APPRECIATE IT IF WE DIDN'T DISCUSS HER RIGHT NOW.
SO, ARE YOU GIRLS GOING TO LET ME UNPACK, OR WHAT?
AW, WE'LL LEAVE BEFORE HE GETS BACK. FIRST, YOU GOTTA TELL US ALL ABOUT YOUR HONEYMOON!
BUT LEAVE OUT THE BEDROOM STUFF. THAT SHIT'S OBVIOUS...
PLINK PLANK PLUNK PLONK PLONK PLINK PLONK
ELL, FRANCE WAS OK. TELL JACK, BUT I STILL LD HAVE RATHER GONE TO MEXICO.
ME AN' HOPEY ALMOST WENT TO TIJUANA YESTERDAY.
YEAH, DEL WANTED US TO SMUGGLE SOME DOPE FOR HIM OUTTA THERE...
BUT, WE CHICKENED OUT AT THE LAST MINUTE.
WHAT DO YOU MEAN "WE"? YOU CHICKENED OUT!
SO DID YOU!
OK! PARTY'S OVER! I HAVE TO UNPACK! NOW!

YEAH, THAT'S MOM ALL RIGHT! SHE'S ALL GLAMOUR NOW 'CAUSE SHE GOT A JOB AT THE UNEMPLOYMENT OFFICE.

NO KIDDING? SO, HOW IS LIFE IN MONTOYA, LATELY? OR SHOULD I SAY, "DAIRYTOWN"?

KINDA DEAD. IT ISN'T HALF AS COOL AS HOPPERS. AT LEAST YOU HAVE CUTE GUYS HERE.

YEAH, BUT AS ALL THINGS GO, YOU NEVER KNOW WHICH ONES ARE GONNA BE TRULY NICE.

EAH? HOW UT THE GUY H THE ONE BROW YOU E TALKING TO?

OH, SURE. SPEEDY WILL SHOW YOU A GREAT TIME. FIRST, HE'LL SHOW YOU HIS FAVORITE TATTOOS...

TATTOOS, HUH? YOU THINK HE'LL SHOW THEM TO ME? HUH, PERLITA?

OH, STOP, ESTHER! HE'S... ESTHER!

SHIT...

WHAT WERE YOU TRYING TO DO, FINISH THAT KEG ALL BY YOURSELF?

YEAH, I WAS HOPING I'D DROWN MYSELF AFTER A WHILE, SO THEN I'D... NEVER MIND.

SO, HOW LONG WILL HOPEY BE GONE?

TWO WHOLE FUCKING MONTHS! CAN YOU BELIEVE THAT SHIT?

≈URP≈

¡PERLITA! MAGGIE!

⑤

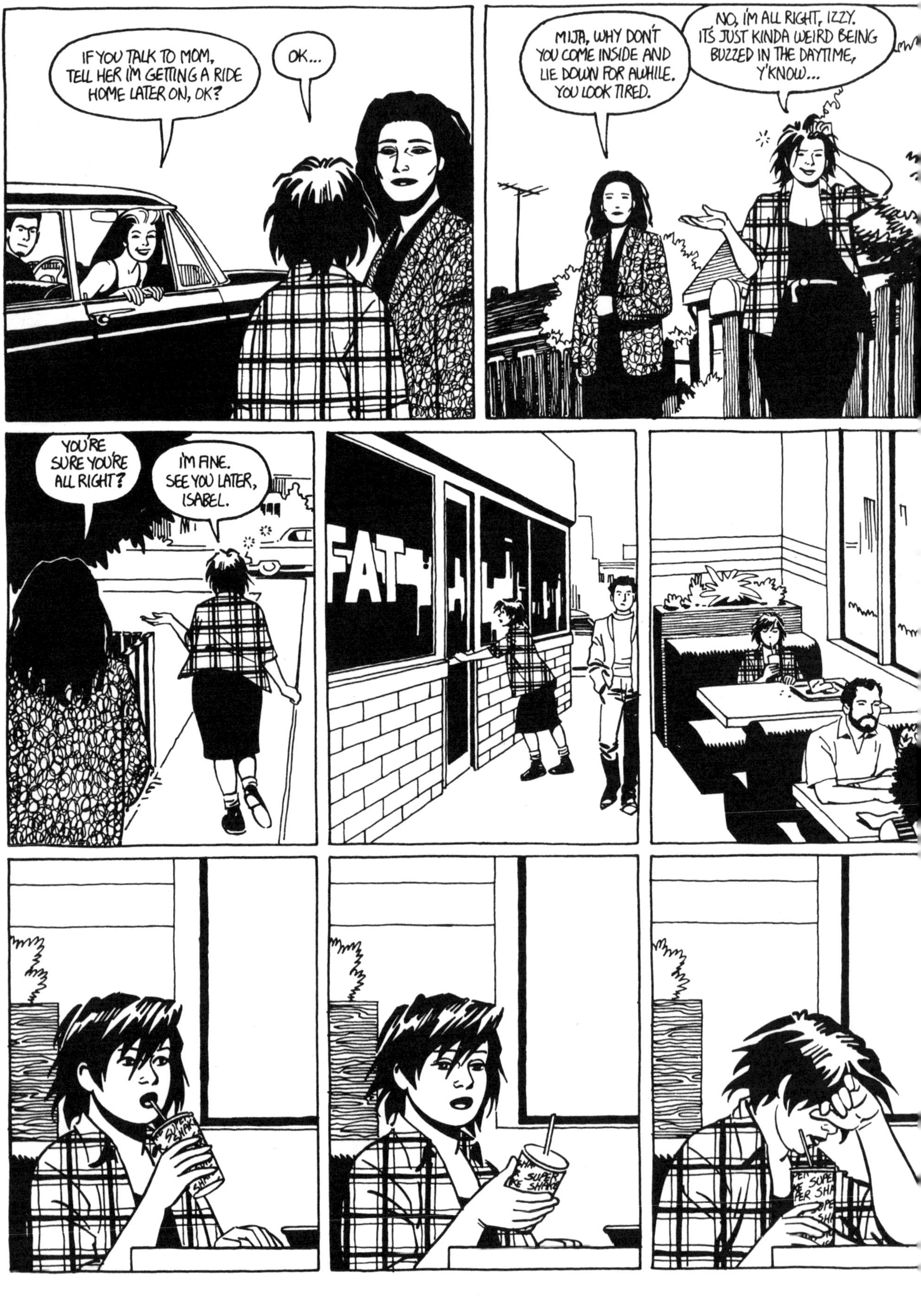
IF YOU TALK TO MOM, TELL HER I'M GETTING A RIDE HOME LATER ON, OK?
OK...
MIJA, WHY DON'T YOU COME INSIDE AND LIE DOWN FOR AWHILE. YOU LOOK TIRED.
NO, I'M ALL RIGHT, IZZY. IT'S JUST KINDA WEIRD BEING BUZZED IN THE DAYTIME, Y'KNOW...
YOU'RE SURE YOU'RE ALL RIGHT?
I'M FINE. SEE YOU LATER, ISABEL.
FAT

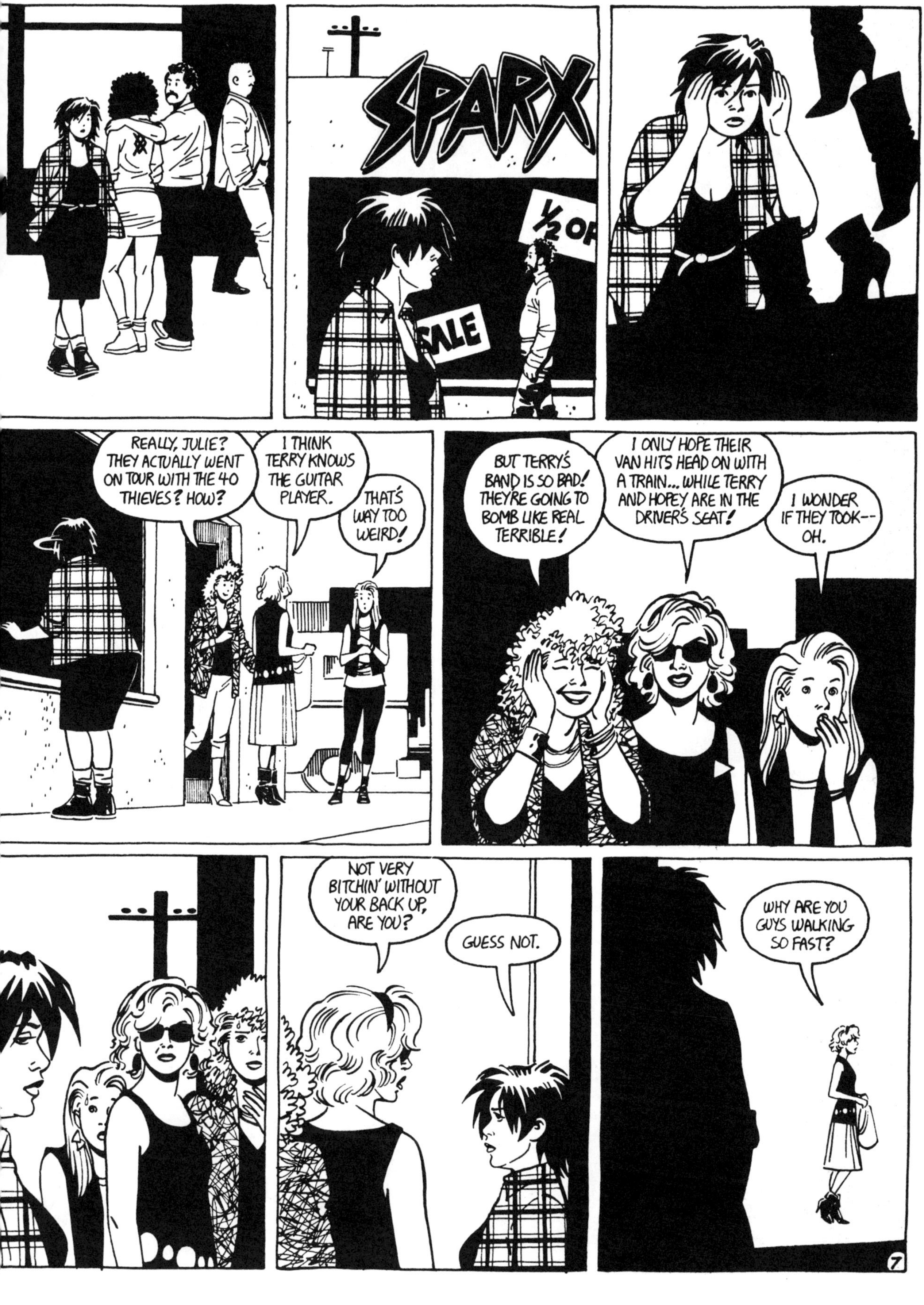
SPARX
½ OF
SALE
REALLY, JULIE? THEY ACTUALLY WENT ON TOUR WITH THE 40 THIEVES? HOW?
I THINK TERRY KNOWS THE GUITAR PLAYER.
THAT'S WAY TOO WEIRD!
BUT TERRY'S BAND IS SO BAD! THEY'RE GOING TO BOMB LIKE REAL TERRIBLE!
I ONLY HOPE THEIR VAN HITS HEAD ON WITH A TRAIN... WHILE TERRY AND HOPEY ARE IN THE DRIVER'S SEAT!
I WONDER IF THEY TOOK-- OH.
NOT VERY BITCHIN' WITHOUT YOUR BACK UP, ARE YOU?
GUESS NOT.
WHY ARE YOU GUYS WALKING SO FAST?

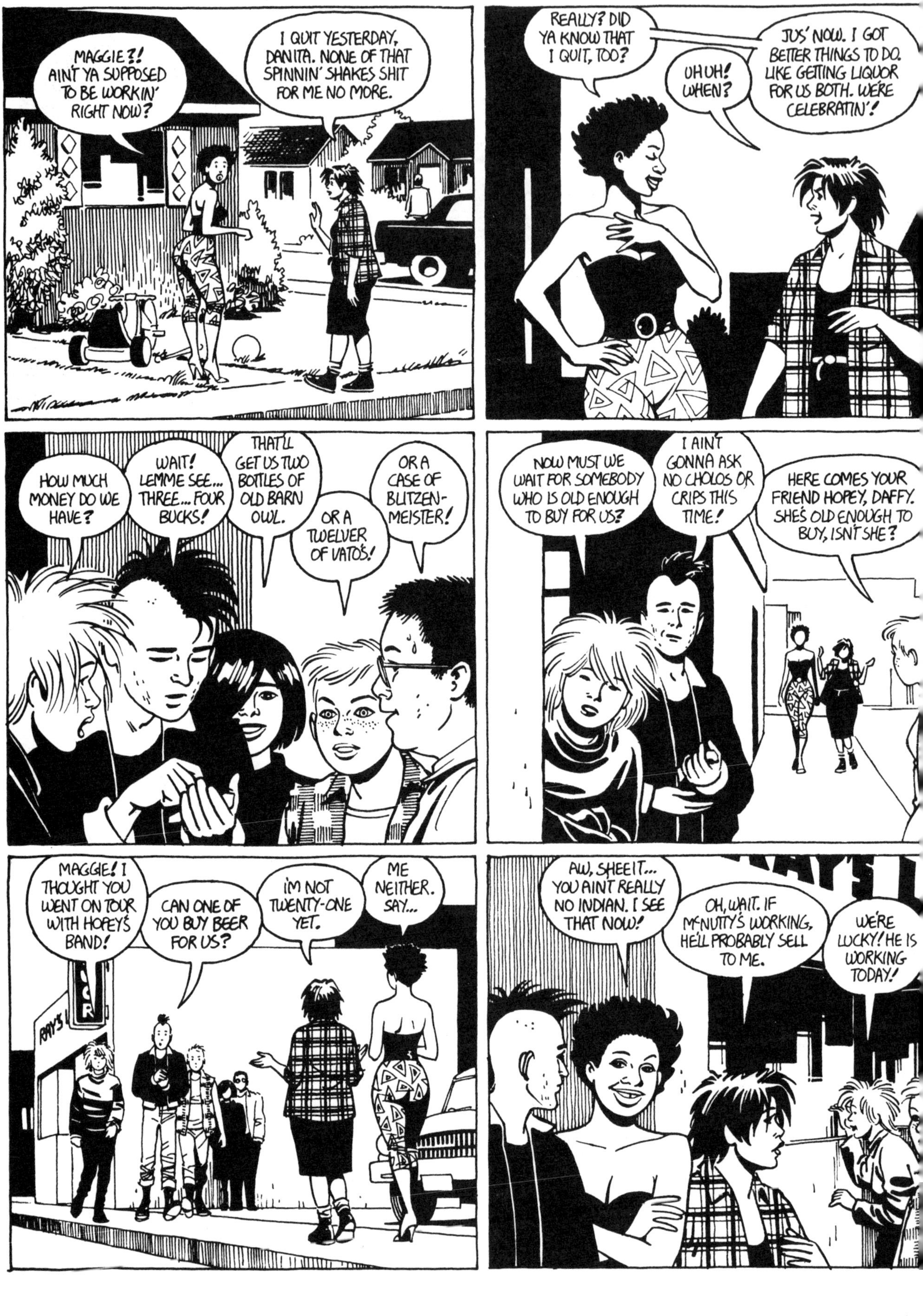
MAGGIE ?! AIN'T YA SUPPOSED TO BE WORKIN' RIGHT NOW?
I QUIT YESTERDAY, DANITA. NONE OF THAT SPINNIN' SHAKES SHIT FOR ME NO MORE.
REALLY? DID YA KNOW THAT I QUIT, TOO?
UH UH! WHEN?
JUS' NOW. I GOT BETTER THINGS TO DO. LIKE GETTING LIQUOR FOR US BOTH. WE'RE CELEBRATIN'!
HOW MUCH MONEY DO WE HAVE?
WAIT! LEMME SEE... THREE... FOUR BUCKS!
THAT'LL GET US TWO BOTTLES OF OLD BARN OWL.
OR A TWELVER OF VATO'S!
OR A CASE OF BLITZEN-MEISTER!
NOW MUST WE WAIT FOR SOMEBODY WHO IS OLD ENOUGH TO BUY FOR US?
I AIN'T GONNA ASK NO CHOLOS OR CRIPS THIS TIME!
HERE COMES YOUR FRIEND HOPEY, DAFFY. SHE'S OLD ENOUGH TO BUY, ISN'T SHE?
MAGGIE! I THOUGHT YOU WENT ON TOUR WITH HOPEY'S BAND!
CAN ONE OF YOU BUY BEER FOR US?
I'M NOT TWENTY-ONE YET.
ME NEITHER. SAY...
RAY'S
AW, SHEEIT... YOU AINT REALLY NO INDIAN. I SEE THAT NOW!
OH, WAIT. IF McNUTTY'S WORKING, HE'LL PROBABLY SELL TO ME.
WE'RE LUCKY! HE IS WORKING TODAY!

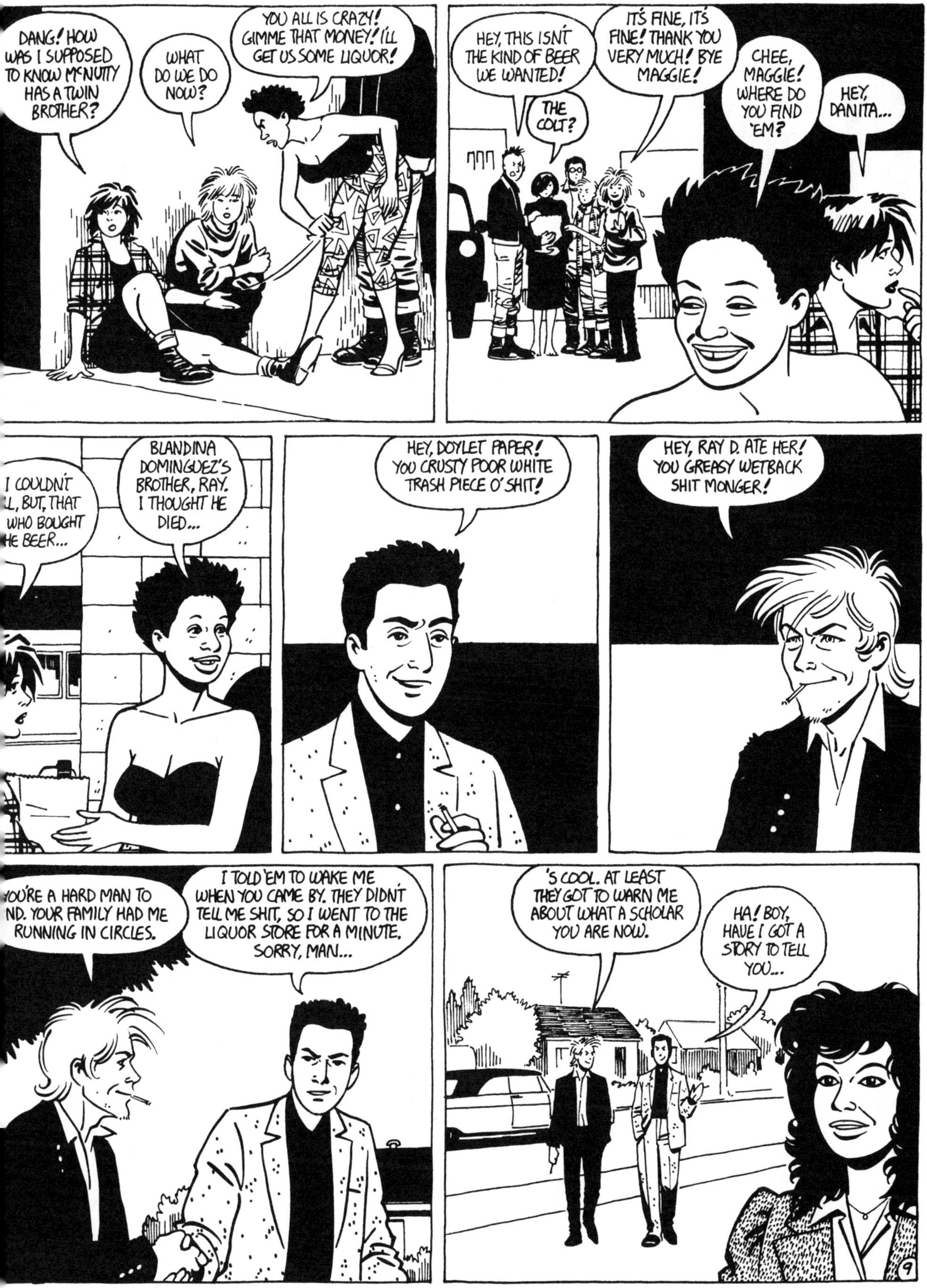
DANG! HOW WAS I SUPPOSED TO KNOW McNUTTY HAS A TWIN BROTHER?
WHAT DO WE DO NOW?
YOU ALL IS CRAZY! GIMME THAT MONEY! I'LL GET US SOME LIQUOR!
HEY, THIS ISN'T THE KIND OF BEER WE WANTED!
THE COLT?
IT'S FINE, IT'S FINE! THANK YOU VERY MUCH! BYE MAGGIE!
CHEE, MAGGIE! WHERE DO YOU FIND 'EM?
HEY, DANITA...
I COULDN'T ...L, BUT, THAT ... WHO BOUGHT ...HE BEER...
BLANDINA DOMINGUEZ'S BROTHER, RAY. I THOUGHT HE DIED...
HEY, DOYLET PAPER! YOU CRUSTY POOR WHITE TRASH PIECE O' SHIT!
HEY, RAY D. ATE HER! YOU GREASY WETBACK SHIT MONGER!
...OU'RE A HARD MAN TO ...ND. YOUR FAMILY HAD ME RUNNING IN CIRCLES.
I TOLD 'EM TO WAKE ME WHEN YOU CAME BY. THEY DIDN'T TELL ME SHIT, SO I WENT TO THE LIQUOR STORE FOR A MINUTE. SORRY, MAN...
'S COOL. AT LEAST THEY GOT TO WARN ME ABOUT WHAT A SCHOLAR YOU ARE NOW.
HA! BOY, HAVE I GOT A STORY TO TELL YOU...
9

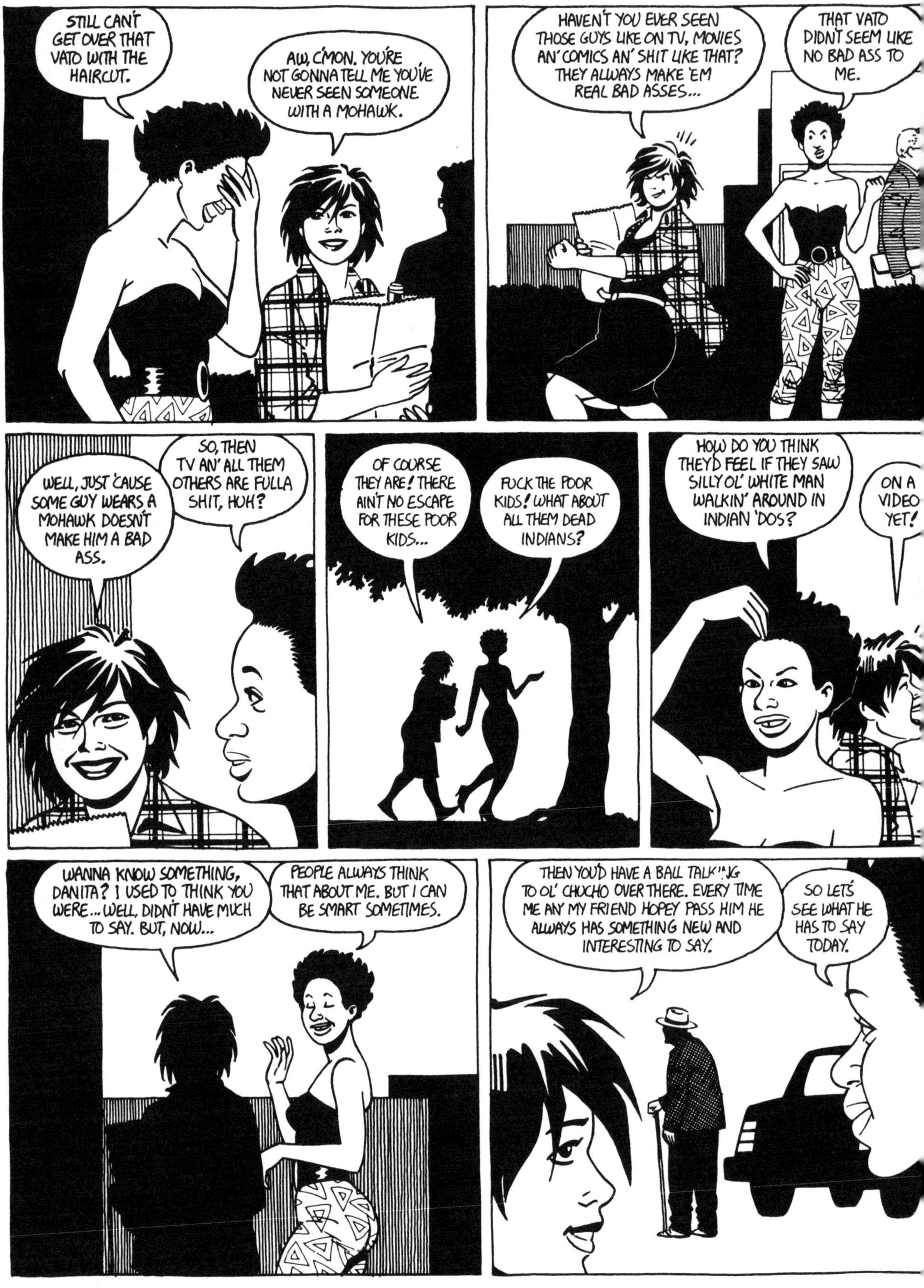
STILL CAN'T GET OVER THAT VATO WITH THE HAIRCUT.
AW, C'MON. YOU'RE NOT GONNA TELL ME YOU'VE NEVER SEEN SOMEONE WITH A MOHAWK.
HAVEN'T YOU EVER SEEN THOSE GUYS LIKE ON TV, MOVIES AN' COMICS AN' SHIT LIKE THAT? THEY ALWAYS MAKE 'EM REAL BAD ASSES...
THAT VATO DIDN'T SEEM LIKE NO BAD ASS TO ME.
WELL, JUST 'CAUSE SOME GUY WEARS A MOHAWK DOESN'T MAKE HIM A BAD ASS.
SO, THEN TV AN' ALL THEM OTHERS ARE FULLA SHIT, HUH?
OF COURSE THEY ARE! THERE AIN'T NO ESCAPE FOR THESE POOR KIDS...
FUCK THE POOR KIDS! WHAT ABOUT ALL THEM DEAD INDIANS?
HOW DO YOU THINK THEY'D FEEL IF THEY SAW SILLY OL' WHITE MAN WALKIN' AROUND IN INDIAN 'DOS?
ON A VIDEO YET!
WANNA KNOW SOMETHING, DANITA? I USED TO THINK YOU WERE... WELL, DIDN'T HAVE MUCH TO SAY. BUT, NOW...
PEOPLE ALWAYS THINK THAT ABOUT ME. BUT I CAN BE SMART SOMETIMES.
THEN YOU'D HAVE A BALL TALKING TO OL' CHUCHO OVER THERE. EVERY TIME ME AN' MY FRIEND HOPEY PASS HIM HE ALWAYS HAS SOMETHING NEW AND INTERESTING TO SAY.
SO LET'S SEE WHAT HE HAS TO SAY TODAY.

11

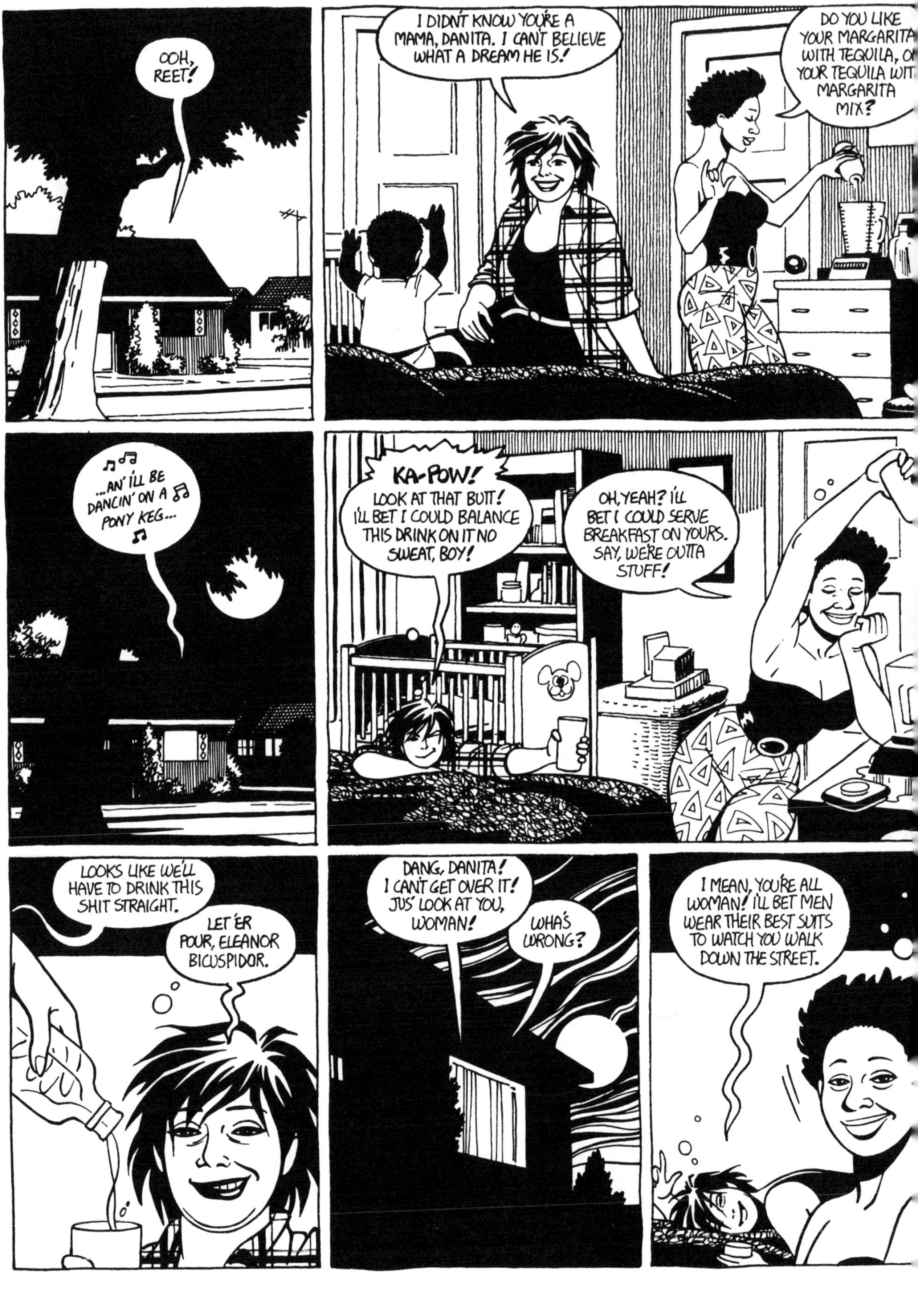
OOH, REET!
I DIDN'T KNOW YOU'RE A MAMA, DANITA. I CAN'T BELIEVE WHAT A DREAM HE IS!
DO YOU LIKE YOUR MARGARITA WITH TEQUILA, OR YOUR TEQUILA WITH MARGARITA MIX?
...AN' I'LL BE DANCIN' ON A PONY KEG...
KA-POW!
LOOK AT THAT BUTT! I'LL BET I COULD BALANCE THIS DRINK ON IT NO SWEAT, BOY!
OH, YEAH? I'LL BET I COULD SERVE BREAKFAST ON YOURS. SAY, WE'RE OUTTA STUFF!
LOOKS LIKE WE'LL HAVE TO DRINK THIS SHIT STRAIGHT.
LET 'ER POUR, ELEANOR BICUSPIDOR.
DANG, DANITA! I CAN'T GET OVER IT! JUS' LOOK AT YOU, WOMAN!
WHA'S WRONG?
I MEAN, YOU'RE ALL WOMAN! I'LL BET MEN WEAR THEIR BEST SUITS TO WATCH YOU WALK DOWN THE STREET.

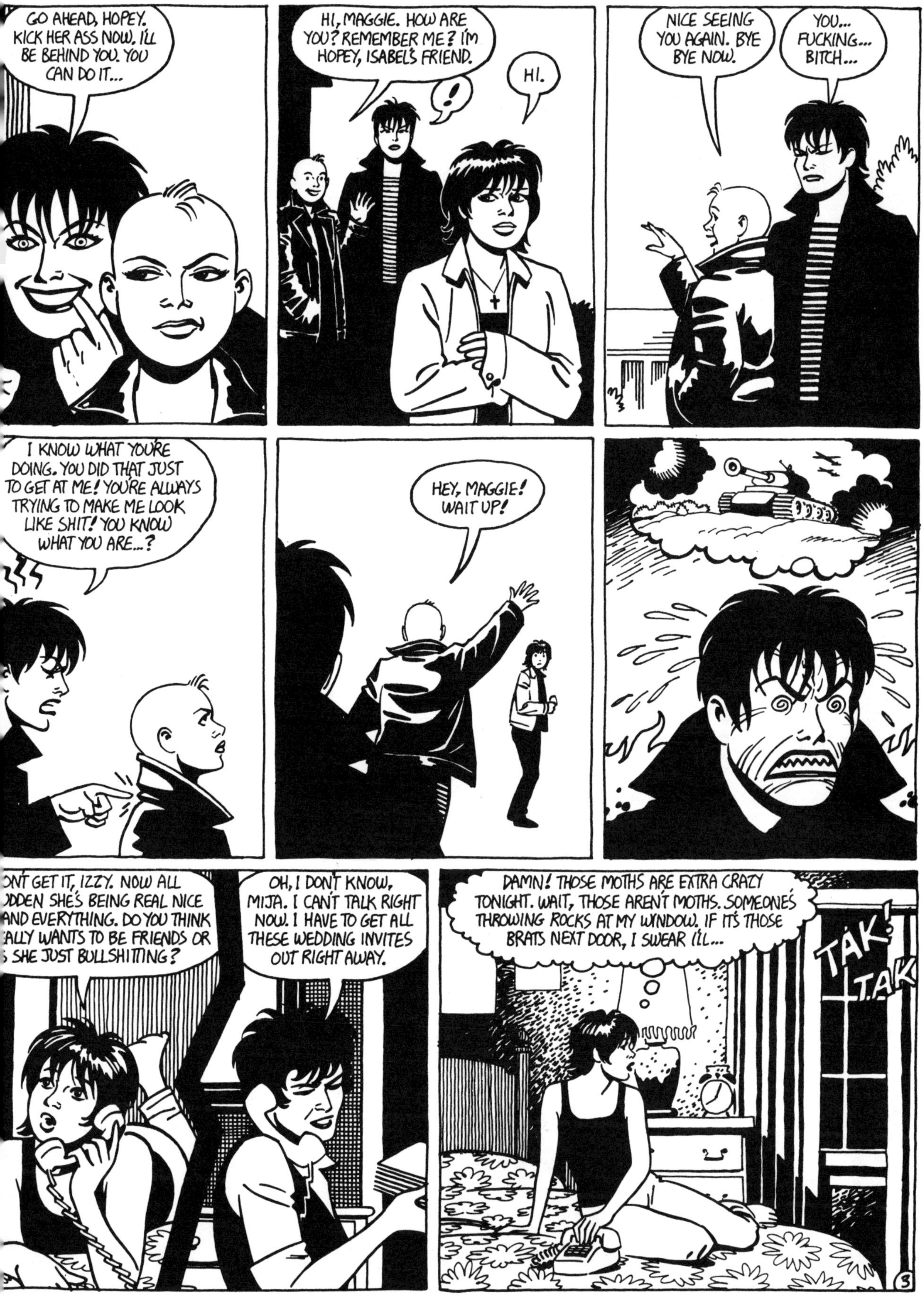
GO AHEAD, HOPEY. KICK HER ASS NOW. I'LL BE BEHIND YOU. YOU CAN DO IT...
HI, MAGGIE. HOW ARE YOU? REMEMBER ME? I'M HOPEY, ISABEL'S FRIEND.
!
HI.
NICE SEEING YOU AGAIN. BYE BYE NOW.
YOU... FUCKING... BITCH...
I KNOW WHAT YOU'RE DOING. YOU DID THAT JUST TO GET AT ME! YOU'RE ALWAYS TRYING TO MAKE ME LOOK LIKE SHIT! YOU KNOW WHAT YOU ARE...?
HEY, MAGGIE! WAIT UP!
ON'T GET IT, IZZY. NOW ALL DDEN SHE'S BEING REAL NICE AND EVERYTHING. DO YOU THINK ALLY WANTS TO BE FRIENDS OR S SHE JUST BULLSHITTING?
OH, I DON'T KNOW, MIJA. I CAN'T TALK RIGHT NOW. I HAVE TO GET ALL THESE WEDDING INVITES OUT RIGHT AWAY.
DAMN! THOSE MOTHS ARE EXTRA CRAZY TONIGHT. WAIT, THOSE AREN'T MOTHS. SOMEONE'S THROWING ROCKS AT MY WINDOW. IF IT'S THOSE BRATS NEXT DOOR, I SWEAR I'LL...
TAK! TAK
3

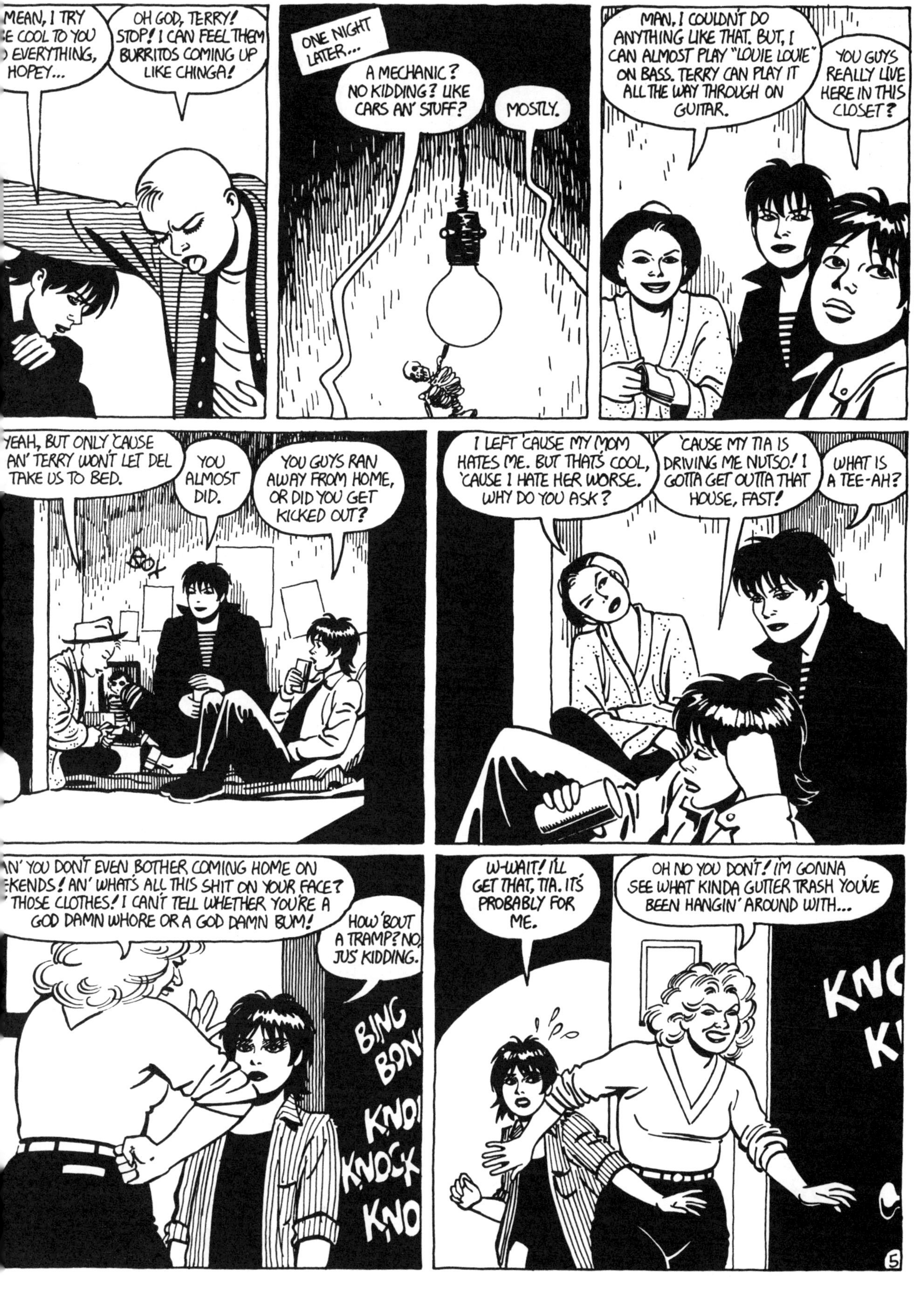
MEAN, I TRY
E COOL TO YOU
D EVERYTHING,
HOPEY...
OH GOD, TERRY! STOP! I CAN FEEL THEM BURRITOS COMING UP LIKE CHINGA!
ONE NIGHT LATER...
A MECHANIC? NO KIDDING? LIKE CARS AN' STUFF?
MOSTLY.
MAN, I COULDN'T DO ANYTHING LIKE THAT. BUT, I CAN ALMOST PLAY "LOUIE LOUIE" ON BASS. TERRY CAN PLAY IT ALL THE WAY THROUGH ON GUITAR.
YOU GUYS REALLY LIVE HERE IN THIS CLOSET?
YEAH, BUT ONLY 'CAUSE AN' TERRY WON'T LET DEL TAKE US TO BED.
YOU ALMOST DID.
YOU GUYS RAN AWAY FROM HOME, OR DID YOU GET KICKED OUT?
I LEFT 'CAUSE MY MOM HATES ME. BUT THAT'S COOL, 'CAUSE I HATE HER WORSE. WHY DO YOU ASK?
'CAUSE MY TIA IS DRIVING ME NUTSO! I GOTTA GET OUTTA THAT HOUSE, FAST!
WHAT IS A TEE-AH?
N' YOU DON'T EVEN BOTHER COMING HOME ON
EKENDS! AN' WHAT'S ALL THIS SHIT ON YOUR FACE? THOSE CLOTHES! I CAN'T TELL WHETHER YOU'RE A GOD DAMN WHORE OR A GOD DAMN BUM!
HOW 'BOUT A TRAMP? NO, JUS' KIDDING.
BING BON
KNO
KNOCK
KNO
W-WAIT! I'LL GET THAT, TIA. IT'S PROBABLY FOR ME.
OH NO YOU DON'T! I'M GONNA SEE WHAT KINDA GUTTER TRASH YOU'VE BEEN HANGIN' AROUND WITH...
KNO
K

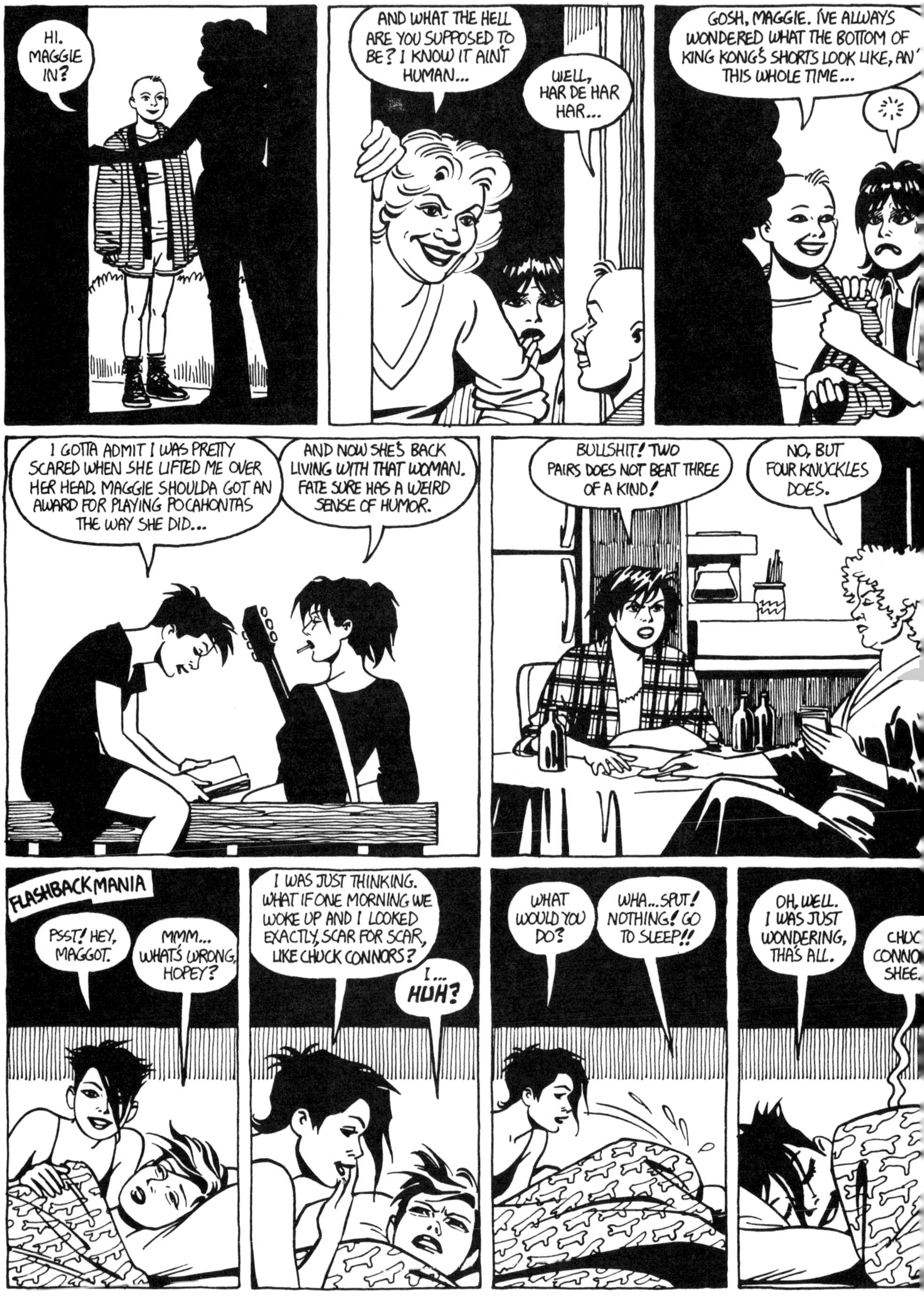

HI. MAGGIE IN?
AND WHAT THE HELL ARE YOU SUPPOSED TO BE? I KNOW IT AIN'T HUMAN...
WELL, HAR DE HAR HAR...
GOSH, MAGGIE. I'VE ALWAYS WONDERED WHAT THE BOTTOM OF KING KONG'S SHORTS LOOK LIKE, AN' THIS WHOLE TIME...
I GOTTA ADMIT I WAS PRETTY SCARED WHEN SHE LIFTED ME OVER HER HEAD. MAGGIE SHOULDA GOT AN AWARD FOR PLAYING POCAHONTAS THE WAY SHE DID...
AND NOW SHE'S BACK LIVING WITH THAT WOMAN. FATE SURE HAS A WEIRD SENSE OF HUMOR.
BULLSHIT! TWO PAIRS DOES NOT BEAT THREE OF A KIND!
NO, BUT FOUR KNUCKLES DOES.
FLASHBACK MANIA
PSST! HEY, MAGGOT.
MMM... WHAT'S WRONG, HOPEY?
I WAS JUST THINKING. WHAT IF ONE MORNING WE WOKE UP AND I LOOKED EXACTLY, SCAR FOR SCAR, LIKE CHUCK CONNORS?
I... HUH?
WHAT WOULD YOU DO?
WHA...SPUT! NOTHING! GO TO SLEEP!!
OH, WELL. I WAS JUST WONDERING, THAT'S ALL.
CHUC CONNO SHEE.

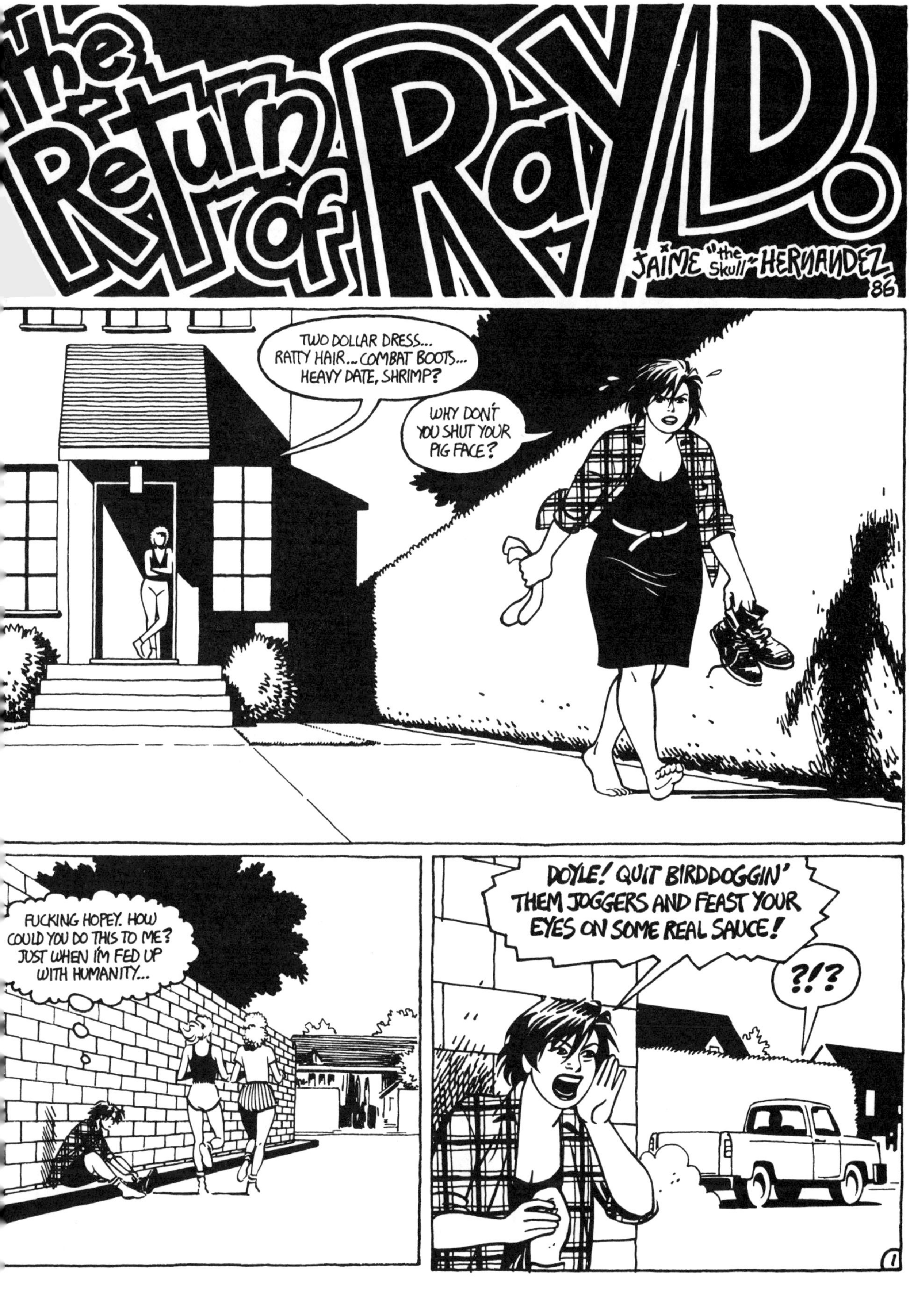
the Return of Ray D.
JAIME "the Skull" HERNANDEZ 86
TWO DOLLAR DRESS... RATTY HAIR... COMBAT BOOTS... HEAVY DATE, SHRIMP?
WHY DON'T YOU SHUT YOUR PIG FACE?
FUCKING HOPEY. HOW COULD YOU DO THIS TO ME? JUST WHEN I'M FED UP WITH HUMANITY...
DOYLE! QUIT BIRDDOGGIN' THEM JOGGERS AND FEAST YOUR EYES ON SOME REAL SAUCE!
?!?
1

NINA/GODMOTHER

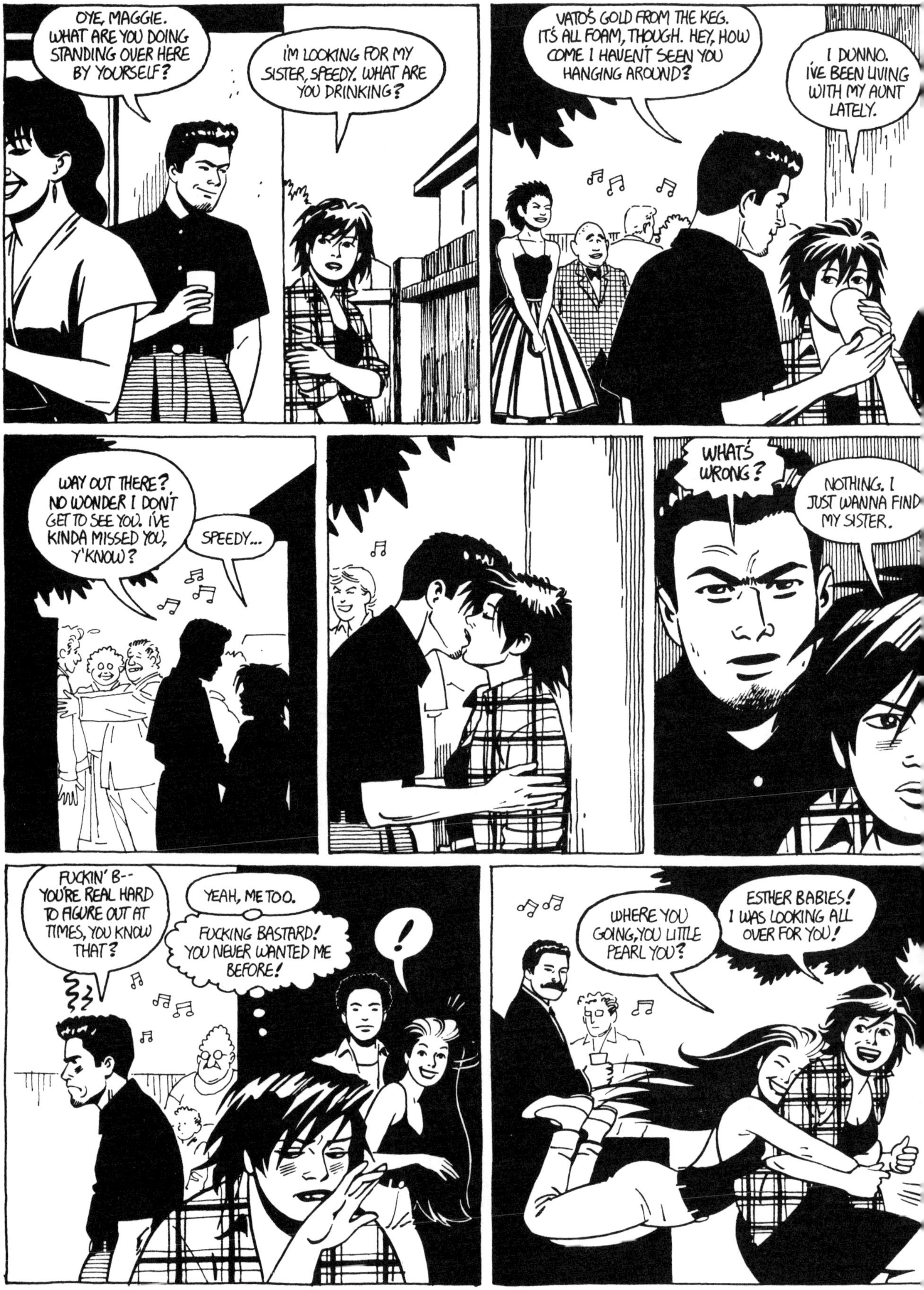
OYE, MAGGIE. WHAT ARE YOU DOING STANDING OVER HERE BY YOURSELF?
I'M LOOKING FOR MY SISTER, SPEEDY. WHAT ARE YOU DRINKING?
VATO'S GOLD FROM THE KEG. IT'S ALL FOAM, THOUGH. HEY, HOW COME I HAVEN'T SEEN YOU HANGING AROUND?
I DUNNO. I'VE BEEN LIVING WITH MY AUNT LATELY.
WAY OUT THERE? NO WONDER I DON'T GET TO SEE YOU. I'VE KINDA MISSED YOU, Y'KNOW?
SPEEDY...
WHAT'S WRONG?
NOTHING. I JUST WANNA FIND MY SISTER.
FUCKIN' B-- YOU'RE REAL HARD TO FIGURE OUT AT TIMES, YOU KNOW THAT?
YEAH, ME TOO.
FUCKING BASTARD! YOU NEVER WANTED ME BEFORE!
!
WHERE YOU GOING, YOU LITTLE PEARL YOU?
ESTHER BABIES! I WAS LOOKING ALL OVER FOR YOU!

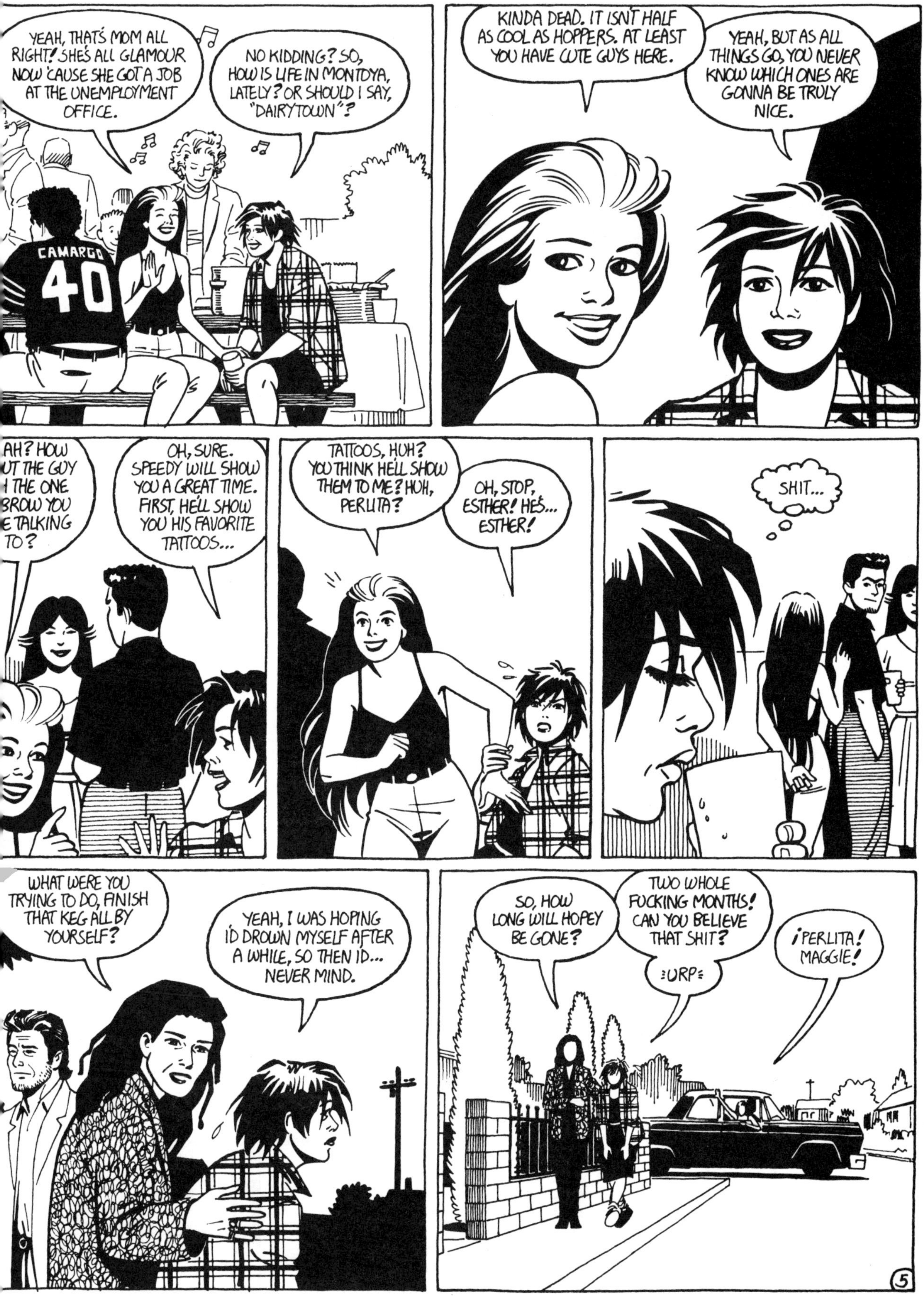
YEAH, THAT'S MOM ALL RIGHT! SHE'S ALL GLAMOUR NOW 'CAUSE SHE GOT A JOB AT THE UNEMPLOYMENT OFFICE.
NO KIDDING? SO, HOW IS LIFE IN MONTOYA, LATELY? OR SHOULD I SAY, "DAIRYTOWN"?
CAMARGO 40
KINDA DEAD. IT ISN'T HALF AS COOL AS HOPPERS. AT LEAST YOU HAVE CUTE GUYS HERE.
YEAH, BUT AS ALL THINGS GO, YOU NEVER KNOW WHICH ONES ARE GONNA BE TRULY NICE.
AH? HOW UT THE GUY I THE ONE BROW YOU E TALKING TO?
OH, SURE. SPEEDY WILL SHOW YOU A GREAT TIME. FIRST, HE'LL SHOW YOU HIS FAVORITE TATTOOS...
TATTOOS, HUH? YOU THINK HE'LL SHOW THEM TO ME? HUH, PERLITA?
OH, STOP, ESTHER! HE'S... ESTHER!
SHIT...
WHAT WERE YOU TRYING TO DO, FINISH THAT KEG ALL BY YOURSELF?
YEAH, I WAS HOPING I'D DROWN MYSELF AFTER A WHILE, SO THEN I'D... NEVER MIND.
SO, HOW LONG WILL HOPEY BE GONE?
TWO WHOLE FUCKING MONTHS! CAN YOU BELIEVE THAT SHIT?
URP
¡PERLITA! MAGGIE!

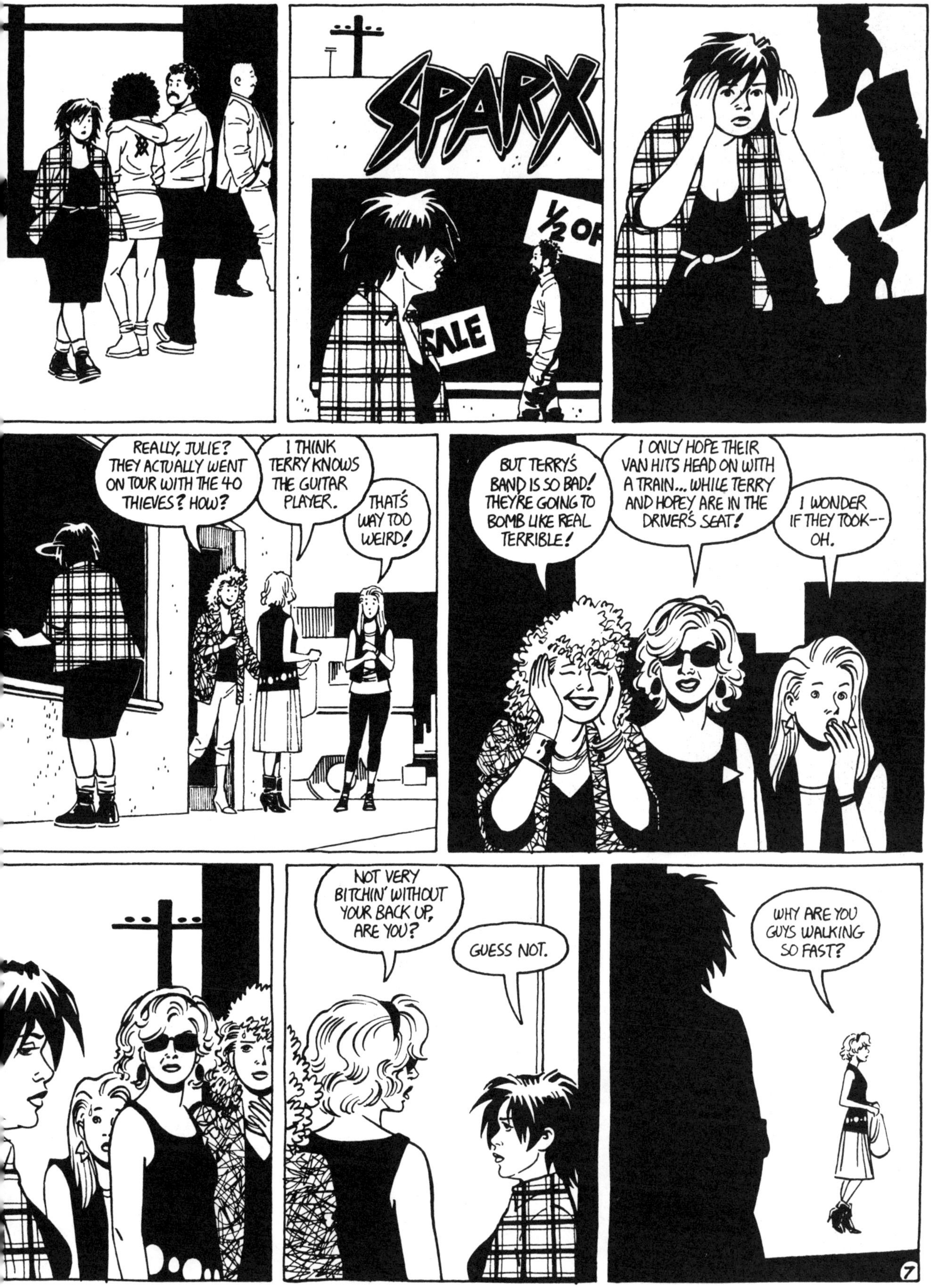
SPARX
1/2 OF
SALE
REALLY, JULIE? THEY ACTUALLY WENT ON TOUR WITH THE 40 THIEVES? HOW?
I THINK TERRY KNOWS THE GUITAR PLAYER.
THAT'S WAY TOO WEIRD!
BUT TERRY'S BAND IS SO BAD! THEY'RE GOING TO BOMB LIKE REAL TERRIBLE!
I ONLY HOPE THEIR VAN HITS HEAD ON WITH A TRAIN... WHILE TERRY AND HOPEY ARE IN THE DRIVER'S SEAT!
I WONDER IF THEY TOOK-- OH.
NOT VERY BITCHIN' WITHOUT YOUR BACK UP, ARE YOU?
GUESS NOT.
WHY ARE YOU GUYS WALKING SO FAST?

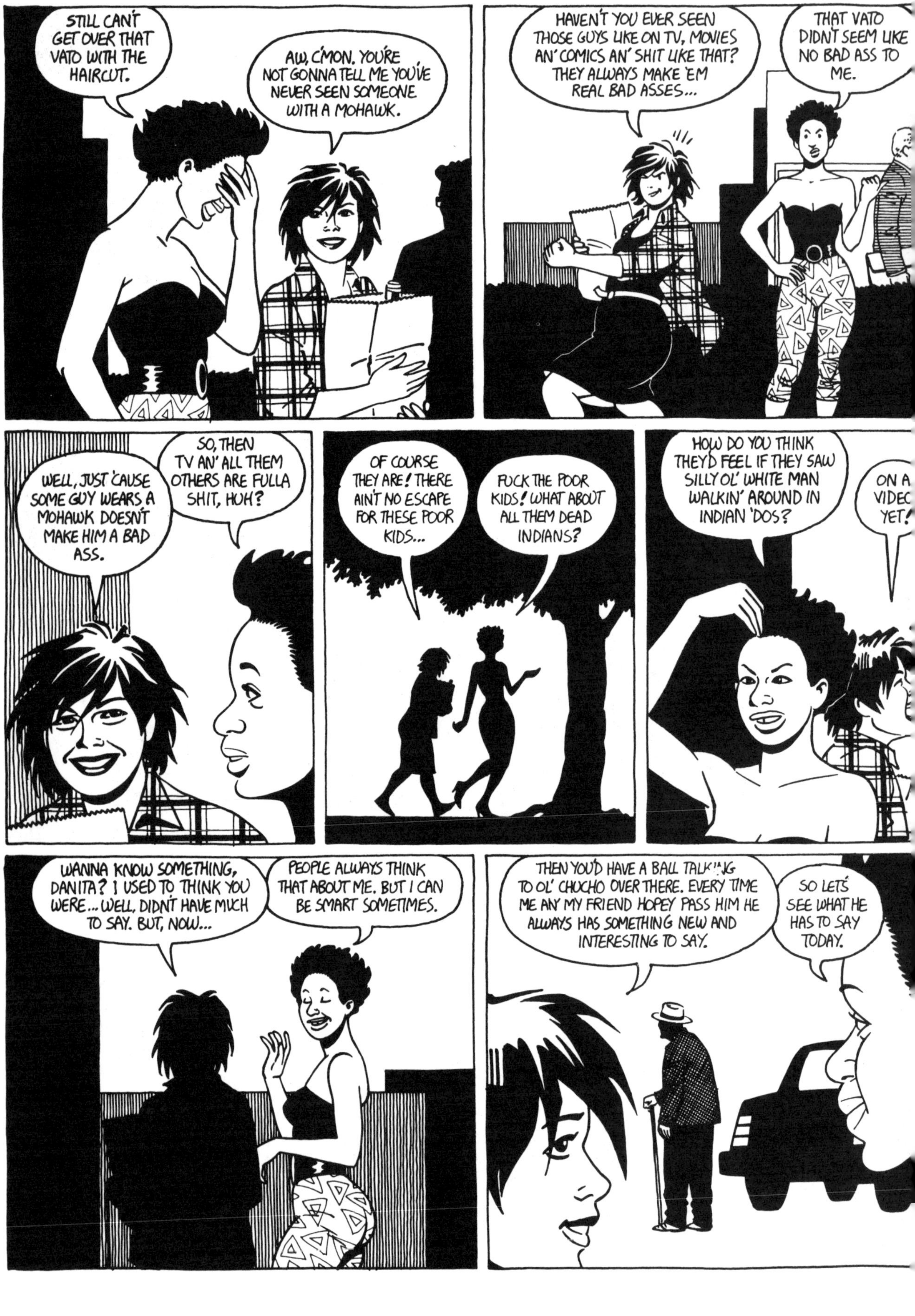

STILL CAN'T GET OVER THAT VATO WITH THE HAIRCUT.
AW, C'MON. YOU'RE NOT GONNA TELL ME YOU'VE NEVER SEEN SOMEONE WITH A MOHAWK.
HAVEN'T YOU EVER SEEN THOSE GUYS LIKE ON TV, MOVIES AN' COMICS AN' SHIT LIKE THAT? THEY ALWAYS MAKE 'EM REAL BAD ASSES...
THAT VATO DIDN'T SEEM LIKE NO BAD ASS TO ME.
WELL, JUST 'CAUSE SOME GUY WEARS A MOHAWK DOESN'T MAKE HIM A BAD ASS.
SO, THEN TV AN' ALL THEM OTHERS ARE FULLA SHIT, HUH?
OF COURSE THEY ARE! THERE AIN'T NO ESCAPE FOR THESE POOR KIDS...
FUCK THE POOR KIDS! WHAT ABOUT ALL THEM DEAD INDIANS?
HOW DO YOU THINK THEY'D FEEL IF THEY SAW SILLY OL' WHITE MAN WALKIN' AROUND IN INDIAN 'DOS?
ON A VIDEC YET!
WANNA KNOW SOMETHING, DANITA? I USED TO THINK YOU WERE... WELL, DIDN'T HAVE MUCH TO SAY. BUT, NOW...
PEOPLE ALWAYS THINK THAT ABOUT ME. BUT I CAN BE SMART SOMETIMES.
THEN YOU'D HAVE A BALL TALKING TO OL' CHUCHO OVER THERE. EVERY TIME ME ANY MY FRIEND HOPEY PASS HIM HE ALWAYS HAS SOMETHING NEW AND INTERESTING TO SAY.
SO LET'S SEE WHAT HE HAS TO SAY TODAY.

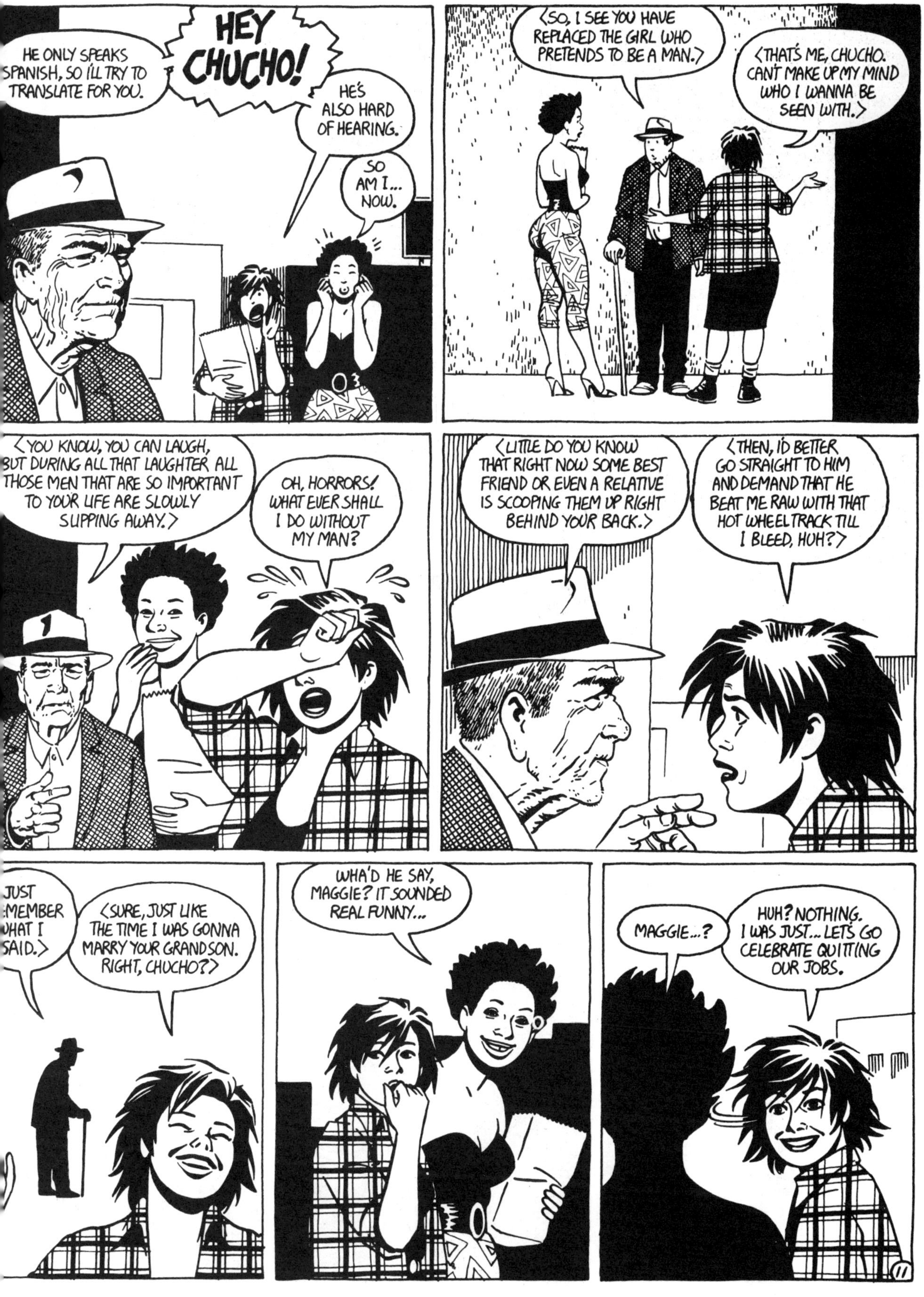
HE ONLY SPEAKS SPANISH, SO I'LL TRY TO TRANSLATE FOR YOU.
HEY CHUCHO!
HE'S ALSO HARD OF HEARING.
SO AM I... NOW.
<SO, I SEE YOU HAVE REPLACED THE GIRL WHO PRETENDS TO BE A MAN.>
<THAT'S ME, CHUCHO. CAN'T MAKE UP MY MIND WHO I WANNA BE SEEN WITH.>
<YOU KNOW, YOU CAN LAUGH, BUT DURING ALL THAT LAUGHTER ALL THOSE MEN THAT ARE SO IMPORTANT TO YOUR LIFE ARE SLOWLY SLIPPING AWAY.>
OH, HORRORS! WHAT EVER SHALL I DO WITHOUT MY MAN?
<LITTLE DO YOU KNOW THAT RIGHT NOW SOME BEST FRIEND OR EVEN A RELATIVE IS SCOOPING THEM UP RIGHT BEHIND YOUR BACK.>
<THEN, I'D BETTER GO STRAIGHT TO HIM AND DEMAND THAT HE BEAT ME RAW WITH THAT HOT WHEEL TRACK TILL I BLEED, HUH?>
JUST EMEMBER WHAT I SAID.>
<SURE, JUST LIKE THE TIME I WAS GONNA MARRY YOUR GRANDSON. RIGHT, CHUCHO?>
WHA'D HE SAY, MAGGIE? IT SOUNDED REAL FUNNY...
MAGGIE...?
HUH? NOTHING. I WAS JUST... LET'S GO CELEBRATE QUITTING OUR JOBS.

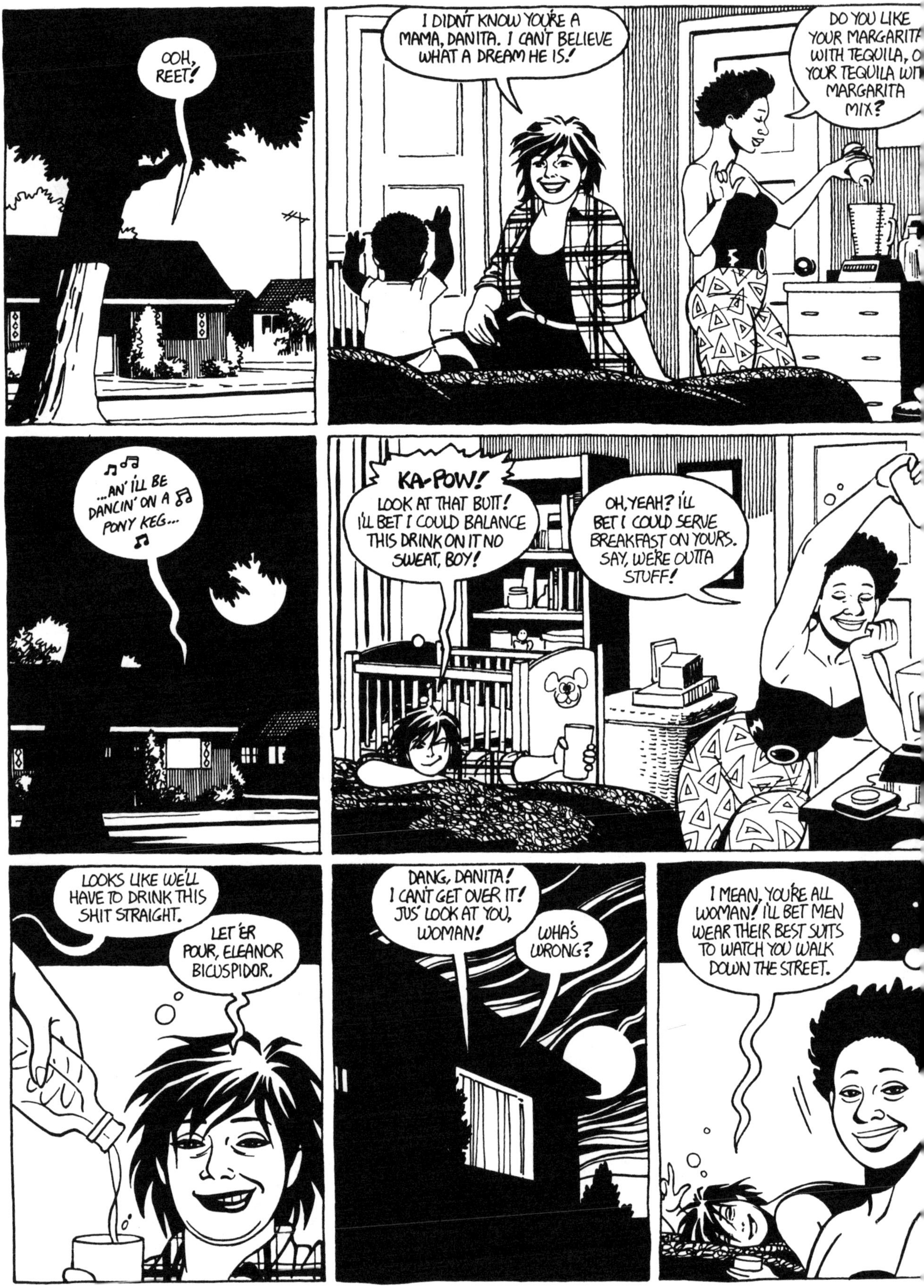

OOH, REET!
I DIDN'T KNOW YOU'RE A MAMA, DANITA. I CAN'T BELIEVE WHAT A DREAM HE IS!
DO YOU LIKE YOUR MARGARITA WITH TEQUILA, OR YOUR TEQUILA WITH MARGARITA MIX?
...AN' I'LL BE DANCIN' ON A PONY KEG...
KA-POW!
LOOK AT THAT BUTT! I'LL BET I COULD BALANCE THIS DRINK ON IT NO SWEAT, BOY!
OH, YEAH? I'LL BET I COULD SERVE BREAKFAST ON YOURS. SAY, WE'RE OUTTA STUFF!
LOOKS LIKE WE'LL HAVE TO DRINK THIS SHIT STRAIGHT.
LET 'ER POUR, ELEANOR BICUSPIDOR.
DANG, DANITA! I CAN'T GET OVER IT! JUS' LOOK AT YOU, WOMAN!
WHA'S WRONG?
I MEAN, YOU'RE ALL WOMAN! I'LL BET MEN WEAR THEIR BEST SUITS TO WATCH YOU WALK DOWN THE STREET.

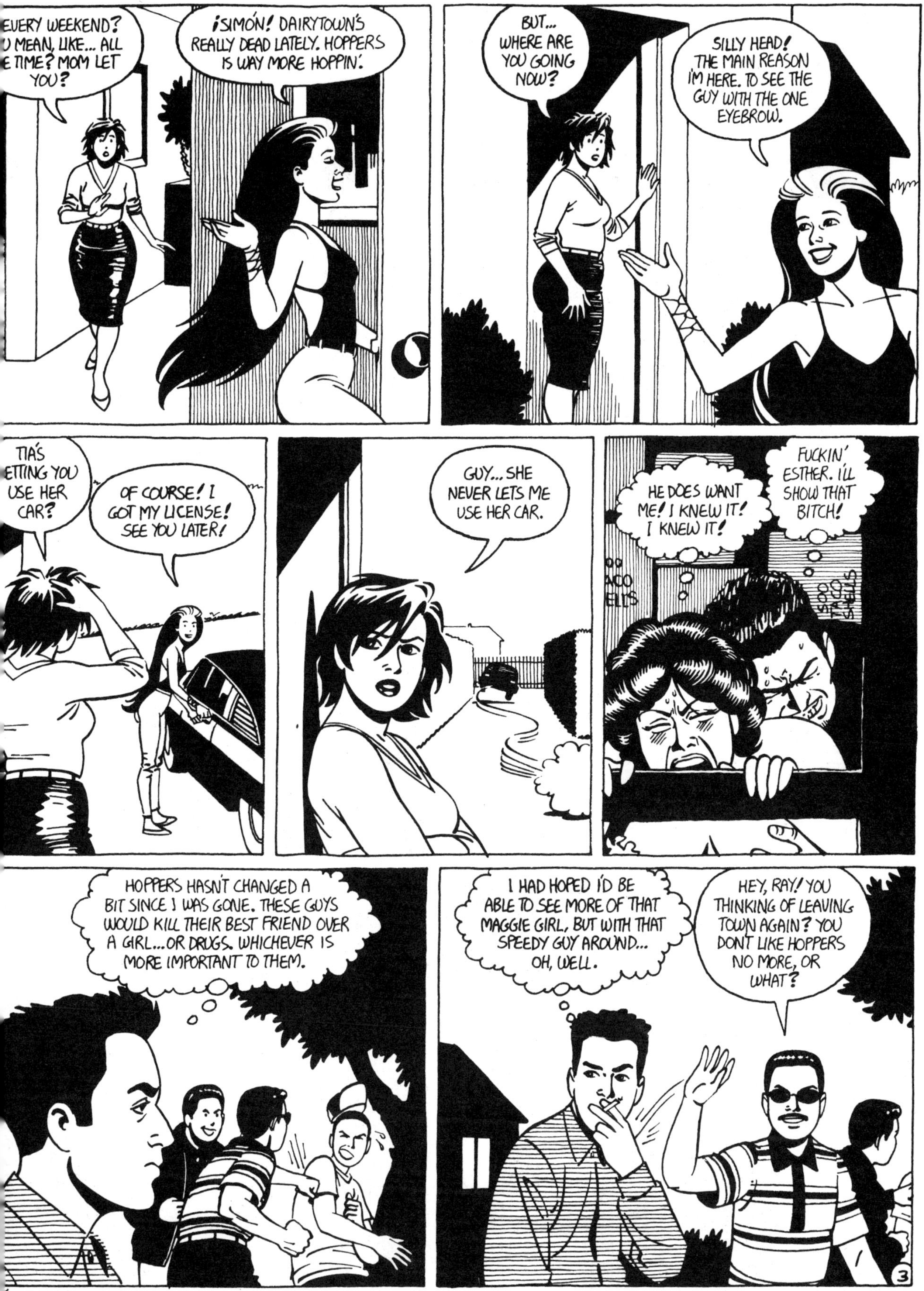
EVERY WEEKEND? U MEAN, LIKE... ALL E TIME? MOM LET YOU?
¡SIMÓN! DAIRYTOWN'S REALLY DEAD LATELY. HOPPERS IS WAY MORE HOPPIN'.
BUT... WHERE ARE YOU GOING NOW?
SILLY HEAD! THE MAIN REASON I'M HERE. TO SEE THE GUY WITH THE ONE EYEBROW.
TIA'S ETTING YOU USE HER CAR?
OF COURSE! I GOT MY LICENSE! SEE YOU LATER!
GUY... SHE NEVER LETS ME USE HER CAR.
HE DOES WANT ME! I KNEW IT! I KNEW IT!
FUCKIN' ESTHER. I'LL SHOW THAT BITCH!
HOPPERS HASN'T CHANGED A BIT SINCE I WAS GONE. THESE GUYS WOULD KILL THEIR BEST FRIEND OVER A GIRL...OR DRUGS. WHICHEVER IS MORE IMPORTANT TO THEM.
I HAD HOPED I'D BE ABLE TO SEE MORE OF THAT MAGGIE GIRL, BUT WITH THAT SPEEDY GUY AROUND... OH, WELL.
HEY, RAY! YOU THINKING OF LEAVING TOWN AGAIN? YOU DON'T LIKE HOPPERS NO MORE, OR WHAT?

*OF COURSE!

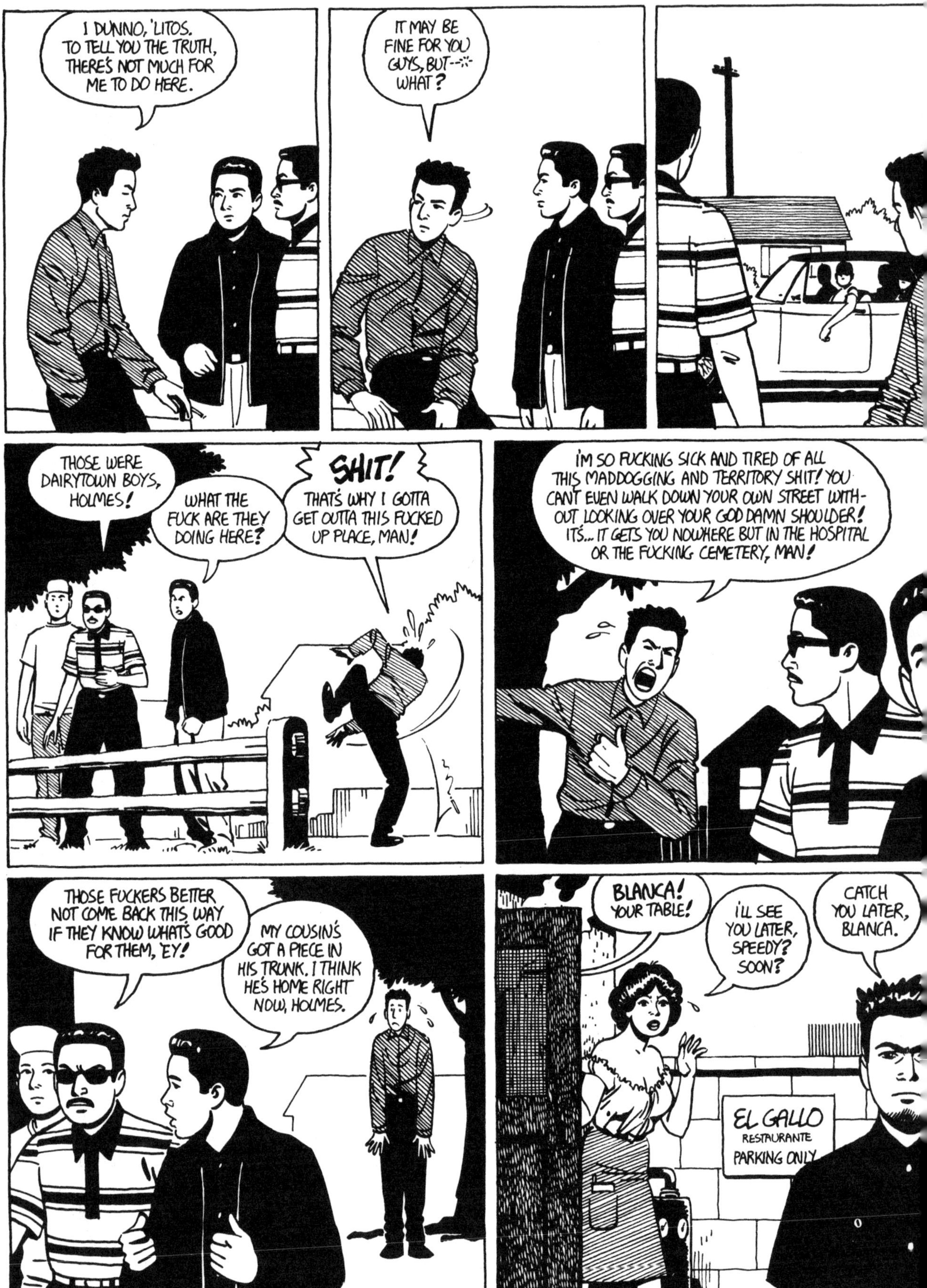
I DUNNO, 'LITOS. TO TELL YOU THE TRUTH, THERE'S NOT MUCH FOR ME TO DO HERE.
IT MAY BE FINE FOR YOU GUYS, BUT-- WHAT?
THOSE WERE DAIRYTOWN BOYS, HOLMES!
WHAT THE FUCK ARE THEY DOING HERE?
SHIT!
THAT'S WHY I GOTTA GET OUTTA THIS FUCKED UP PLACE, MAN!
I'M SO FUCKING SICK AND TIRED OF ALL THIS MADDOGGING AND TERRITORY SHIT! YOU CAN'T EVEN WALK DOWN YOUR OWN STREET WITH-OUT LOOKING OVER YOUR GOD DAMN SHOULDER! IT'S... IT GETS YOU NOWHERE BUT IN THE HOSPITAL OR THE FUCKING CEMETERY, MAN!
THOSE FUCKERS BETTER NOT COME BACK THIS WAY IF THEY KNOW WHAT'S GOOD FOR THEM, 'EY!
MY COUSIN'S GOT A PIECE IN HIS TRUNK. I THINK HE'S HOME RIGHT NOW, HOLMES.
BLANCA! YOUR TABLE!
I'LL SEE YOU LATER, SPEEDY? SOON?
CATCH YOU LATER, BLANCA.
EL GALLO
RESTAURANTE
PARKING ONLY

PIECE/GUN

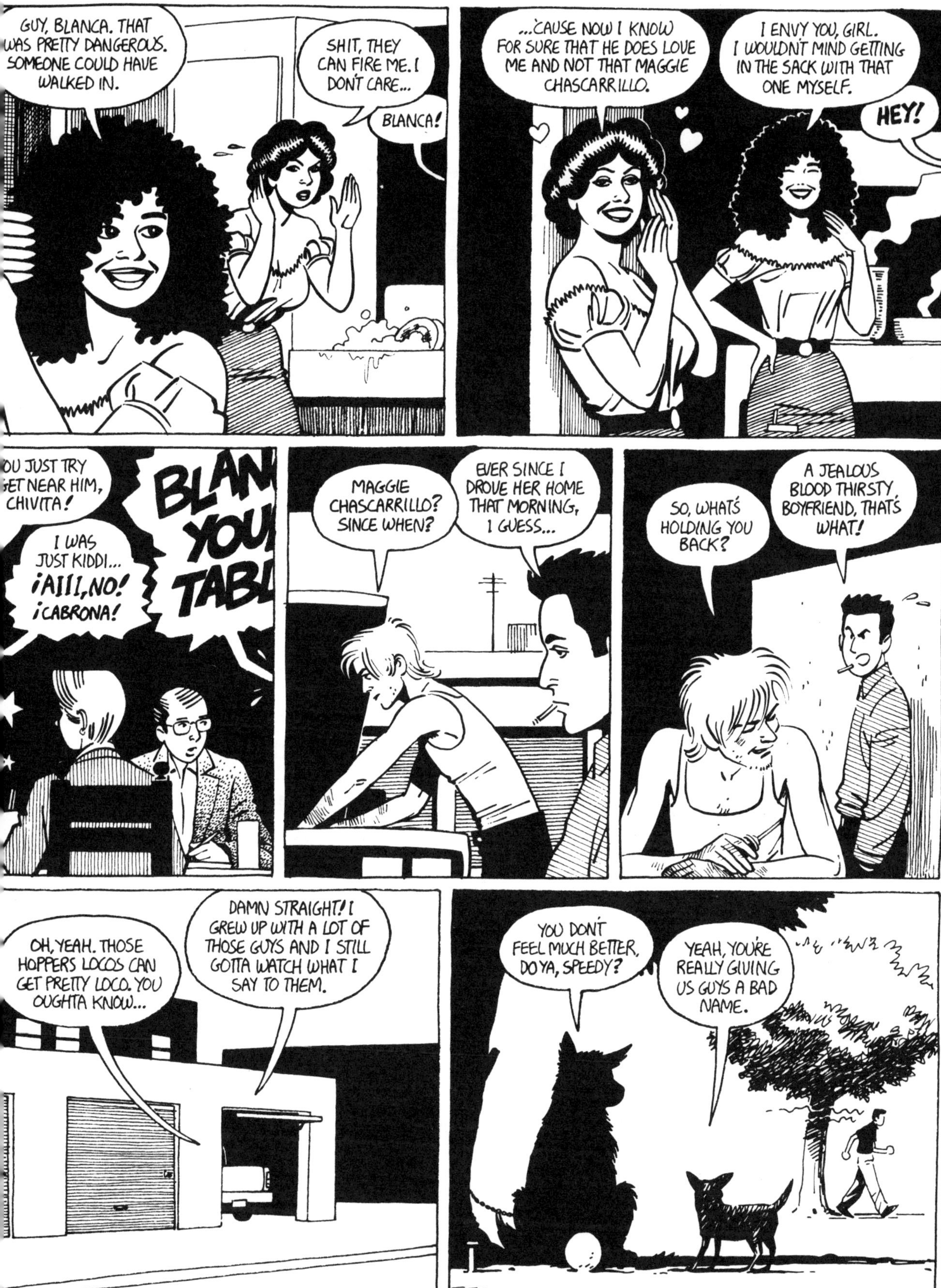
GUY, BLANCA. THAT WAS PRETTY DANGEROUS. SOMEONE COULD HAVE WALKED IN.
SHIT, THEY CAN FIRE ME. I DON'T CARE...
BLANCA!
...'CAUSE NOW I KNOW FOR SURE THAT HE DOES LOVE ME AND NOT THAT MAGGIE CHASCARRILLO.
I ENVY YOU, GIRL. I WOULDN'T MIND GETTING IN THE SACK WITH THAT ONE MYSELF.
HEY!
OU JUST TRY GET NEAR HIM, CHIVITA!
I WAS JUST KIDDI... ¡AIII, NO! ¡CABRONA!
BLAN YOU TABL
MAGGIE CHASCARRILLO? SINCE WHEN?
EVER SINCE I DROVE HER HOME THAT MORNING, I GUESS...
SO, WHAT'S HOLDING YOU BACK?
A JEALOUS BLOOD THIRSTY BOYFRIEND, THAT'S WHAT!
OH, YEAH. THOSE HOPPERS LOCOS CAN GET PRETTY LOCO. YOU OUGHTA KNOW...
DAMN STRAIGHT! I GREW UP WITH A LOT OF THOSE GUYS AND I STILL GOTTA WATCH WHAT I SAY TO THEM.
YOU DON'T FEEL MUCH BETTER, DO YA, SPEEDY?
YEAH, YOU'RE REALLY GIVING US GUYS A BAD NAME.

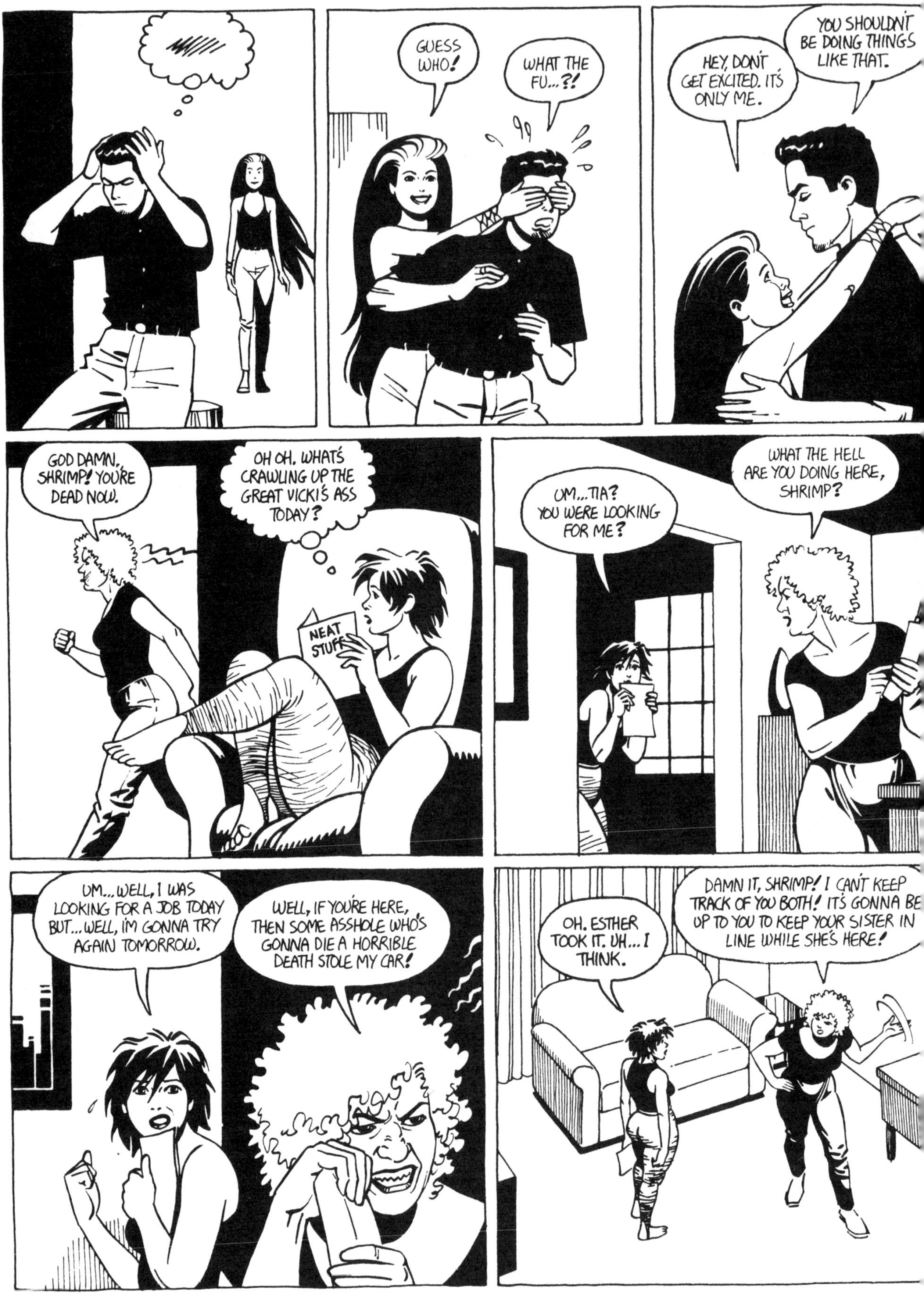
GUESS WHO!
WHAT THE FU...?!
HEY, DON'T GET EXCITED. IT'S ONLY ME.
YOU SHOULDN'T BE DOING THINGS LIKE THAT.
GOD DAMN, SHRIMP! YOU'RE DEAD NOW.
OH OH. WHAT'S CRAWLING UP THE GREAT VICKI'S ASS TODAY?
NEAT STUFF
UM... TIA? YOU WERE LOOKING FOR ME?
WHAT THE HELL ARE YOU DOING HERE, SHRIMP?
UM... WELL, I WAS LOOKING FOR A JOB TODAY BUT... WELL, I'M GONNA TRY AGAIN TOMORROW.
WELL, IF YOU'RE HERE, THEN SOME ASSHOLE WHO'S GONNA DIE A HORRIBLE DEATH STOLE MY CAR!
OH. ESTHER TOOK IT. UH... I THINK.
DAMN IT, SHRIMP! I CAN'T KEEP TRACK OF YOU BOTH! IT'S GONNA BE UP TO YOU TO KEEP YOUR SISTER IN LINE WHILE SHE'S HERE!

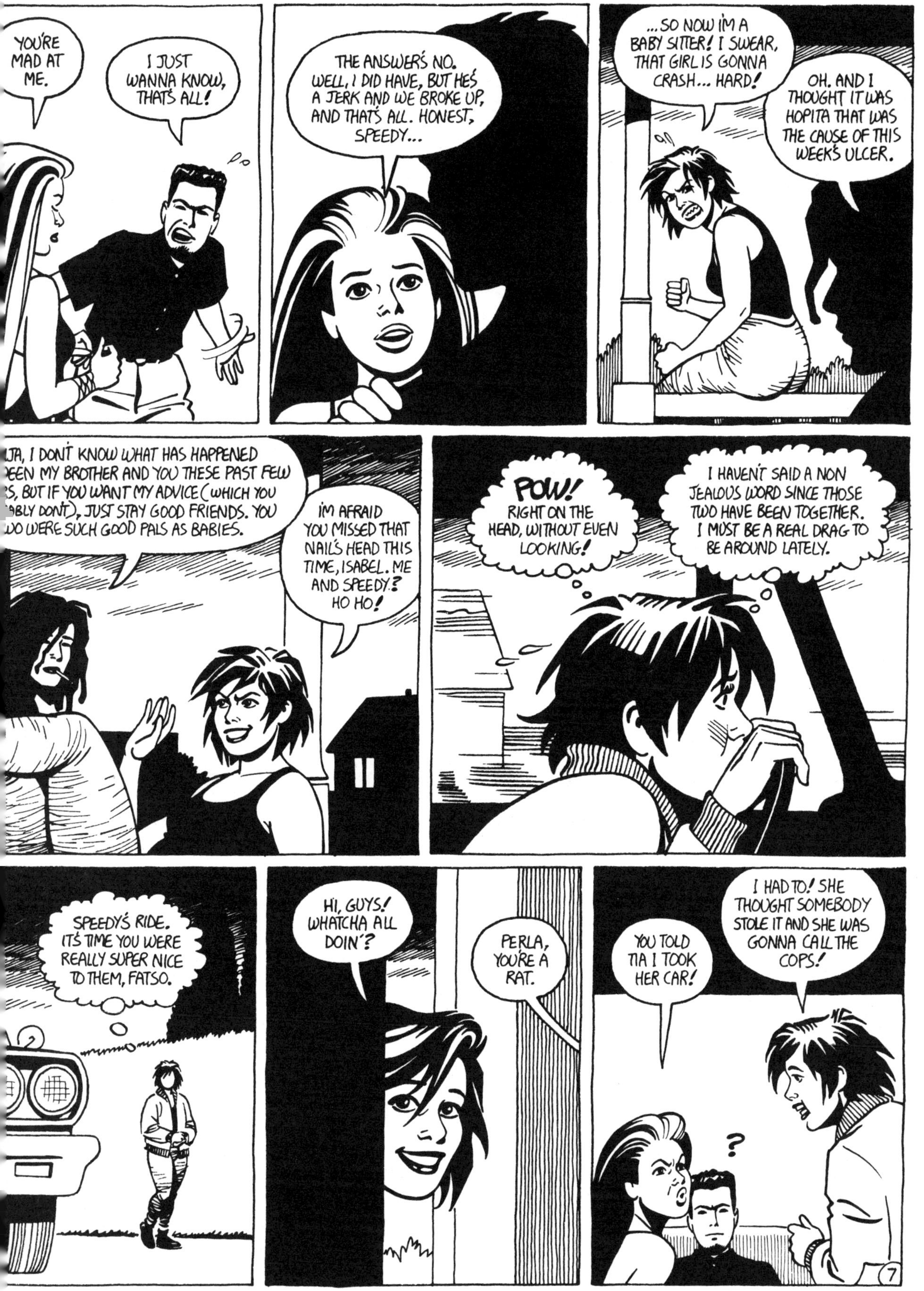

YOU'RE MAD AT ME.
I JUST WANNA KNOW, THAT'S ALL!
THE ANSWER'S NO. WELL, I DID HAVE, BUT HE'S A JERK AND WE BROKE UP, AND THAT'S ALL. HONEST, SPEEDY...
...SO NOW I'M A BABY SITTER! I SWEAR, THAT GIRL IS GONNA CRASH... HARD!
OH. AND I THOUGHT IT WAS HOPITA THAT WAS THE CAUSE OF THIS WEEK'S ULCER.
JA, I DON'T KNOW WHAT HAS HAPPENED EEN MY BROTHER AND YOU THESE PAST FEW S, BUT IF YOU WANT MY ADVICE (WHICH YOU ABLY DON'T), JUST STAY GOOD FRIENDS. YOU O WERE SUCH GOOD PALS AS BABIES.
I'M AFRAID YOU MISSED THAT NAIL'S HEAD THIS TIME, ISABEL. ME AND SPEEDY? HO HO!
POW! RIGHT ON THE HEAD, WITHOUT EVEN LOOKING!
I HAVEN'T SAID A NON JEALOUS WORD SINCE THOSE TWO HAVE BEEN TOGETHER. I MUST BE A REAL DRAG TO BE AROUND LATELY.
SPEEDY'S RIDE. IT'S TIME YOU WERE REALLY SUPER NICE TO THEM, FATSO.
HI, GUYS! WHATCHA ALL DOIN'?
PERLA, YOU'RE A RAT.
YOU TOLD TIA I TOOK HER CAR!
I HAD TO! SHE THOUGHT SOMEBODY STOLE IT AND SHE WAS GONNA CALL THE COPS!
?
7

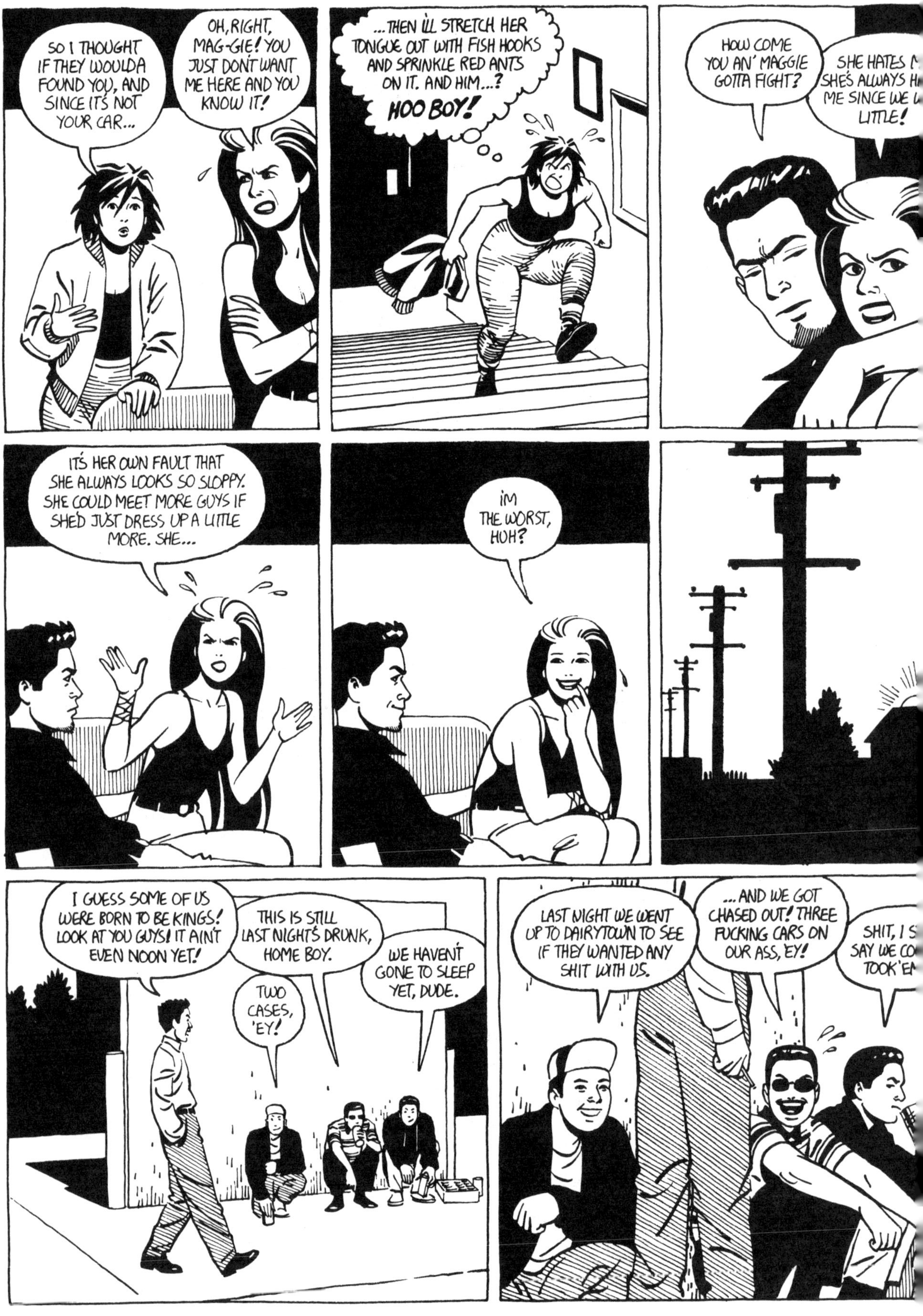
SO I THOUGHT IF THEY WOULDA FOUND YOU, AND SINCE IT'S NOT YOUR CAR...
OH, RIGHT, MAG-GIE! YOU JUST DON'T WANT ME HERE AND YOU KNOW IT!
...THEN I'LL STRETCH HER TONGUE OUT WITH FISH HOOKS AND SPRINKLE RED ANTS ON IT. AND HIM...? HOO BOY!
HOW COME YOU AN' MAGGIE GOTTA FIGHT?
SHE HATES SHE'S ALWAYS ME SINCE WE LITTLE!
IT'S HER OWN FAULT THAT SHE ALWAYS LOOKS SO SLOPPY. SHE COULD MEET MORE GUYS IF SHE'D JUST DRESS UP A LITTLE MORE. SHE...
I'M THE WORST, HUH?
I GUESS SOME OF US WERE BORN TO BE KINGS! LOOK AT YOU GUYS! IT AIN'T EVEN NOON YET!
THIS IS STILL LAST NIGHT'S DRUNK, HOME BOY.
TWO CASES, 'EY!
WE HAVEN'T GONE TO SLEEP YET, DUDE.
LAST NIGHT WE WENT UP TO DAIRYTOWN TO SEE IF THEY WANTED ANY SHIT WITH US.
...AND WE GOT CHASED OUT! THREE FUCKING CARS ON OUR ASS, 'EY!
SHIT, I SAY WE

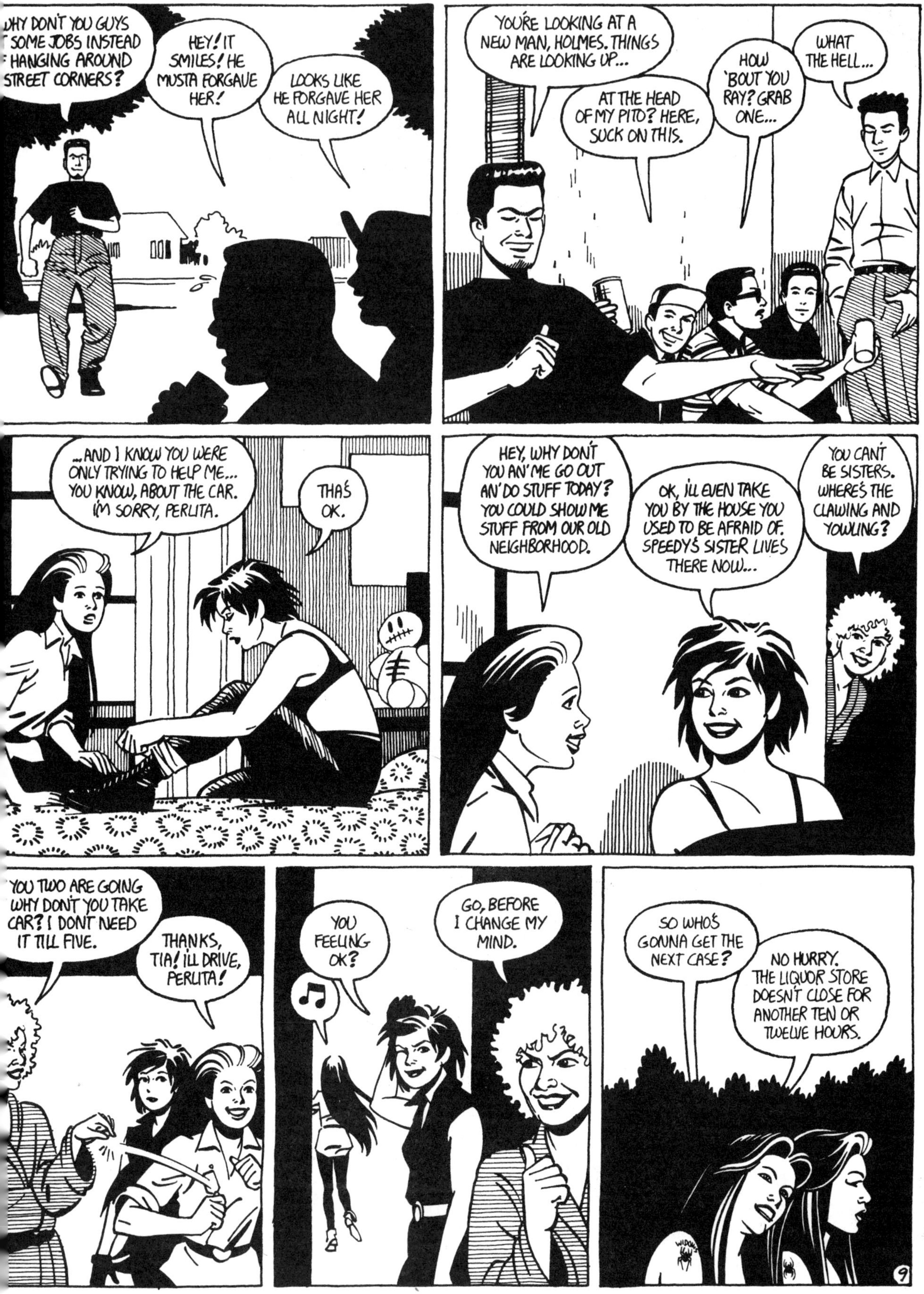

WHY DON'T YOU GUYS T SOME JOBS INSTEAD F HANGING AROUND STREET CORNERS?
HEY! IT SMILES! HE MUSTA FORGAVE HER!
LOOKS LIKE HE FORGAVE HER ALL NIGHT!
YOU'RE LOOKING AT A NEW MAN, HOLMES. THINGS ARE LOOKING UP...
AT THE HEAD OF MY PITO? HERE, SUCK ON THIS.
HOW 'BOUT YOU RAY? GRAB ONE...
WHAT THE HELL...
...AND I KNOW YOU WERE ONLY TRYING TO HELP ME... YOU KNOW, ABOUT THE CAR. I'M SORRY, PERLITA.
THA'S OK.
HEY, WHY DON'T YOU AN' ME GO OUT AN' DO STUFF TODAY? YOU COULD SHOW ME STUFF FROM OUR OLD NEIGHBORHOOD.
OK, I'LL EVEN TAKE YOU BY THE HOUSE YOU USED TO BE AFRAID OF. SPEEDY'S SISTER LIVES THERE NOW...
YOU CAN'T BE SISTERS. WHERE'S THE CLAWING AND YOWLING?
YOU TWO ARE GOING WHY DON'T YOU TAKE CAR? I DONT NEED IT TILL FIVE.
THANKS, TIA! I'LL DRIVE, PERLITA!
YOU FEELING OK?
GO, BEFORE I CHANGE MY MIND.
SO WHO'S GONNA GET THE NEXT CASE?
NO HURRY. THE LIQUOR STORE DOESN'T CLOSE FOR ANOTHER TEN OR TWELVE HOURS.
WIDOWS

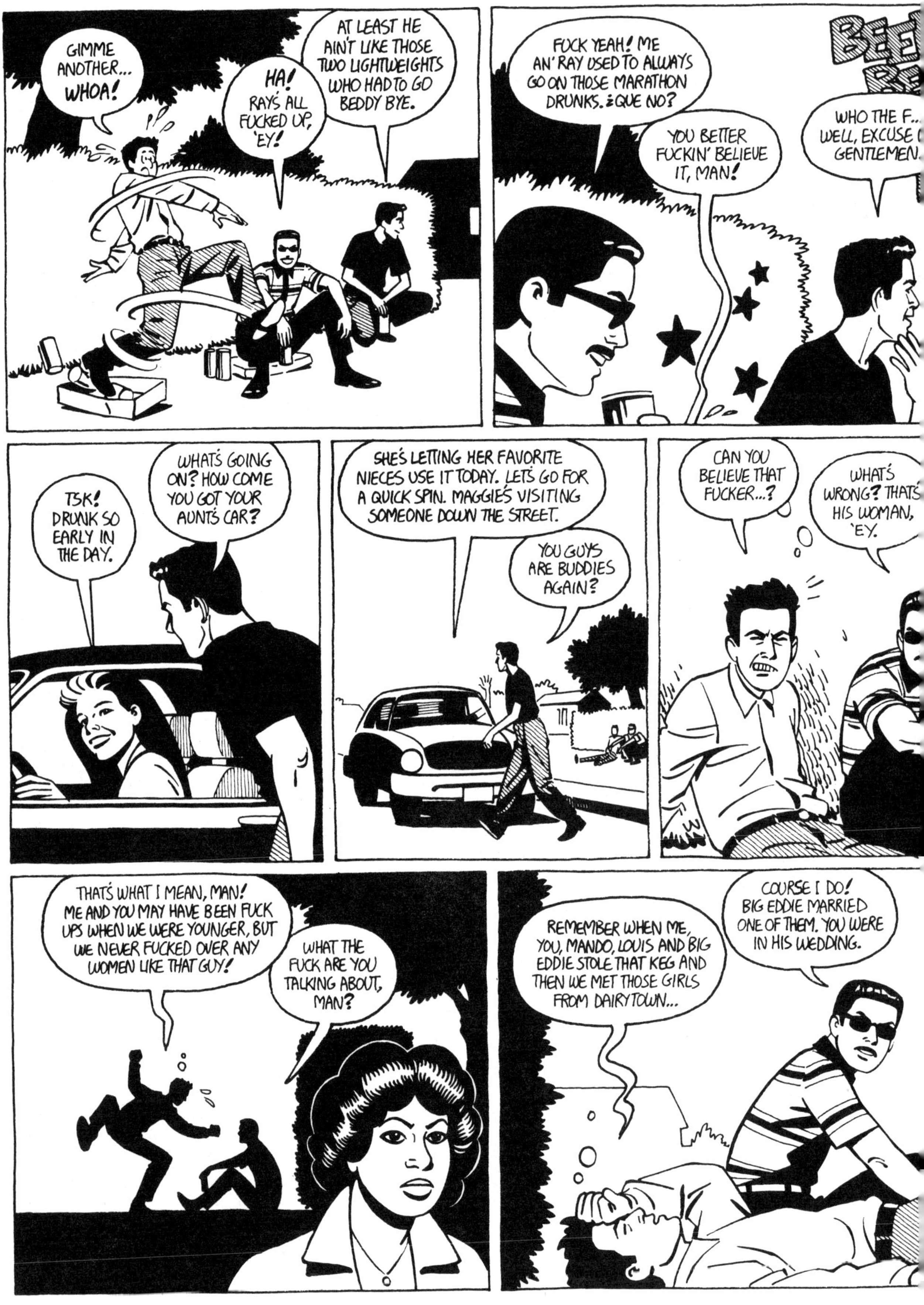

GIMME ANOTHER... WHOA!
HA! RAY'S ALL FUCKED UP, 'EY!
AT LEAST HE AIN'T LIKE THOSE TWO LIGHTWEIGHTS WHO HAD TO GO BEDDY BYE.
FUCK YEAH! ME AN' RAY USED TO ALWAYS GO ON THOSE MARATHON DRUNKS. ¿QUE NO?
YOU BETTER FUCKIN' BELIEVE IT, MAN!
WHO THE F... WELL, EXCUSE GENTLEMEN.
TSK! DRUNK SO EARLY IN THE DAY.
WHAT'S GOING ON? HOW COME YOU GOT YOUR AUNT'S CAR?
SHE'S LETTING HER FAVORITE NIECES USE IT TODAY. LET'S GO FOR A QUICK SPIN. MAGGIE'S VISITING SOMEONE DOWN THE STREET.
YOU GUYS ARE BUDDIES AGAIN?
CAN YOU BELIEVE THAT FUCKER...?
WHAT'S WRONG? THAT'S HIS WOMAN, 'EY.
THAT'S WHAT I MEAN, MAN! ME AND YOU MAY HAVE BEEN FUCK UPS WHEN WE WERE YOUNGER, BUT WE NEVER FUCKED OVER ANY WOMEN LIKE THAT GUY!
WHAT THE FUCK ARE YOU TALKING ABOUT, MAN?
REMEMBER WHEN ME, YOU, MANDO, LOUIS AND BIG EDDIE STOLE THAT KEG AND THEN WE MET THOSE GIRLS FROM DAIRYTOWN...
COURSE I DO! BIG EDDIE MARRIED ONE OF THEM. YOU WERE IN HIS WEDDING.

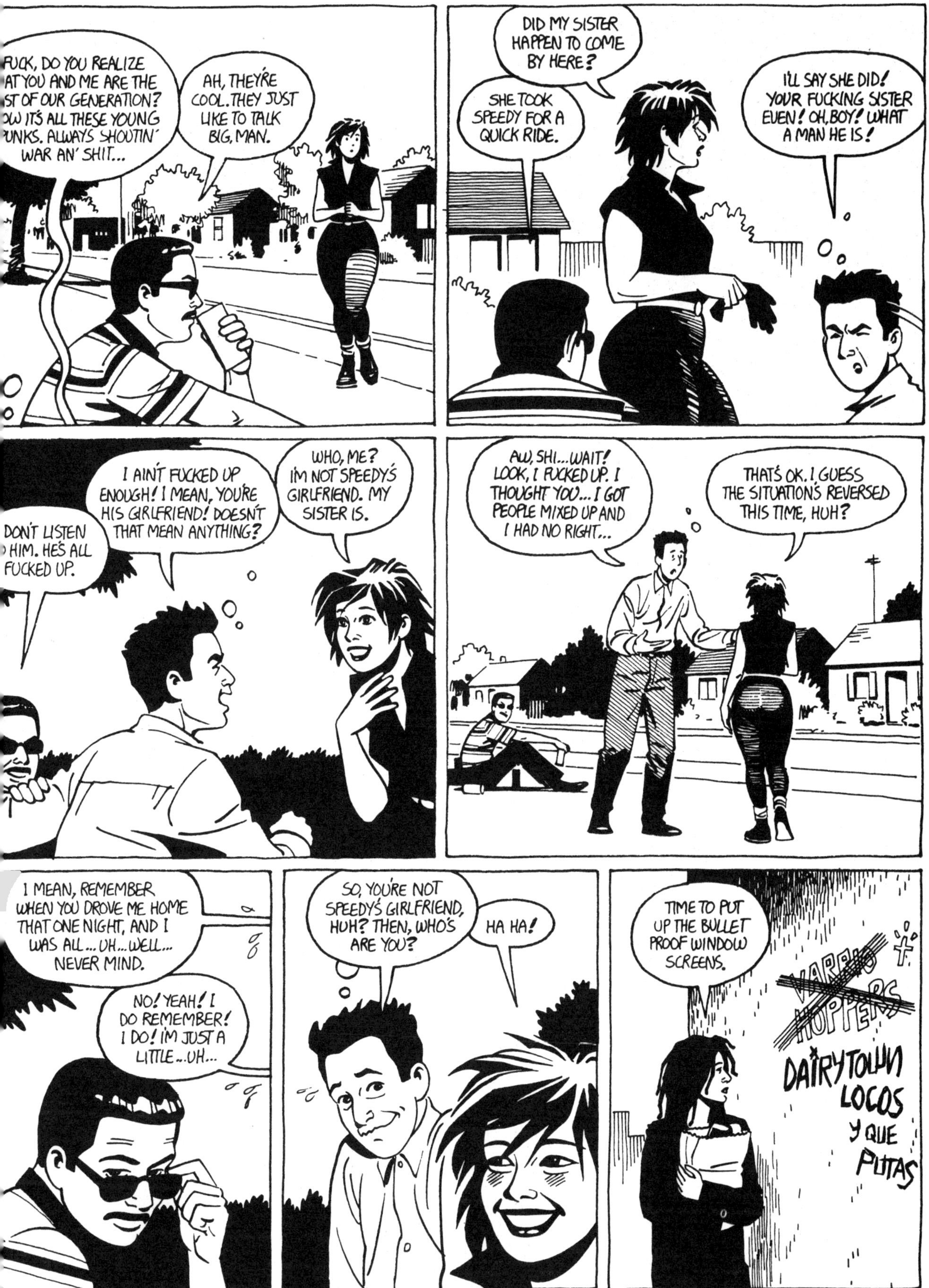
FUCK, DO YOU REALIZE AT YOU AND ME ARE THE ST OF OUR GENERATION? OW IT'S ALL THESE YOUNG PUNKS. ALWAYS SHOUTIN' WAR AN' SHIT...
AH, THEY'RE COOL. THEY JUST LIKE TO TALK BIG, MAN.
DID MY SISTER HAPPEN TO COME BY HERE?
SHE TOOK SPEEDY FOR A QUICK RIDE.
I'LL SAY SHE DID! YOUR FUCKING SISTER EVEN! OH, BOY! WHAT A MAN HE IS!
DON'T LISTEN HIM. HE'S ALL FUCKED UP.
I AIN'T FUCKED UP ENOUGH! I MEAN, YOU'RE HIS GIRLFRIEND! DOESN'T THAT MEAN ANYTHING?
WHO, ME? I'M NOT SPEEDY'S GIRLFRIEND. MY SISTER IS.
AW, SHI... WAIT! LOOK, I FUCKED UP. I THOUGHT YOU... I GOT PEOPLE MIXED UP AND I HAD NO RIGHT...
THAT'S OK. I GUESS THE SITUATION'S REVERSED THIS TIME, HUH?
I MEAN, REMEMBER WHEN YOU DROVE ME HOME THAT ONE NIGHT, AND I WAS ALL... UH... WELL... NEVER MIND.
NO! YEAH! I DO REMEMBER! I DO! I'M JUST A LITTLE... UH...
SO, YOU'RE NOT SPEEDY'S GIRLFRIEND, HUH? THEN, WHO'S ARE YOU?
HA HA!
TIME TO PUT UP THE BULLET PROOF WINDOW SCREENS.
VARRIO HOPPERS
DAIRYTOWN LOCOS Y QUE PUTAS

END OF PART ONE

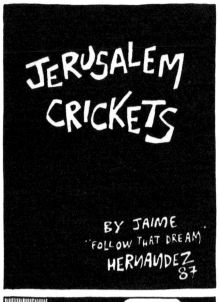

JERUSALEM CRICKETS

BY JAIME
"FOLLOW THAT DREAM"
HERNANDEZ 87

TERRY, I GOTTA HELP LOAD UP OUR SHIT!

IT CAN WAIT. COME ON.

YOU HAVE A CHOICE. TELEPHONE OR LETTER.

LETTER.

WHY ARE YOU SO ANXIOUS FOR ME TO WRITE THE MAGPIE? YOU HATE HER!

YFM

YOU HAVE TO CLEAR MY GOOD NAME, LOVE...

I JUST KNOW SHE THINKS I'M THE ONE RESPONSIBLE FOR LEAVING HER BEHIND ON THIS TOUR.

I KNEW IT WAS MORE THAN JUST THINKING OF MAGGIE...

I AM THINKING OF MAGGIE. SHE STILL MUST BE HEARTBROKEN WITHOUT A WORD FROM YOU YET.

SURE, SURE, OK.

DAMN! HOW DOES ANYONE START ONE OF THESE THINGS?

"DEAREST MAGPIE..."

"SORRY I COULDN'T GET IN TOUCH WITH YOU EARLIER, BUT THIS PAST MONTH HAS BEEN VERY HECTIC FOR OUR BAND..."

HOW DO YOU SPELL "HECTIC"?

"BY THE WAY, WE'RE ALSO SORRY YOU COULDN'T COME WITH US, BUT WE HAD TO GET AN EARLY START, AND YOU..."

SHE'S NOT GONNA BUY THAT!

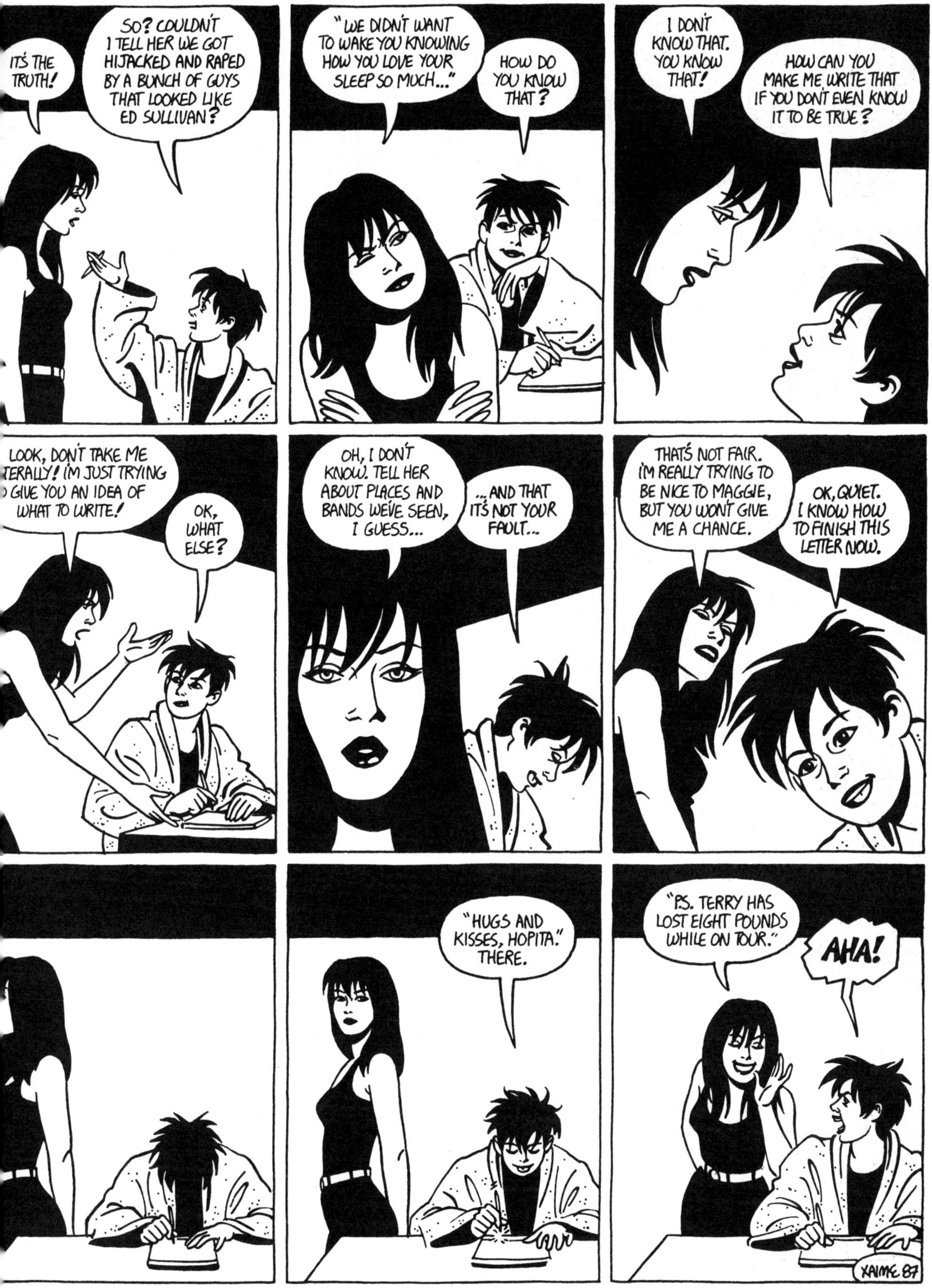
IT'S THE TRUTH!
SO? COULDN'T I TELL HER WE GOT HIJACKED AND RAPED BY A BUNCH OF GUYS THAT LOOKED LIKE ED SULLIVAN?
"WE DIDN'T WANT TO WAKE YOU KNOWING HOW YOU LOVE YOUR SLEEP SO MUCH..."
HOW DO YOU KNOW THAT?
I DON'T KNOW THAT. YOU KNOW THAT!
HOW CAN YOU MAKE ME WRITE THAT IF YOU DON'T EVEN KNOW IT TO BE TRUE?
LOOK, DON'T TAKE ME ITERALLY! I'M JUST TRYING O GIVE YOU AN IDEA OF WHAT TO WRITE!
OK, WHAT ELSE?
OH, I DON'T KNOW. TELL HER ABOUT PLACES AND BANDS WE'VE SEEN, I GUESS...
...AND THAT IT'S NOT YOUR FAULT...
THAT'S NOT FAIR. I'M REALLY TRYING TO BE NICE TO MAGGIE, BUT YOU WON'T GIVE ME A CHANCE.
OK, QUIET. I KNOW HOW TO FINISH THIS LETTER NOW.
"HUGS AND KISSES, HOPITA." THERE.
"P.S. TERRY HAS LOST EIGHT POUNDS WHILE ON TOUR."
AHA!
XAIME 87

VIDALOCA2

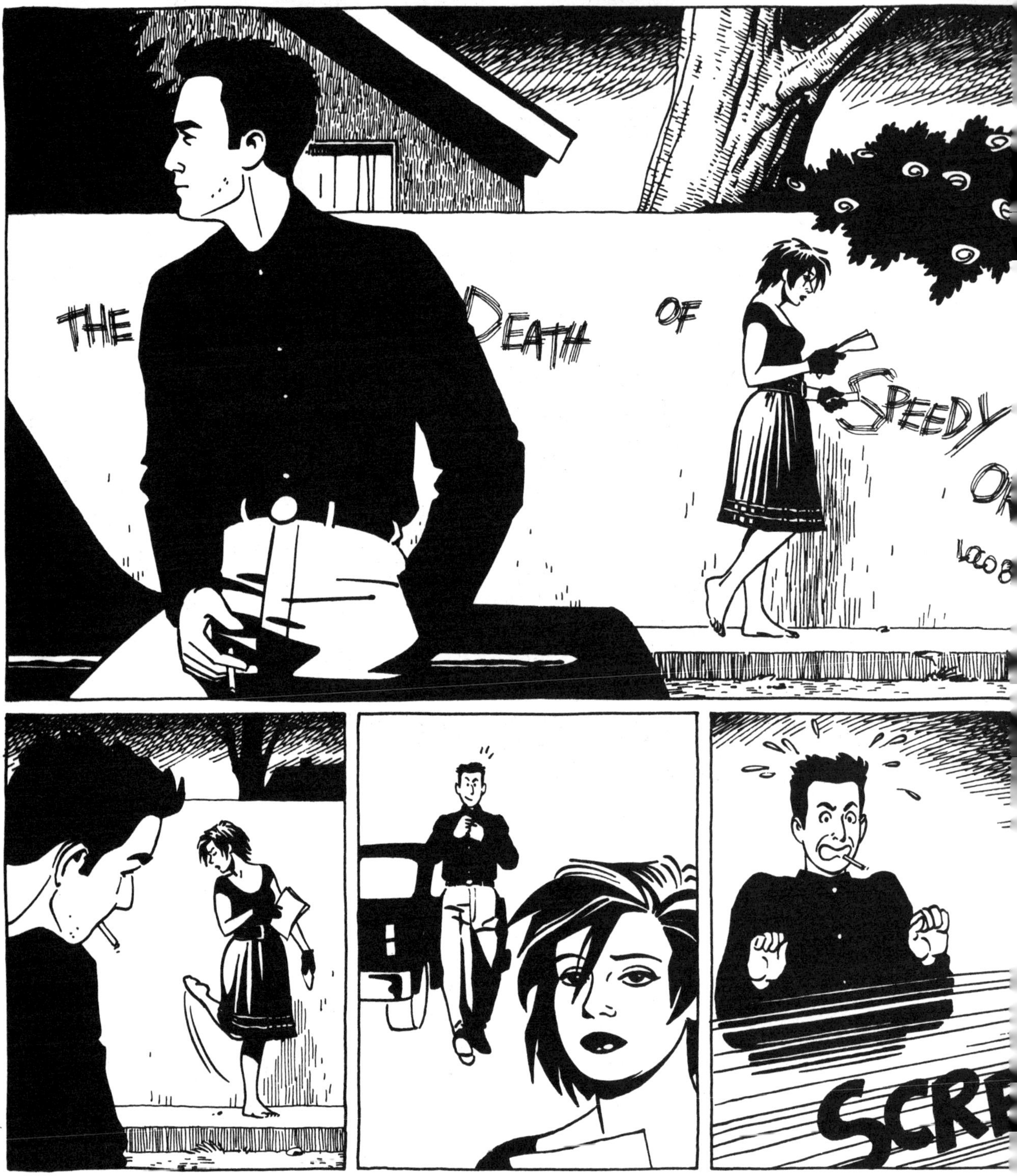
THE DEATH OF SPEEDY

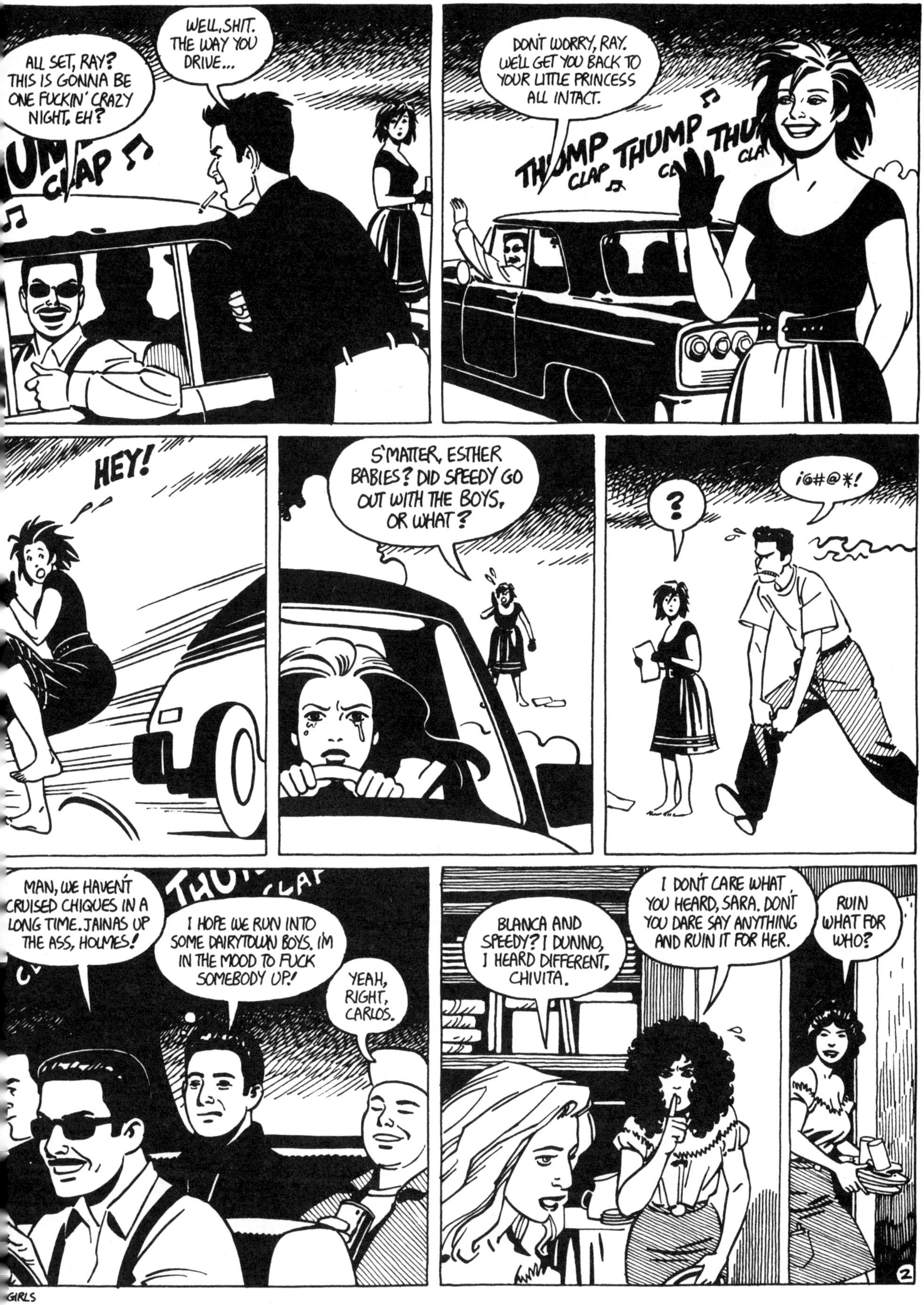

ALL SET, RAY? THIS IS GONNA BE ONE FUCKIN' CRAZY NIGHT, EH?
WELL, SHIT. THE WAY YOU DRIVE...
CLAP
DON'T WORRY, RAY. WE'LL GET YOU BACK TO YOUR LITTLE PRINCESS ALL INTACT.
THUMP CLAP THUMP
HEY!
S'MATTER, ESTHER BABIES? DID SPEEDY GO OUT WITH THE BOYS, OR WHAT?
?
¡@#@*!
MAN, WE HAVEN'T CRUISED CHIQUES IN A LONG TIME. JAINAS UP THE ASS, HOLMES!
I HOPE WE RUN INTO SOME DAIRYTOWN BOYS. I'M IN THE MOOD TO FUCK SOMEBODY UP!
YEAH, RIGHT, CARLOS.
BLANCA AND SPEEDY? I DUNNO, I HEARD DIFFERENT, CHIVITA.
I DON'T CARE WHAT YOU HEARD, SARA. DON'T YOU DARE SAY ANYTHING AND RUIN IT FOR HER.
RUIN WHAT FOR WHO?

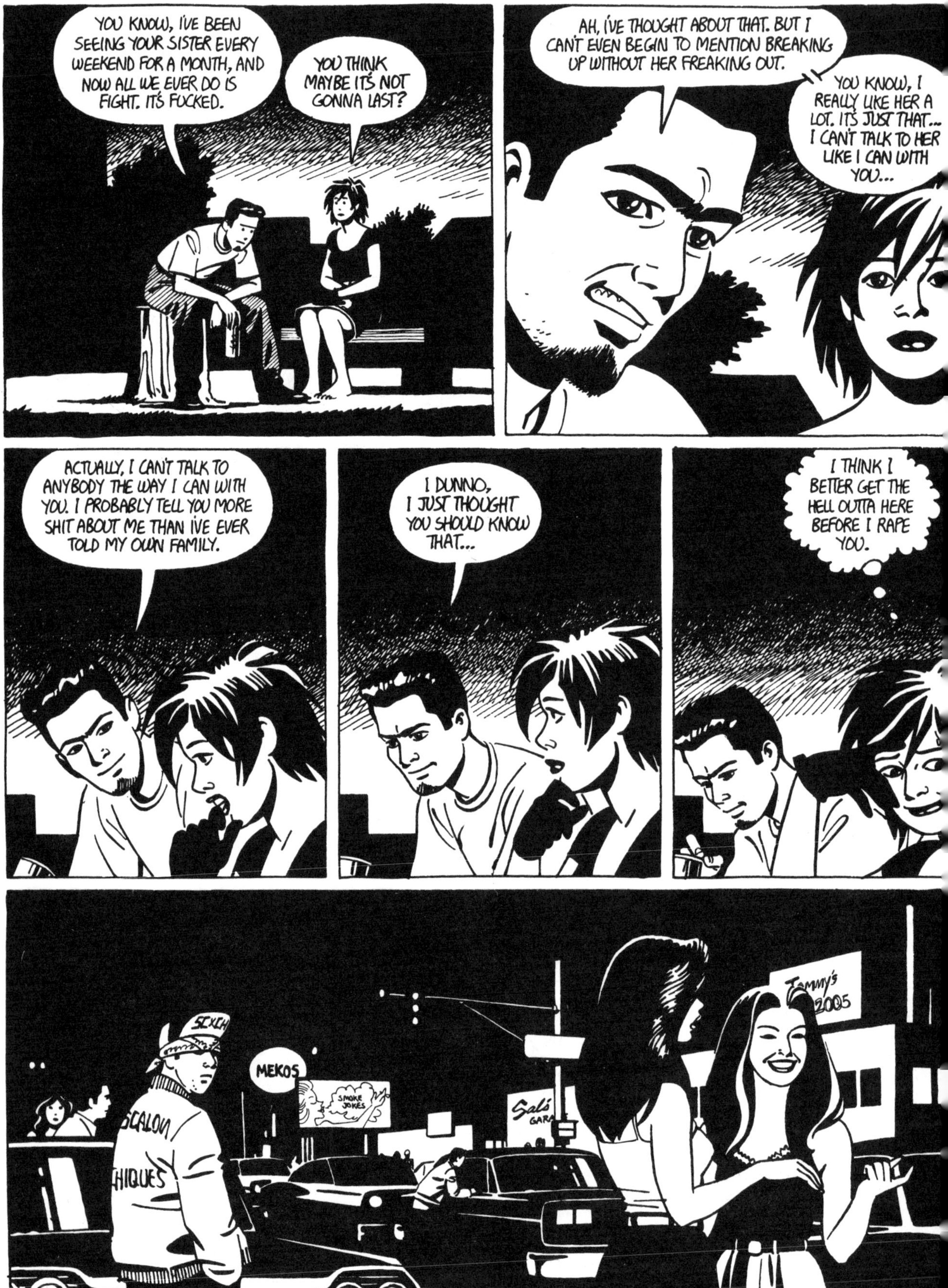
YOU KNOW, I'VE BEEN SEEING YOUR SISTER EVERY WEEKEND FOR A MONTH, AND NOW ALL WE EVER DO IS FIGHT. IT'S FUCKED.
YOU THINK MAYBE IT'S NOT GONNA LAST?
AH, I'VE THOUGHT ABOUT THAT. BUT I CAN'T EVEN BEGIN TO MENTION BREAKING UP WITHOUT HER FREAKING OUT.
YOU KNOW, I REALLY LIKE HER A LOT. IT'S JUST THAT... I CAN'T TALK TO HER LIKE I CAN WITH YOU...
ACTUALLY, I CAN'T TALK TO ANYBODY THE WAY I CAN WITH YOU. I PROBABLY TELL YOU MORE SHIT ABOUT ME THAN I'VE EVER TOLD MY OWN FAMILY.
I DUNNO, I JUST THOUGHT YOU SHOULD KNOW THAT...
I THINK I BETTER GET THE HELL OUTTA HERE BEFORE I RAPE YOU.
MEKOS
SMOKE JOKES
2005

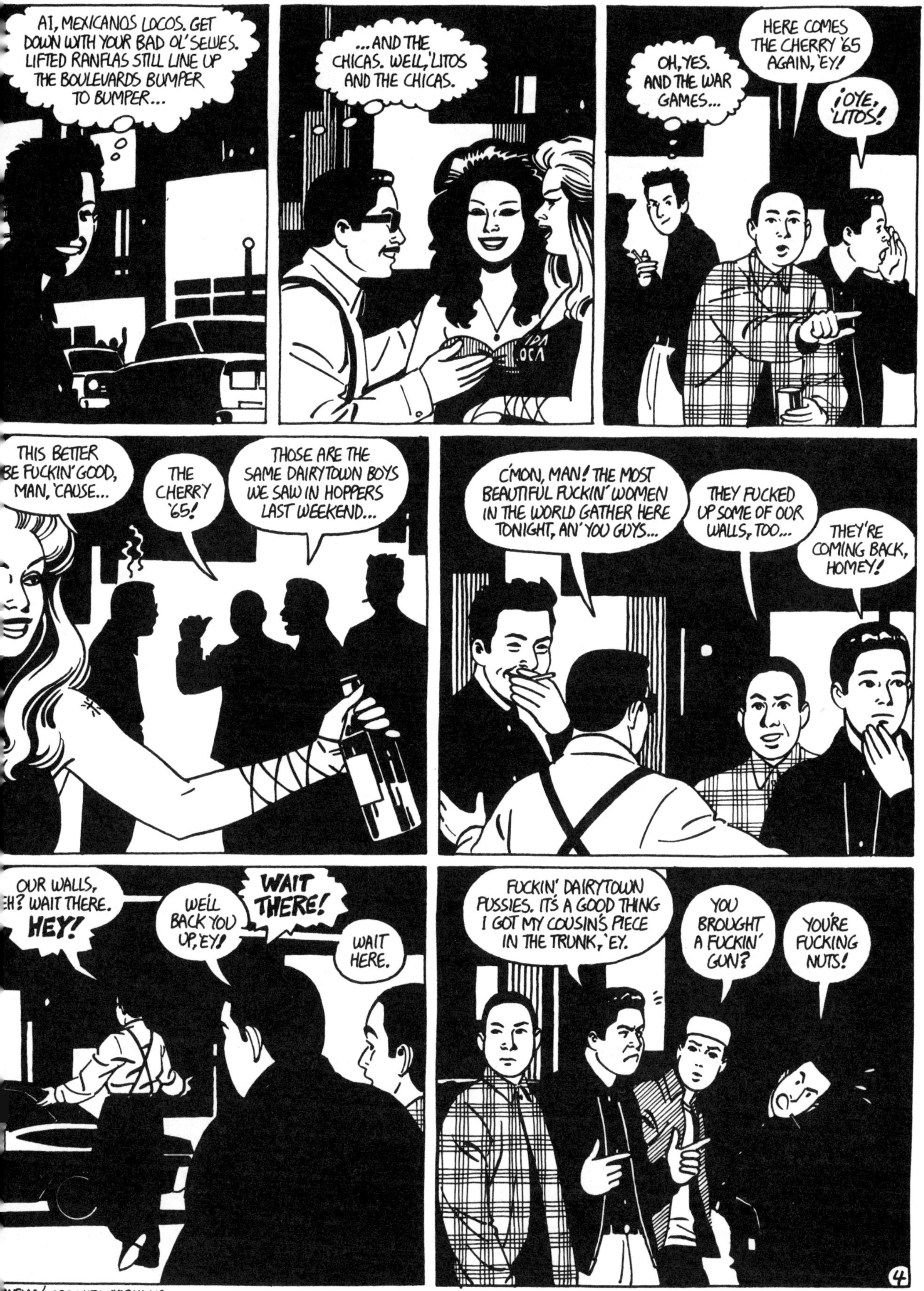
AI, MEXICANOS LOCOS. GET DOWN WITH YOUR BAD OL' SELVES. LIFTED RANFLAS STILL LINE UP THE BOULEVARDS BUMPER TO BUMPER...
...AND THE CHICAS. WELL, 'LITOS AND THE CHICAS.
OH, YES. AND THE WAR GAMES...
HERE COMES THE CHERRY '65 AGAIN, 'EY!
¡OYE, 'LITOS!
THIS BETTER BE FUCKIN' GOOD, MAN, 'CAUSE...
THE CHERRY '65!
THOSE ARE THE SAME DAIRYTOWN BOYS WE SAW IN HOPPERS LAST WEEKEND...
C'MON, MAN! THE MOST BEAUTIFUL FUCKIN' WOMEN IN THE WORLD GATHER HERE TONIGHT, AN' YOU GUYS...
THEY FUCKED UP SOME OF OUR WALLS, TOO...
THEY'RE COMING BACK, HOMEY!
OUR WALLS, EH? WAIT THERE. HEY!
WE'LL BACK YOU UP, 'EY!
WAIT THERE!
WAIT HERE.
FUCKIN' DAIRYTOWN PUSSIES. IT'S A GOOD THING I GOT MY COUSIN'S PIECE IN THE TRUNK, 'EY.
YOU BROUGHT A FUCKIN' GUN?
YOU'RE FUCKING NUTS!

RANFLAS/CARS WITH HYDRAULICS

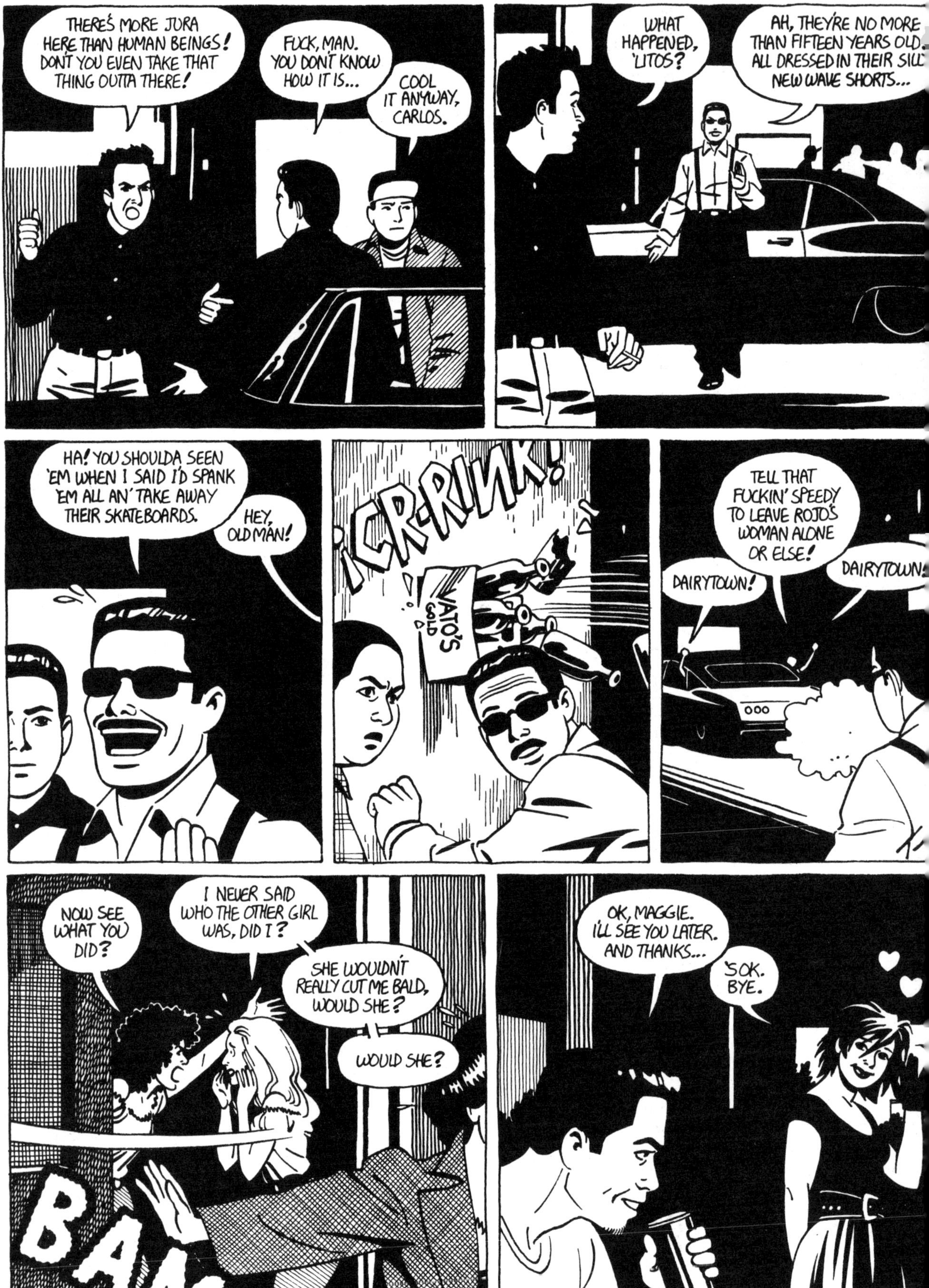

THERE'S MORE JURA HERE THAN HUMAN BEINGS! DON'T YOU EVEN TAKE THAT THING OUTTA THERE!
FUCK, MAN. YOU DON'T KNOW HOW IT IS...
COOL IT ANYWAY, CARLOS.
WHAT HAPPENED, 'LITOS?
AH, THEY'RE NO MORE THAN FIFTEEN YEARS OLD. ALL DRESSED IN THEIR SILL NEW WAVE SHORTS...
HA! YOU SHOULDA SEEN 'EM WHEN I SAID I'D SPANK 'EM ALL AN' TAKE AWAY THEIR SKATEBOARDS.
HEY, OLD MAN!
¡CR-RINK!
VATO'S GOLD
TELL THAT FUCKIN' SPEEDY TO LEAVE ROJO'S WOMAN ALONE OR ELSE!
DAIRYTOWN!
DAIRYTOWN!
NOW SEE WHAT YOU DID?
I NEVER SAID WHO THE OTHER GIRL WAS, DID I?
SHE WOULDN'T REALLY CUT ME BALD, WOULD SHE?
WOULD SHE?
BA
OK, MAGGIE. I'LL SEE YOU LATER. AND THANKS...
'S OK. BYE.

JURA/POLICE

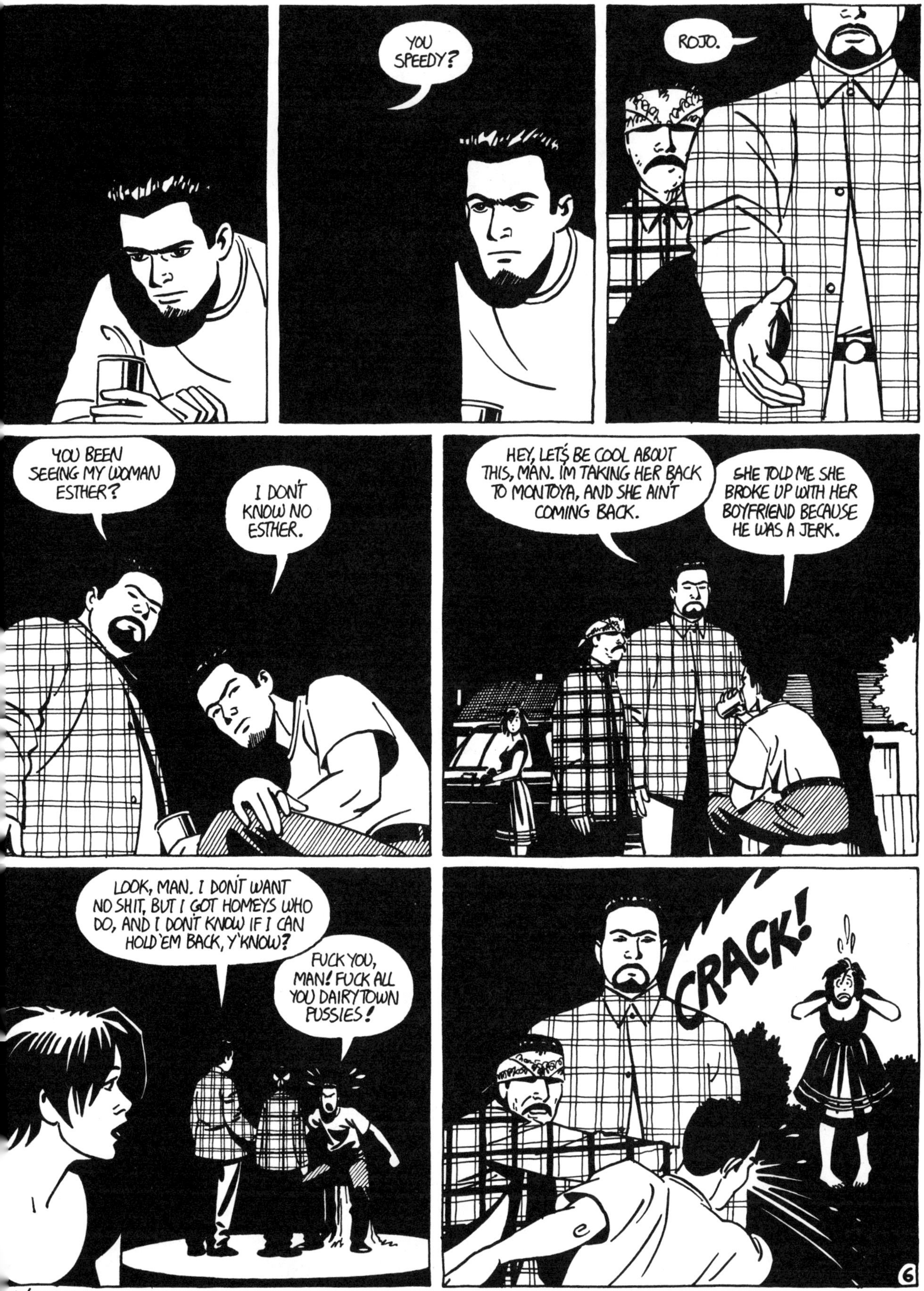
YOU SPEEDY?
ROJO.
YOU BEEN SEEING MY WOMAN ESTHER?
I DON'T KNOW NO ESTHER.
HEY, LET'S BE COOL ABOUT THIS, MAN. I'M TAKING HER BACK TO MONTOYA, AND SHE AIN'T COMING BACK.
SHE TOLD ME SHE BROKE UP WITH HER BOYFRIEND BECAUSE HE WAS A JERK.
LOOK, MAN. I DON'T WANT NO SHIT, BUT I GOT HOMEYS WHO DO, AND I DON'T KNOW IF I CAN HOLD 'EM BACK, Y'KNOW?
FUCK YOU, MAN! FUCK ALL YOU DAIRYTOWN PUSSIES!
CRACK!
6

A/ DAIRYTOWN

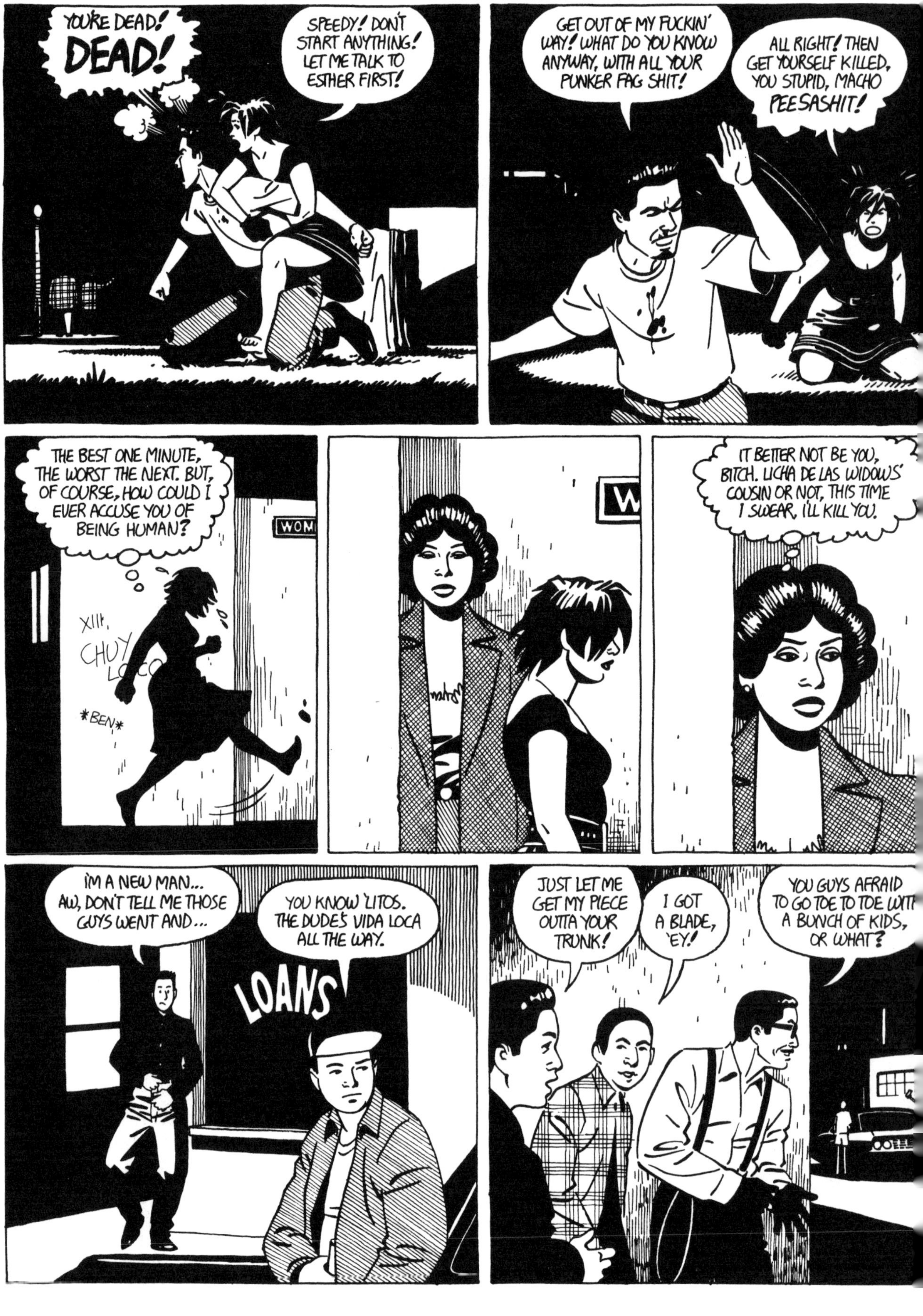
YOU'RE DEAD! DEAD!
SPEEDY! DON'T START ANYTHING! LET ME TALK TO ESTHER FIRST!
GET OUT OF MY FUCKIN' WAY! WHAT DO YOU KNOW ANYWAY, WITH ALL YOUR PUNKER FAG SHIT!
ALL RIGHT! THEN GET YOURSELF KILLED, YOU STUPID, MACHO PEESASHIT!
THE BEST ONE MINUTE, THE WORST THE NEXT. BUT, OF COURSE, HOW COULD I EVER ACCUSE YOU OF BEING HUMAN?
WOM
XIII
CHUY LOCO
BEN
W
IT BETTER NOT BE YOU, BITCH. LICHA DE LAS WIDOWS' COUSIN OR NOT, THIS TIME I SWEAR, I'LL KILL YOU.
I'M A NEW MAN... AW, DON'T TELL ME THOSE GUYS WENT AND...
YOU KNOW 'LITOS. THE DUDE'S VIDA LOCA ALL THE WAY.
LOANS
JUST LET ME GET MY PIECE OUTTA YOUR TRUNK!
I GOT A BLADE, 'EY!
YOU GUYS AFRAID TO GO TOE TO TOE WITH A BUNCH OF KIDS, OR WHAT?

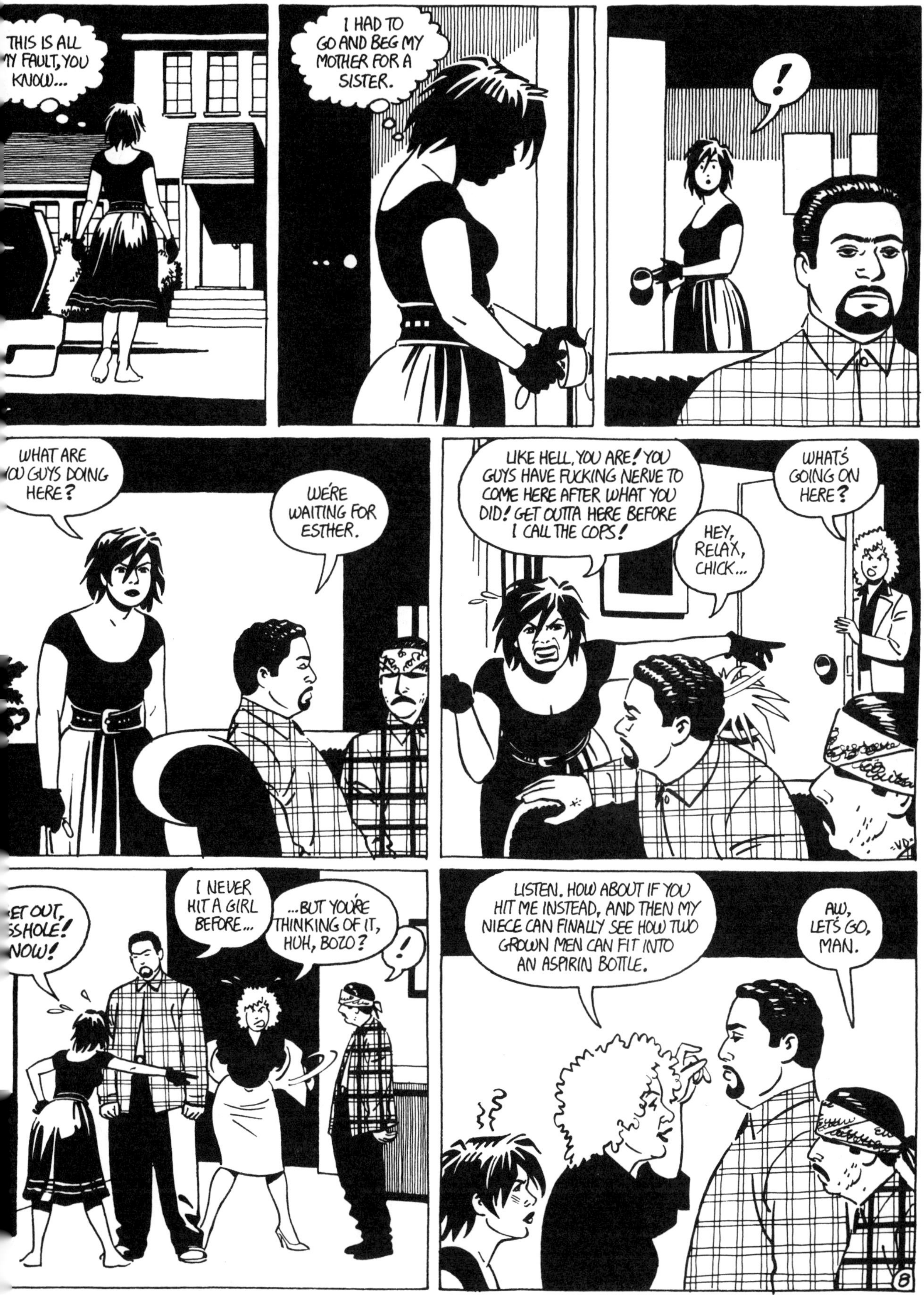
THIS IS ALL MY FAULT, YOU KNOW...
I HAD TO GO AND BEG MY MOTHER FOR A SISTER.
!
WHAT ARE YOU GUYS DOING HERE?
WE'RE WAITING FOR ESTHER.
LIKE HELL, YOU ARE! YOU GUYS HAVE FUCKING NERVE TO COME HERE AFTER WHAT YOU DID! GET OUTTA HERE BEFORE I CALL THE COPS!
HEY, RELAX, CHICK...
WHAT'S GOING ON HERE?
ET OUT, SSHOLE! NOW!
I NEVER HIT A GIRL BEFORE...
...BUT YOU'RE THINKING OF IT, HUH, BOZO?
!
LISTEN. HOW ABOUT IF YOU HIT ME INSTEAD, AND THEN MY NIECE CAN FINALLY SEE HOW TWO GROWN MEN CAN FIT INTO AN ASPIRIN BOTTLE.
AW, LET'S GO, MAN.
8

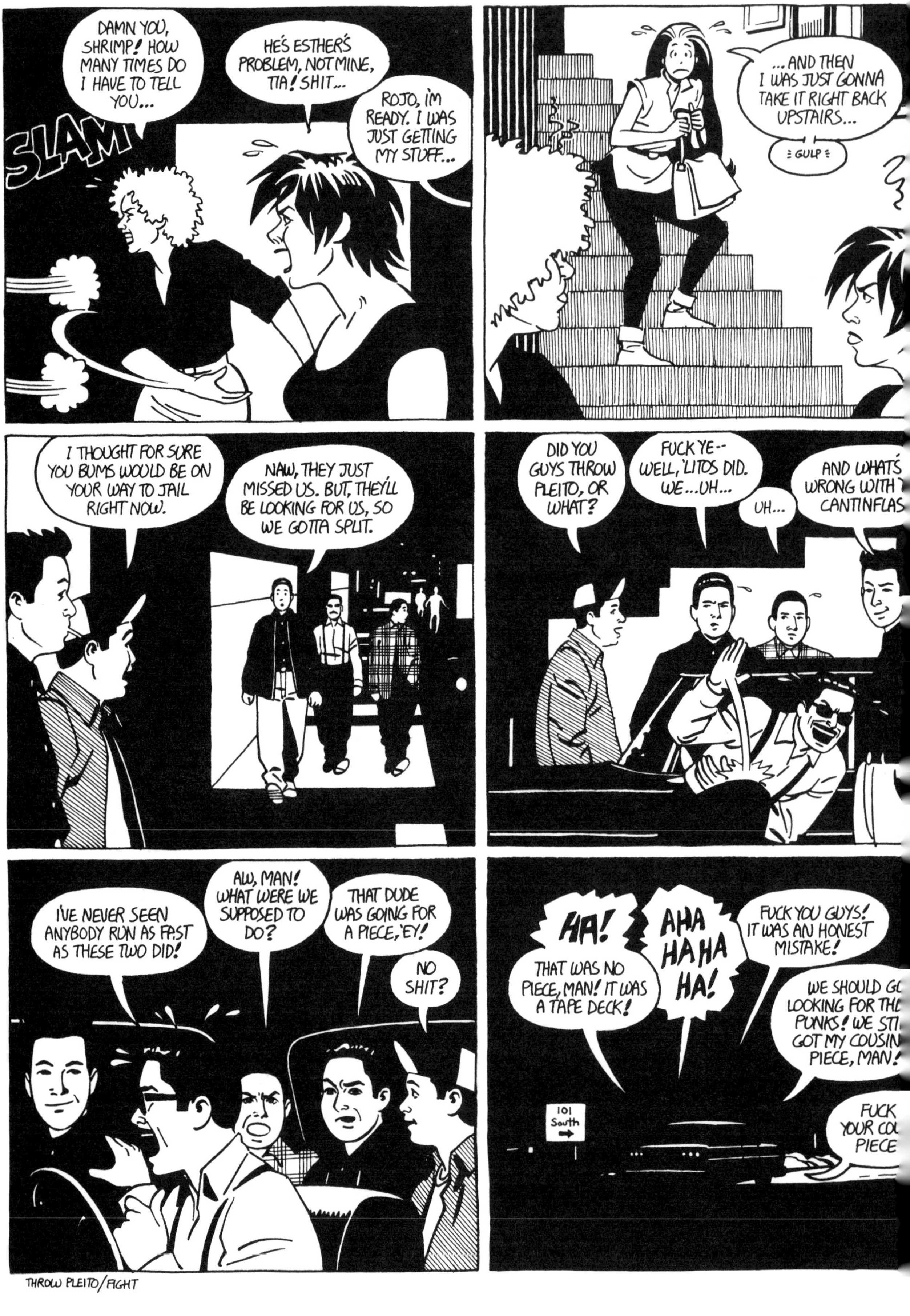
DAMN YOU, SHRIMP! HOW MANY TIMES DO I HAVE TO TELL YOU...
SLAM
HE'S ESTHER'S PROBLEM, NOT MINE, TIA! SHIT...
ROJO, I'M READY. I WAS JUST GETTING MY STUFF...
...AND THEN I WAS JUST GONNA TAKE IT RIGHT BACK UPSTAIRS...
GULP
I THOUGHT FOR SURE YOU BUMS WOULD BE ON YOUR WAY TO JAIL RIGHT NOW.
NAW, THEY JUST MISSED US. BUT, THEY'LL BE LOOKING FOR US, SO WE GOTTA SPLIT.
DID YOU GUYS THROW PLEITO, OR WHAT?
FUCK YE-- WELL, 'LITOS DID. WE...UH...
UH...
AND WHAT'S WRONG WITH
CANTINFLAS
I'VE NEVER SEEN ANYBODY RUN AS FAST AS THESE TWO DID!
AW, MAN! WHAT WERE WE SUPPOSED TO DO?
THAT DUDE WAS GOING FOR A PIECE, 'EY!
NO SHIT?
HA!
THAT WAS NO PIECE, MAN! IT WAS A TAPE DECK!
AHA HA HA HA!
FUCK YOU GUYS! IT WAS AN HONEST MISTAKE!
WE SHOULD
LOOKING FOR
PUNKS! WE
GOT MY
PIECE, MAN!
101 South
FUCK
YOUR

THROW PLEITO/FIGHT

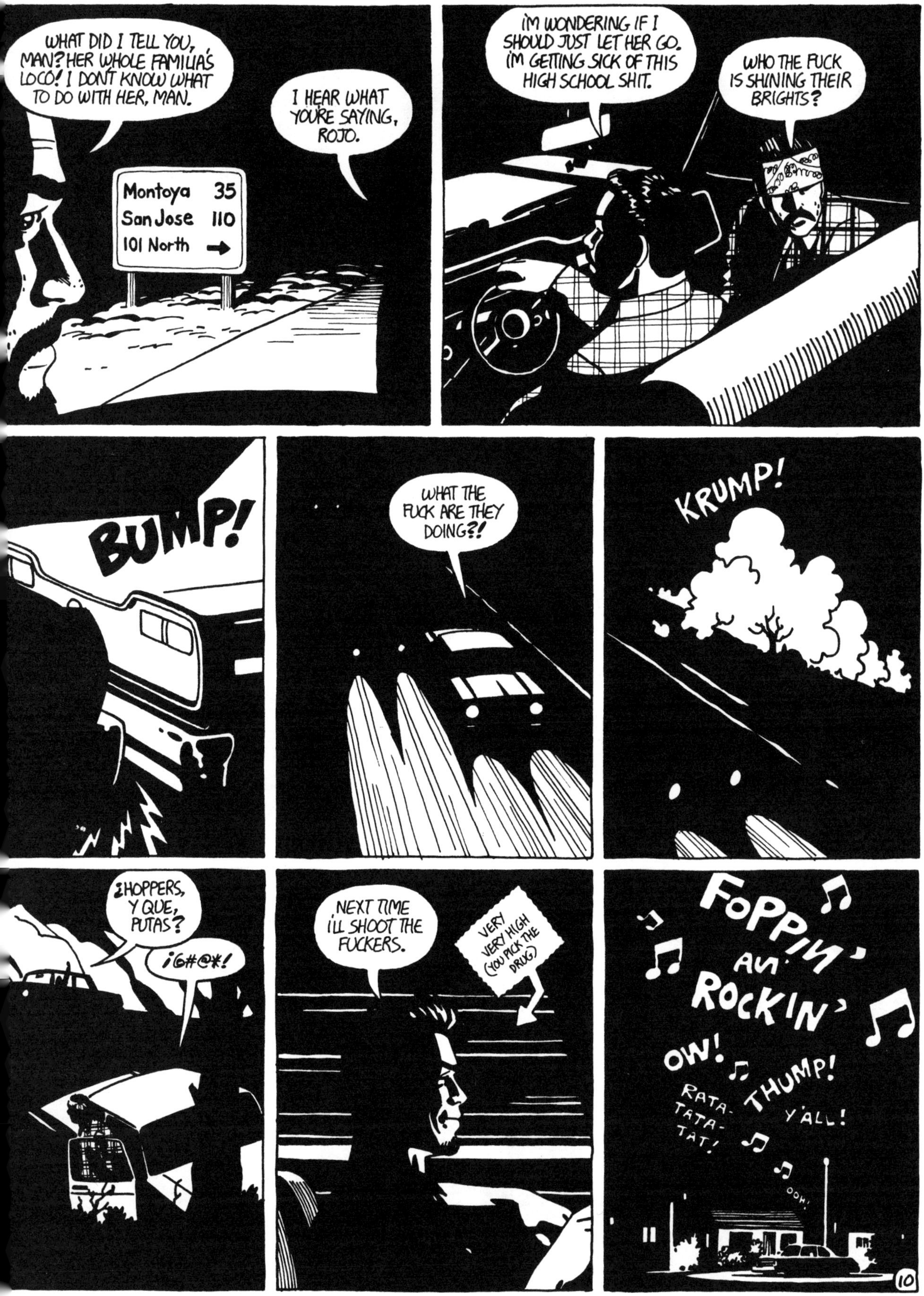
WHAT DID I TELL YOU, MAN? HER WHOLE FAMILIA'S LOCO! I DON'T KNOW WHAT TO DO WITH HER, MAN.
I HEAR WHAT YOU'RE SAYING, ROJO.
Montoya 35
San Jose 110
101 North
I'M WONDERING IF I SHOULD JUST LET HER GO. I'M GETTING SICK OF THIS HIGH SCHOOL SHIT.
WHO THE FUCK IS SHINING THEIR BRIGHTS?
BUMP!
WHAT THE FUCK ARE THEY DOING?!
KRUMP!
¿HOPPERS, Y QUE, PUTAS?
¡G#@*!
NEXT TIME I'LL SHOOT THE FUCKERS.
VERY VERY HIGH (YOU PICK THE DRUG)
FOPPIN' AN' ROCKIN'
OW!
THUMP!
RATA-TATA-TAT!
Y'ALL!
OOH!

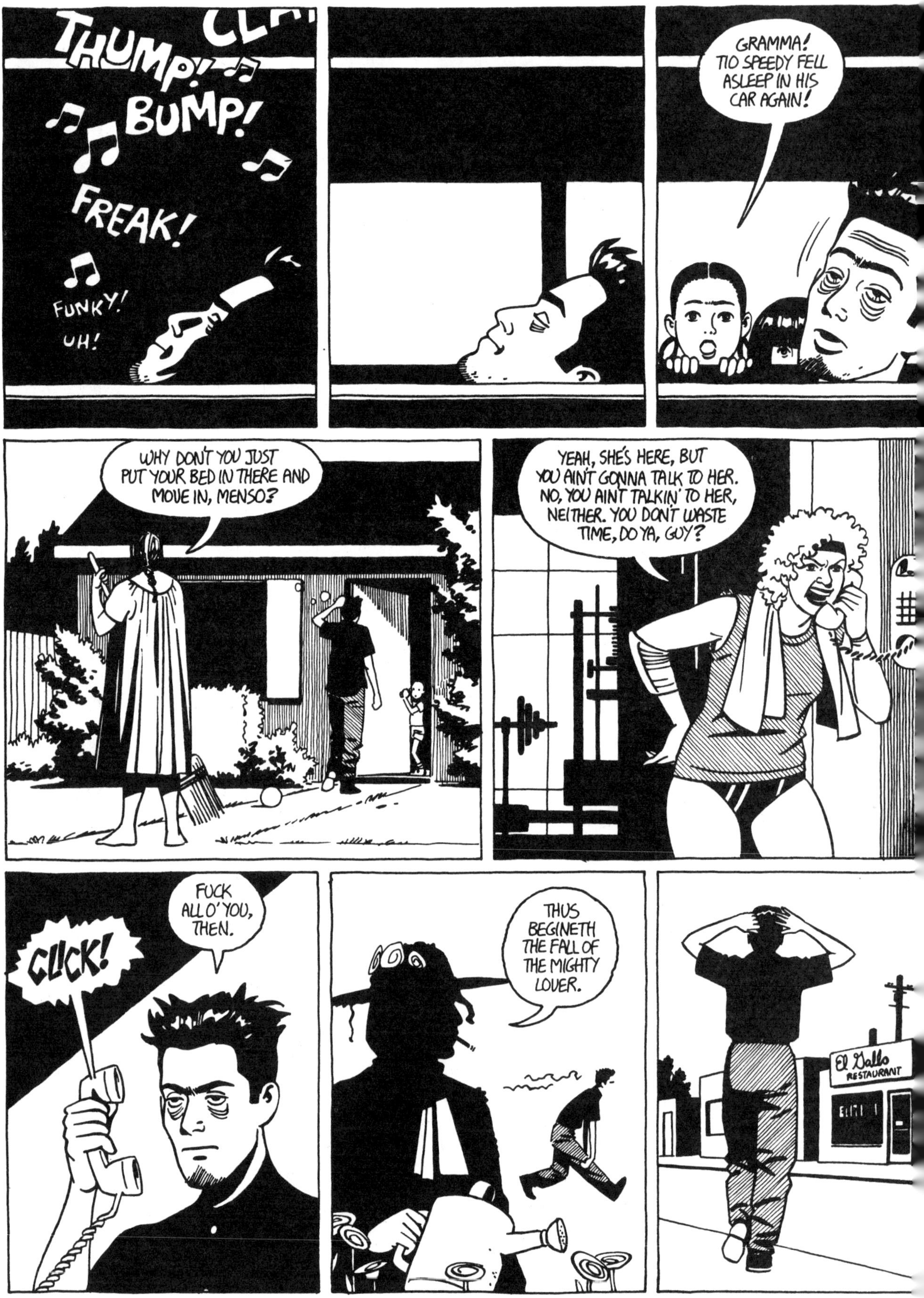
THUMP!
CLA
BUMP!
FREAK!
FUNKY!
UH!
GRAMMA! TIO SPEEDY FELL ASLEEP IN HIS CAR AGAIN!
WHY DON'T YOU JUST PUT YOUR BED IN THERE AND MOVE IN, MENSO?
YEAH, SHE'S HERE, BUT YOU AIN'T GONNA TALK TO HER. NO, YOU AIN'T TALKIN' TO HER, NEITHER. YOU DON'T WASTE TIME, DO YA, GUY?
CLICK!
FUCK ALL O' YOU, THEN.
THUS BEGINETH THE FALL OF THE MIGHTY LOVER.
El Gallo
RESTAURANT

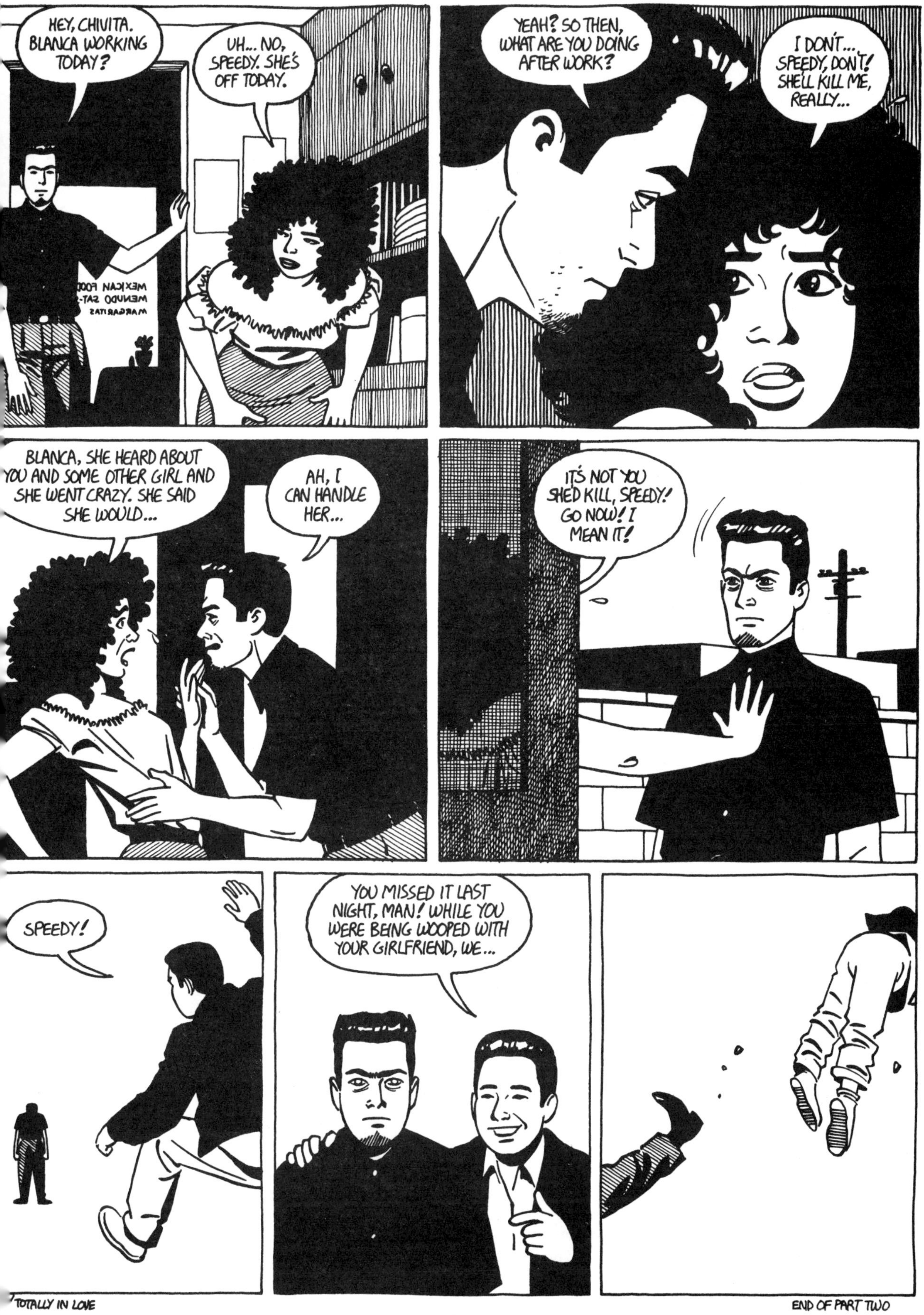
HEY, CHIVITA. BLANCA WORKING TODAY?
UH... NO, SPEEDY. SHE'S OFF TODAY.
MEXICAN FOOD MENUDO SAT-S MARGARITAS
YEAH? SO THEN, WHAT ARE YOU DOING AFTER WORK?
I DON'T... SPEEDY, DON'T! SHE'LL KILL ME, REALLY...
BLANCA, SHE HEARD ABOUT YOU AND SOME OTHER GIRL AND SHE WENT CRAZY. SHE SAID SHE WOULD...
AH, I CAN HANDLE HER...
IT'S NOT YOU SHE'D KILL, SPEEDY! GO NOW! I MEAN IT!
SPEEDY!
YOU MISSED IT LAST NIGHT, MAN! WHILE YOU WERE BEING WOOPED WITH YOUR GIRLFRIEND, WE...

END OF PART TWO

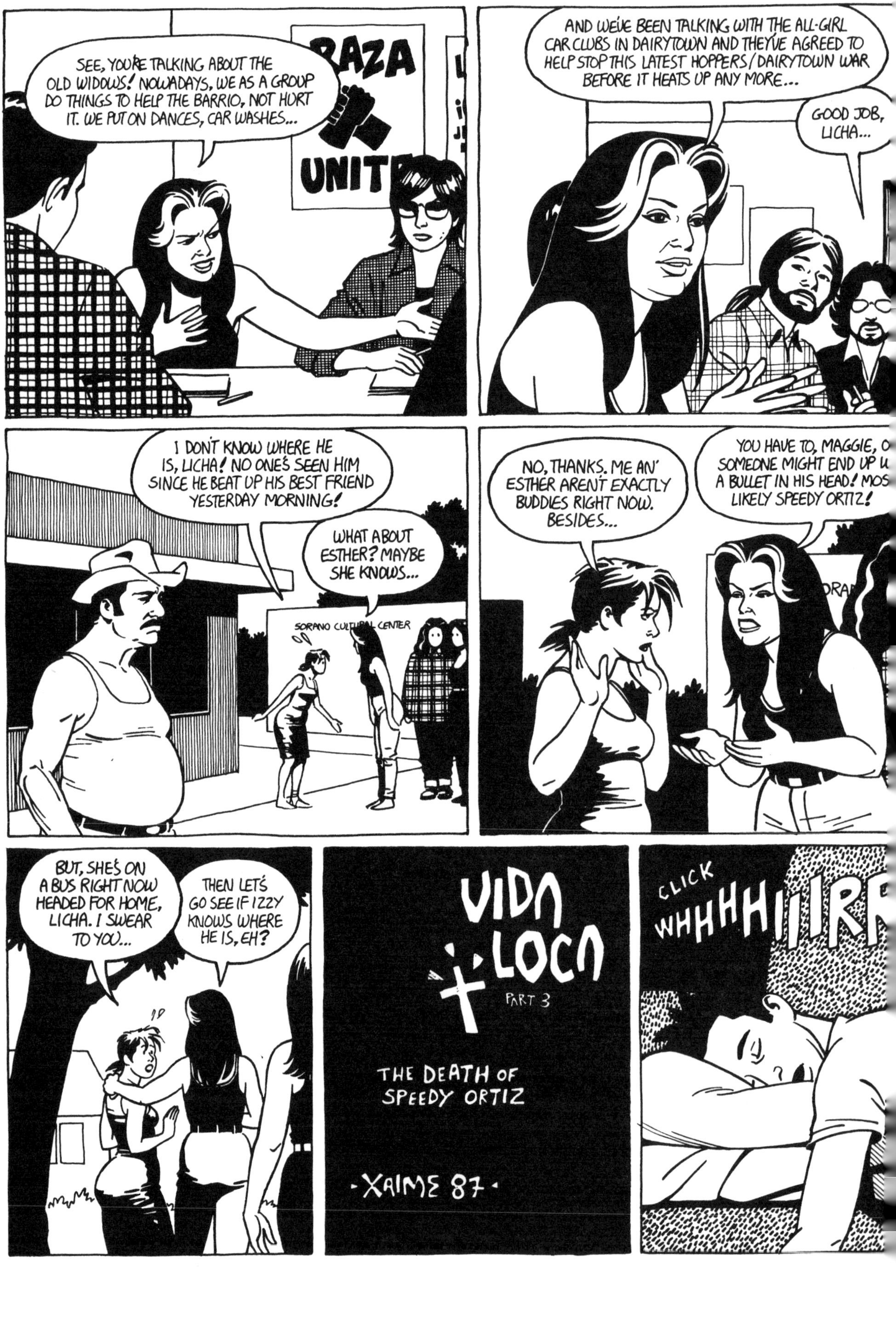

RAZA UNIT
SEE, YOU'RE TALKING ABOUT THE OLD WIDOWS! NOWADAYS, WE AS A GROUP DO THINGS TO HELP THE BARRIO, NOT HURT IT. WE PUT ON DANCES, CAR WASHES...
AND WE'VE BEEN TALKING WITH THE ALL-GIRL CAR CLUBS IN DAIRYTOWN AND THEY'VE AGREED TO HELP STOP THIS LATEST HOPPERS/DAIRYTOWN WAR BEFORE IT HEATS UP ANY MORE...
GOOD JOB, LICHA...
I DON'T KNOW WHERE HE IS, LICHA! NO ONE'S SEEN HIM SINCE HE BEAT UP HIS BEST FRIEND YESTERDAY MORNING!
WHAT ABOUT ESTHER? MAYBE SHE KNOWS...
SORANO CULTURAL CENTER
NO, THANKS. ME AN' ESTHER AREN'T EXACTLY BUDDIES RIGHT NOW. BESIDES...
YOU HAVE TO, MAGGIE, O SOMEONE MIGHT END UP W A BULLET IN HIS HEAD! MOS LIKELY SPEEDY ORTIZ!
BUT, SHE'S ON A BUS RIGHT NOW HEADED FOR HOME, LICHA. I SWEAR TO YOU...
THEN LET'S GO SEE IF IZZY KNOWS WHERE HE IS, EH?
VIDA LOCA
PART 3
THE DEATH OF SPEEDY ORTIZ
XAIME 87
CLICK
WHHHHIIRR

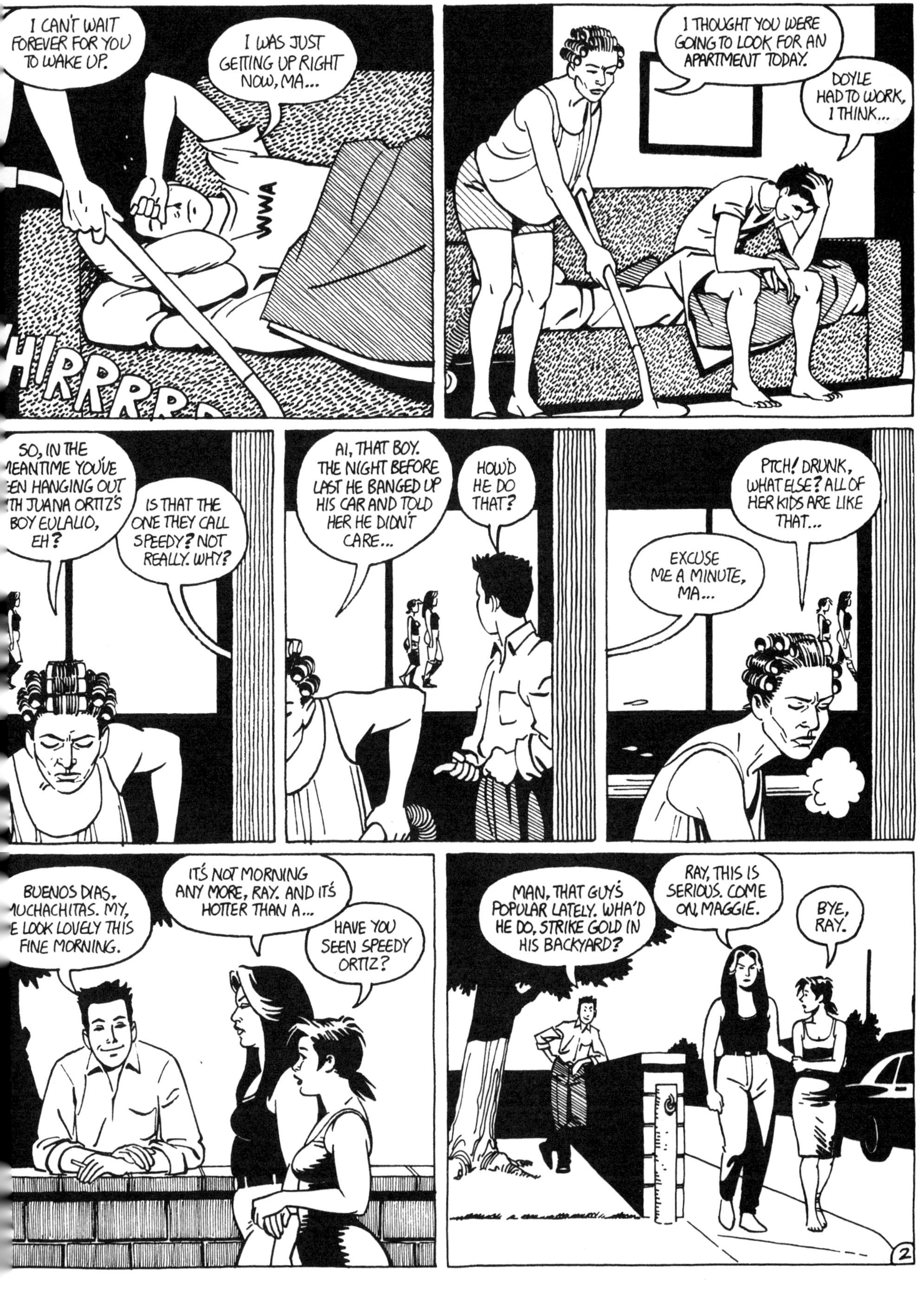
I CAN'T WAIT FOREVER FOR YOU TO WAKE UP.
I WAS JUST GETTING UP RIGHT NOW, MA...
WWA
HIRRRRD
I THOUGHT YOU WERE GOING TO LOOK FOR AN APARTMENT TODAY.
DOYLE HAD TO WORK, I THINK...
SO, IN THE MEANTIME YOU'VE BEEN HANGING OUT WITH JUANA ORTIZ'S BOY EULALIO, EH?
IS THAT THE ONE THEY CALL SPEEDY? NOT REALLY. WHY?
AI, THAT BOY. THE NIGHT BEFORE LAST HE BANGED UP HIS CAR AND TOLD HER HE DIDN'T CARE...
HOW'D HE DO THAT?
PTCH! DRUNK, WHAT ELSE? ALL OF HER KIDS ARE LIKE THAT...
EXCUSE ME A MINUTE, MA...
BUENOS DIAS, MUCHACHITAS. MY, YOU LOOK LOVELY THIS FINE MORNING.
IT'S NOT MORNING ANY MORE, RAY. AND IT'S HOTTER THAN A...
HAVE YOU SEEN SPEEDY ORTIZ?
MAN, THAT GUY'S POPULAR LATELY. WHA'D HE DO, STRIKE GOLD IN HIS BACKYARD?
RAY, THIS IS SERIOUS. COME ON, MAGGIE.
BYE, RAY.

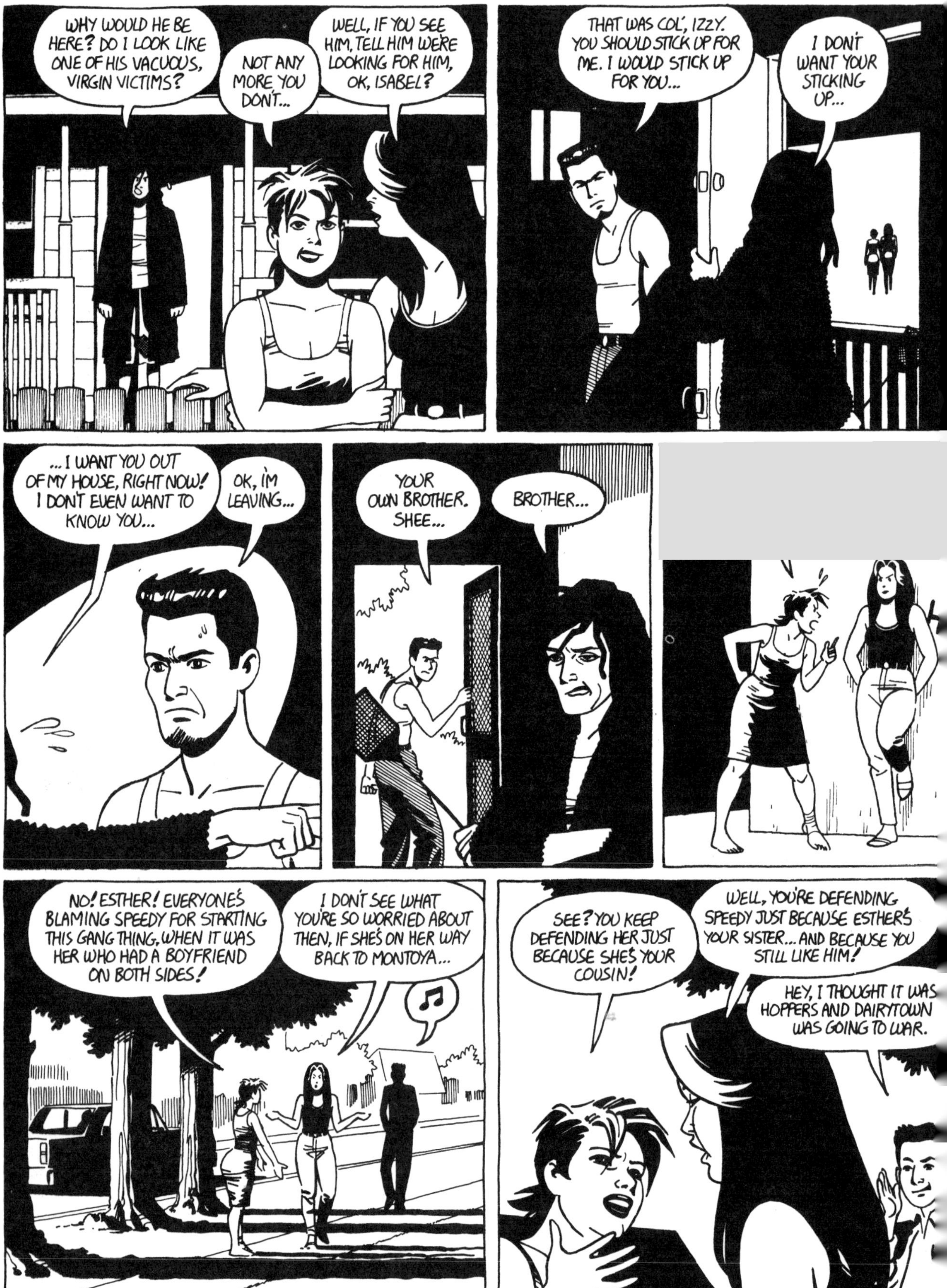
WHY WOULD HE BE HERE? DO I LOOK LIKE ONE OF HIS VACUOUS, VIRGIN VICTIMS?
NOT ANY MORE YOU DON'T...
WELL, IF YOU SEE HIM, TELL HIM WE'RE LOOKING FOR HIM, OK, ISABEL?
THAT WAS COL', IZZY. YOU SHOULD STICK UP FOR ME. I WOULD STICK UP FOR YOU...
I DON'T WANT YOUR STICKING UP...
...I WANT YOU OUT OF MY HOUSE, RIGHT NOW! I DON'T EVEN WANT TO KNOW YOU...
OK, I'M LEAVING...
YOUR OWN BROTHER. SHEE...
BROTHER...
NO! ESTHER! EVERYONE'S BLAMING SPEEDY FOR STARTING THIS GANG THING, WHEN IT WAS HER WHO HAD A BOYFRIEND ON BOTH SIDES!
I DON'T SEE WHAT YOU'RE SO WORRIED ABOUT THEN, IF SHE'S ON HER WAY BACK TO MONTOYA...
♫
SEE? YOU KEEP DEFENDING HER JUST BECAUSE SHE'S YOUR COUSIN!
WELL, YOU'RE DEFENDING SPEEDY JUST BECAUSE ESTHER'S YOUR SISTER... AND BECAUSE YOU STILL LIKE HIM!
HEY, I THOUGHT IT WAS HOPPERS AND DAIRYTOWN WAS GOING TO WAR.

MONTOYA/DAIRYTOWN

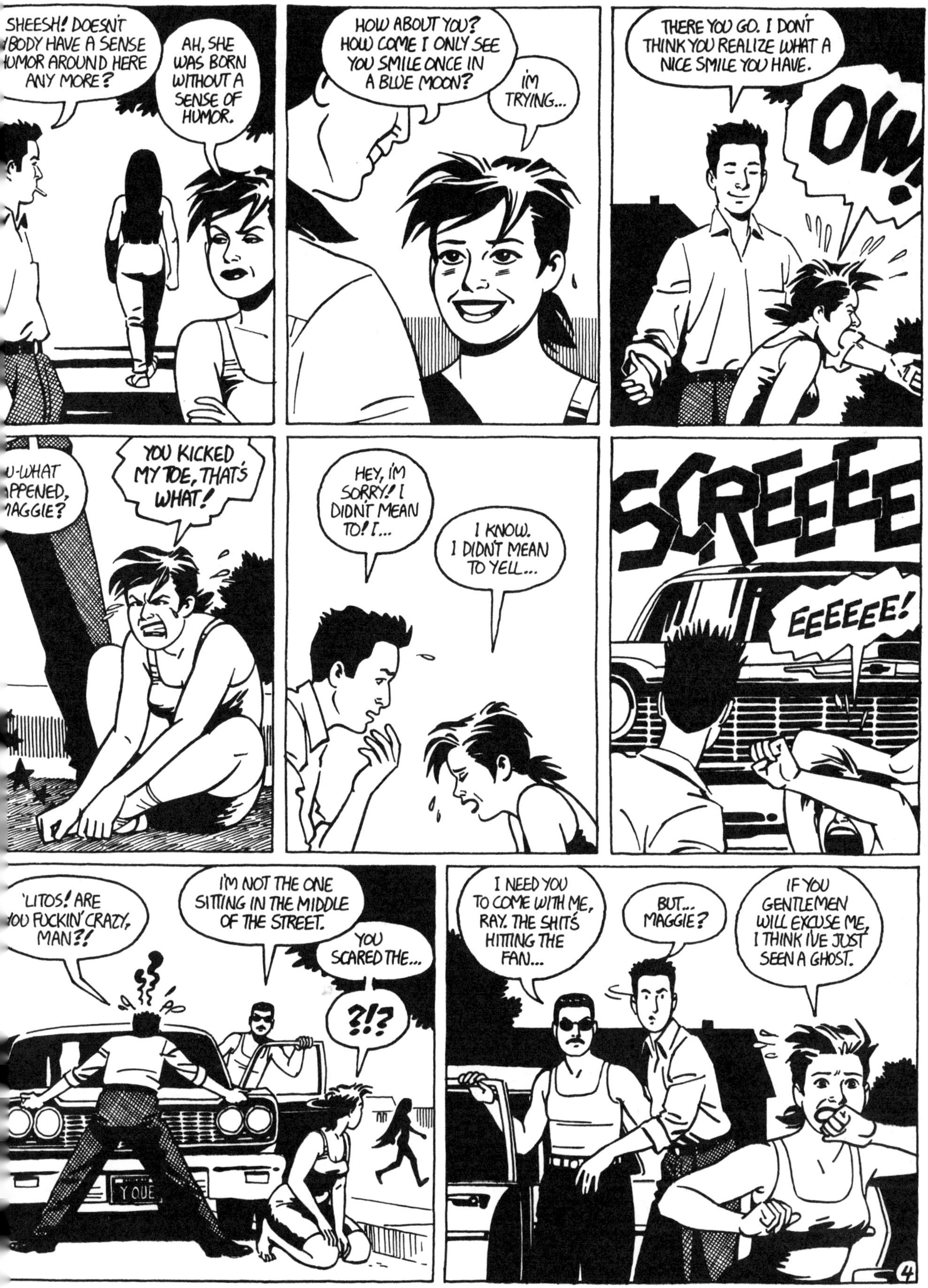
SHEESH! DOESN'T YBODY HAVE A SENSE HUMOR AROUND HERE ANY MORE?
AH, SHE WAS BORN WITHOUT A SENSE OF HUMOR.
HOW ABOUT YOU? HOW COME I ONLY SEE YOU SMILE ONCE IN A BLUE MOON?
I'M TRYING...
THERE YOU GO. I DON'T THINK YOU REALIZE WHAT A NICE SMILE YOU HAVE.
OW!
U-WHAT APPENED, MAGGIE?
YOU KICKED MY TOE, THAT'S WHAT!
HEY, I'M SORRY! I DIDN'T MEAN TO! I...
I KNOW. I DIDN'T MEAN TO YELL...
SCREEEE
EEEEEE!
'LITOS! ARE YOU FUCKIN' CRAZY, MAN?!
I'M NOT THE ONE SITTING IN THE MIDDLE OF THE STREET.
YOU SCARED THE...
?!?
Y QUE
I NEED YOU TO COME WITH ME, RAY. THE SHIT'S HITTING THE FAN...
BUT... MAGGIE?
IF YOU GENTLEMEN WILL EXCUSE ME, I THINK I'VE JUST SEEN A GHOST.
4

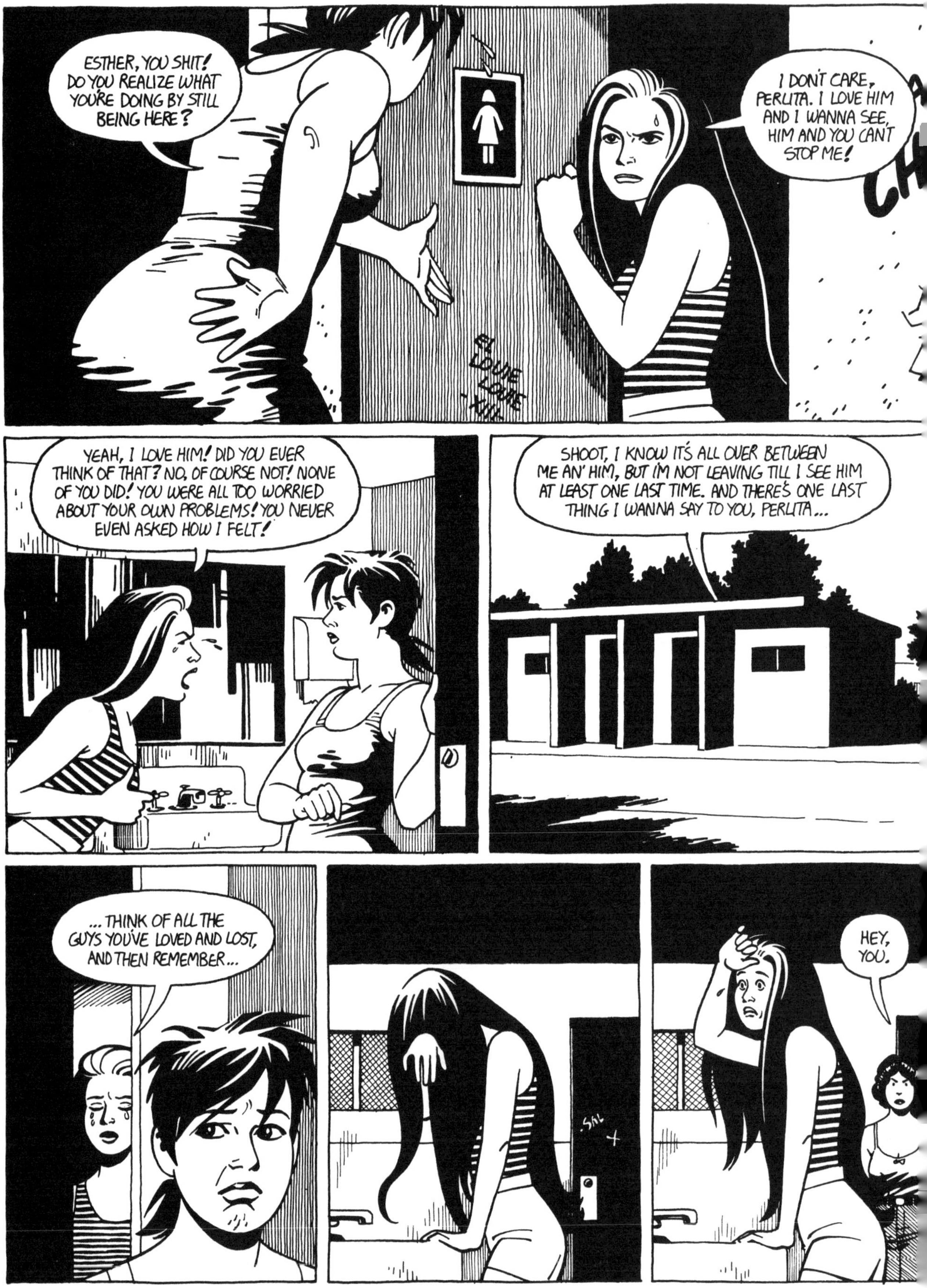
ESTHER, YOU SHIT! DO YOU REALIZE WHAT YOU'RE DOING BY STILL BEING HERE?
I DON'T CARE, PERLITA. I LOVE HIM AND I WANNA SEE, HIM AND YOU CAN'T STOP ME!
YEAH, I LOVE HIM! DID YOU EVER THINK OF THAT? NO, OF COURSE NOT! NONE OF YOU DID! YOU WERE ALL TOO WORRIED ABOUT YOUR OWN PROBLEMS! YOU NEVER EVEN ASKED HOW I FELT!
SHOOT, I KNOW IT'S ALL OVER BETWEEN ME AN' HIM, BUT I'M NOT LEAVING TILL I SEE HIM AT LEAST ONE LAST TIME. AND THERE'S ONE LAST THING I WANNA SAY TO YOU, PERLITA...
...THINK OF ALL THE GUYS YOU'VE LOVED AND LOST, AND THEN REMEMBER...
HEY, YOU.

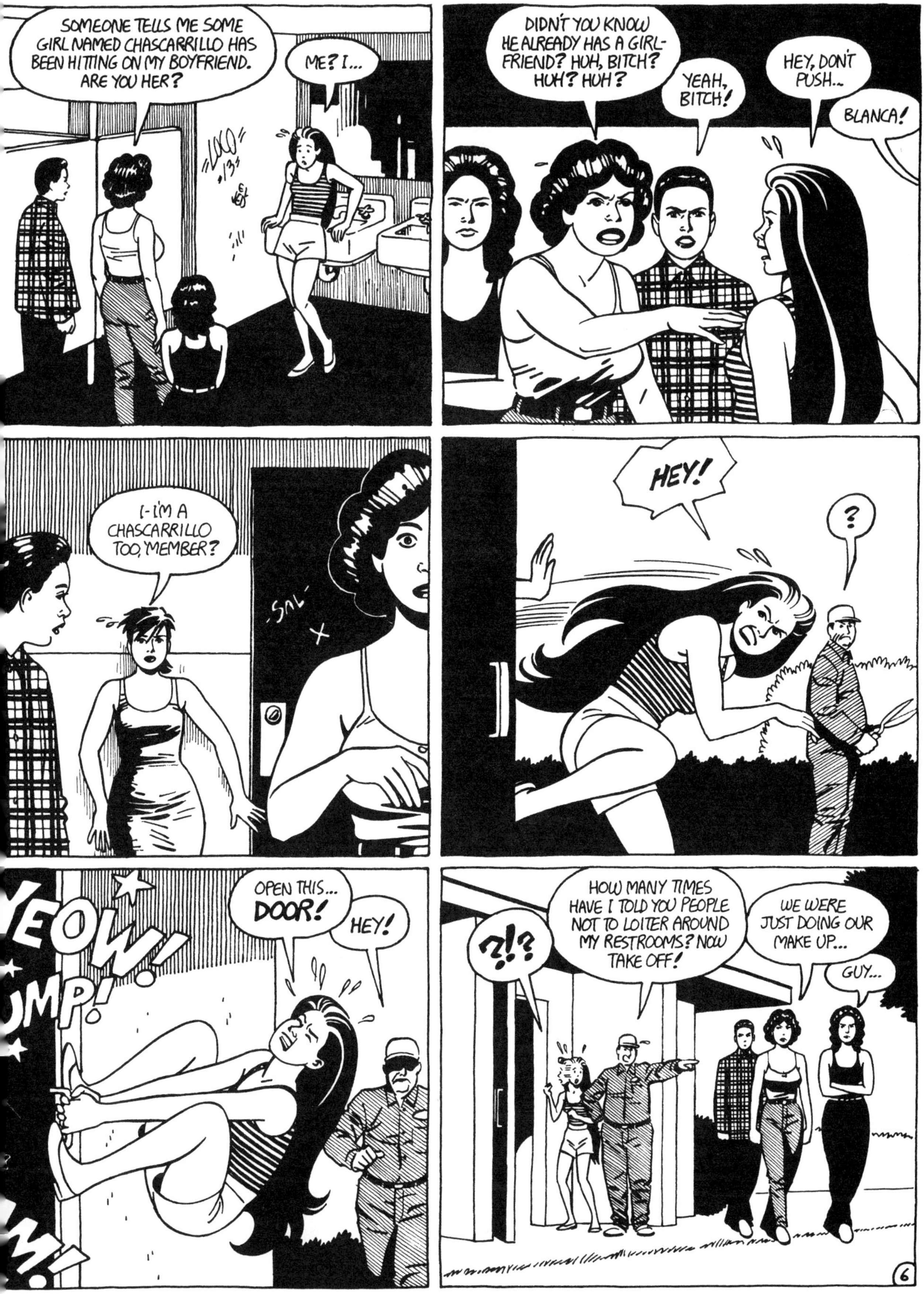

SOMEONE TELLS ME SOME GIRL NAMED CHASCARRILLO HAS BEEN HITTING ON MY BOYFRIEND. ARE YOU HER?
ME? I...
DIDN'T YOU KNOW HE ALREADY HAS A GIRL-FRIEND? HUH, BITCH? HUH? HUH?
YEAH, BITCH!
HEY, DON'T PUSH...
BLANCA!
I-I'M A CHASCARRILLO TOO, 'MEMBER?
HEY!
?
YEOW!
UMP!
OPEN THIS... DOOR!
HEY!
?!?
HOW MANY TIMES HAVE I TOLD YOU PEOPLE NOT TO LOITER AROUND MY RESTROOMS? NOW TAKE OFF!
WE WERE JUST DOING OUR MAKE UP...
GUY...

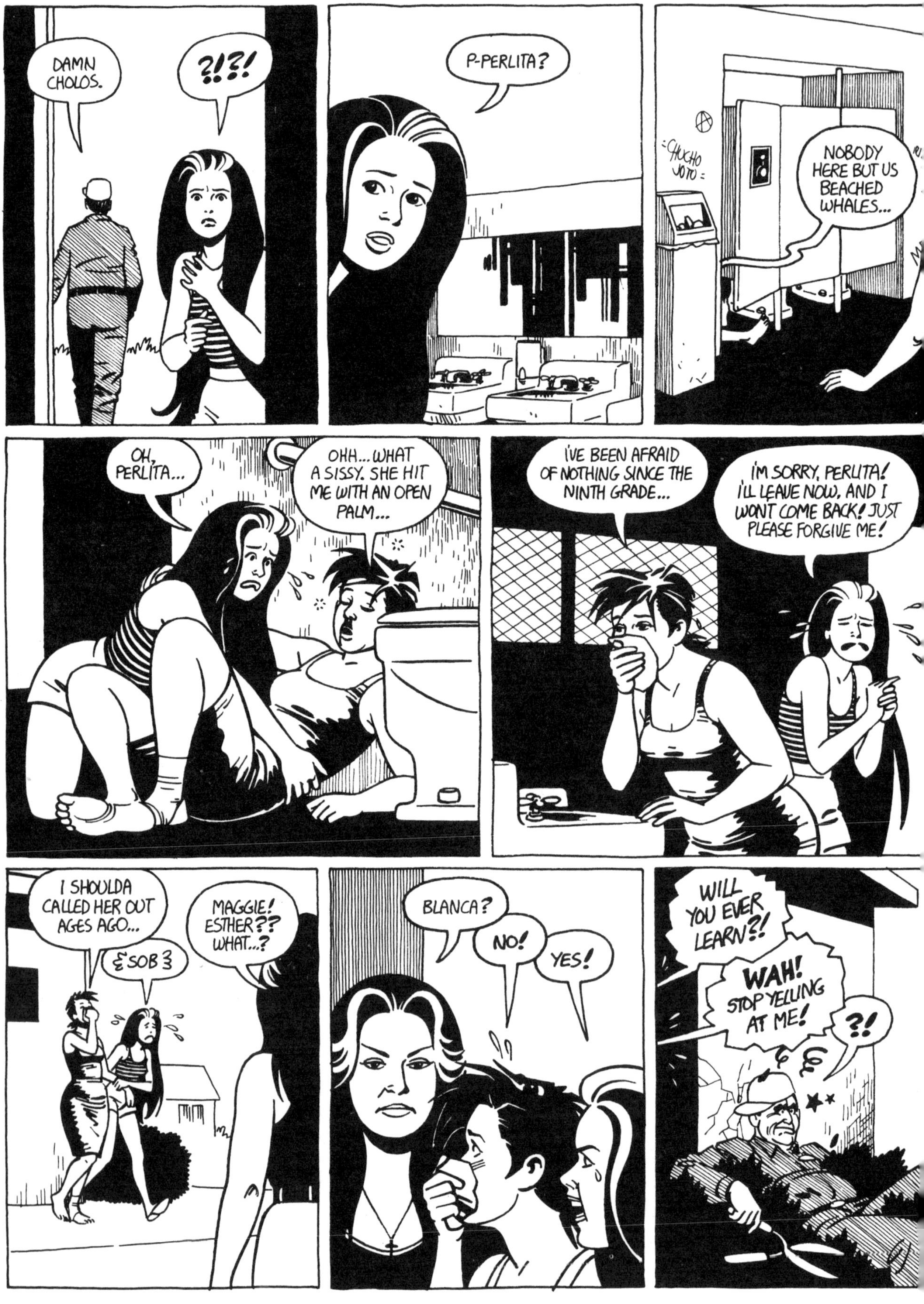
DAMN CHOLOS.
?!?!
P-PERLITA?
:CHUCHO JOTO:
NOBODY HERE BUT US BEACHED WHALES...
OH, PERLITA...
OHH... WHAT A SISSY. SHE HIT ME WITH AN OPEN PALM...
I'VE BEEN AFRAID OF NOTHING SINCE THE NINTH GRADE...
I'M SORRY, PERLITA! I'LL LEAVE NOW, AND I WON'T COME BACK! JUST PLEASE FORGIVE ME!
I SHOULDA CALLED HER OUT AGES AGO...
SOB
MAGGIE! ESTHER?? WHAT...?
BLANCA?
NO!
YES!
WILL YOU EVER LEARN?!
WAH! STOP YELLING AT ME!
?!

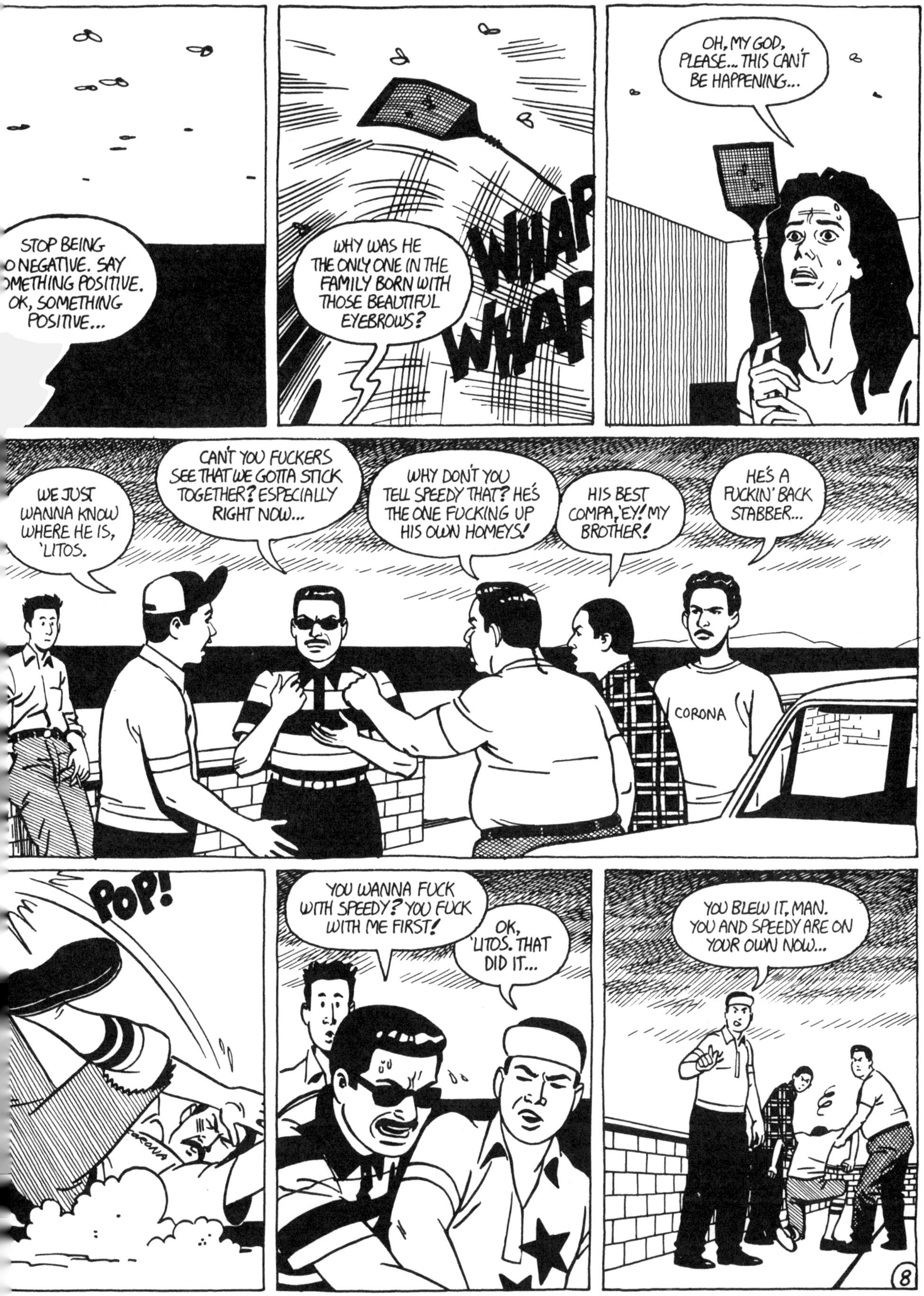
STOP BEING O NEGATIVE. SAY OMETHING POSITIVE. OK, SOMETHING POSITIVE...
WHY WAS HE THE ONLY ONE IN THE FAMILY BORN WITH THOSE BEAUTIFUL EYEBROWS?
WHAP WHAP
OH, MY GOD, PLEASE... THIS CAN'T BE HAPPENING...
WE JUST WANNA KNOW WHERE HE IS, 'LITOS.
CAN'T YOU FUCKERS SEE THAT WE GOTTA STICK TOGETHER? ESPECIALLY RIGHT NOW...
WHY DON'T YOU TELL SPEEDY THAT? HE'S THE ONE FUCKING UP HIS OWN HOMEYS!
HIS BEST COMPA, 'EY! MY BROTHER!
HE'S A FUCKIN' BACK STABBER...
CORONA
POP!
YOU WANNA FUCK WITH SPEEDY? YOU FUCK WITH ME FIRST!
OK, 'LITOS. THAT DID IT...
YOU BLEW IT, MAN. YOU AND SPEEDY ARE ON YOUR OWN NOW...

ISABEL, I COULD HEAR YOU ALL THE WAY FROM MY... AI...

EVERYTHING'S FINE... NOTHING'S FINE... AND LIFE GOES CHUGGIN' ON LIKE A SEVENTY-FOUR CHEVY VEGA...

HAVE YOU EVER GONE TO BED AT NIGHT, AND EVERYTHING WAS FINE? THERE WAS NOT A SAFER PLACE IN THE WORLD... LIFE WAS SIMPLY BEAUTIFUL... BEAUTIFUL...

ISABEL, I THINK YOU BETTER GET DOWN...

THEN JUST ONE NIGHT LATER, IN THE SAME SITUATION, NOTHING IS FINE. NOT EVEN TWENTY LOCKS ON YOUR DOORS AND WINDOWS CAN SAVE YOU FROM THE HORRORS OF THIS COLD, VICIOUS WORLD... INSECURITY RUNS WILD... HOW THE HELL CAN ANYONE SURVIVE?

C'MO

EVERY NIGHT WE HEAR THE SIRENS, THE POPS... FIRE CRACKERS? BOX CARS COUPLING AT THE TRAIN STATION? FARM SHOTS IN THE FIELDS? GUN SHOTS? ARE WE EVER CERTAIN? DO WE EVEN CHECK? NO...

NO, WE'RE JUST GLAD IT SOUNDS A MILE AWAY AND NOT DOWN OUR STREET. AH, LIFE GOES CHUGGIN' ON... LIKE A GOD DAMN SEVENTY-FOUR CHEVY VEGA...

YOU GET SOME SLEE... GET OUTSIDE I'LL BE RIGHT OUT!

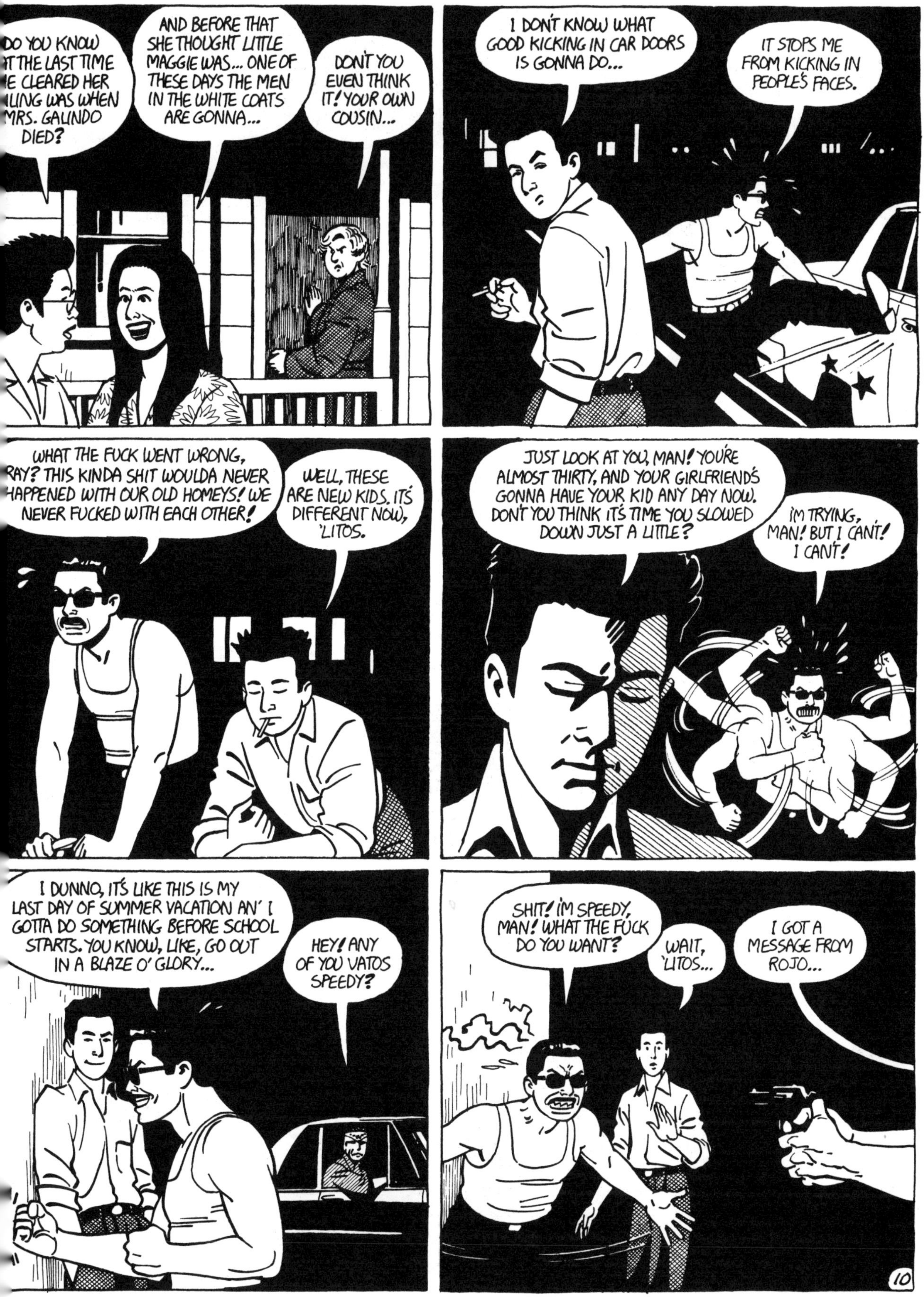
DO YOU KNOW IT THE LAST TIME E CLEARED HER ILING WAS WHEN MRS. GALINDO DIED?
AND BEFORE THAT SHE THOUGHT LITTLE MAGGIE WAS... ONE OF THESE DAYS THE MEN IN THE WHITE COATS ARE GONNA...
DON'T YOU EVEN THINK IT! YOUR OWN COUSIN...
I DON'T KNOW WHAT GOOD KICKING IN CAR DOORS IS GONNA DO...
IT STOPS ME FROM KICKING IN PEOPLE'S FACES.
WHAT THE FUCK WENT WRONG, RAY? THIS KINDA SHIT WOULDA NEVER HAPPENED WITH OUR OLD HOMEYS! WE NEVER FUCKED WITH EACH OTHER!
WELL, THESE ARE NEW KIDS. IT'S DIFFERENT NOW, 'LITOS.
JUST LOOK AT YOU, MAN! YOU'RE ALMOST THIRTY, AND YOUR GIRLFRIEND'S GONNA HAVE YOUR KID ANY DAY NOW. DON'T YOU THINK IT'S TIME YOU SLOWED DOWN JUST A LITTLE?
I'M TRYING, MAN! BUT I CAN'T! I CAN'T!
I DUNNO, IT'S LIKE THIS IS MY LAST DAY OF SUMMER VACATION AN' I GOTTA DO SOMETHING BEFORE SCHOOL STARTS. YOU KNOW, LIKE, GO OUT IN A BLAZE O' GLORY...
HEY! ANY OF YOU VATOS SPEEDY?
SHIT! I'M SPEEDY, MAN! WHAT THE FUCK DO YOU WANT?
WAIT, 'LITOS...
I GOT A MESSAGE FROM ROJO...

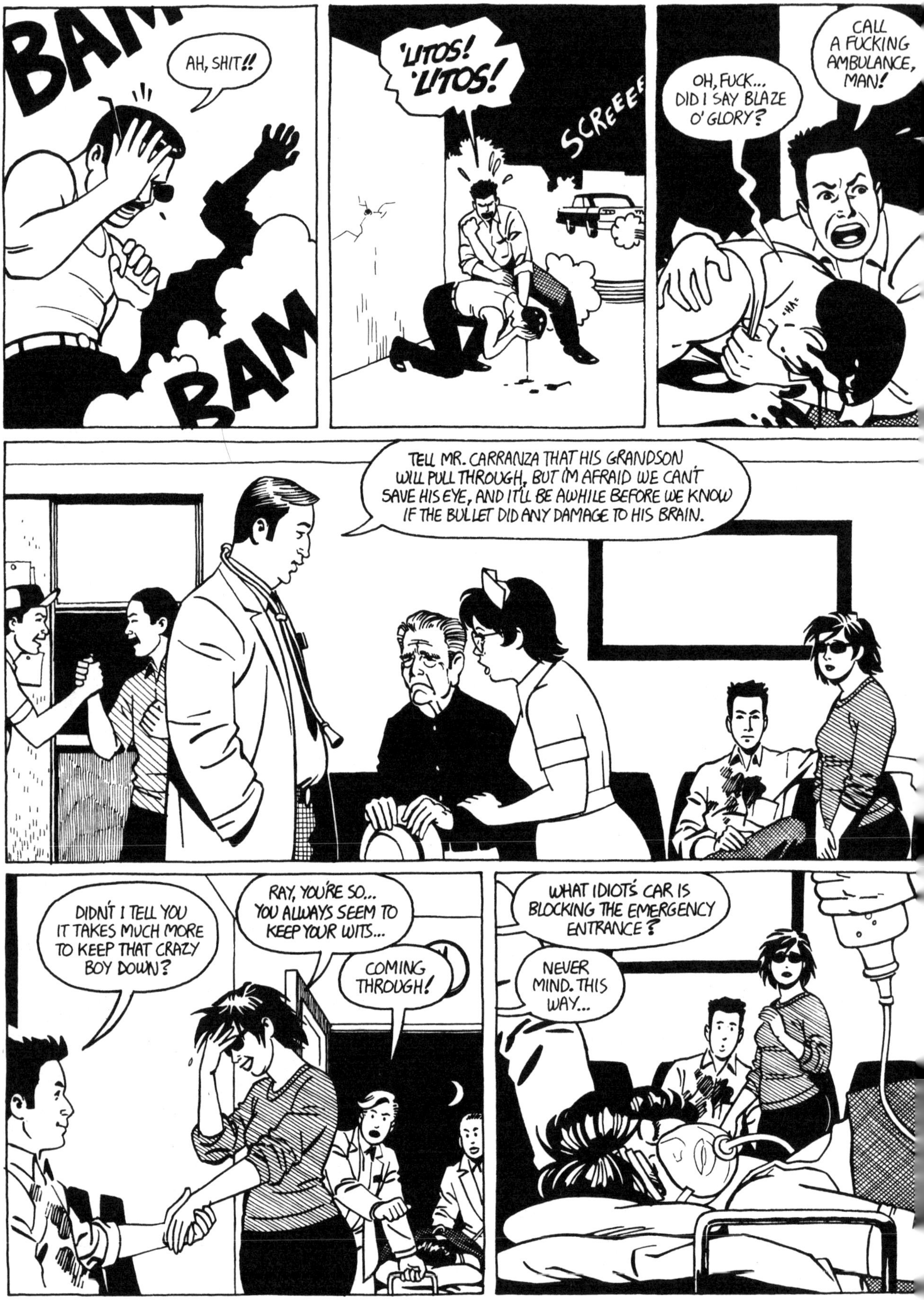
BAM
AH, SHIT!!
BAM
'LITOS! 'LITOS!
SCREEEE
OH, FUCK... DID I SAY BLAZE O' GLORY?
CALL A FUCKING AMBULANCE, MAN!
HA
TELL MR. CARRANZA THAT HIS GRANDSON WILL PULL THROUGH, BUT I'M AFRAID WE CAN'T SAVE HIS EYE, AND IT'LL BE AWHILE BEFORE WE KNOW IF THE BULLET DID ANY DAMAGE TO HIS BRAIN.
DIDN'T I TELL YOU IT TAKES MUCH MORE TO KEEP THAT CRAZY BOY DOWN?
RAY, YOU'RE SO... YOU ALWAYS SEEM TO KEEP YOUR WITS...
COMING THROUGH!
WHAT IDIOT'S CAR IS BLOCKING THE EMERGENCY ENTRANCE?
NEVER MIND. THIS WAY...

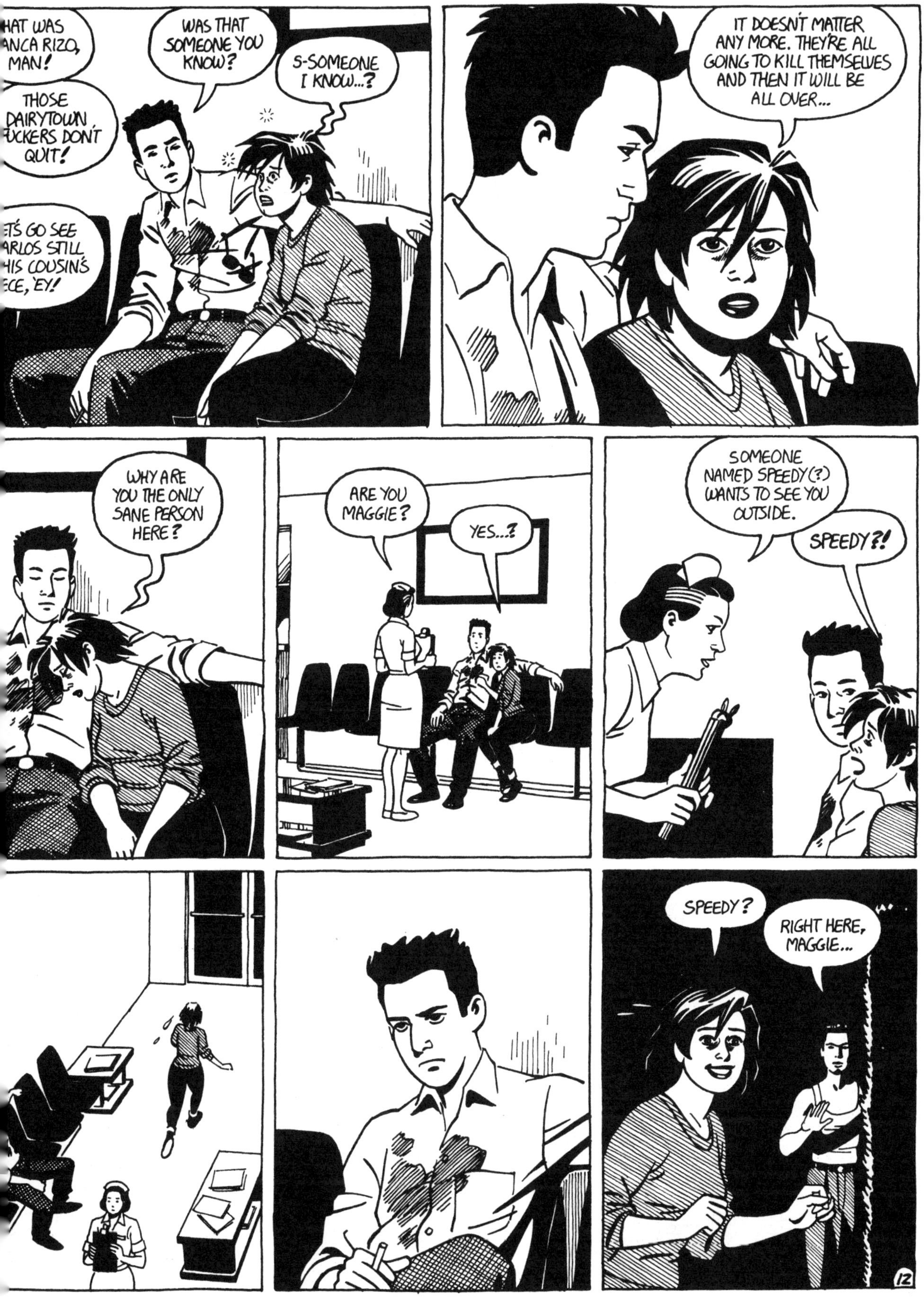

HAT WAS
ANCA RIZO,
MAN!
WAS THAT SOMEONE YOU KNOW?
S-SOMEONE I KNOW...?
THOSE DAIRYTOWN
UCKERS DON'T QUIT!
ET'S GO SEE
ARLOS STILL
HIS COUSIN'S
ECE, 'EY!
IT DOESN'T MATTER ANY MORE. THEY'RE ALL GOING TO KILL THEMSELVES AND THEN IT WILL BE ALL OVER...
WHY ARE YOU THE ONLY SANE PERSON HERE?
ARE YOU MAGGIE?
YES...?
SOMEONE NAMED SPEEDY (?) WANTS TO SEE YOU OUTSIDE.
SPEEDY?!
SPEEDY?
RIGHT HERE, MAGGIE...

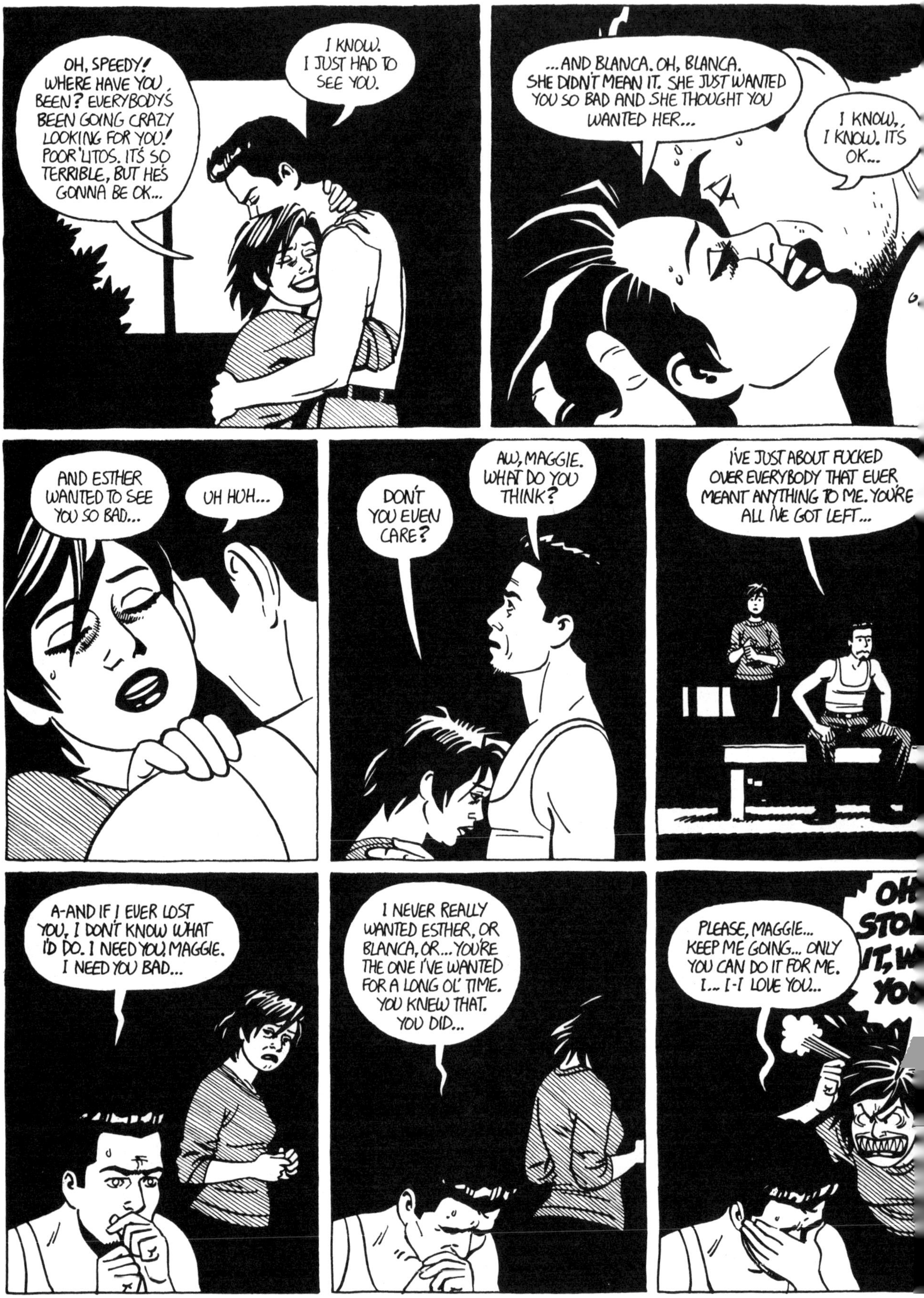
OH, SPEEDY! WHERE HAVE YOU BEEN? EVERYBODY'S BEEN GOING CRAZY LOOKING FOR YOU! POOR 'LITOS. IT'S SO TERRIBLE, BUT HE'S GONNA BE OK...
I KNOW. I JUST HAD TO SEE YOU.
...AND BLANCA. OH, BLANCA. SHE DIDN'T MEAN IT. SHE JUST WANTED YOU SO BAD AND SHE THOUGHT YOU WANTED HER...
I KNOW, I KNOW. IT'S OK...
AND ESTHER WANTED TO SEE YOU SO BAD...
UH HUH...
DON'T YOU EVEN CARE?
AW, MAGGIE. WHAT DO YOU THINK?
I'VE JUST ABOUT FUCKED OVER EVERYBODY THAT EVER MEANT ANYTHING TO ME. YOU'RE ALL I'VE GOT LEFT...
A-AND IF I EVER LOST YOU, I DON'T KNOW WHAT I'D DO. I NEED YOU, MAGGIE. I NEED YOU BAD...
I NEVER REALLY WANTED ESTHER, OR BLANCA, OR... YOU'RE THE ONE I'VE WANTED FOR A LONG OL' TIME. YOU KNEW THAT. YOU DID...
PLEASE, MAGGIE... KEEP ME GOING... ONLY YOU CAN DO IT FOR ME. I... I-I LOVE YOU...
OH

DON'T YOU DARE PUT THIS ON ME! DAMN YOU, SPEEDY! AREN'T YOU GUYS ALL SICK AND TIRED OF WATCHING ME MAKE AN ALL-STAR ASS OF MYSELF? AREN'T YOU? I AM!

I DON'T WANT TO WANT YOU ANY MORE, SPEEDY. I DON'T WANT TO WANT RAND RACE ANY MORE. I CAN'T... I CAN'T DO IT ANY MORE. IT HURTS TOO MUCH...

EMERGENCY

ISN'T THAT THAT ORTIZ KID'S CAR?

YEAH, WHAT'S HE UP TO SO LATE, OR SHOULD I SAY SO EARLY?

SAY, BUDDY! YOU CAN'T PARK HERE! C'MON, LET'S GO! MOVE IT, BAH-TOE...

AW, JEEZ... JERRY, GET ON THE RADIO...

WHAT'S UP?

14

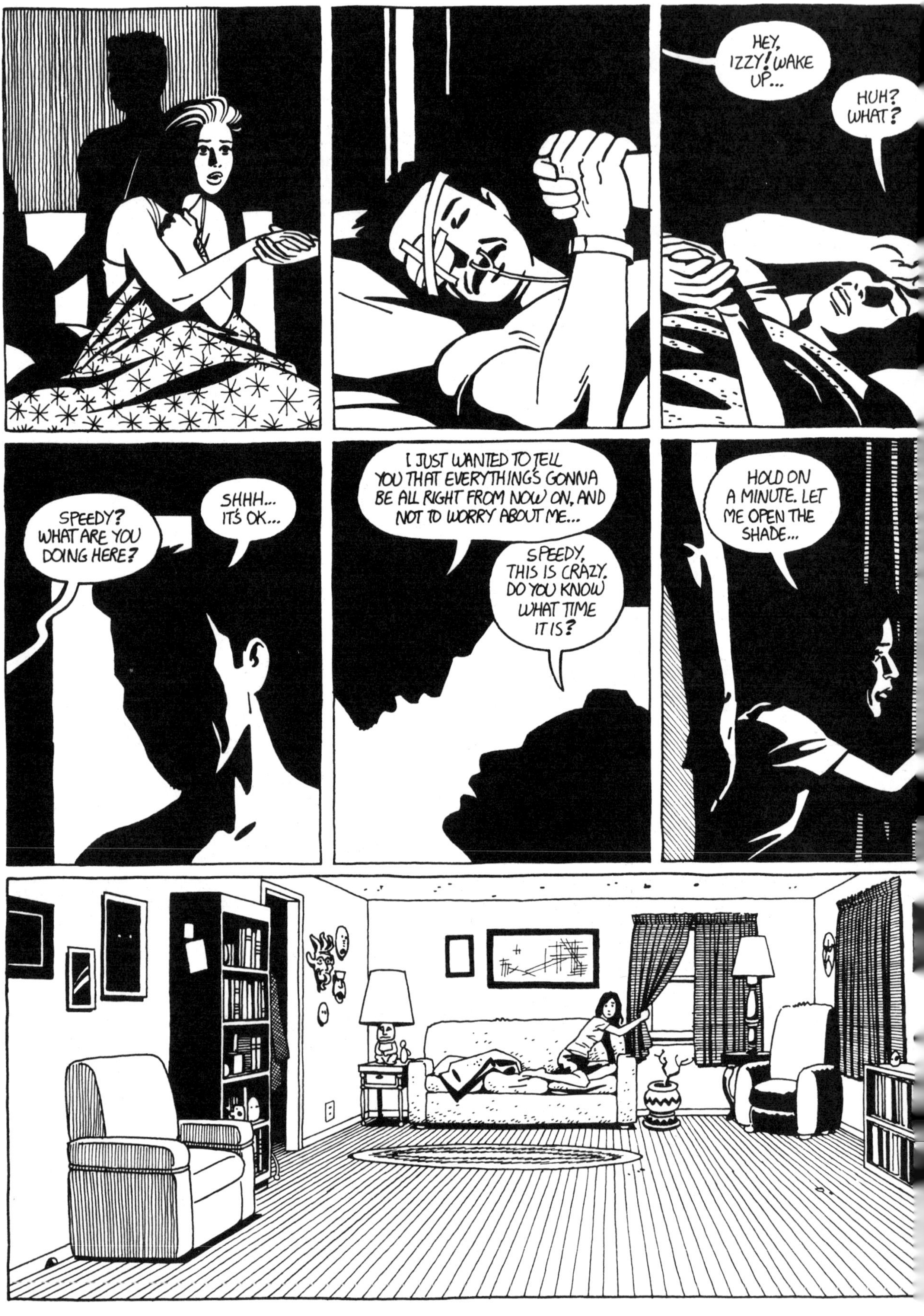
HEY, IZZY! WAKE UP...
HUH? WHAT?
SPEEDY? WHAT ARE YOU DOING HERE?
SHHH... IT'S OK...
I JUST WANTED TO TELL YOU THAT EVERYTHING'S GONNA BE ALL RIGHT FROM NOW ON, AND NOT TO WORRY ABOUT ME...
SPEEDY, THIS IS CRAZY. DO YOU KNOW WHAT TIME IT IS?
HOLD ON A MINUTE. LET ME OPEN THE SHADE...

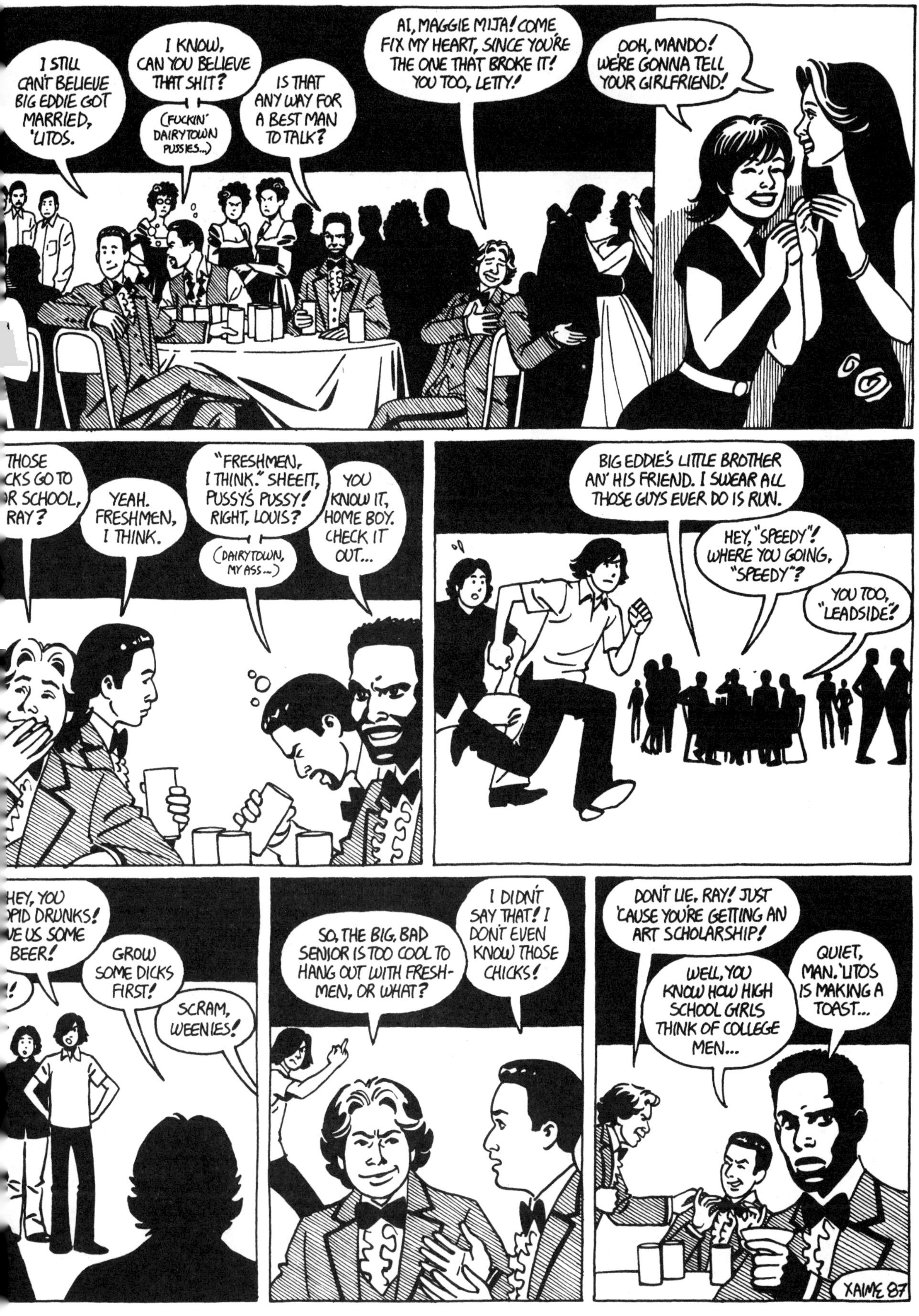
I STILL CAN'T BELIEVE BIG EDDIE GOT MARRIED, 'LITOS.
I KNOW, CAN YOU BELIEVE THAT SHIT?
(FUCKIN' DAIRYTOWN PUSSIES...)
IS THAT ANY WAY FOR A BEST MAN TO TALK?
AI, MAGGIE MIJA! COME FIX MY HEART, SINCE YOU'RE THE ONE THAT BROKE IT! YOU TOO, LETTY!
OOH, MANDO! WE'RE GONNA TELL YOUR GIRLFRIEND!
THOSE
CKS GO TO
R SCHOOL,
RAY?
YEAH. FRESHMEN, I THINK.
"FRESHMEN, I THINK." SHEEIT, PUSSY'S PUSSY! RIGHT, LOUIS?
(DAIRYTOWN, MY ASS...)
YOU KNOW IT, HOME BOY. CHECK IT OUT...
BIG EDDIE'S LITTLE BROTHER AN' HIS FRIEND. I SWEAR ALL THOSE GUYS EVER DO IS RUN.
HEY, "SPEEDY"! WHERE YOU GOING, "SPEEDY"?
YOU TOO, "LEADSIDE"!
HEY, YOU
PID DRUNKS!
VE US SOME
BEER!
GROW SOME DICKS FIRST!
SCRAM, WEENIES!
SO, THE BIG, BAD SENIOR IS TOO COOL TO HANG OUT WITH FRESH-MEN, OR WHAT?
I DIDN'T SAY THAT! I DON'T EVEN KNOW THOSE CHICKS!
DON'T LIE, RAY! JUST 'CAUSE YOU'RE GETTING AN ART SCHOLARSHIP!
WELL, YOU KNOW HOW HIGH SCHOOL GIRLS THINK OF COLLEGE MEN...
QUIET, MAN. 'LITOS IS MAKING A TOAST...
XAIME 87

THE NIGHT APE SEX CAME HOME TO PLAY

XAIM

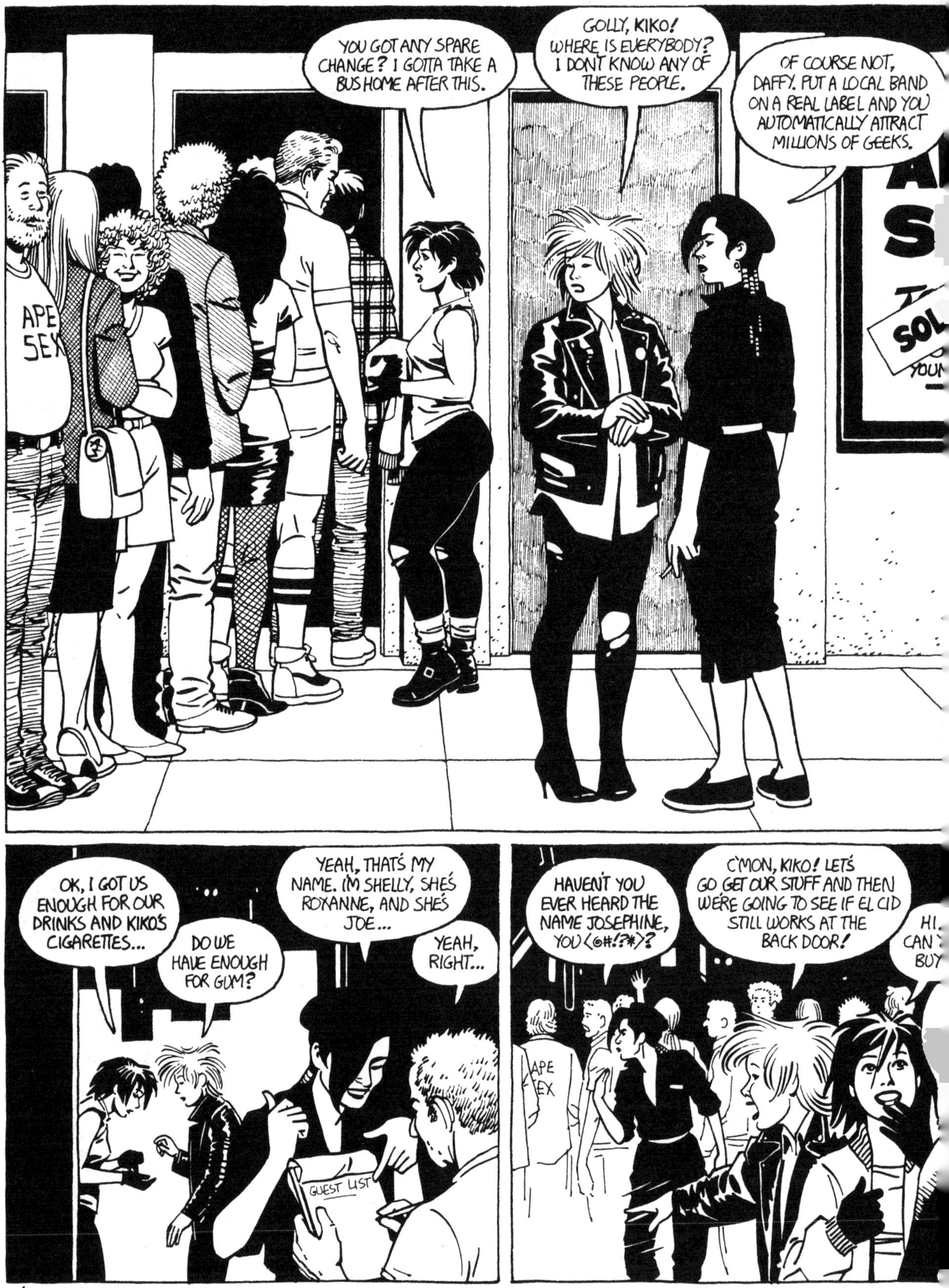

YOU GOT ANY SPARE CHANGE? I GOTTA TAKE A BUS HOME AFTER THIS.
GOLLY, KIKO! WHERE IS EVERYBODY? I DON'T KNOW ANY OF THESE PEOPLE.
OF COURSE NOT, DAFFY. PUT A LOCAL BAND ON A REAL LABEL AND YOU AUTOMATICALLY ATTRACT MILLIONS OF GEEKS.
APE SEX
OK, I GOT US ENOUGH FOR OUR DRINKS AND KIKO'S CIGARETTES...
DO WE HAVE ENOUGH FOR GUM?
YEAH, THAT'S MY NAME. I'M SHELLY, SHE'S ROXANNE, AND SHE'S JOE...
YEAH, RIGHT...
GUEST LIST
HAVEN'T YOU EVER HEARD THE NAME JOSEPHINE, YOU <@#!?*>?
C'MON, KIKO! LET'S GO GET OUR STUFF AND THEN WE'RE GOING TO SEE IF EL CID STILL WORKS AT THE BACK DOOR!
HI.

<JAPANESE>

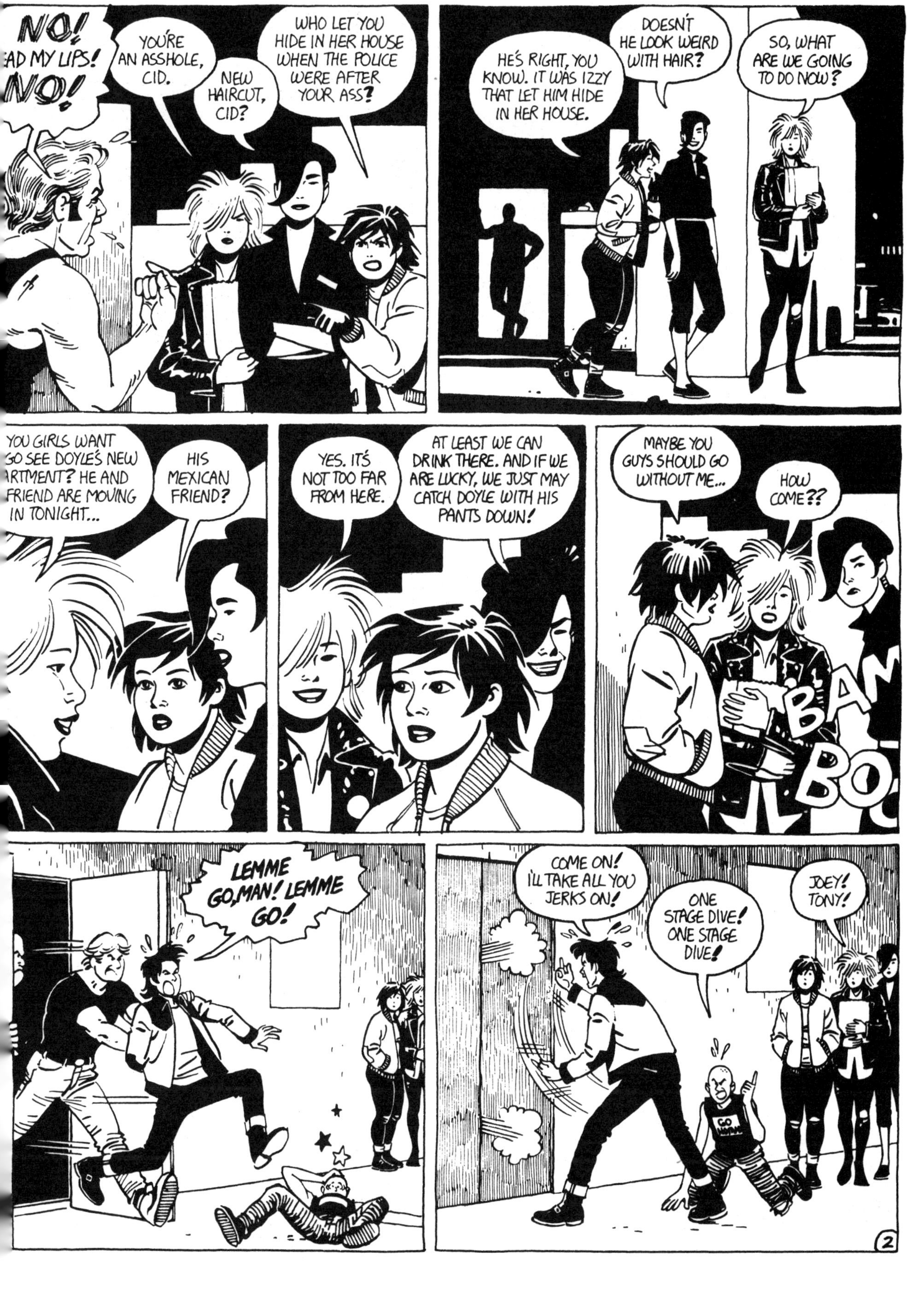
NO! READ MY LIPS! NO!
YOU'RE AN ASSHOLE, CID.
NEW HAIRCUT, CID?
WHO LET YOU HIDE IN HER HOUSE WHEN THE POLICE WERE AFTER YOUR ASS?
HE'S RIGHT, YOU KNOW. IT WAS IZZY THAT LET HIM HIDE IN HER HOUSE.
DOESN'T HE LOOK WEIRD WITH HAIR?
SO, WHAT ARE WE GOING TO DO NOW?
YOU GIRLS WANT TO GO SEE DOYLE'S NEW APARTMENT? HE AND A FRIEND ARE MOVING IN TONIGHT...
HIS MEXICAN FRIEND?
YES. IT'S NOT TOO FAR FROM HERE.
AT LEAST WE CAN DRINK THERE. AND IF WE ARE LUCKY, WE JUST MAY CATCH DOYLE WITH HIS PANTS DOWN!
MAYBE YOU GUYS SHOULD GO WITHOUT ME...
HOW COME??
BAM
BO
LEMME GO, MAN! LEMME GO!
COME ON! I'LL TAKE ALL YOU JERKS ON!
ONE STAGE DIVE! ONE STAGE DIVE!
JOEY! TONY!
GO

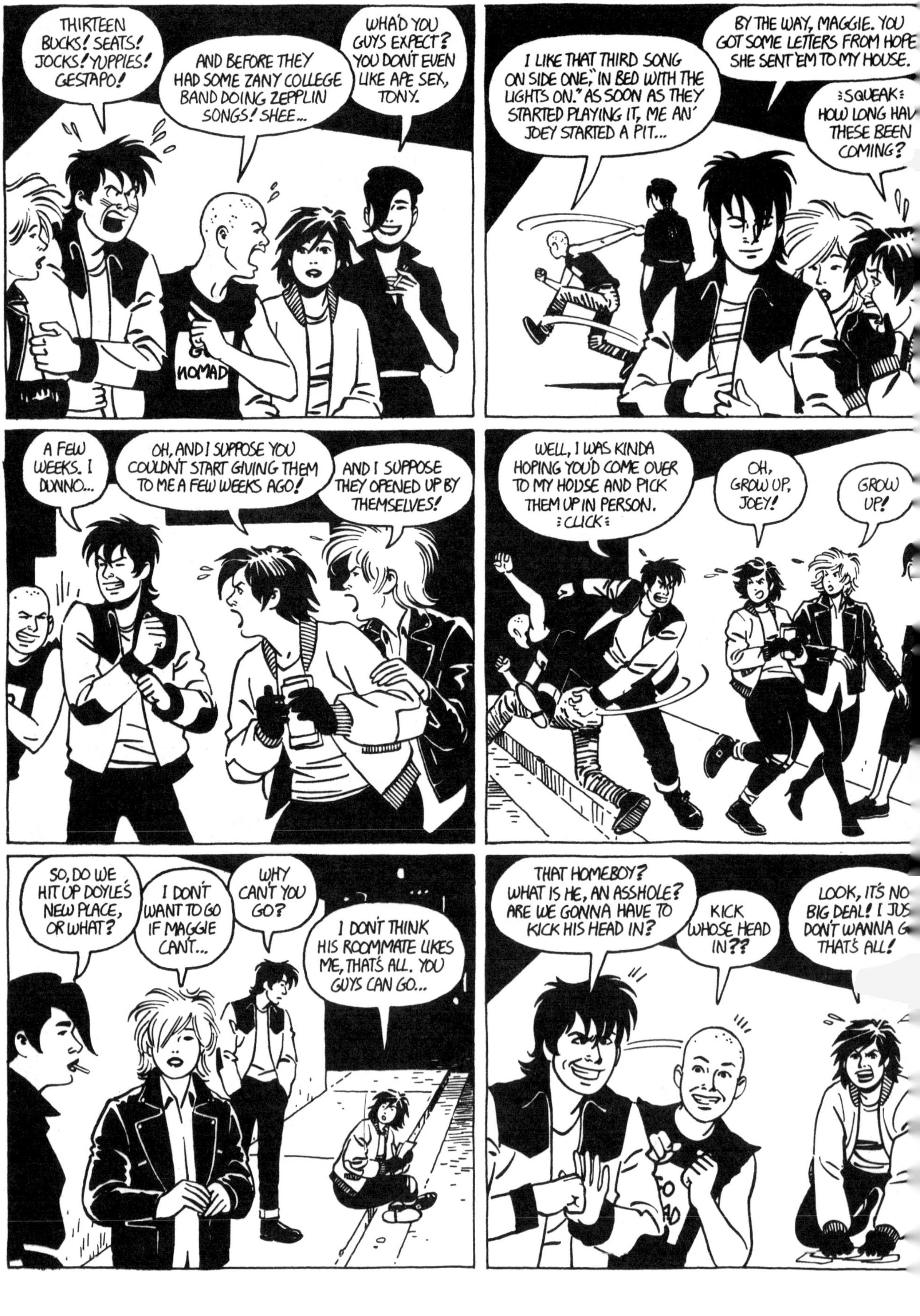
THIRTEEN BUCKS! SEATS! JOCKS! YUPPIES! GESTAPO!
AND BEFORE THEY HAD SOME ZANY COLLEGE BAND DOING ZEPPLIN SONGS! SHEE...
WHA'D YOU GUYS EXPECT? YOU DON'T EVEN LIKE APE SEX, TONY.
NOMAD
I LIKE THAT THIRD SONG ON SIDE ONE, "IN BED WITH THE LIGHTS ON." AS SOON AS THEY STARTED PLAYING IT, ME AN' JOEY STARTED A PIT...
BY THE WAY, MAGGIE. YOU GOT SOME LETTERS FROM HOPE SHE SENT 'EM TO MY HOUSE.
:SQUEAK: HOW LONG HAV THESE BEEN COMING?
A FEW WEEKS. I DUNNO...
OH, AND I SUPPOSE YOU COULDN'T START GIVING THEM TO ME A FEW WEEKS AGO!
AND I SUPPOSE THEY OPENED UP BY THEMSELVES!
WELL, I WAS KINDA HOPING YOU'D COME OVER TO MY HOUSE AND PICK THEM UP IN PERSON. :CLICK:
OH, GROW UP, JOEY!
GROW UP!
SO, DO WE HIT UP DOYLE'S NEW PLACE, OR WHAT?
I DON'T WANT TO GO IF MAGGIE CAN'T...
WHY CAN'T YOU GO?
I DON'T THINK HIS ROOMMATE LIKES ME, THAT'S ALL. YOU GUYS CAN GO...
THAT HOMEBOY? WHAT IS HE, AN ASSHOLE? ARE WE GONNA HAVE TO KICK HIS HEAD IN?
KICK WHOSE HEAD IN??
LOOK, IT'S NO BIG DEAL! I JUS DON'T WANNA G THAT'S ALL!

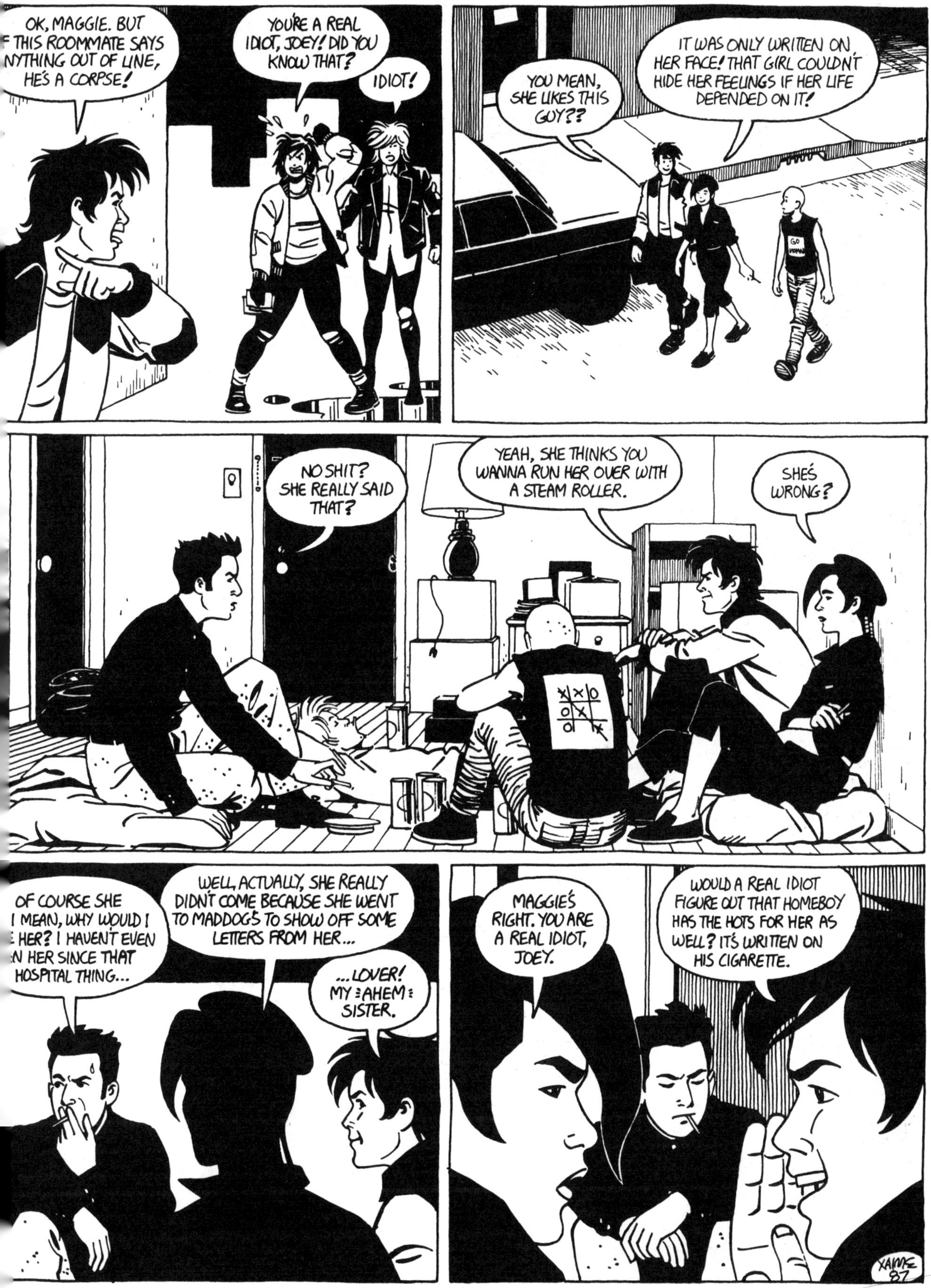
OK, MAGGIE. BUT IF THIS ROOMMATE SAYS ANYTHING OUT OF LINE, HE'S A CORPSE!
YOU'RE A REAL IDIOT, JOEY! DID YOU KNOW THAT?
IDIOT!
YOU MEAN, SHE LIKES THIS GUY??
IT WAS ONLY WRITTEN ON HER FACE! THAT GIRL COULDN'T HIDE HER FEELINGS IF HER LIFE DEPENDED ON IT!
GO WOMAN
NO SHIT? SHE REALLY SAID THAT?
YEAH, SHE THINKS YOU WANNA RUN HER OVER WITH A STEAM ROLLER.
SHE'S WRONG?
OF COURSE SHE ... I MEAN, WHY WOULD I ... HER? I HAVEN'T EVEN ... HER SINCE THAT HOSPITAL THING...
WELL, ACTUALLY, SHE REALLY DIDN'T COME BECAUSE SHE WENT TO MADDOG'S TO SHOW OFF SOME LETTERS FROM HER...
...LOVER! MY AHEM SISTER.
MAGGIE'S RIGHT. YOU ARE A REAL IDIOT, JOEY.
WOULD A REAL IDIOT FIGURE OUT THAT HOMEBOY HAS THE HOTS FOR HER AS WELL? IT'S WRITTEN ON HIS CIGARETTE.
XAIME 87

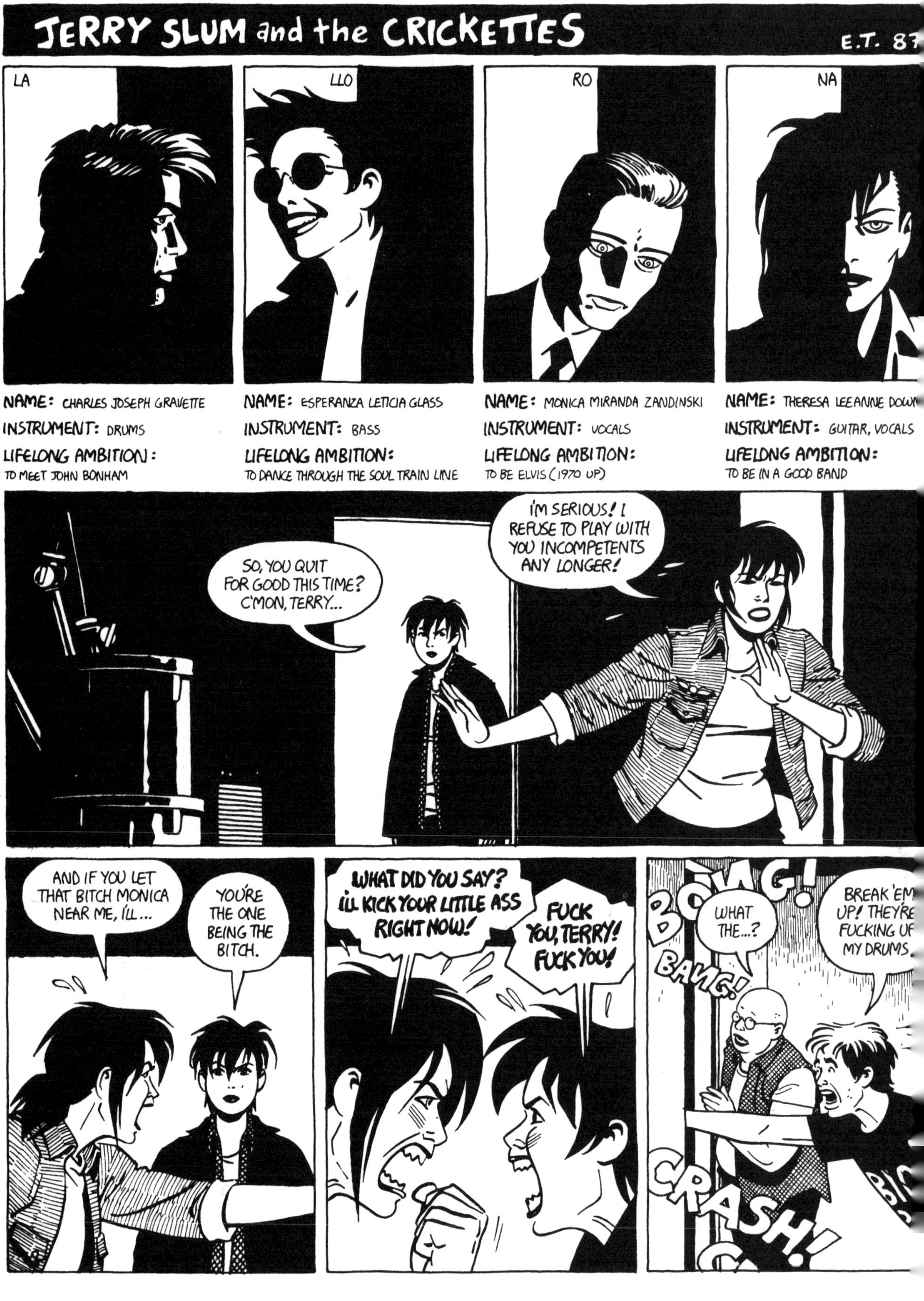
JERRY SLUM and the CRICKETTES
E.T. 87
LA
LLO
RO
NA
NAME: CHARLES JOSEPH GRAVETTE
INSTRUMENT: DRUMS
LIFELONG AMBITION: TO MEET JOHN BONHAM
NAME: ESPERANZA LETICIA GLASS
INSTRUMENT: BASS
LIFELONG AMBITION: TO DANCE THROUGH THE SOUL TRAIN LINE
NAME: MONICA MIRANDA ZANDINSKI
INSTRUMENT: VOCALS
LIFELONG AMBITION: TO BE ELVIS (1970 UP)
NAME: THERESA LEEANNE DOWN
INSTRUMENT: GUITAR, VOCALS
LIFELONG AMBITION: TO BE IN A GOOD BAND
SO, YOU QUIT FOR GOOD THIS TIME? C'MON, TERRY...
I'M SERIOUS! I REFUSE TO PLAY WITH YOU INCOMPETENTS ANY LONGER!
AND IF YOU LET THAT BITCH MONICA NEAR ME, I'LL...
YOU'RE THE ONE BEING THE BITCH.
WHAT DID YOU SAY? I'LL KICK YOUR LITTLE ASS RIGHT NOW!
FUCK YOU, TERRY! FUCK YOU!
WHAT THE...?
BREAK 'EM UP! THEY'RE FUCKING UP MY DRUMS
BANG!
CRASH!

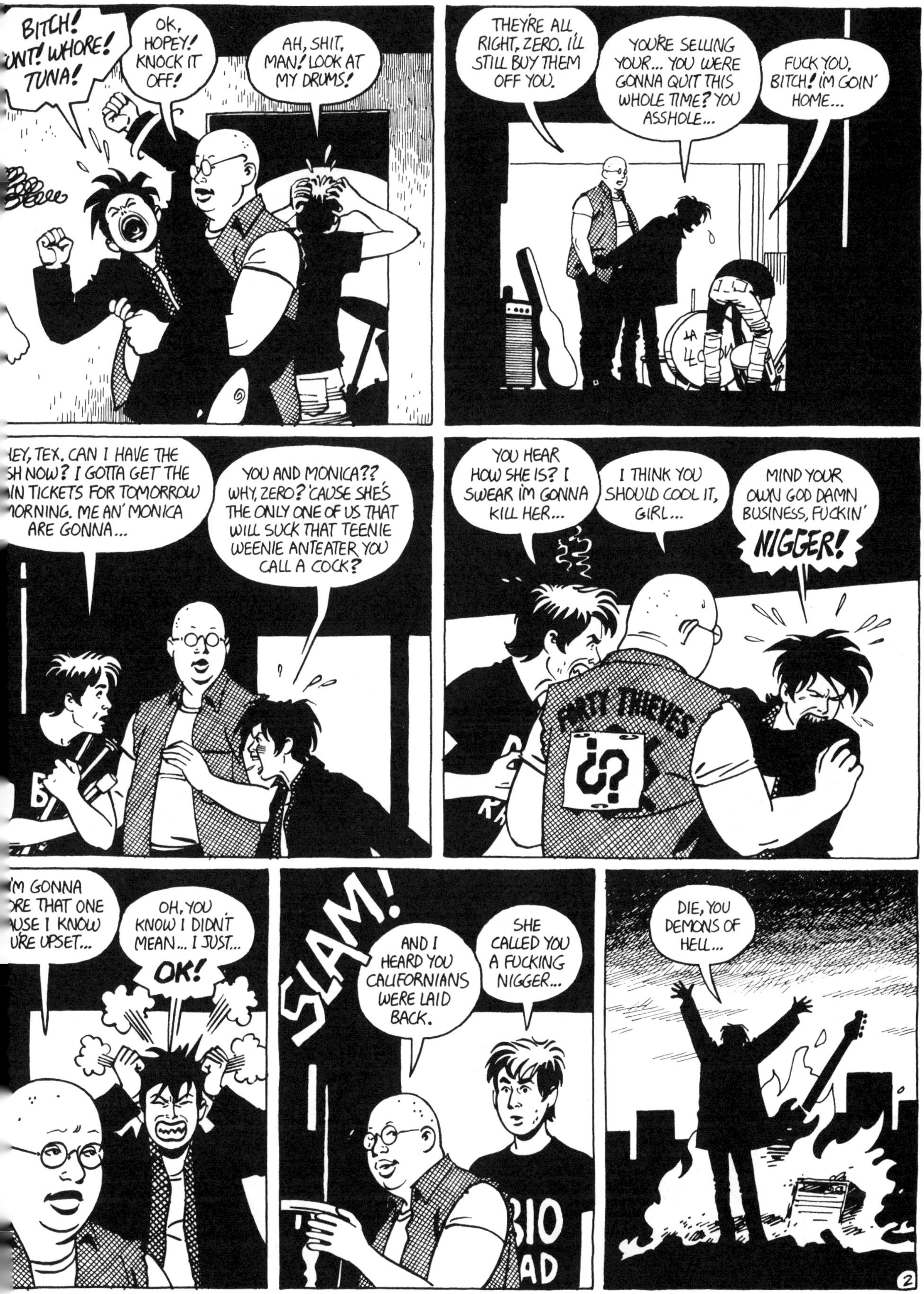
BITCH! UNT! WHORE! TUNA!
OK, HOPEY! KNOCK IT OFF!
AH, SHIT, MAN! LOOK AT MY DRUMS!
THEY'RE ALL RIGHT, ZERO. I'LL STILL BUY THEM OFF YOU.
YOU'RE SELLING YOUR... YOU WERE GONNA QUIT THIS WHOLE TIME? YOU ASSHOLE...
FUCK YOU, BITCH! I'M GOIN' HOME...
HEY, TEX. CAN I HAVE THE SH NOW? I GOTTA GET THE AIN TICKETS FOR TOMORROW MORNING. ME AN' MONICA ARE GONNA...
YOU AND MONICA?? WHY, ZERO? 'CAUSE SHE'S THE ONLY ONE OF US THAT WILL SUCK THAT TEENIE WEENIE ANTEATER YOU CALL A COCK?
YOU HEAR HOW SHE IS? I SWEAR I'M GONNA KILL HER...
I THINK YOU SHOULD COOL IT, GIRL...
MIND YOUR OWN GOD DAMN BUSINESS, FUCKIN' NIGGER!
FORTY THIEVES
I'M GONNA ORE THAT ONE AUSE I KNOW U'RE UPSET...
OH, YOU KNOW I DIDN'T MEAN... I JUST...
OK!
SLAM!
AND I HEARD YOU CALIFORNIANS WERE LAID BACK.
SHE CALLED YOU A FUCKING NIGGER...
DIE, YOU DEMONS OF HELL...

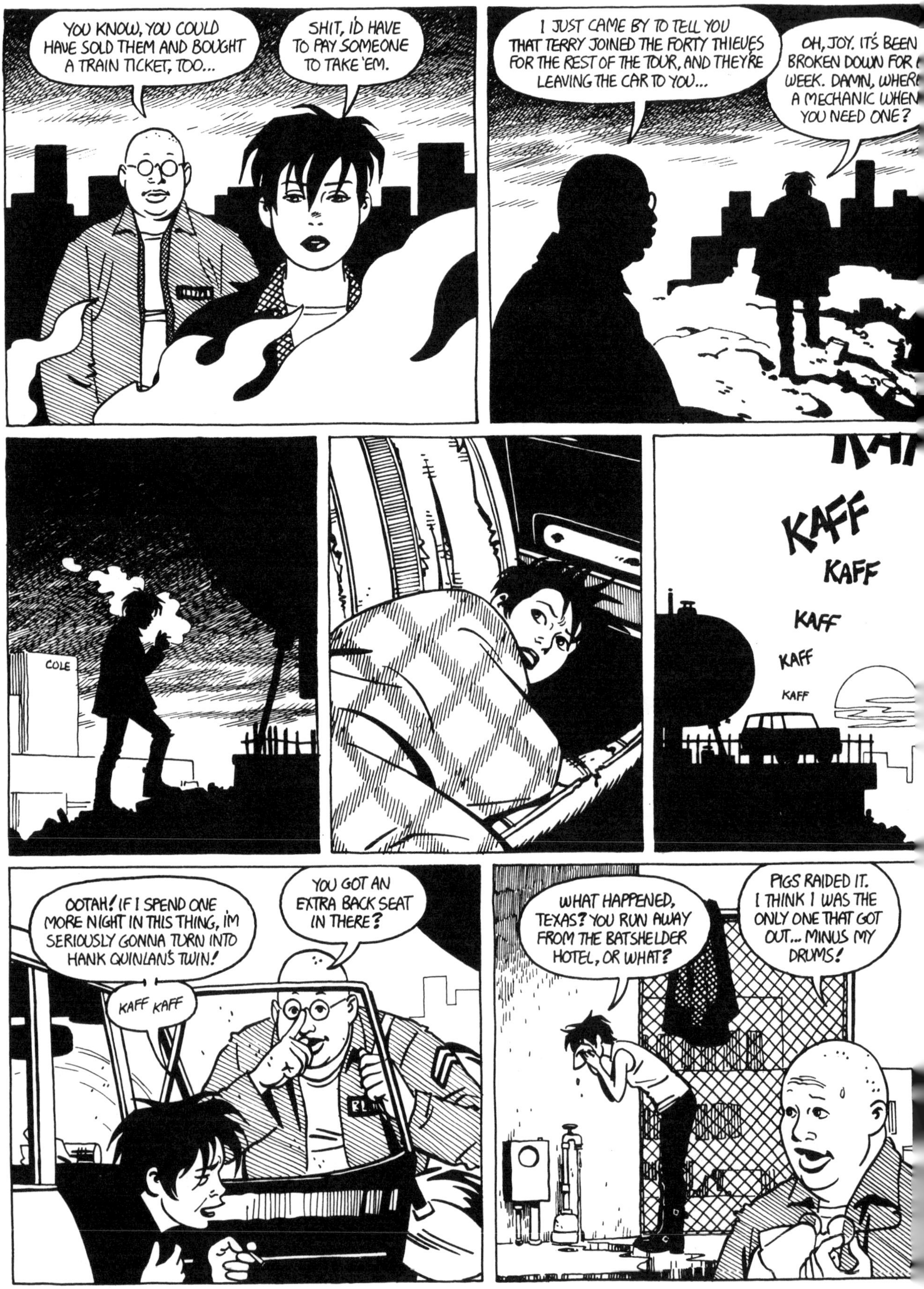
YOU KNOW, YOU COULD HAVE SOLD THEM AND BOUGHT A TRAIN TICKET, TOO...
SHIT, I'D HAVE TO PAY SOMEONE TO TAKE 'EM.
I JUST CAME BY TO TELL YOU THAT TERRY JOINED THE FORTY THIEVES FOR THE REST OF THE TOUR, AND THEY'RE LEAVING THE CAR TO YOU...
OH, JOY. IT'S BEEN BROKEN DOWN FOR WEEK. DAMN, WHER A MECHANIC WHEN YOU NEED ONE?
COLE
KAFF
KAFF
KAFF
KAFF
KAFF
OOTAH! IF I SPEND ONE MORE NIGHT IN THIS THING, I'M SERIOUSLY GONNA TURN INTO HANK QUINLAN'S TWIN!
KAFF KAFF
YOU GOT AN EXTRA BACK SEAT IN THERE?
WHAT HAPPENED, TEXAS? YOU RUN AWAY FROM THE BATSHELDER HOTEL, OR WHAT?
PIGS RAIDED IT. I THINK I WAS THE ONLY ONE THAT GOT OUT... MINUS MY DRUMS!

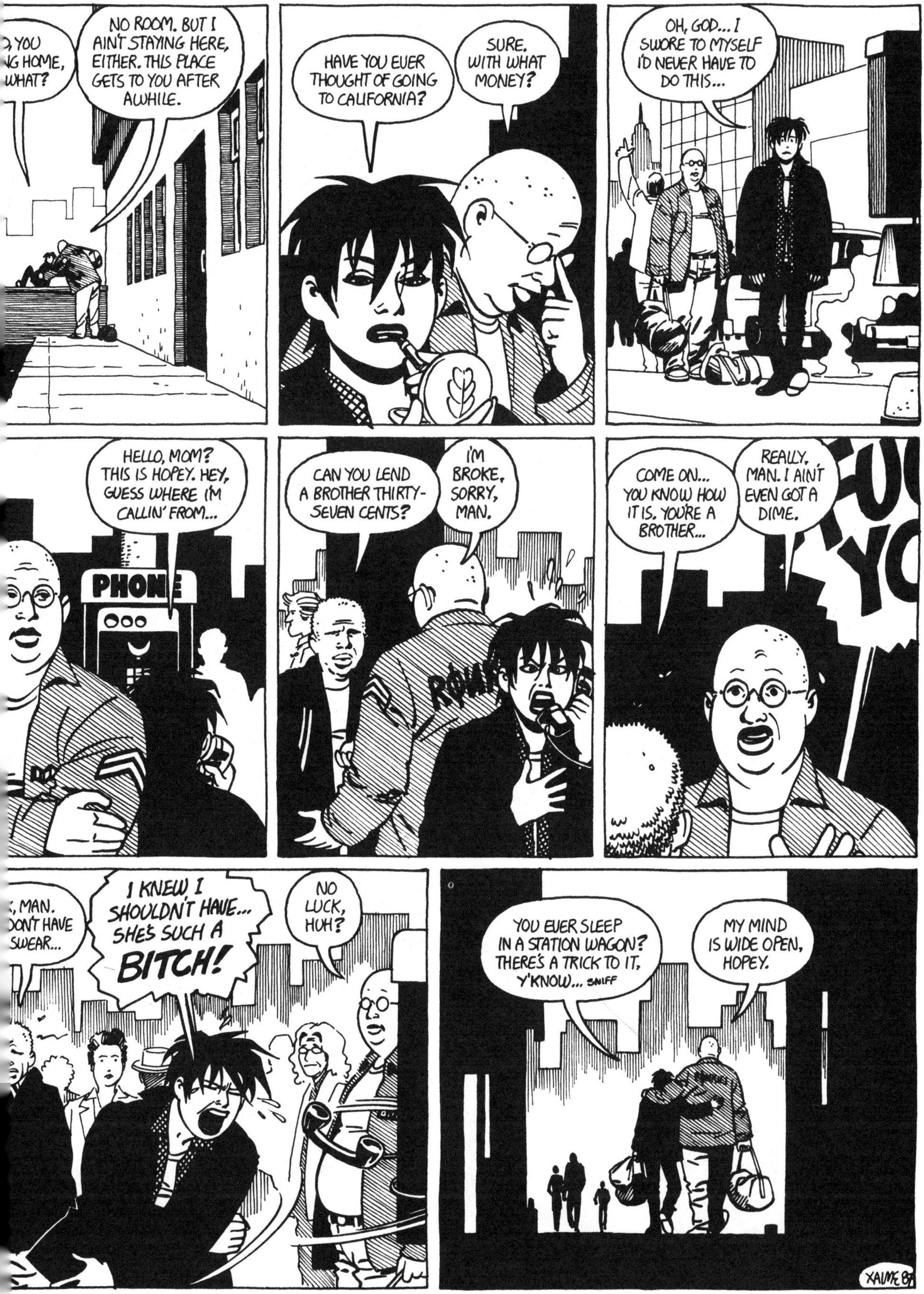

…, YOU …NG HOME, …WHAT?
NO ROOM. BUT I AIN'T STAYING HERE, EITHER. THIS PLACE GETS TO YOU AFTER AWHILE.
HAVE YOU EVER THOUGHT OF GOING TO CALIFORNIA?
SURE. WITH WHAT MONEY?
OH, GOD... I SWORE TO MYSELF I'D NEVER HAVE TO DO THIS...
HELLO, MOM? THIS IS HOPEY. HEY, GUESS WHERE I'M CALLIN' FROM...
PHONE
CAN YOU LEND A BROTHER THIRTY-SEVEN CENTS?
I'M BROKE, SORRY, MAN.
COME ON... YOU KNOW HOW IT IS. YOU'RE A BROTHER...
REALLY, MAN. I AIN'T EVEN GOT A DIME.
…, MAN. …DON'T HAVE …SWEAR...
I KNEW I SHOULDN'T HAVE... SHE'S SUCH A BITCH!
NO LUCK, HUH?
YOU EVER SLEEP IN A STATION WAGON? THERE'S A TRICK TO IT, Y'KNOW... SNIFF
MY MIND IS WIDE OPEN, HOPEY.
XAIME 89

A Mess of Skin...

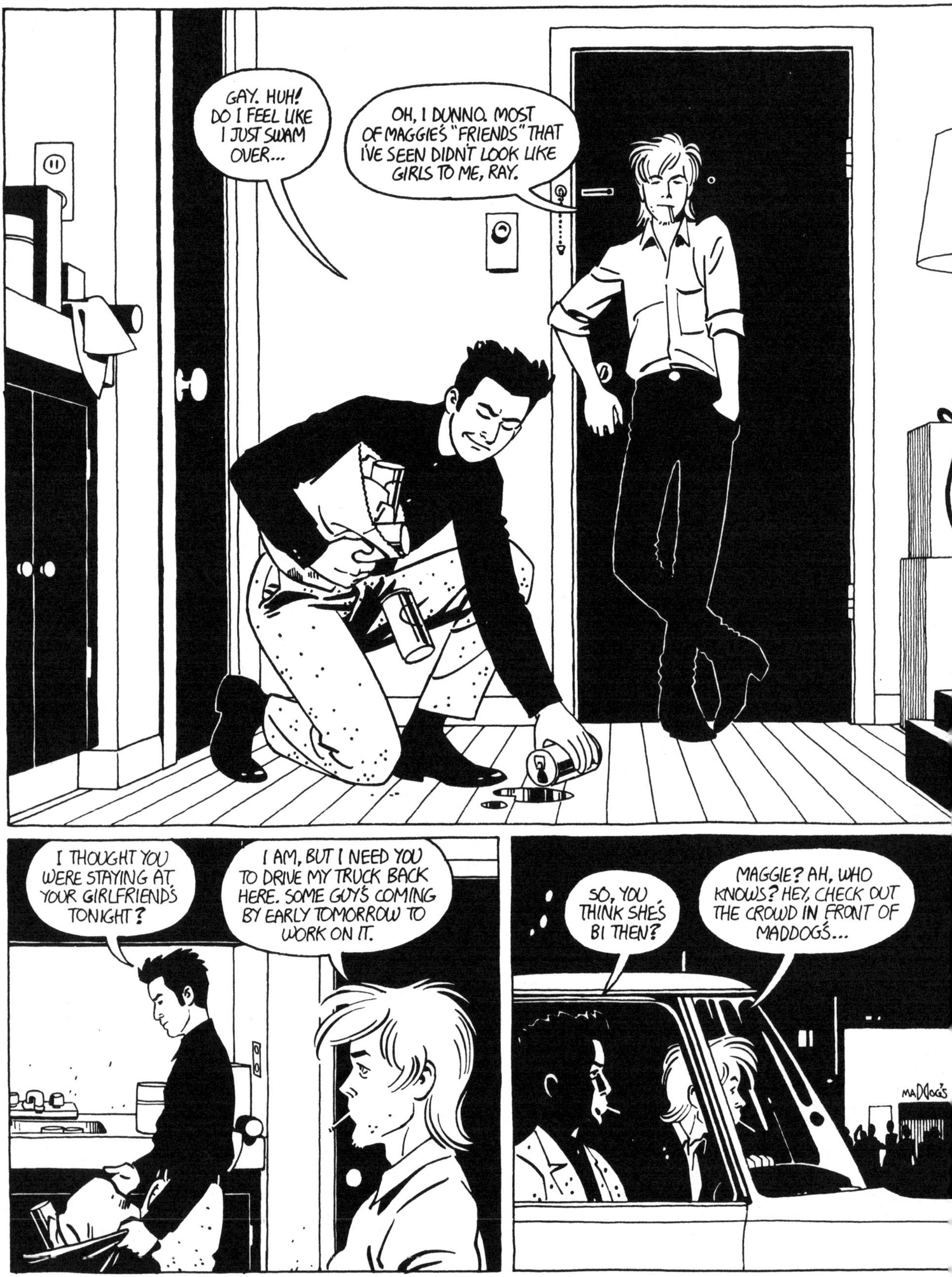
GAY. HUH! DO I FEEL LIKE I JUST SWAM OVER...
OH, I DUNNO. MOST OF MAGGIE'S "FRIENDS" THAT I'VE SEEN DIDN'T LOOK LIKE GIRLS TO ME, RAY.
I THOUGHT YOU WERE STAYING AT YOUR GIRLFRIEND'S TONIGHT?
I AM, BUT I NEED YOU TO DRIVE MY TRUCK BACK HERE. SOME GUY'S COMING BY EARLY TOMORROW TO WORK ON IT.
SO, YOU THINK SHE'S BI THEN?
MAGGIE? AH, WHO KNOWS? HEY, CHECK OUT THE CROWD IN FRONT OF MADDOG'S...
MADDOG'S

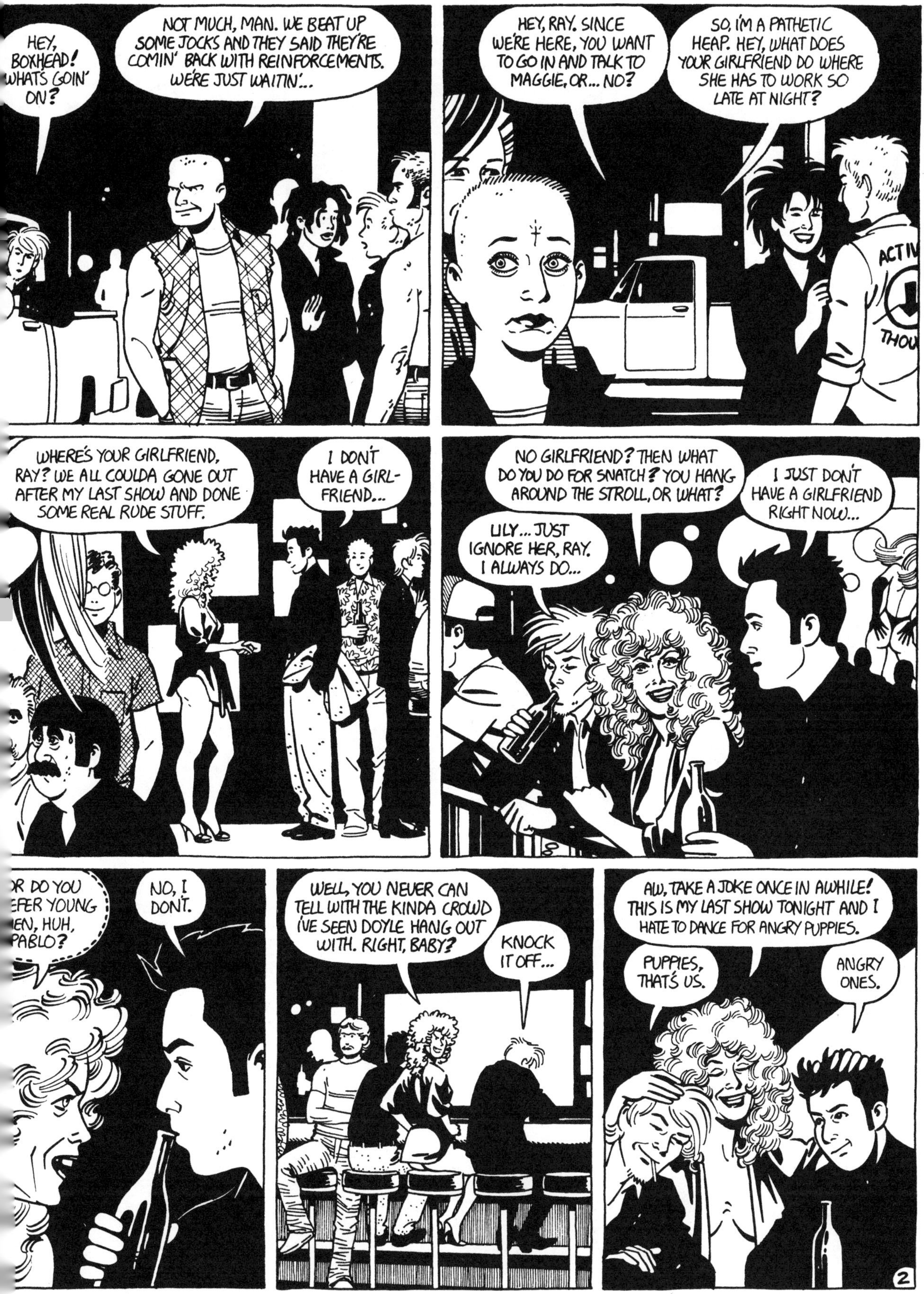
HEY, BOXHEAD! WHAT'S GOIN' ON?
NOT MUCH, MAN. WE BEAT UP SOME JOCKS AND THEY SAID THEY'RE COMIN' BACK WITH REINFORCEMENTS. WE'RE JUST WAITIN'...
HEY, RAY. SINCE WE'RE HERE, YOU WANT TO GO IN AND TALK TO MAGGIE, OR... NO?
SO, I'M A PATHETIC HEAP. HEY, WHAT DOES YOUR GIRLFRIEND DO WHERE SHE HAS TO WORK SO LATE AT NIGHT?
WHERE'S YOUR GIRLFRIEND, RAY? WE ALL COULDA GONE OUT AFTER MY LAST SHOW AND DONE SOME REAL RUDE STUFF.
I DON'T HAVE A GIRL-FRIEND...
NO GIRLFRIEND? THEN WHAT DO YOU DO FOR SNATCH? YOU HANG AROUND THE STROLL, OR WHAT?
I JUST DON'T HAVE A GIRLFRIEND RIGHT NOW...
LILY... JUST IGNORE HER, RAY. I ALWAYS DO...
OR DO YOU EFER YOUNG IEN, HUH, PABLO?
NO, I DON'T.
WELL, YOU NEVER CAN TELL WITH THE KINDA CROWD I'VE SEEN DOYLE HANG OUT WITH. RIGHT, BABY?
KNOCK IT OFF...
AW, TAKE A JOKE ONCE IN AWHILE! THIS IS MY LAST SHOW TONIGHT AND I HATE TO DANCE FOR ANGRY PUPPIES.
PUPPIES, THAT'S US.
ANGRY ONES.
2

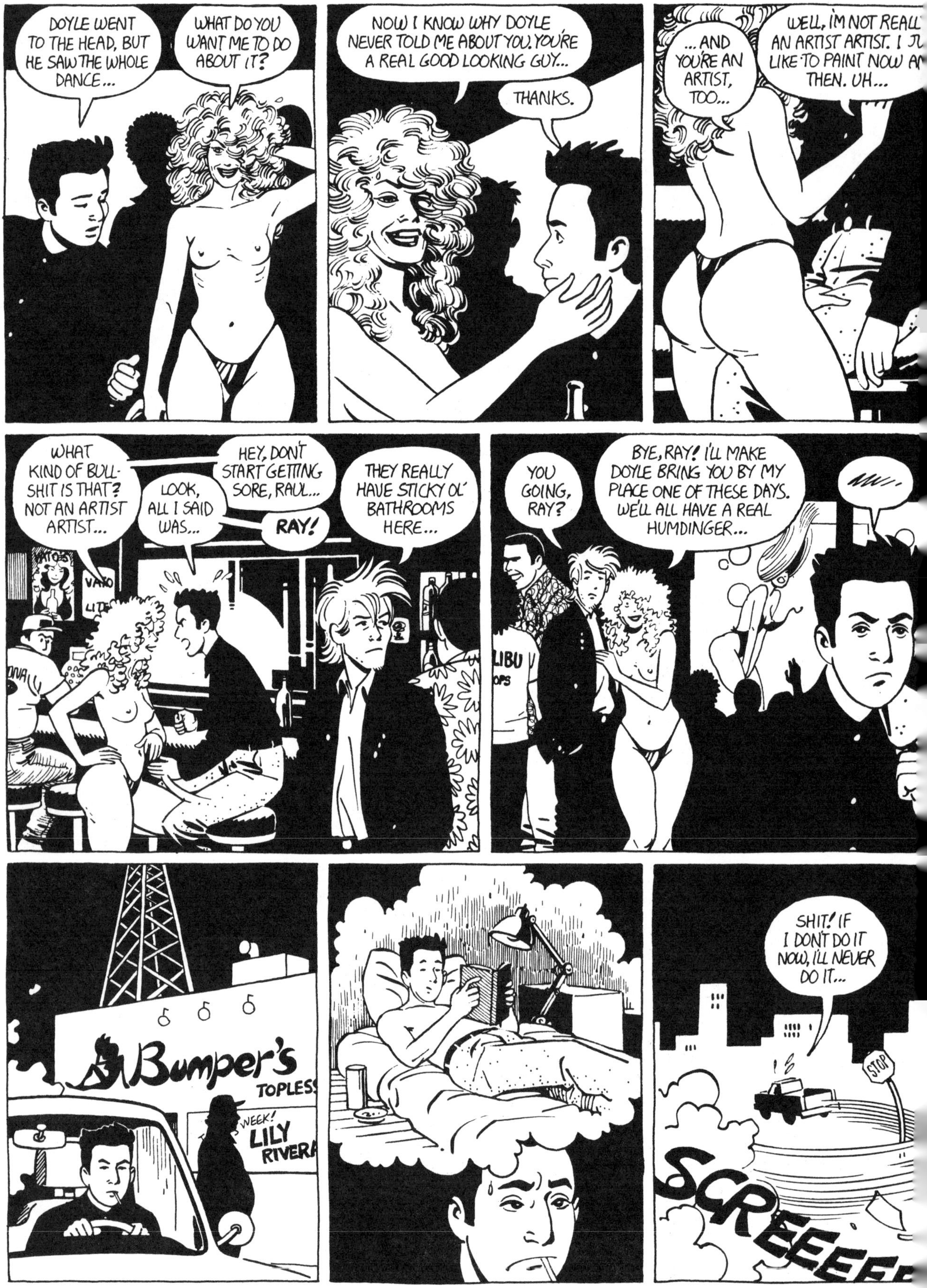
DOYLE WENT TO THE HEAD, BUT HE SAW THE WHOLE DANCE...
WHAT DO YOU WANT ME TO DO ABOUT IT?
NOW I KNOW WHY DOYLE NEVER TOLD ME ABOUT YOU. YOU'RE A REAL GOOD LOOKING GUY...
THANKS.
...AND YOU'RE AN ARTIST, TOO...
WELL, I'M NOT REALL AN ARTIST ARTIST. I JU LIKE TO PAINT NOW A THEN. UH...
WHAT KIND OF BULL-SHIT IS THAT? NOT AN ARTIST ARTIST...
LOOK, ALL I SAID WAS...
HEY, DON'T START GETTING SORE, RAUL...
RAY!
THEY REALLY HAVE STICKY OL' BATHROOMS HERE...
YOU GOING, RAY?
BYE, RAY! I'LL MAKE DOYLE BRING YOU BY MY PLACE ONE OF THESE DAYS. WE'LL ALL HAVE A REAL HUMDINGER...
Bumper's
TOPLESS
WEEK!
LILY RIVERA
SHIT! IF I DON'T DO IT NOW, I'LL NEVER DO IT...
STOP
SCREEEEE

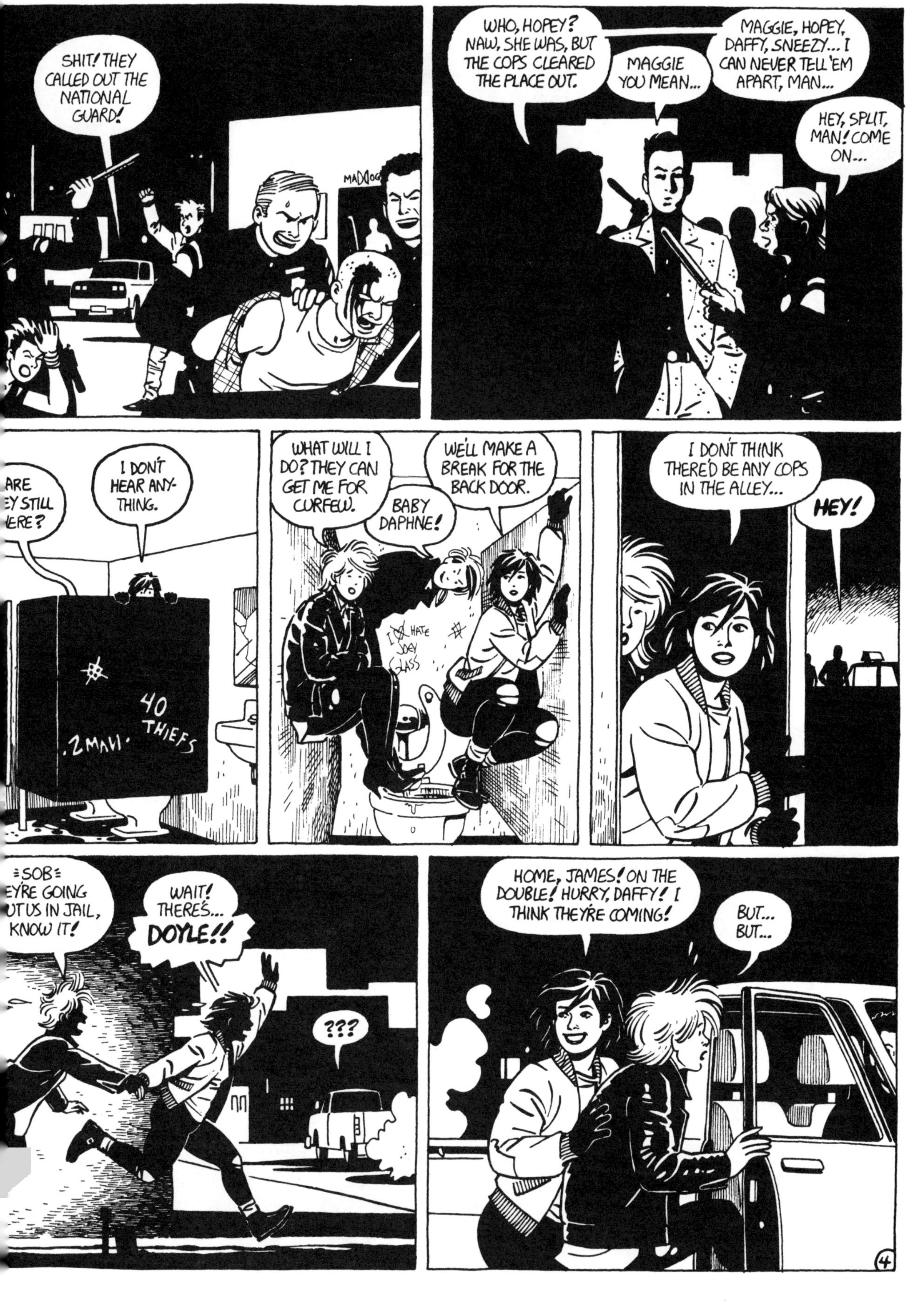
SHIT! THEY CALLED OUT THE NATIONAL GUARD!
MADDOG
WHO, HOPEY? NAW, SHE WAS, BUT THE COPS CLEARED THE PLACE OUT.
MAGGIE YOU MEAN...
MAGGIE, HOPEY, DAFFY, SNEEZY... I CAN NEVER TELL 'EM APART, MAN...
HEY, SPLIT, MAN! COME ON...
ARE EY STILL HERE?
I DON'T HEAR ANY-THING.
40 THIEFS
.2MAH.
WHAT WILL I DO? THEY CAN GET ME FOR CURFEW.
BABY DAPHNE!
WE'LL MAKE A BREAK FOR THE BACK DOOR.
I HATE JOEY GLASS
I DON'T THINK THERE'D BE ANY COPS IN THE ALLEY...
HEY!
SOB
EY'RE GOING UT US IN JAIL, KNOW IT!
WAIT! THERE'S... DOYLE!!
???
HOME, JAMES! ON THE DOUBLE! HURRY, DAFFY! I THINK THEY'RE COMING!
BUT... BUT...

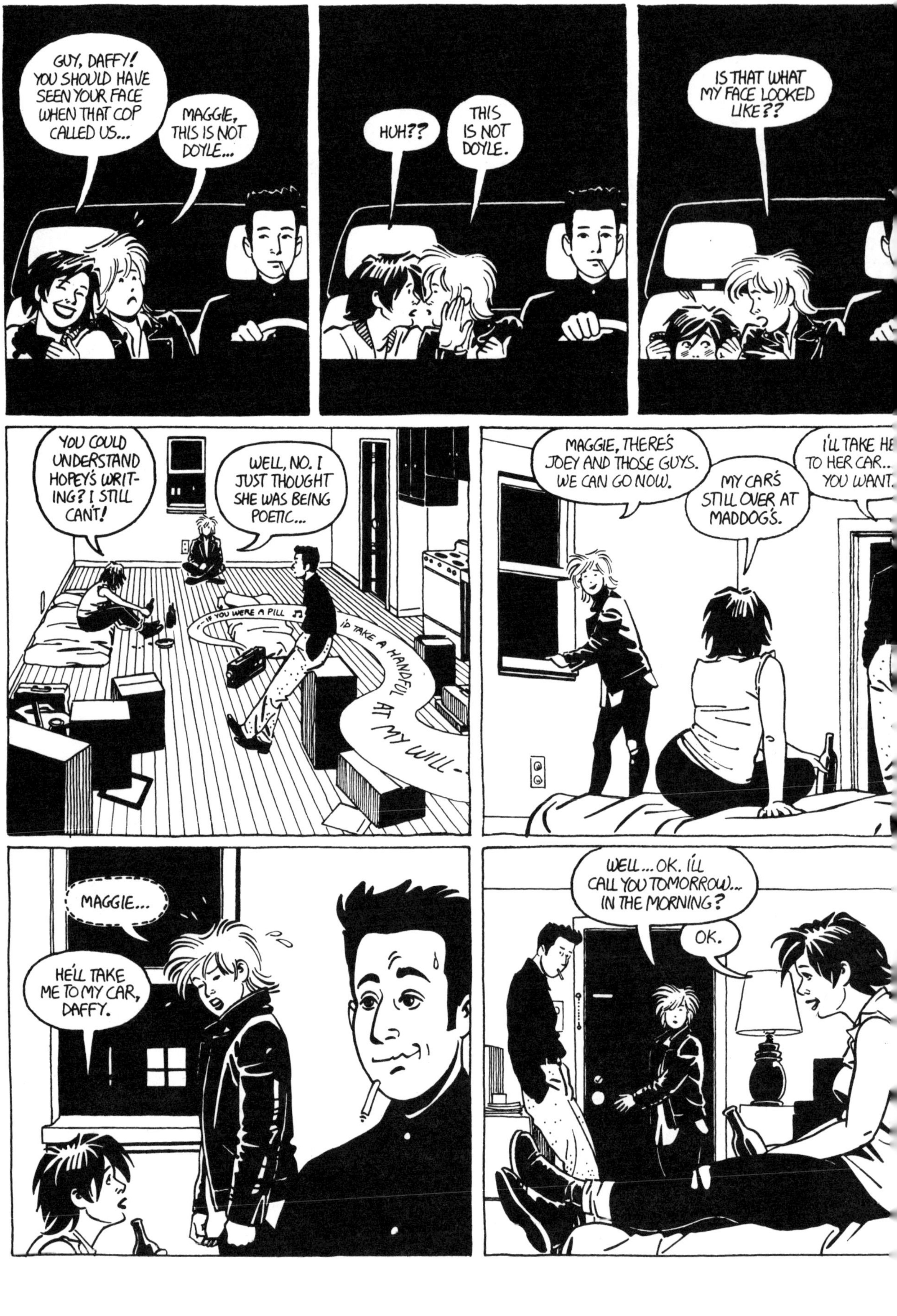
GUY, DAFFY! YOU SHOULD HAVE SEEN YOUR FACE WHEN THAT COP CALLED US...
MAGGIE, THIS IS NOT DOYLE...
HUH??
THIS IS NOT DOYLE.
IS THAT WHAT MY FACE LOOKED LIKE??
YOU COULD UNDERSTAND HOPEY'S WRITING? I STILL CAN'T!
WELL, NO. I JUST THOUGHT SHE WAS BEING POETIC...
IF YOU WERE A PILL
I'D TAKE A HANDFUL AT MY WILL
MAGGIE, THERE'S JOEY AND THOSE GUYS. WE CAN GO NOW.
MY CAR'S STILL OVER AT MADDOG'S.
I'LL TAKE HE TO HER CAR... YOU WANT.
MAGGIE...
HE'LL TAKE ME TO MY CAR, DAFFY.
WELL... OK. I'LL CALL YOU TOMORROW... IN THE MORNING?
OK.

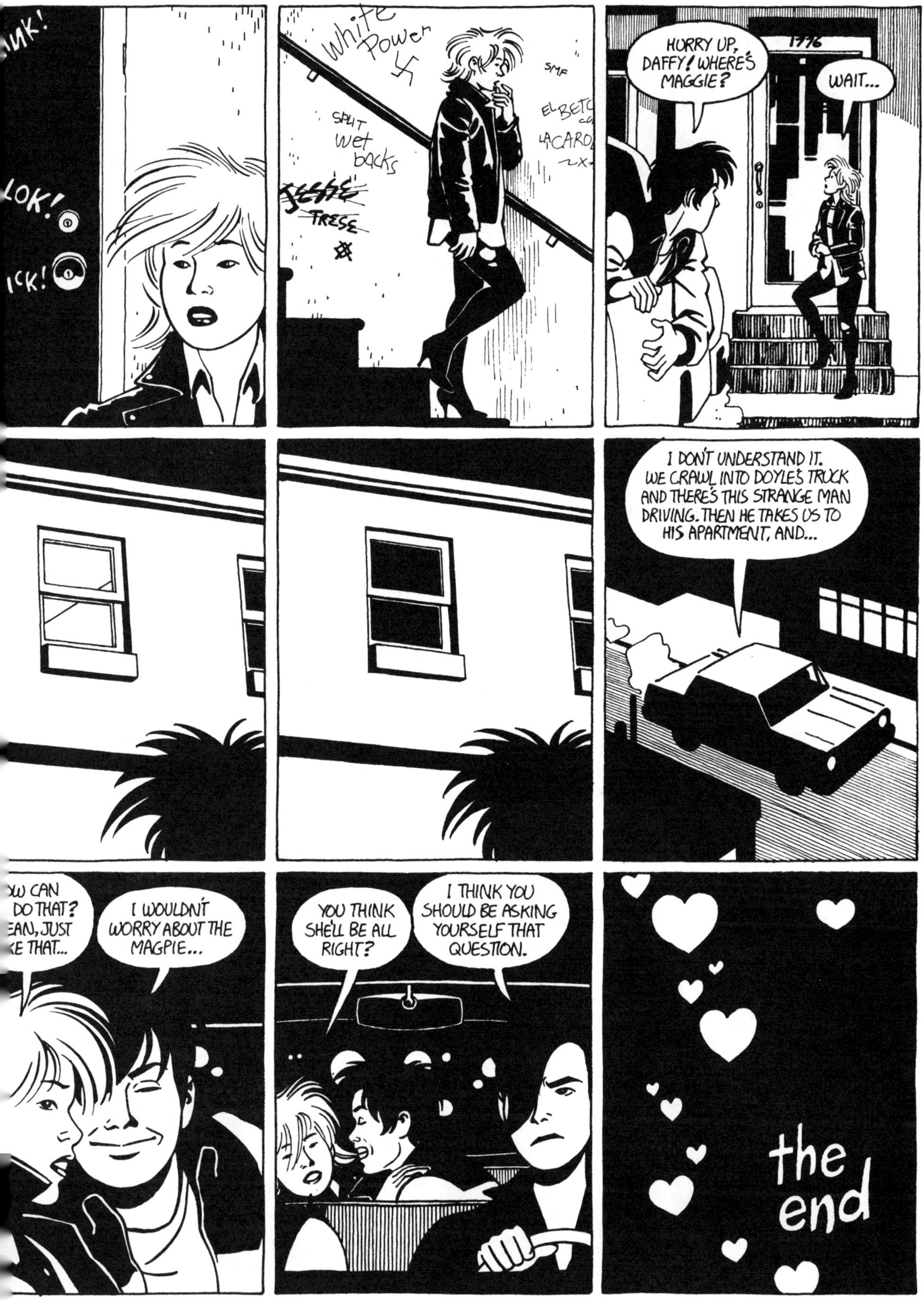
white Power
SPLIT wet backs
TRESE
SMF
HURRY UP, DAFFY! WHERE'S MAGGIE?
1776
WAIT...
I DON'T UNDERSTAND IT. WE CRAWL INTO DOYLE'S TRUCK AND THERE'S THIS STRANGE MAN DRIVING. THEN HE TAKES US TO HIS APARTMENT, AND...
I WOULDN'T WORRY ABOUT THE MAGPIE...
YOU THINK SHE'LL BE ALL RIGHT?
I THINK YOU SHOULD BE ASKING YOURSELF THAT QUESTION.
the end

ALL THIS AND *PENNY,* TOO...

...A MILLION MILES FROM HOME

HYMEH 87

HI. WHERE WERE YOU LAST NIGHT?

SLEPT IN THE CAR AGAIN.

THIS IS GETTING RIDICULOUS. I'M ABOUT TO GIVE UP AND CALL MY PARENTS...

DON'T YOU STILL WANNA GO TO CALIFORNIA WITH ME?

WELL, SURE I DO. BUT WE'VE BARELY MOVED FIFTY MILES WEST IN THE PAST TWO WEEKS!

WELL, SHIT! IT'D BE A LOT EASIER IF WE HAD MONEY TO TRAVEL WITH!

WAIT A SECOND...

WHEN IN BADGEPORT, VISIT

Costiga
MANOR EAST

ALSO • COSTIGAN MANOR W
IN SAKATOOTH, WA
• COSTIGAN MANOR SOU
IN MUSKRATICA, TX
• COSTIGAN MANOR NOF
IN ST. MOSE, IL

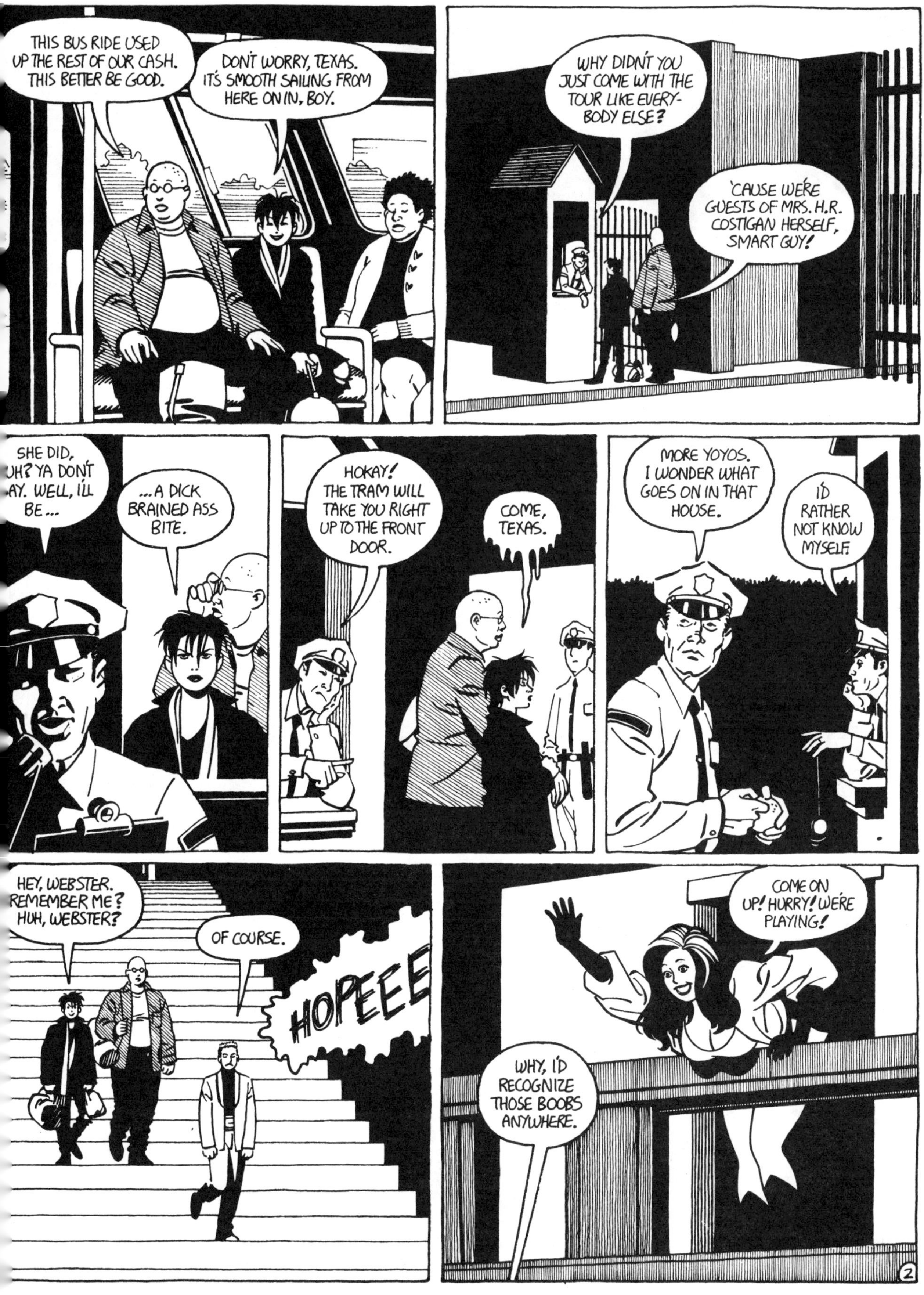

THIS BUS RIDE USED UP THE REST OF OUR CASH. THIS BETTER BE GOOD.
DON'T WORRY, TEXAS. IT'S SMOOTH SAILING FROM HERE ON IN, BOY.
WHY DIDN'T YOU JUST COME WITH THE TOUR LIKE EVERY-BODY ELSE?
'CAUSE WE'RE GUESTS OF MRS. H.R. COSTIGAN HERSELF, SMART GUY!
SHE DID, UH? YA DON'T AY. WELL, I'LL BE...
...A DICK BRAINED ASS BITE.
HOKAY! THE TRAM WILL TAKE YOU RIGHT UP TO THE FRONT DOOR.
COME, TEXAS.
MORE YOYOS. I WONDER WHAT GOES ON IN THAT HOUSE.
I'D RATHER NOT KNOW MYSELF.
HEY, WEBSTER. REMEMBER ME? HUH, WEBSTER?
OF COURSE.
HOPEEE
COME ON UP! HURRY! WE'RE PLAYING!
WHY, I'D RECOGNIZE THOSE BOOBS ANYWHERE.
2

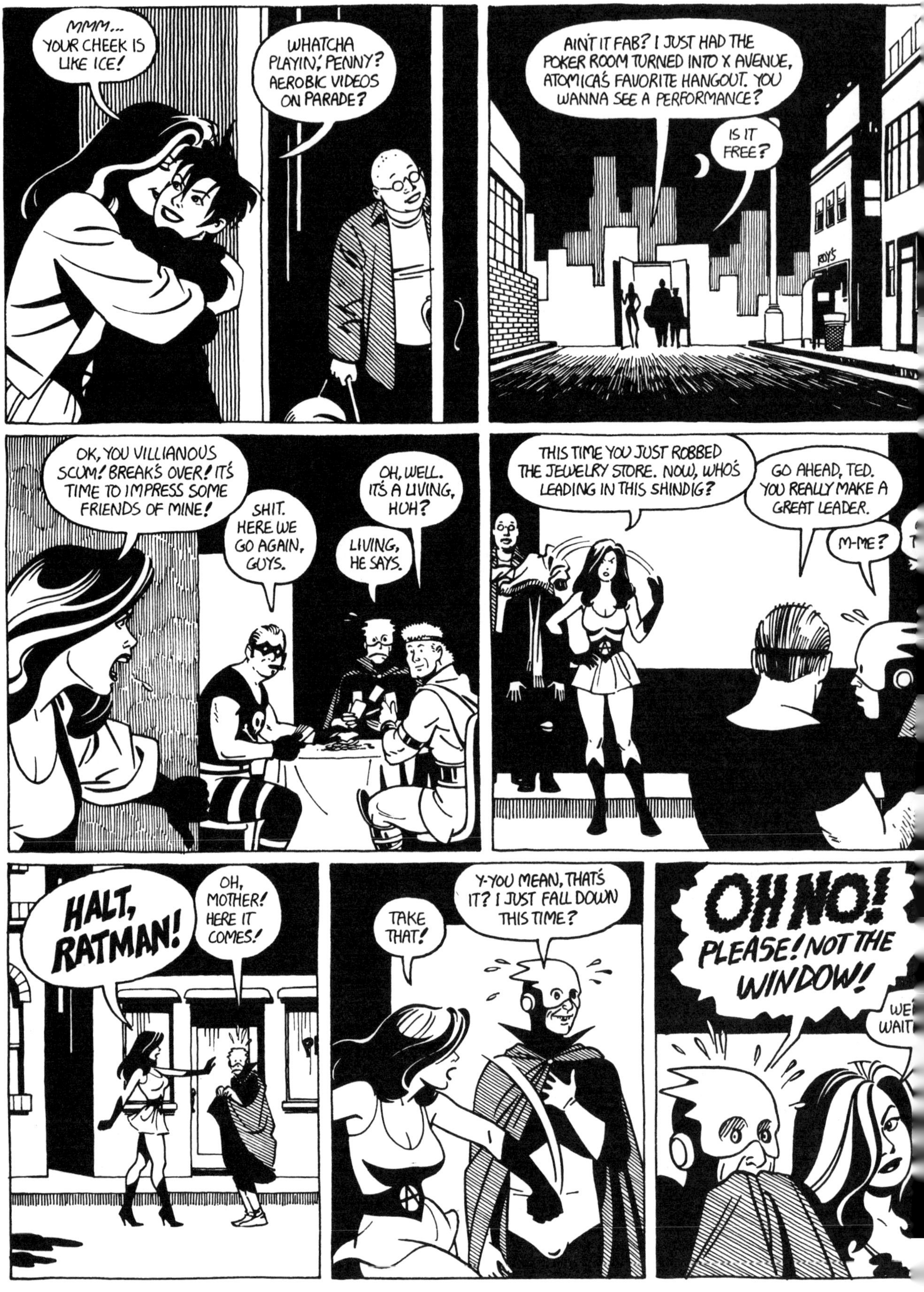
MMM... YOUR CHEEK IS LIKE ICE!
WHATCHA PLAYIN', PENNY? AEROBIC VIDEOS ON PARADE?
AIN'T IT FAB? I JUST HAD THE POKER ROOM TURNED INTO X AVENUE, ATOMICA'S FAVORITE HANGOUT. YOU WANNA SEE A PERFORMANCE?
IS IT FREE?
ROY'S
OK, YOU VILLIANOUS SCUM! BREAK'S OVER! IT'S TIME TO IMPRESS SOME FRIENDS OF MINE!
SHIT. HERE WE GO AGAIN, GUYS.
OH, WELL. IT'S A LIVING, HUH?
LIVING, HE SAYS.
THIS TIME YOU JUST ROBBED THE JEWELRY STORE. NOW, WHO'S LEADING IN THIS SHINDIG?
GO AHEAD, TED. YOU REALLY MAKE A GREAT LEADER.
M-ME?
HALT, RATMAN!
OH, MOTHER! HERE IT COMES!
TAKE THAT!
Y-YOU MEAN, THAT'S IT? I JUST FALL DOWN THIS TIME?
OH NO! PLEASE! NOT THE WINDOW!

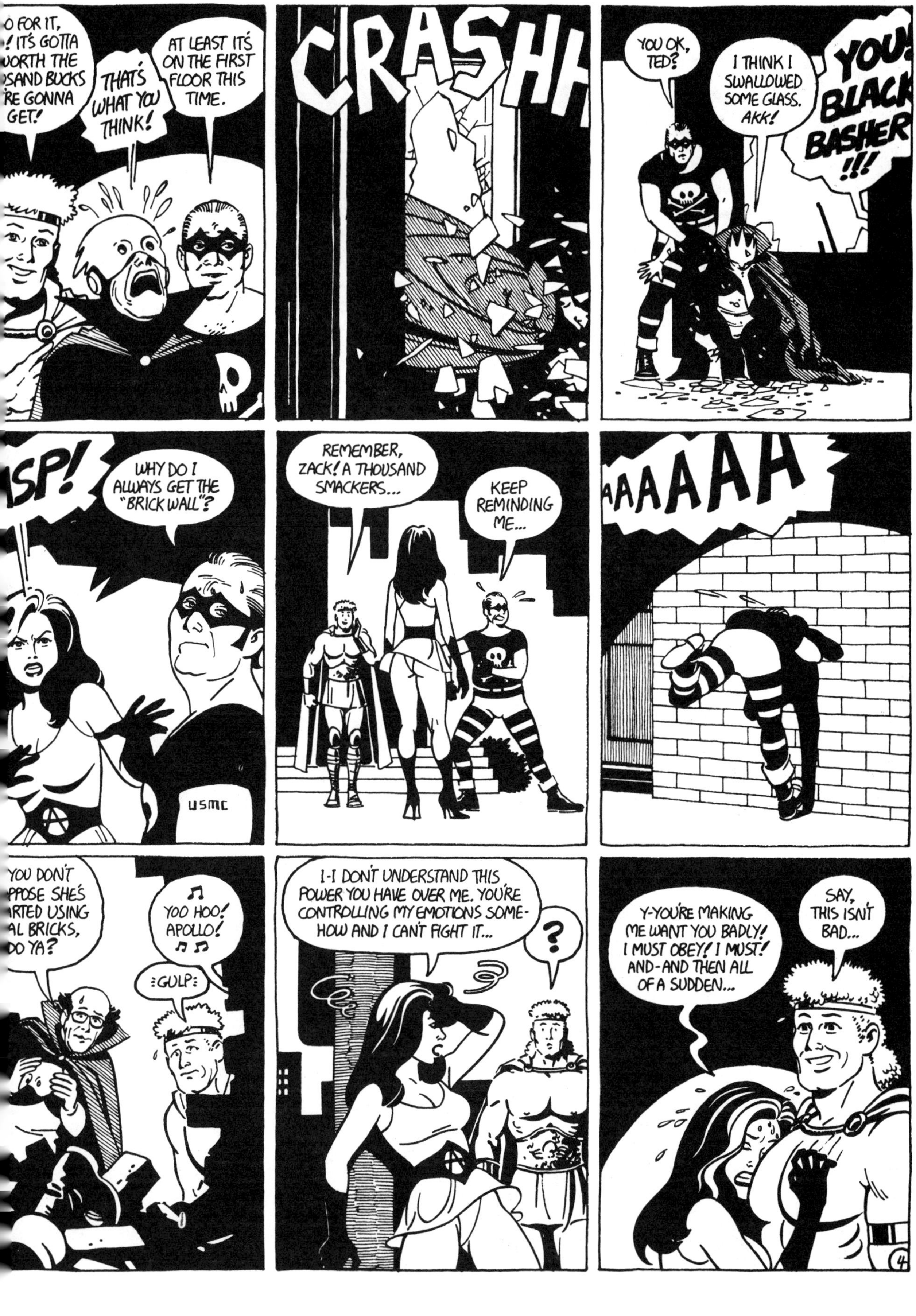

O FOR IT, ! IT'S GOTTA WORTH THE SAND BUCKS RE GONNA GET!
THAT'S WHAT YOU THINK!
AT LEAST IT'S ON THE FIRST FLOOR THIS TIME.
CRASHH
YOU OK, TED?
I THINK I SWALLOWED SOME GLASS. AKK!
YOU! BLACK BASHER!!!
SP!
WHY DO I ALWAYS GET THE "BRICK WALL"?
USMC
REMEMBER, ZACK! A THOUSAND SMACKERS...
KEEP REMINDING ME...
AAAAAA
YOU DON'T PPOSE SHE'S RTED USING L BRICKS, DO YA?
YOO HOO! APOLLO!
GULP
I-I DON'T UNDERSTAND THIS POWER YOU HAVE OVER ME. YOU'RE CONTROLLING MY EMOTIONS SOMEHOW AND I CAN'T FIGHT IT...
?
Y-YOU'RE MAKING ME WANT YOU BADLY! I MUST OBEY! I MUST! AND-AND THEN ALL OF A SUDDEN...
SAY, THIS ISN'T BAD...
4

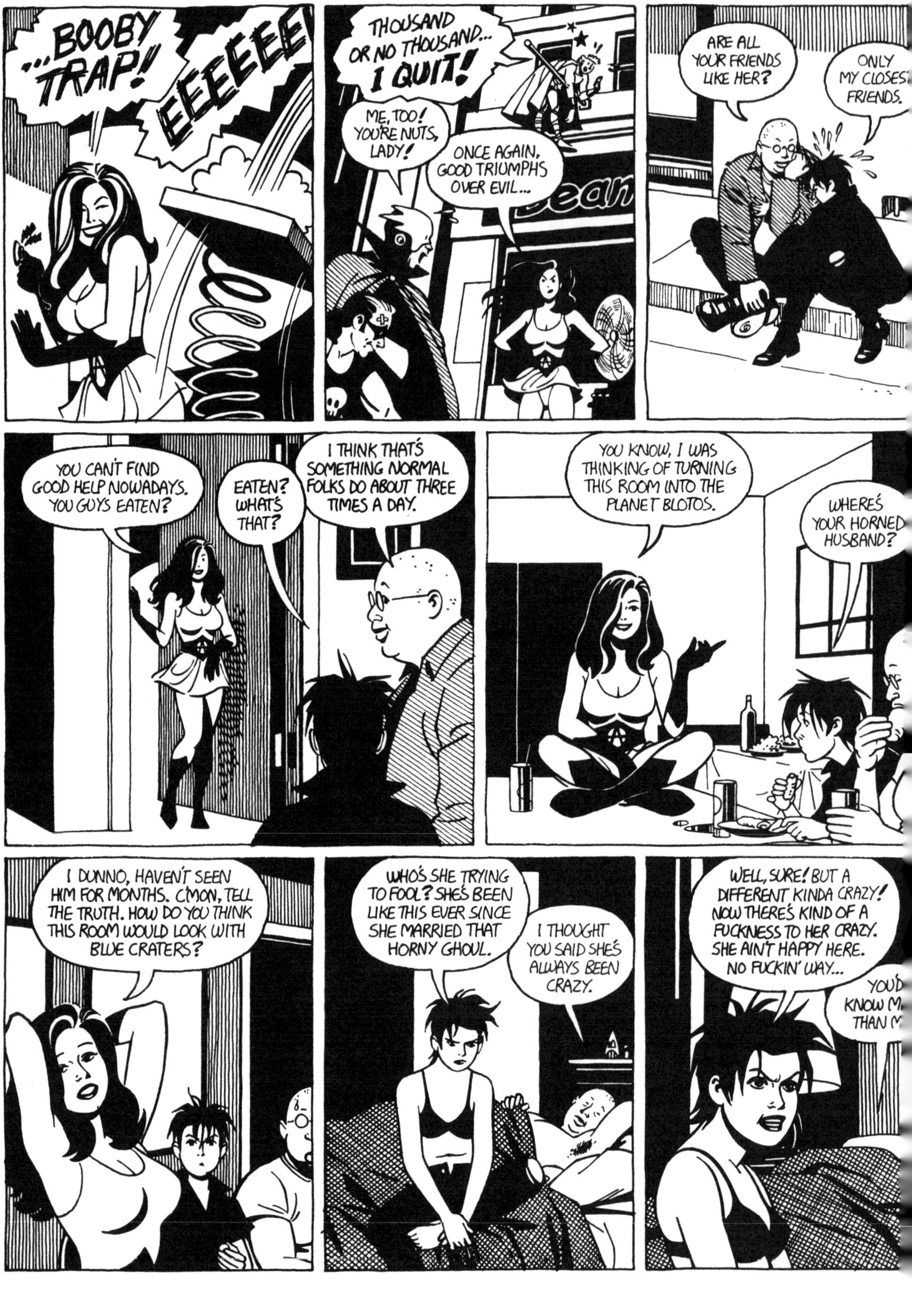
...BOOBY TRAP!
EEEEEE
THOUSAND OR NO THOUSAND... I QUIT!
ME, TOO! YOU'RE NUTS, LADY!
ONCE AGAIN, GOOD TRIUMPHS OVER EVIL...
ARE ALL YOUR FRIENDS LIKE HER?
ONLY MY CLOSEST FRIENDS.
YOU CAN'T FIND GOOD HELP NOWADAYS. YOU GUYS EATEN?
EATEN? WHAT'S THAT?
I THINK THAT'S SOMETHING NORMAL FOLKS DO ABOUT THREE TIMES A DAY.
YOU KNOW, I WAS THINKING OF TURNING THIS ROOM INTO THE PLANET BLOTOS.
WHERE'S YOUR HORNED HUSBAND?
I DUNNO, HAVEN'T SEEN HIM FOR MONTHS. C'MON, TELL THE TRUTH. HOW DO YOU THINK THIS ROOM WOULD LOOK WITH BLUE CRATERS?
WHO'S SHE TRYING TO FOOL? SHE'S BEEN LIKE THIS EVER SINCE SHE MARRIED THAT HORNY GHOUL.
I THOUGHT YOU SAID SHE'S ALWAYS BEEN CRAZY.
WELL, SURE! BUT A DIFFERENT KINDA CRAZY! NOW THERE'S KIND OF A FUCKNESS TO HER CRAZY. SHE AIN'T HAPPY HERE. NO FUCKIN' WAY...

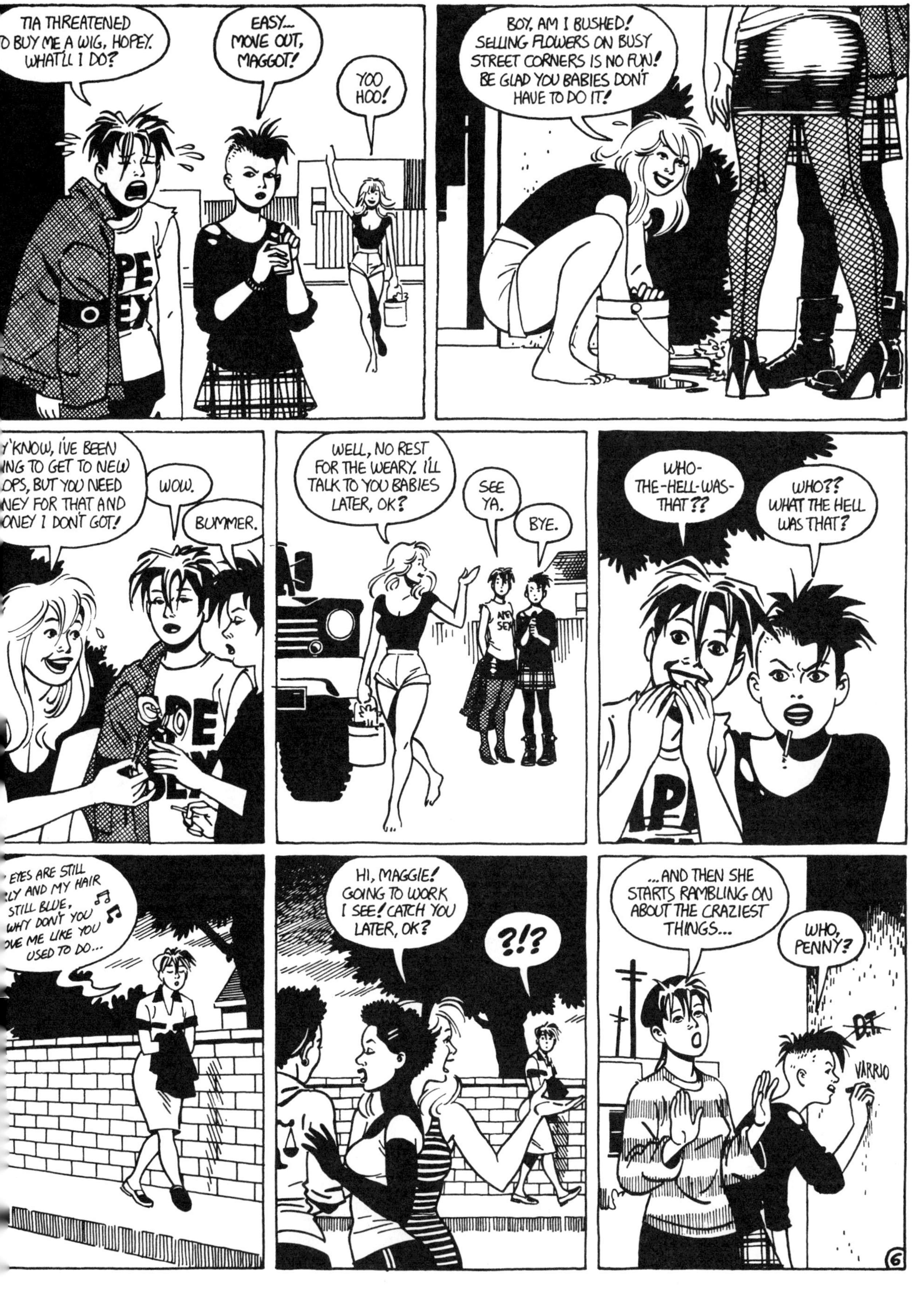
TIA THREATENED
O BUY ME A WIG, HOPEY. WHAT'LL I DO?
EASY... MOVE OUT, MAGGOT!
YOO HOO!
BOY, AM I BUSHED! SELLING FLOWERS ON BUSY STREET CORNERS IS NO FUN! BE GLAD YOU BABIES DON'T HAVE TO DO IT!
Y'KNOW, I'VE BEEN
NG TO GET TO NEW
OPS, BUT YOU NEED
NEY FOR THAT AND
ONEY I DON'T GOT!
WOW.
BUMMER.
WELL, NO REST FOR THE WEARY. I'LL TALK TO YOU BABIES LATER, OK?
SEE YA.
BYE.
WHO-THE-HELL-WAS-THAT??
WHO?? WHAT THE HELL WAS THAT?
EYES ARE STILL
RLY AND MY HAIR
STILL BLUE,
WHY DON'T YOU
OVE ME LIKE YOU
USED TO DO...
HI, MAGGIE! GOING TO WORK I SEE! CATCH YOU LATER, OK?
?!?
...AND THEN SHE STARTS RAMBLING ON ABOUT THE CRAZIEST THINGS...
WHO, PENNY?
D.T.
VARRIO

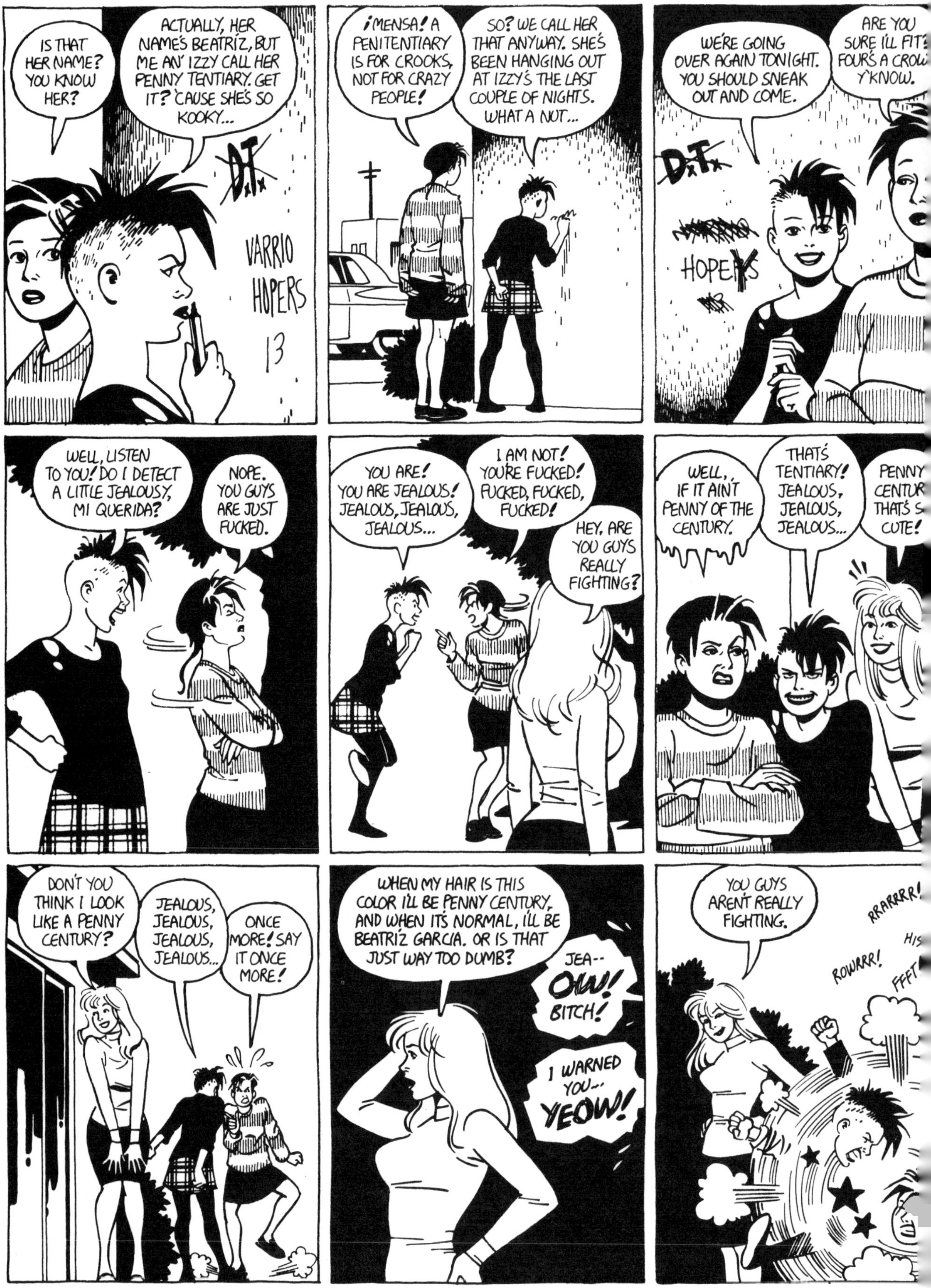

IS THAT HER NAME? YOU KNOW HER?
ACTUALLY, HER NAME'S BEATRÍZ, BUT ME AN' IZZY CALL HER PENNY TENTIARY. GET IT? 'CAUSE SHE'S SO KOOKY...
D.T.
VARRIO HOPERS 13
¡MENSA! A PENITENTIARY IS FOR CROOKS, NOT FOR CRAZY PEOPLE!
SO? WE CALL HER THAT ANYWAY. SHE'S BEEN HANGING OUT AT IZZY'S THE LAST COUPLE OF NIGHTS. WHAT A NUT...
WE'RE GOING OVER AGAIN TONIGHT. YOU SHOULD SNEAK OUT AND COME.
ARE YOU SURE I'LL FIT? FOUR'S A CROW Y'KNOW.
D.T.
HOPERS
WELL, LISTEN TO YOU! DO I DETECT A LITTLE JEALOUSY, MI QUERIDA?
NOPE. YOU GUYS ARE JUST FUCKED.
YOU ARE! YOU ARE JEALOUS! JEALOUS, JEALOUS, JEALOUS...
I AM NOT! YOU'RE FUCKED! FUCKED, FUCKED, FUCKED!
HEY, ARE YOU GUYS REALLY FIGHTING?
WELL, IF IT AIN'T PENNY OF THE CENTURY.
THAT'S TENTIARY! JEALOUS, JEALOUS, JEALOUS...
PENNY CENTUR THAT'S S CUTE!
DON'T YOU THINK I LOOK LIKE A PENNY CENTURY?
JEALOUS, JEALOUS, JEALOUS, JEALOUS...
ONCE MORE! SAY IT ONCE MORE!
WHEN MY HAIR IS THIS COLOR I'LL BE PENNY CENTURY, AND WHEN IT'S NORMAL, I'LL BE BEATRÍZ GARCIA. OR IS THAT JUST WAY TOO DUMB?
JEA-- OW! BITCH!
I WARNED YOU... YEOW!
YOU GUYS AREN'T REALLY FIGHTING.
RRARRRR!
HIS
ROWRRR!
FFFT

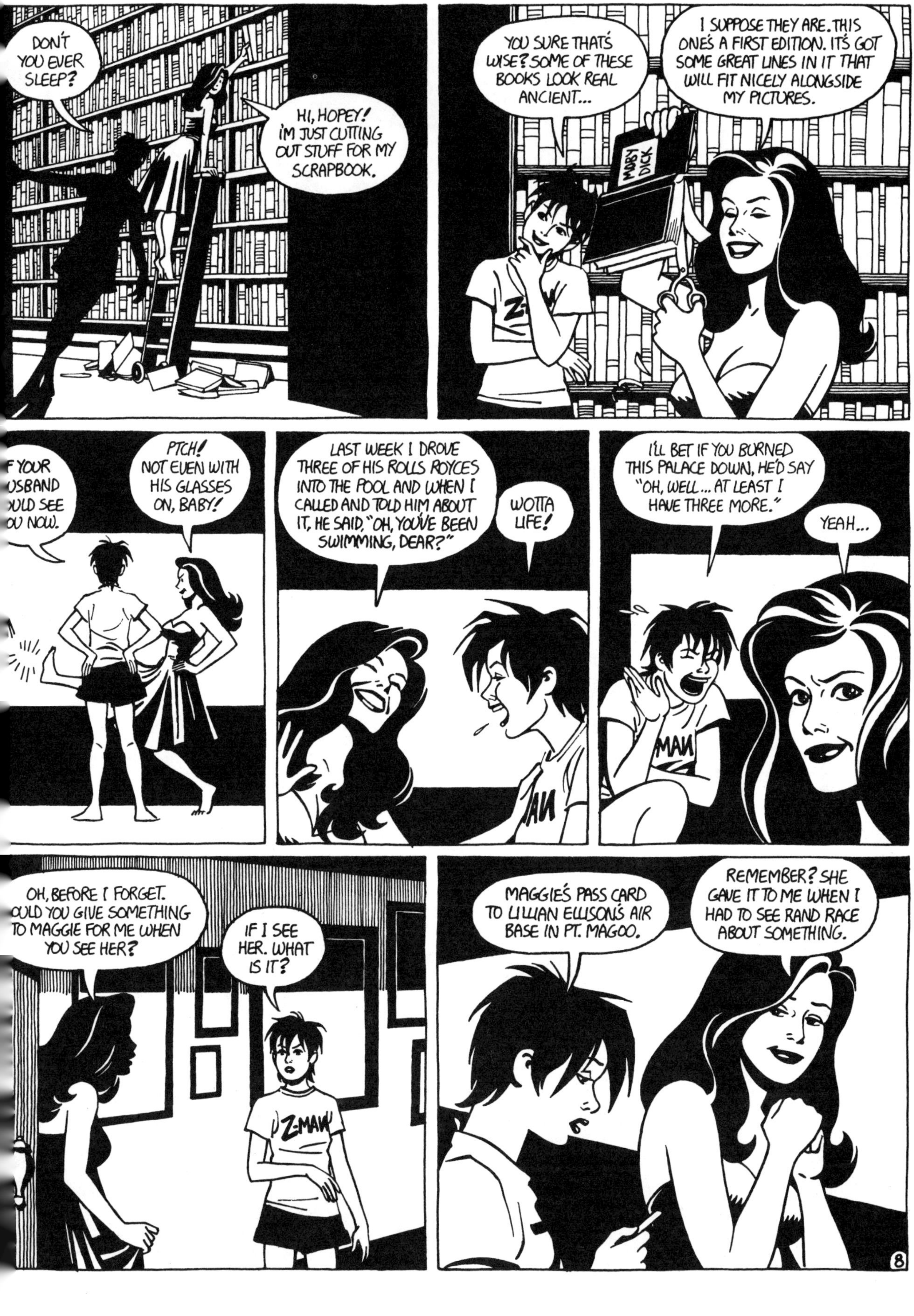
DON'T YOU EVER SLEEP?
HI, HOPEY! I'M JUST CUTTING OUT STUFF FOR MY SCRAPBOOK.
YOU SURE THAT'S WISE? SOME OF THESE BOOKS LOOK REAL ANCIENT...
I SUPPOSE THEY ARE. THIS ONE'S A FIRST EDITION. IT'S GOT SOME GREAT LINES IN IT THAT WILL FIT NICELY ALONGSIDE MY PICTURES.
MOBY DICK
Z-MAN
F YOUR USBAND OULD SEE OU NOW.
PTCH! NOT EVEN WITH HIS GLASSES ON, BABY!
LAST WEEK I DROVE THREE OF HIS ROLLS ROYCES INTO THE POOL AND WHEN I CALLED AND TOLD HIM ABOUT IT, HE SAID, "OH, YOU'VE BEEN SWIMMING, DEAR?"
WOTTA LIFE!
I'LL BET IF YOU BURNED THIS PALACE DOWN, HE'D SAY "OH, WELL... AT LEAST I HAVE THREE MORE."
YEAH...
OH, BEFORE I FORGET. OULD YOU GIVE SOMETHING TO MAGGIE FOR ME WHEN YOU SEE HER?
IF I SEE HER. WHAT IS IT?
Z-MAN
MAGGIE'S PASS CARD TO LILLIAN ELLISON'S AIR BASE IN PT. MAGOO.
REMEMBER? SHE GAVE IT TO ME WHEN I HAD TO SEE RAND RACE ABOUT SOMETHING.

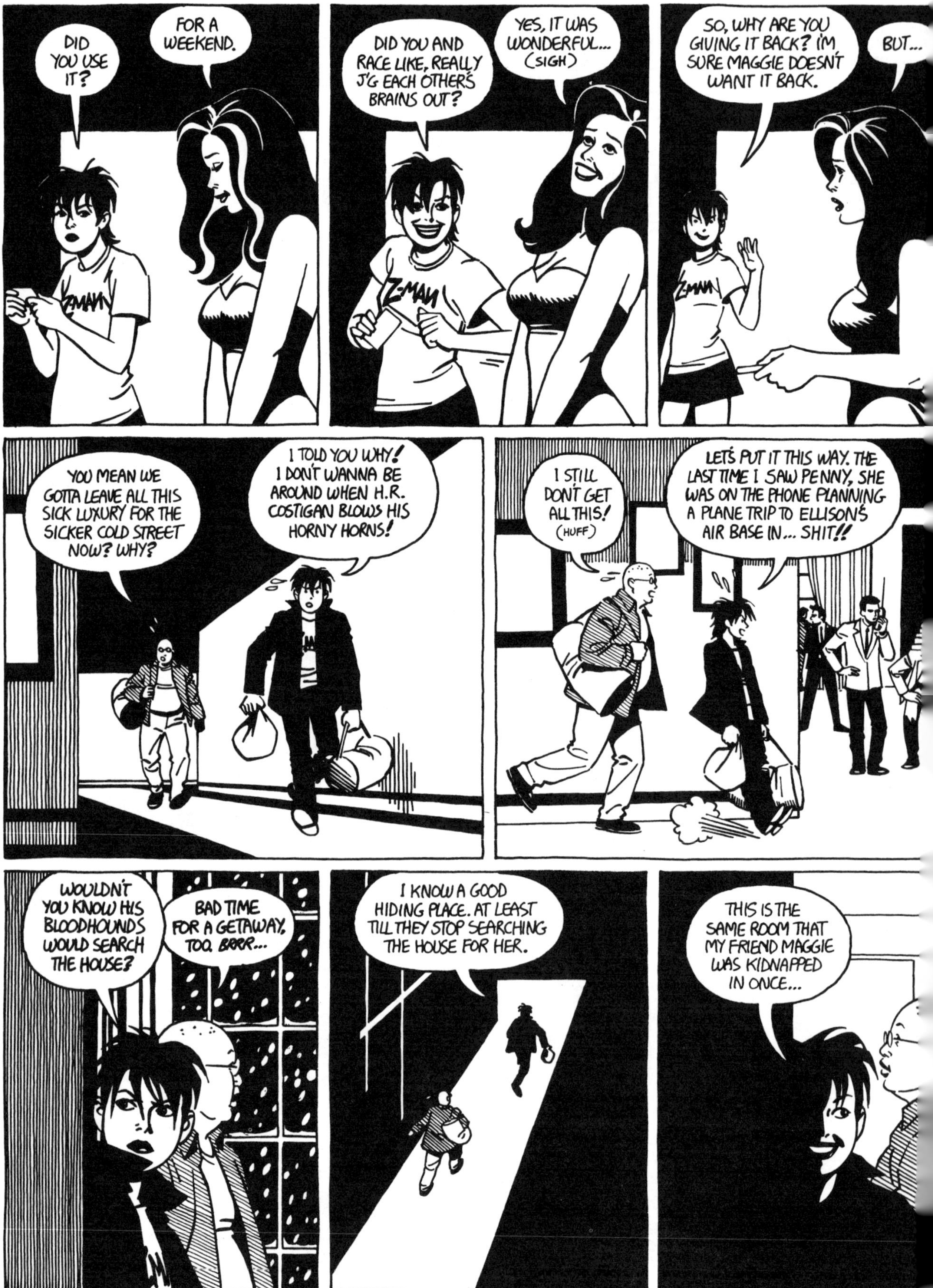
DID YOU USE IT?
FOR A WEEKEND.
DID YOU AND RACE LIKE, REALLY J'G EACH OTHER'S BRAINS OUT?
YES, IT WAS WONDERFUL... (SIGH)
SO, WHY ARE YOU GIVING IT BACK? I'M SURE MAGGIE DOESN'T WANT IT BACK.
BUT...
YOU MEAN WE GOTTA LEAVE ALL THIS SICK LUXURY FOR THE SICKER COLD STREET NOW? WHY?
I TOLD YOU WHY! I DON'T WANNA BE AROUND WHEN H.R. COSTIGAN BLOWS HIS HORNY HORNS!
I STILL DON'T GET ALL THIS! (HUFF)
LET'S PUT IT THIS WAY. THE LAST TIME I SAW PENNY, SHE WAS ON THE PHONE PLANNING A PLANE TRIP TO ELLISON'S AIR BASE IN... SHIT!!
WOULDN'T YOU KNOW HIS BLOODHOUNDS WOULD SEARCH THE HOUSE?
BAD TIME FOR A GETAWAY, TOO. BRRR...
I KNOW A GOOD HIDING PLACE. AT LEAST TILL THEY STOP SEARCHING THE HOUSE FOR HER.
THIS IS THE SAME ROOM THAT MY FRIEND MAGGIE WAS KIDNAPPED IN ONCE...

J'G/JUG (PRONOUNCED JIG)

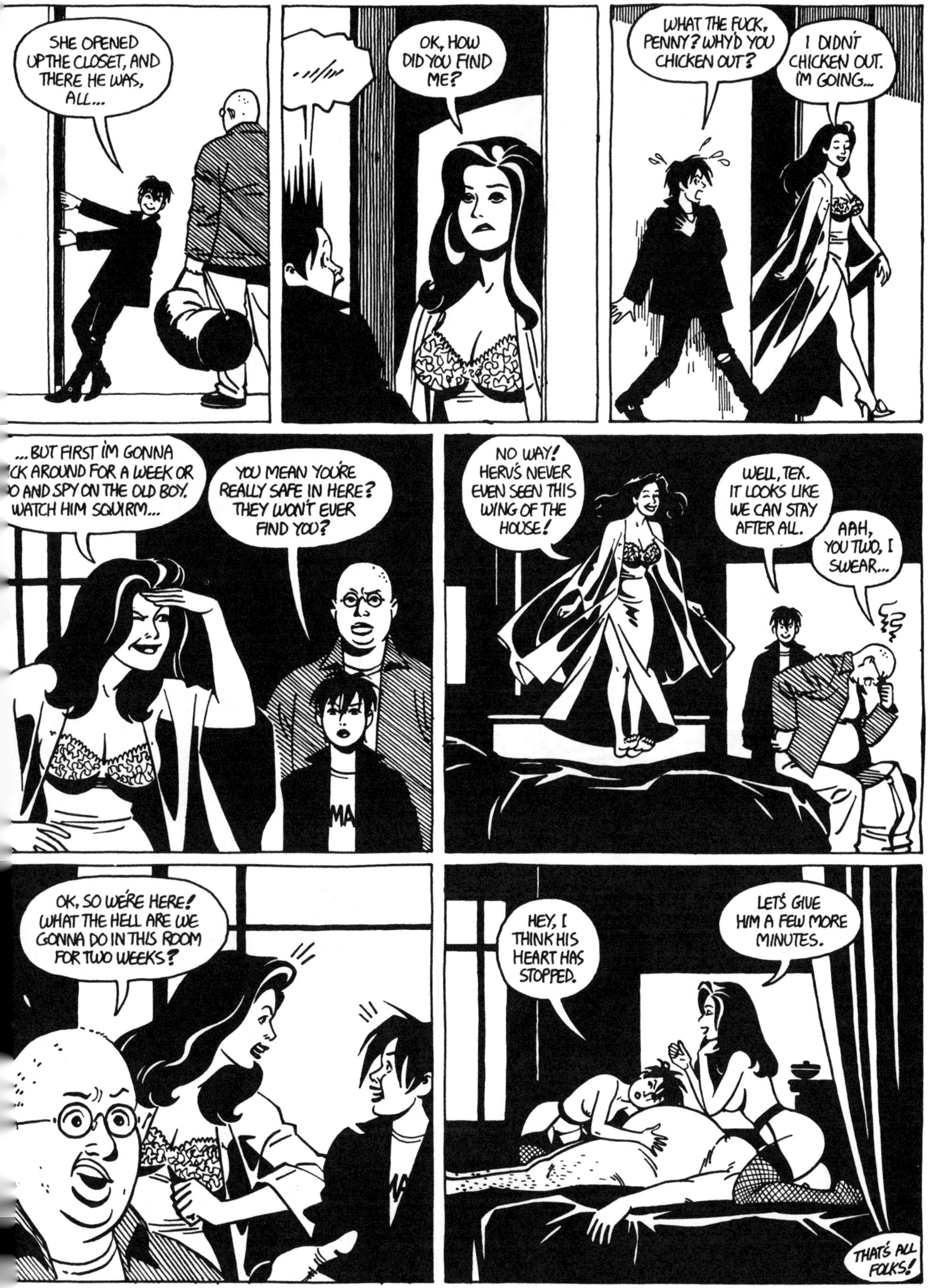
SHE OPENED UP THE CLOSET, AND THERE HE WAS, ALL...
OK, HOW DID YOU FIND ME?
WHAT THE FUCK, PENNY? WHY'D YOU CHICKEN OUT?
I DIDN'T CHICKEN OUT. I'M GOING...
...BUT FIRST I'M GONNA
ICK AROUND FOR A WEEK OR
O AND SPY ON THE OLD BOY. WATCH HIM SQUIRM...
YOU MEAN YOU'RE REALLY SAFE IN HERE? THEY WON'T EVER FIND YOU?
NO WAY! HERV'S NEVER EVEN SEEN THIS WING OF THE HOUSE!
WELL, TEX. IT LOOKS LIKE WE CAN STAY AFTER ALL.
AAH, YOU TWO, I SWEAR...
OK, SO WE'RE HERE! WHAT THE HELL ARE WE GONNA DO IN THIS ROOM FOR TWO WEEKS?
HEY, I THINK HIS HEART HAS STOPPED.
LET'S GIVE HIM A FEW MORE MINUTES.
THAT'S ALL FOLKS!

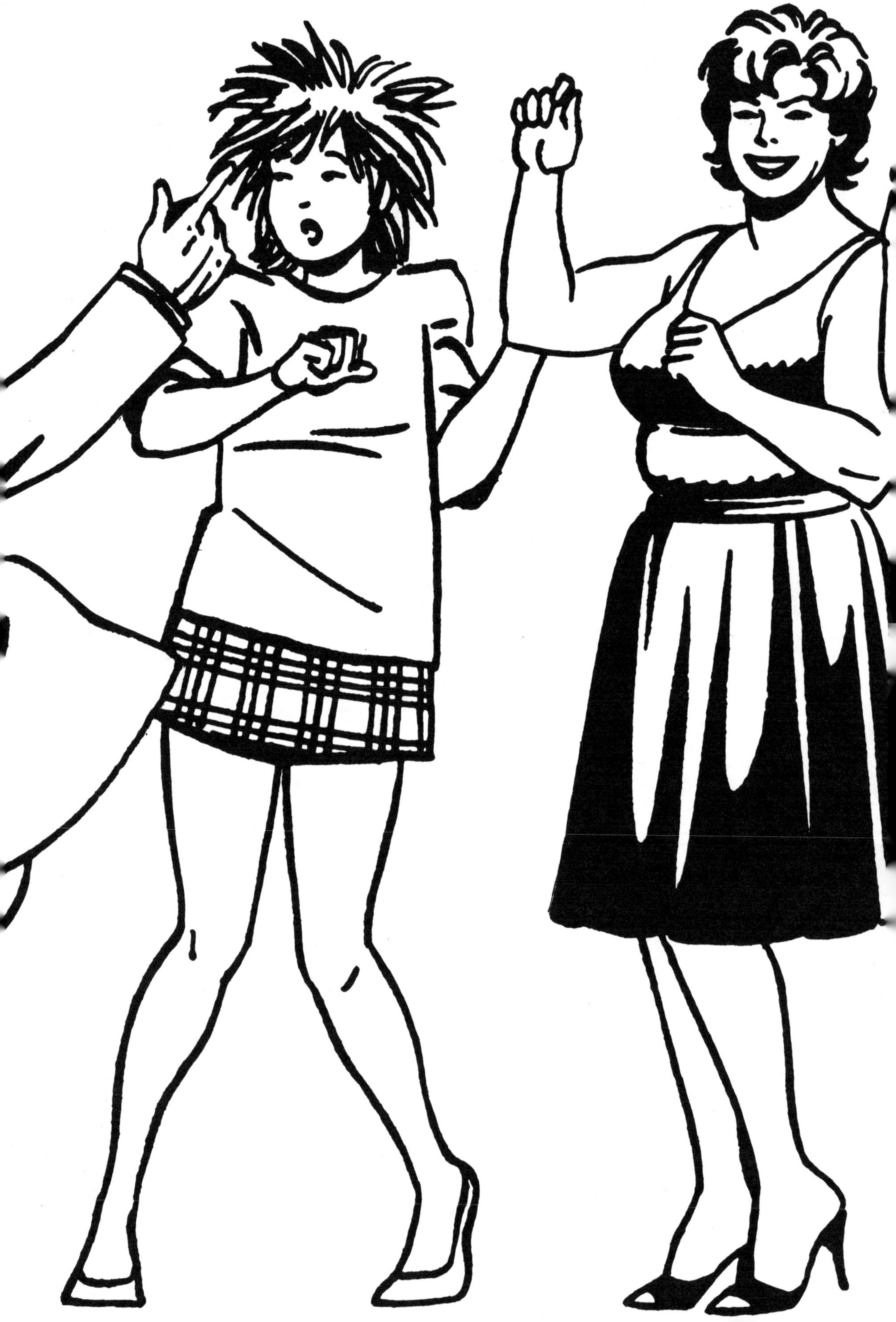